The Madison Cafe

The Madison Cafe

A Novel

John McClurken

WATERMAIN

Copyright © 2018 by John McClurken

Published in the United States by Watermain Press

ISBN 978-0-692-09836-3

Library of Congress Cataloging-in-Publication data is forthcoming.

Book Design by Sunam Mah

First Edition

1 3 5 7 9 10 8 6 4 2

Printed in the United States of America

For Peggy

My One and Only

"Ah me!" said he, "What might have been is not what is!"
— R. Wilfer, *Our Mutual Friend*

PART I

One Morning in the Alley

Every morning Katherine walked from her house to work, down the alley between Main Street and Cedar Street. One day in early June, 1986, it was just beginning to get light at five-thirty as she went out the back door and started into the alley. Ahead, she saw the dark hulk of a man stumbling towards her and, as the distance closed, she recognized one of the town's notable drunks, Axel Maise, staggering slowly up the alley.

Now a few feet away, he mumbled, " Come on little girl, let's go have a beer."

Dressed as always in a plaid shirt, blue jeans, and brown Frye hiking boots, Katherine had an air of an outdoor toughness and she wasn't intimidated in spite of being shorter and over a hundred pounds lighter than the smelly drunk.

She moved to the far right side of the alley, giving Maise a wide berth. He stumbled towards her and caught her left arm at the wrist, pulling at her and growling, "Come here you little bitch."

Katherine shook off his grip and turned towards him. She grabbed both his arms and kneed him in the crotch. When he bent forward in pain, she kneed him again in the face, scoring a direct hit on his bulbous nose which made a crisp snapping noise as it broke. She pushed him down on his back and put her right foot on his Adam's apple, applying enough pressure to make him gag.

"You get one warning and this it dirt bag. Don't come near me again," she growled. She kicked him in the side, scoring a direct hit on his left kidney, then turned and continued down the alley to the back door of the Madison Café, where she let herself in and went to work.

Maude Doud witnessed the whole thing. She was half a block away, across a vacant lot on Cedar Street with her Cairn Terrier, Rascal. She watched Katherine Baker make short work of Axel Maise, leaving him unconscious in the alley. Maude walked home in a hurry and called the town constable at home. She knew Will McCann wasn't on duty yet and she should have called 911, but it was a good time to remind him she was on the town council and chairman of the Public Safety Committee so she could go right to the top if she wanted. She took some satisfaction hearing Will grumble when she told him Axel Maise was passed out in the alley between the Madison Café and Lou's Scenic Tavern.

The stricken drunk lay in the alley another twenty minutes before Will's deputy, Charley Sizemore, arrived. With help from Wally Berger and Ray Kesecker, who were headed for breakfast at the Madison Café, Charley got Axel Maise into the back of his patrol car. By then, Maude and Rascal had returned to their perch on Cedar Street and watched, just to make sure the town's streets and alleys were cleaned up as the new day began.

The morning talk about Axel Maise being found beat up and unconscious in the alley was the number one topic at the Madison Café for less than five minutes. Being passed out in public was nothing new for the deadbeat drunk and everyone assumed it was one of his drinking buddies from Lou's Scenic Tavern who'd pummeled him.

The one person who'd witnessed the incident in the alley that morning kept her mouth shut. Later that afternoon, when Maude Doud ran into Will McCann at the bank and learned that Axel Maise was on his way to the Veterans Hospital in Seattle, she told the constable "good riddance to bad rubbish." In addition to his broken nose and bruised kidney, his liver was in a life-threatening stage of cirrhosis. He wouldn't be back in Cedar Mills. Maude decided it was time to introduce herself to Katherine Baker.

You Can Go Home Again

The Madison Café is located on the west end of the downtown business district of Cedar Mills, an area that spans two long blocks along Main

Street. It's open for breakfast and lunch from six o'clock in the morning until two o'clock in the afternoon. Dinner isn't served and the café isn't open on weekends. Horace Greeley Martin, the Madison's owner, is proud of the restaurant's reputation for breakfast where one of the specialties is buttermilk pancakes made with a closely held secret recipe known only to the head cook, Katherine Baker, and her assistant, Larry Bradford. Greeley himself doesn't know how to make the batter.

Katherine Baker has been the Madison Café's cook since the beginning. The beginning being over a year ago after Greeley bought the old Star Theater building which included the Sunny Jim Grill. He left the long-shuttered theater untouched but remodeled the small restaurant, updating the kitchen and adding a large dining area in the rear. He also added an office on the second floor, in the front, and an apartment in the rear.

Katherine had left Cedar Mills over a decade before. She'd run off to Los Angeles on the night of her high school graduation with one of her teachers, Art Fletcher. Back then she was Katy Owling, the oldest daughter of Reverend Ron Owling and his wife Susan. Her sudden departure shook the foundations of the Owling family and the Cedar Mills Presbyterian Church over which her father had presided for three years.

Katy was an honor student with a full scholarship to study voice and piano at Mills College in the Bay Area that fall. When she suddenly disappeared on graduation night, the Owlings were convinced she'd been kidnapped. But then they found the note from Katy telling them she was in love with Art. He had show business connections in Los Angeles. He was going to make her a star. She would write as soon as they were settled.

The rest of Katy Owling's story has been told a thousand times, in myriad ways. It's enough to say that not long after arriving in Los Angeles, Katy was alone and pregnant, homeless on the streets of Los Angeles, and Art was gone. A couple years later, one of the Dalrymple boys from Cedar Mills said they'd seen Art Fletcher at Dutch Harbor working in a salmon cannery.

Katy found refuge at the Catholic Sisters of Mercy home for women. She gave her daughter up for adoption when the baby was born. A few months later she was working as a dancer and backup singer for a disco band in a seaman's dive in San Pedro. Not long after that, she married the band's bass player who called himself Chauncey Baker.

Katy spent the next two years with Chauncey, dancing in cheap clubs from San Bernadino to Barstow and beyond, living on booze, cocaine, and pills. She eventually regained consciousness in the Tulare County Jail where she was serving a six-month sentence for drunk driving and attempted vehicular manslaughter. Three months of her time was suspended and her record was expunged when she completed a job training program in culinary arts at the local community college. Chauncey had decamped and Katy's marriage was annulled when her lawyer found out Chauncey's legal name was Marvin Buckley.

After her release, she became Katherine Baker, short order cook, a sober short order cook. Her shoulder-length blonde hair was now short and brown. She wore clear-lens glasses with tortoise shell frames. She dressed in plaid shirts, blue jeans, and brown hiking boots. She was wary of making friends and had lost touch with her family. She was quiet and hard working, always showing up on time and working with a single-minded focus that impressed and sometimes threatened those around her.

Over the years, she worked her way north through the Great Valley on U.S. 99 and then toward Oregon along Interstate 5, working in cafes, grills, and truck stops. She liked the work and she liked the independence. She could move on whenever she wanted, easily finding another job in the next town that suited her. By the time she landed at Nolan Beane's Log Cabin Restaurant in Roseburg, Oregon, she was journeyman cook. But she found there was more to learn and spent the next two years at Roseburg in what could be called a post-graduate fellowship, studying logging camp cuisine.

In Roseburg, Katherine started thinking about Cedar Mills. One night on a whim, she got her younger sister Karen's phone number from Information and called her. The call was short. Karen made it clear she had no interest in rekindling a relationship with her older sister.

"So why'd you call me?" Karen had asked, sounding defensive and resentful. "I'm not going to loan you any money if that's what you want."

"I just called to see how you were. I don't need anything."

"I'm doing great," Karen said sarcastically. "Not that you should care. I got my nursing degree. Just started working for a doctor in Ferndale."

Karen told her that after Katy had run off, the family left Cedar Mills the next year. Not long after that, their parents divorced. Pastor Ron Owling had drifted from church to church as a temporary pastor, calling himself a "Rent a Reverend."

"He finally disappeared. Haven't heard from him in years," Karen said.

She said their mother Susan had joined a group of fundamentalist Sanitarians led by the guru Mitchell Lodong, who preached that communal bathing several times a day brought one closer to God. She was living in Lodong's commune at Catchall, a small town between Index and Gold Bar on the road to Stevens Pass.

"So we're all just hunky dory, thanks to you," Karen barked. "Anything else you need to know?"

"I'm really sorry I bothered you," Katherine said and hung up.

But she kept thinking about Cedar Mills and eventually said goodbye to Nolan Beane and the Log Cabin Restaurant. She headed north to the Olympic Peninsula, thinking by now Katy Owling would be long forgotten. And even if she wasn't, no one would know Katherine Baker was that little tramp who'd run off with one of her high school teachers.

By an act of fortuitous coincidence, she arrived at Cedar Mills the week Greeley Martin was interviewing for a cook at his new Madison Café. When he interviewed Katherine, Greeley was skeptical about her ability to run the kitchen of his new restaurant. Katherine suggested he call Roseburg and get a reference from her former employer, Nolan Beane.

Katherine's old boss got right to the point, telling Greeley, "Hire her son, and don't let her go."

Greeley offered her the job on the spot, confessing that he didn't know much about running a restaurant so he hoped she did.

A New Friendship

The day after Katherine's confrontation with Axel Maise in the alley, Maude Doud knocked on Katherine's front door late in the afternoon. She wanted to tell her she was proud of what Katherine had done. She heard the piano as she came up the steps. When she knocked, there was an extended silence before Katherine finally opened the door.

Maude did all the talking as Katherine stared at her: Of course Katherine didn't know her, she was Greeley's aunt. She knew Katherine worked at the café. Greeley thought the world of her. They were neighbors, she lived two houses down on the other side of Second Avenue, the house with the noisy little dog in the yard. That's Rascal. She should have come and introduced herself before. She'd brought Katherine some just-baked chocolate chip cookies.

"Thank you Mrs. Doud," Katherine said. "I've seen you at the restaurant, I know you're Greeley's aunt. Would you like to come in."

Would she like to come in? Of course she'd like to come in. She couldn't think of anything more she wanted than to get inside Katherine's house. "Well, just for a minute, dear," Maude answered, brushing past Katherine with the determination of a life insurance salesman. "I'll put the cookies in the kitchen." She charged through the little house on a scouting sortie, taking in everything as she swept through the living room and dining room.

"I haven't seen the inside of this house since Greeley finished remodeling," Maude said. "This is the third house he's bought and rented out. For an ex-English teacher, Greeley's quite the businessman."

"It was very nice of him to rent it to me." Katherine said. "I've lived in single rooms for so long, I don't know what to do with all this space."

Maude said she couldn't stay, but then decided to sit a for minute after Katherine offered her a cup of coffee. They sat on a well-worn sofa covered with a blanket facing a weathered coffee table. Against the wall behind them was a bookshelf filled with paperback books. On the coffee table were *Three Centuries of American Poetry* and Stephen Crane's *The Red Badge of Courage*, along with the latest copy of *North Coast Passages*, the journal of the Cedar County Historical Society. A vintage Kimball baby grand piano occupied the rest of the living room.

"So there it is," Maude sighed, "Luther Moody's piano. Bless his heart. It doesn't seem he's been gone for over a year now."

Katherine told Maude how surprised she'd been when Greeley offered it to her after Luther had left it to him in his will along with a large collection of sheet music and an old piano tuning kit. Greely told her he didn't want any of it. The piano would probably end up as firewood if she didn't take it.

Then a few days later, Greeley, his Uncle Larry and his dad, Lonnie, along with Walt Beaver and his two boys, Matt and Harley, showed up with the piano and twenty-seven cardboard boxes of sheet music loaded on one of the old Ford flatbeds from Lonnie's lumber yard.

Maude got up and walked into the dining room while Katherine talked. Except for an oil stove in one corner, a brown rectangular metal box that was expected to heat the entire house, the dining room was bare. The kitchen was furnished with a small chrome-legged table with a Formica top and two wooden chairs. Despite its emptiness, the house was clean and neat. Maude resisted the urge to be brazenly rude and wander into the two bedrooms and bathroom that opened off the dining room. She returned to the living room and pointed to the piano, where an old weathered book of Czerny etudes was open on the music stand.

"I think the piano's found a good home. All Luther ever did when he wasn't playing at the American Legion, was sit at home and play that piano for hours. And now I hear you playing when I'm out with Rascal. You sound pretty good."

"Not really," Katherine answered. "I used to play years ago but I'm rusty."

Maude sat down on the sofa. "I see Greeley made sure you have a copy of that historical society journal," she said. "Greeley's the society president and editor, you know. That and the café have kept him going after his wife Janis died."

"He thought I'd be interested in his article about Luther Moody since I've got his piano."

"Luther Moody was one of strangest people to come out of this town. Nice, but weird as a three-legged rooster."

"I've started reading the article. I hope you don't say anything to Greeley, but it's pretty boring." Katherine said.

"You're not telling me anything. All you need to know is that Luther Moody left town for the Army after high school and never came back. Well, not until his mother was near death years later. I heard the whole story from his brother Rex, who was here from San Francisco for Luther's funeral. After the Army, Luther played piano in a nightclub in Seattle and then spent years with Corky Carlsson and The All Stars, playing around the state. He was calling himself Dallas Moody when he came home to take care of his mother, but none of us let him get away with that. He left here as Luther and would always be Luther. Spent the next few years playing on weekends at the American Legion. When he wasn't there he was home playing that piano day and night. Finally drank himself to death."

"Sounds sad," Katherine said. "But I can tell this piano has been loved just by the way the keyboard feels."

"Anyway, I came over to tell you I saw what happened in the alley when Axel Maise grabbed you. I was over on Cedar Street with Rascal. We saw what went down."

Katherine blushed, "I really didn't. . ."

"Let me finish, dear," Maude interrupted. "I'm happy you took care of that old snake. You deserve a medal for pulverizing him once and for all. I'm on the town council and I've been trying to get him run out of town for years. Pardon my French, but screw due process when it comes to trash like that. Anyway, you were well within your rights. He assaulted you. So now he's gone, and I've come to say thank you."

Katherine was silent.

"You don't have to say anything. And don't worry, it's between you, me and the fence post. You're going to have to give me a few lessons in self-defense sometime. There. Now I've told you." Maude said with a sigh. "Would you do me a favor before I go? Would you play something for me?"

Katherine walked over to the piano and closed the Czerny. She sat for a moment and then started playing softly from memory. It was Mozart, a piece of the "Piano Concerto 23 in A Major," the plaintive andante, saturated with sadness and regret. When she finished, Katherine hung her head for a few seconds and then looked over at Maude with a smile. "Julia Howe, my piano teacher in Iowa loved to hear me play that."

"Beautiful." Maude said, getting up and walking to the door with her back to Katherine, telling herself those weren't tears in her eyes.

Katherine followed her onto the front steps.

"Thank you for the cookies, Mrs. Doud," Katherine said. "And about what happened the other day. . ."

"Not one more word about it. It's behind us now." Maude said, pausing for a moment as she turned back toward Katherine. "I want to be your friend. Let me know if there's anything I can do for you."

Inspired by Maude's comments about Luther Moody, Katherine sat on the sofa, picked up *North Coast Passages* and looked through it carefully for the first time. She was surprised to see the names of people she knew from the cafe. Ezra Franklin, the insurance agent, had written a short piece about the spelling of a local river, "Greywolf or Graywolf: The Naming of a River." Marilyn Smallwood, the owner of Mountain View Cleaners and a morning regular at The Table, had written an article entitled, "Early Peninsula Transportation: Footwear Styles of the Coastal Salish Indians."

After Greeley's article on Moody, which took up half the journal, there was a tribute to Bert Peck, the Bateman's Bread truck driver and his wife Ina for their "generous contribution" of the "Sydney Dickens Bible" which was to be sold at auction for the start of a society trust fund. Katherine stretched out on the sofa and started reading "Luther 'Dallas' Moody, A Man and His Piano" again. This time she got as far as Luther quitting his job at the Northern Lights Club in Seattle's Arctic Hotel to join Corky Carlsson and The All Stars before she nodded off to sleep.

Katherine's Piano

Katherine Baker's baby grand piano started life known by its maker as "Kimball Compact Grand Piano, Serial No. 1891-9183." It came out of Kimball's Chicago works in 1891 already sold and crated for shipment. Taken to Rock Island, Illinois by rail and transported by barge down the Mississippi River to New Orleans, the piano was put aboard the newly christened *Arundhati Star*, a passenger steamer built at Martineau Shipyards in the Crescent City. The ship was bound for India and the waters around Bombay where it served as the flagship for a small fleet of vessels owned by Kumar Mahindra. The piano was the centerpiece of the ship's grand salon which was intended as an entertainment venue for officers of the British Raj in order to further advance Mahindra's favor with the colonial government.

The *Arundhati Star* sailed in Bombay waters from 1892 until 1895, functioning as a private yacht for Kumar Mahindra, his wife, and their guests, who were selected by how beneficial they could be to the advancement of Mahindra's wealth and power. Then, during the unrest of 1895 when a wave of nationalism boiled over into riots, the shipping magnate, who was considered an arm of the colonial regime, made plans to escape with his family aboard the *Arundhati Star*. He began moving the family's most precious belongings on board the ship in advance of any threats to their safety.

But their plan to escape failed. Mahindra and his wife were both stabbed to death when a mob of Hindi nationalists invaded their estate. Their two-year old daughter, Indira, was spared and was adopted by her godfather, Sir William Butterworth, a vice-governor of Bombay. As executor of the Mahindra estate, Butterworth sold everything and put the money into a trust for young Indira. He sent the little girl to London to be raised by his sister Lydia and her husband Montgomery Naismith, an international banker of considerable wealth.

The *Arundhati Star* was sold in 1896 to Cyrus Milton of San Francisco who was expanding his shipping operations north into Puget Sound. By 1897, the ship had been renamed the *Arctic Maid* and with the Kimball Compact Grand Piano, Serial No. 1891-9183, still aboard but abjectly shoved into a corner of the grand salon, she was sailing the crowded route from Seattle to Alaska, hauling men and supplies back and forth during the Klondike gold rush.

Cyrus Milton made a fortune during the Stampede and he used some of it to build the Arctic Hotel in downtown Seattle when the gold rush ended in 1899. A "presidential suite" was constructed on the top floor of the twelve-story hotel with panoramic views of Elliott Bay and the Olympic Mountains beyond. Construction of the hotel was completed in 1900. Then, after thousands of miles on three oceans and as many continents, the Kimball baby grand piano was moved from the *Arctic Maid* to the Arctic Hotel's presidential suite.

The piano had been played by hundreds of hands in those nine years. It had led the singing of ballads and bawdy songs of Kiplingesque soldiers on the South Asian subcontinent and ethereal Hindi melodies sung by fey young Indian men for the entertainment of their colonial overlords. Dance hall songs had been pounded out on the piano by Klondike whores and boozed-up barroom balladeers running away to seek their fortune in the Yukon. Then years passed while it sat as an ornamental part of the furnishings in an elegant room with a view until Luther Moody became its new owner and took it home to Cedar Mills.

But the piano's Indian past was not forgotten. Years later, when the piano occupied Katherine Baker's living room, Kumar Mahindra's grandson, the Indian-Englishman Paul Merrick, began a quest to find the piano and the secrets it held, swearing an oath to do whatever it took to succeed.

Working at the Madison Café

It didn't take long for Katherine to realize that Greeley's declaration of not knowing much about running a restaurant was only the surface of the truth. Most people in her shoes would have walked out when they saw he was clueless about what it would take to turn the Madison Café into a viable business. But Katherine stayed.

After carefully assessing the bleak situation, she told Greeley the café couldn't open in two weeks as he'd announced. It would be at least a month before the place was ready for business. Then she made a list of what had to be done and outlined her plans, tactfully calling it *their* plan of action. Greeley was impressed with her unemotional, businesslike presentation and acceded to her every recommendation, even when it came to additional capital investments in equipment.

When the restaurant did open and business was slow for the first six months, so slow that the ever-optimistic Greeley was starting to have second thoughts about the venture, Katherine maintained a steady, resolute demeanor, never showing any concern that the business might fail. She was the indefatigable cheerleader, making her co-workers feel more optimistic about their jobs than perhaps they should have.

When the busboy Bobby Carr had nothing to do but stand around because all the tables were cleared and all the dishes were washed, Katherine taught him the basics of taking inventory and some other minor tasks that made the dyslexic twenty-year-old, who had been labeled "learning disabled," even more proud he had a job.

Sadie Nixon, the café's only waitress, had been around enough to know when to bail out on a losing proposition but she could see Katherine had paid her dues in the restaurant business which was enough to keep her hanging on a bit longer. When things were quiet, Katherine brought Sadie into the kitchen to make a late breakfast or early lunch, teaching her the balancing-act art of the short order cook. The bond between the two women grew because of it.

Finally business started to pick up and before the first year was over, the place was full in the early morning hours for breakfast and equally busy for lunch. By then, everyone had forgotten about the times when they expected Greeley to abruptly close the restaurant. Everyone had forgotten except Greeley. He knew it was Katherine who had saved the restaurant from going under. To show his gratitude, he promoted her to head cook which came with a salary increase that even surprised Katherine.

So it was when Katherine pummeled Axel Maise in the alley that morning. This was Katherine's world and she was proud of what she'd done. But she also knew her success was due in large part to Greeley Martin's support. There was the house he'd rented to her with a lease agreement that made it a gift. Then he'd surprised her with Luther Moody's old piano which she loved. There'd been countless other things he'd done for her, small but thoughtful things, because he'd taken to heart Nolan Beane's dictum to do whatever it took to keep her from moving on.

Maude and Katherine's Friendship Goes Awry

Maude didn't waste any time developing a friendship with Katherine after her first visit. When she came into the café, Maude made it a point to lean over the service counter into the kitchen and shout a hello to Katherine, who returned the greeting with a tight smile.

Katherine resisted giving the older woman any encouragement, but Maude was Greeley's aunt and snubbing her would be impolite and probably offensive to her boss. So she gave in to Maude's invitations, agreeing to join her on a Saturday outing to the Ravensdale Mall or taking a Sunday drive out along the coast west of Port Smith trying to spot killer whales or spending an afternoon driving around the historic areas of Gosport.

One Saturday afternoon over lunch at the Stuffed Onion Steakhouse after a shopping trip to the mall, Maude was relieved to see Katherine finally laugh out loud when she told her about her new "boyfriend," Milos Grajek, the "Mad Polack."

She told Katherine that a few months ago she'd had to call Will McCann because Grajek would stop at her back yard on his way home from town and yell at her dog Rascal in Polish. The Polish hermit frightened her and she told Will she wanted him arrested for disturbing the peace. But when confronted by the constable, Grajek politely explained he was only trying to teach the dog Polish. He was very sorry he'd caused Maude or the dog any anxiety.

Will arranged a meeting between Maude and Grajek, where in a courtly manner only Europeans are capable of, the Polish émigré apologized to Maude, promising not to shout at her dog again. The two became close friends, so close that the widowed Maude teasingly called him her boyfriend and fixed him dinner at least once a week. She gave Grajek a key to the back door of her house so he could come and go as he pleased, a move that raised the eyebrows of her brother Lonnie and her nephew Greeley.

With stories like this, Katherine's resistance to Maude softened. She started looking forward to hearing the older woman gossip about everyone in town especially about her own family, the Martins. How her brother Lonnie couldn't understand his wife Elizabeth's anger because Greeley had encouraged her younger brother Larry, Greeley's Uncle Larry, to come to Cedar Mills after he'd been released from prison. Elizabeth Martin didn't want her younger brother, now an ex-convict, in her neighborhood and his arrival in town to work at the Madison Café had caused a fissure in the family. Greeley was especially perturbed by his mother's petulance and Lonnie had to play peacemaker between mother and son.

Maude said Greeley had been the only one in the family to support Larry when he was sentenced to four years in Federal prison for tax evasion. Larry's wife divorced him and alienated him from his daughter. His parents turned their back on him, and his older sister Elizabeth, the one who had been his biggest supporter, refused to acknowledge his existence. Only Greeley had kept in touch with his uncle while Larry was incarcerated, offering him a job and a place to live when he was released.

Maude said she didn't know how Katherine felt about having to work with Larry, but she was personally glad he'd come to town, something she could never say to her sister-in-law, because no one was allowed to mention Larry Bradford in Elizabeth Martin's presence. First and foremost to his credit, Maude explained, Larry was a master duplicate bridge player, a skill he had honed during his time at Allenwood. It hadn't taken Maude long to talk him into being her partner at the twice monthly duplicate bridge club at Trinity Episcopal Church. She didn't waste any time in gleefully telling Greeley he'd been benched in favor of his uncle.

"The boy never could count his cards and he insisted on leading away from a king, no matter how many times I told him," she told Katherine. "Larry's been a godsend to me and everyone at Friday night bridge loves him."

But the growing friendship between Katherine and Maude turned sour one Sunday evening after dinner at Maude's when she pulled out an old scrapbook. Sitting next to Katherine on the sofa, she turned to a bookmarked page and passed the book to Katherine, saying with a smile, "I thought it would be fun for you see these."

There were two yellowed newspaper clippings from the *Cedar Mills Gazette*, one on each page. The one on the left detailed the swearing in of the town's mayor, Herschel "King" Doud to his fourth term in office where the entertainment for the evening was a medley of Irish favorites sung by high school student Katy Owling who accompanied herself on the piano. The clipping on the right detailed Maude Doud's installation as Soroptimist Club president with vocal entertainment provided by the high school Swing Time Chorus with a solo by Katy Owling.

Maude said with a wistful smile, "It brings back old memories of good times gone by." Katherine stared at the clippings as Maude continued, "I'll never forget when you moved from Iowa and your father took over the Presbyterian church. It was a blessing to us all when the Owlings moved to town."

Katherine's face was pale. Her hands were shaking. She stood up, handed the scrapbook to Maude, and went to the front door without a word. She turned to Maude as she opened the door, "I don't know what you're trying to prove. Katy Owling's dead," Katherine growled. "I watched her die."

She turned and walked out, quietly closing the door behind her.

Katherine Misses Work

On weekday mornings, Greeley was at the café by four a.m., getting the first coffee going, the grills powered on, and whatever else was on Katherine's morning startup list. Katherine arrived an hour later, about the time Larry, the second cook, came down from his upstairs apartment. Sadie and Bobby Carr arrived just before six when the doors opened.

On Monday morning, following Katherine's dinner with Maude and her tantrum-filled departure, Katherine hadn't shown up by opening time. She'd never been late or missed a day of work. Her absence made everyone anxious. Greeley started pacing around the dining room, furtively looking at the back door each time it opened. Sadie told her first customers, mostly the regulars who occupied The Table, that there'd be coffee but nothing else for a while because they had an electrical problem in the kitchen. Larry told Greeley he could probably get some food out, but it would take a while. Meanwhile Bobby, who was growing increasingly uneasy over Katherine's absence, started running the empty dishwasher and singing "Home on the Range" until Larry redirected him to the storeroom to take inventory.

Finally at seven, Sadie took off her apron and left, telling Greeley she was going to walk up to Katherine's to see what was going on. Greeley told everyone in the dining room they'd be closing for the day because of electrical problems in the kitchen. Then he hung the "Closed" signs on the front and back doors and sat with Larry and Bobby, waiting for news from Sadie.

Katherine's car, an old square-back Toyota station wagon, was parked in front of her house on Cedar Street. Two beaten up brown suitcases were stacked on the passenger-side front seat, plastic garbage bags stuffed with clothes, and paper bags loaded with paperback books filled the back. Sadie knew from experience how easy it is to pick up and leave once you've been a drifter. Sometimes you thought about it for a while and sometimes it happened overnight, you packed up and left. It was obvious Katherine was on her way out of town.

The front door was slightly ajar when Sadie knocked. She heard

Katherine whisper "It's open." She sat cross legged on the living room floor staring at the piano and mumbling, "It won't start. The damn car won't start." Then she fell over on her side in the fetal position, sobbing. Sadie pulled her up onto the sofa. She held Katherine while she continued to cry and murmured, "It's ok, it's ok."

This was how Greeley found them shortly after noon. Sadie told him, "I'm staying here. Someone will have to take Bobby home. You'll have to close the café tomorrow."

"Is there anything I can. . .," he started to ask.

"No. There's nothing you can do," Sadie answered. "I'll call you later."

Greeley walked back down the alley to the café and helped Larry and Bobby shut down the kitchen. Then he hung the "Closed" signs on the front and back doors where they remained the next morning when the first of the morning crowd stood at the back door to the dining room and muttered, "What the hell?"

The Owling Family in Iowa

Reverend Ron Owling and his family had moved to Cedar Mills from Cedar Rapids, Iowa to lead the Cedar Mills Presbyterian Church when, after a reign of thirty years, Reverend Amos Smith had finally relinquished his post as shepherd of a dwindling flock of parishioners. With his wife Susan and their daughters, Katy and Karen, fifteen and twelve respectively, the new pastor brought a breath of fresh air, a regenerative optimism, and hope for a new beginning to the moribund congregation. Pastor Ron, as he preferred to be called, told everyone he met in Cedar Mills that what they might see as problems with the church were to him only opportunities for growth and stepping stones to a new future.

But in spite of all his ecclesiastical boosterism, it had not been easy for the minister to move his family out of their comfortable life in the Midwest to the Olympic Peninsula of Washington state, a remote, undeveloped part of the country. To describe Susan and their daughters as distraught about the end to an idyllic existence would be an understatement. His attempts to convince his wife that the move from one "Cedar" to another "Cedar" must in part be divine intervention, fell on deaf ears. It was divine madness, she told him more than once, even when he insisted he'd been called to Cedar Mills by "the higher authority" to take charge of a foundering church that he and only he could save.

Susan knew all about being "called," having grown up in the Southwest with a Pentecostal preacher for a father and a stoic, obedient wife for a mother. She had worked hard to escape that life and considered her marriage to a newly ordained Presbyterian cleric a step up in the world. They had worked hard together building a life in Cedar Rapids, where fresh out of seminary, Pastor Ron had taken a position as youth minister at the recently formed New Presbyterian Church with the mission to reach out to the students of tiny Coe College.

Fifteen years later, the Cedar Rapids New Presbyterian Church had become an important part of student life at the college. Pastor Ron was not only senior youth minister but was also formally associated with the college as adjunct professor of religious life counseling. Susan had created her own career after the girls started school, and was comfortably settled into her job as office manager at the law firm of McCutcheon & Tarr in downtown Cedar Rapids.

Pastor Ron was known for his exuberant interest in the well-being of the Coe College students, an interest that went well beyond weekly bible study classes, the Sunday service, and monthly Sunday night home-style dinners. He was a counselor, a mentor, and a life coach to all those who needed him. Then in the last two years of his tenure at New Presbyterian, an undercurrent of gossip slowly started to flow that the pastor's energetic activities with some of the female students might be crossing the line of acceptable behavior. It was also rumored his outreach efforts sometimes extended into the dark side of nightlife in Iowa City.

No outright accusations or specific charges were leveled at the popular minister but the rumors continued to grow until a few weeks before commencement in Pastor Ron's sixteenth year at the college, the college president, Bart Mann, together with the head of the East Iowa Presbytery, Carson Markley decided that, innocent or not, Reverend Ron Owling had to go.

"He reminds me of a Baptist, " President Mann told Elder Markley. "They're like cats. They love to raise hell but you can't catch 'em at it."

At commencement that spring, Reverend Owling was awarded the Grover Pickering Award for Outstanding Service to College and Community. In awarding the gold medallion and wall plaque to Pastor Ron, the college president took note of the cleric's bright future, saying he was certain the reverend was destined for even greater accomplishments.

The following week, Carson Markley started having weekly lunches with Pastor Ron and it was apparent to Reverend Owling he was being slowly admitted into the inner circle of church leadership. He was ready to accept whatever Elder Markley laid before him even though moving west to Cedar Mills, Washington had not been on his list of possibilities. But Markley convinced him that he'd built a "shining city on the hill" in Cedar Rapids and now he was being called to build once again, in Cedar Mills. The church needed him.

By the middle of that summer, Ron had finally convinced Susan that they had no choice, his taking charge of a foundering church in the West had been ordained by God. Susan capitulated and worked hard to convince their two daughters their lives were not being completely destroyed. Katy had to accept the fact that she'd no longer have her piano and singing lessons with Julia Howe, and Karen had to hope the Cedar Mills junior high school had a volleyball team.

Prior to their move which was scheduled to take place in September just before Katy would start her sophomore year at the new high school and Karen would start seventh grade, Ron made plans for an exploratory trip to Cedar Mills to make arrangements for a place to live and meet with the elders of his new church. At Susan's suggestion, he agreed to take Katy, hoping it would help ease the pain of the transition to a new home.

Pastor Ron and his oldest daughter left Cedar Rapids before dawn on a Monday in early July, the first day putting in over five hundred miles, stopping in North Platte, Nebraska after a grueling day on Interstate 80. It had been an awkward day. Neither father nor daughter had talked much. Ron's ease at talking with college students and his facility at getting involved in their lives had not translated to his daughters. Katy didn't care, she preferred to stare out the window or read a book, saying "whatever you want to do," when her father suggested they stop.

It was even more awkward when they rented one room with two double beds at the Sedgewick Motel and Restaurant, even though Ron made it seem as though it was hardly uncomfortable to be sharing a room and bathroom with his fifteen-year-old daughter. Katy finally came out of her shell at dinner when her father ordered a glass of red wine while they looked at the menu, asking him with a disapproving tone what he thought he was doing.

"It's nothing new, your mother and I have wine when we go out to dinner," he said. "And besides, it's been a long day, I need to relax."

They ate dinner in silence in spite of Ron's occasional attempts to get his daughter to talk. There was nothing he was going to say to convince her that moving was going to do anything but ruin her life forever, and she didn't want to talk about it. Then he ordered a second glass of wine.

"You're starting to embarrass me," she said disapprovingly.

Ron only smiled.

Back in the motel room, Katy got ready for bed first. Ron had already turned out the lights and was sitting in a chair by the window waiting for his turn in the bathroom. Katy came out in her pajamas, walked over to him, put a hand on his shoulder and told him goodnight, saying she'd try to be better company tomorrow.

When Ron came out of the bathroom into the dark bedroom, he climbed into bed next to Katy.

"Oh my," he exclaimed. "I thought you were in the other bed."

Katy lay in bed with her back to him saying nothing. He moved closer to her, reaching his arm around her and chuckled at his silly mistake while he gave her a hug. Just before he pushed away, she could feel his hardness against her bottom. Did he linger there? Was it a moment too long? But then he was gone, in the other bed, saying good night.

Katy didn't move for a long time, waiting until she thought her father was asleep. Then she crept out of bed and went into the bathroom. She closed the door, stood over the sink and vomited.

The next morning they were on the road again just as the sun was rising over the Nebraska prairie. When Katy flatly told her father that either they'd stay in separate rooms for the rest of the trip or she'd take a Greyhound bus back to Iowa, Ron tried to make a joke of it but he acquiesced and what happened that first night at North Platte didn't happen again.

But Katy never forgot her father's sickeningly sweet wine-infused breath cloaking everything around him, his arm around her in bed, and his body pushing next to hers. It still made her sick to her stomach and it was in the aftermath of that night in Nebraska that her hatred of him began to grow. And later, back home in Cedar Rapids when she tried to tell her mother what her father had done that night in North Platte, Susan Owling dismissed her daughter's story as the product of an over-active imagination.

Sadie Takes Charge

Katherine didn't leave town and the Madison Café opened on Wednesday morning with everyone back at work. The place was soon as busy as normal and nothing was said about Katherine's two-day absence. The only overt recognition from her fellow workers that they were glad she was back came from Bobby Carr who gave her a hug. Greeley, Sadie, and Larry had the good sense to keep their mouths shut. To their credit no one said anything insipid like "let me know if you want to talk about it."

It was Sadie who'd convinced Katherine to stay. She was still at Katherine's on Monday afternoon when she called Greeley and told him to go get the overnight bag her sister Vicki had put together for her and to bring some pizza on the way. When he arrived, she refused to let him in, taking the bag and pizza and saying she'd give him an update in the morning. Sadie spent that night and most of the next day at Katherine's.

Early that evening, Sadie managed to get Katherine into bed by telling her she'd be there beside her. Katherine, still occasionally sobbing, fell asleep in Sadie's arms. During the night Katherine dropped a gold coin she'd clutched in her left hand all day. It fell between them on the bed. Sadie picked it up and held it in the dim light coming from the bathroom. A pyramid with a circled number "8" was etched on one side, around the circle the word "years" were imprinted and outside the pyramid "To Thine Own Self Be True" was printed around the edge. Sadie knew it was a sobriety coin, a treasured talisman for many recovering alcoholics. She reached over and put the coin next to Katherine on her nightstand, sighing, "You're too young to be so old, little girl."

The next morning, Sadie woke to an empty bed and the sounds of the piano in the living room. She lay in bed listening to the andante to Mozart's Piano Concerto 23 in A major. Katherine played it several times before switching to a series of equally lugubrious Chopin nocturnes. Sadie got up and walked into the living room, "My god, don't you know anything cheerful?"

Katherine turned to her with a wan smile and kept playing. "This music makes me feel better," she said.

Sadie shook her head and went to the kitchen. Soon they were sitting at the kitchen table over toast and scrambled eggs.

"After this, I want you to give me a concert," Sadie demanded. "Of stuff I know. Stuff I can sing along with."

So they spent all morning and most of the afternoon around the piano with Sadie occasionally pulling out some of Luther Moody's old sheet music, saying "here play this." Her musical tastes ran to folk, rock and country music of the '60s, '70s and '80s. They sang "Me and Bobby McGee," "Mama Tried," and "Bad, Bad, Leroy Brown," more times than either could count. Late in the afternoon, Sadie called Greeley and told him to bring them something to eat from Jerry Zampini's Chicken in a Basket. She met him on the steps outside and told him to plan on opening the café in the morning.

Katherine and Sadie sat in the kitchen with fried chicken, biscuits, and French fries covering the table. Sadie said she'd told Greeley that he could open the café in the morning and that she was pretty sure Katherine would be back to work.

"I don't want to make you run away," she said. "But we all love you and want you back."

Katherine looked embarrassed, "I'll be there."

Sadie offered to spend the night again but Katherine said no, she'd be fine. Her biggest concern was the car and what she was going to do about unloading it and getting it started.

"Forget about it for now," Sadie told her. "Things will take care of themselves. I'll help you unload it later."

Katherine whispered "Thank you," as they hugged on the front steps.

Sadie said "See you in the morning," and started down the alley to the café where her car was parked.

The Owling Family in Cedar Mills

Any misgivings the Owling family had when leaving Cedar Rapids for their new home in the West were not apparent to the residents of Cedar Mills. The family had left a comfortable and outwardly happy life in the Midwest and ventured into the unknown, wild landscape of the Pacific Northwest but any fear or anxiety on their part took the form of an exuberant embracing of their new life. Their arrival took the Cedar Mills Presbyterian population by storm. They were a unified self-cheerleading team, happy, positive, and kindly curious about learning all they could about their new surroundings.

The Cedar Mills Presbyterian Church elders had been so impressed with the new minister and his delightful daughter on their first trip to Cedar Mills, they'd marshaled the entire congregation to make sure the family had a suitable place to live when they arrived. To that end, two members of the congregation, Carl Wilfong of Wilfong's Variety, and Bud Fitzpatrick of Town and Country Furniture, had donated enough money to buy the abandoned Dutch Mooney farmhouse southwest of town on Cedar River Road. The church members all pitched in to fix up the place and in a few weeks they transformed the old two-story wood frame house into an inviting family home any real estate agent would have loved to put on the market. The finishing touches of a fresh coat of white paint with red trim and a white picket fence around the front yard, were completed only days before the Owlings arrived.

One afternoon in early September, the Owlings pulled into the driveway of the house in their new Jeep Wagoneer with a wood grain exterior, which had been donated by the East Iowa Presbytery in honor of Reverend Ron's many contributions over the years. The Owlings belongings, including Katy's upright piano, had arrived two days before in a Mayflower moving van, the cost of which had been donated by the Coe College board of trustees in honor of Reverend Ron's enriching the spiritual lives of hundreds of Coe students during his fifteen-year tenure at the college.

Reverend Ron Owling would be the first to admit he was no theological savant, nor did he have a flair for dynamic preaching. But as Elder Carson Markley told him back in Cedar Rapids, his strength was in the pastoral side of the ministry which made Pastor Ron an overnight success in Cedar Mills. By the time of his arrival, at least half of the congregation had dropped off the active roles of the church, being driven away by the geriatric Reverend Amos Smith, who found it difficult to finish Sunday worship without dozing off before the end of the service.

Pastor Ron immediately started reversing the congregational atrophy. The new minister rejuvenated the Sunday morning adult bible study group while his wife Susan reorganized the defunct children's Sunday school, enlisting Katy and Karen to help teach classes. With Susan's help, Ron started a lively campaign to rebuild the church choir and after only two months, their recruiting efforts had been so successful there was a waiting list for members to join.

Reverend Owling was a ebullient huckster for God. The messages he posted on the sign in front of the church on Main Street made everyone smile and usually caught the attention of a photographer from one of the local papers. Messages like *Sign Broken. Come Inside for Message.* Or *No Ice Cream. No Milkshakes. Just Great Sundays.*

As a former youth minister, Pastor Ron reached out to the pre-teen and teenagers of his Presbyterian community with an irresistible enthusiasm. With the help of Katy and Karen, they put together a Tuesday night bible study group for pre-teens and Wednesday night group for teens. He cajoled the board of elders for money to buy an old school bus which was used for roller skating parties at the roller rink in Port Smith and trips to Duckabush Hot Springs in the mountains which beckoned with an Olympic-size swimming pool. The Presbyterian Church was suddenly a cool place to be for the kids of Cedar Mills.

By their second year at Cedar Mills, Ron and Susan Owling had become active community members outside the church. Ron joined the Rotary Club and Susan became a member of the Soroptomists, leading more than one person to say "They don't seem like church people."

The Owling daughters excelled in all they did. At school, Karen was a good student but more interested in sports and quickly became a star of the junior high school volleyball team. Katy was an outstanding student who maintained a straight-A grade point average, while taking part in a host of extracurricular activities especially anything connected with the high school music department. Townspeople were impressed that the Owling parents always found time to attend their daughters' school functions, whether it was a soccer game or a school play where more than once, Katy played the lead.

But there was also a dark side to the Owling family's private life after their move to Cedar Mills. Susan Owling slowly started to change from a supportive mother, a cheerleader for her children, to what the younger daughter, Karen, would later describe as a psycho-terrorist, "an aggressive, mean, verbally abusive ogre." And it was Katy who bore the brunt of her mother's scorn which took the form of whispered surprise attacks when Katy least expected it. Susan would quietly come up behind Katy when they were working in the kitchen, or when Katy was doing homework in her bedroom and in a low guttural voice tell Katy she was nothing but a worthless tramp. Susan said she knew that Kathy had tempted her father that night in the Nebraska motel room.

The more Katy succeeded in school the more vicious her mother's verbal attacks became. Susan was obsessed with Katy's underpants, excoriating her for not keeping them clean. In what Katy came to call "an ambush," her mother would whisper, "I know you know how to wipe your bottom so why do I keep seeing those brown stains on your underpants. You're just making more work for me. Or are you're trying to get back at me because you're a mean little troglodyte. I'm the one who has to wash your underpants, so wipe."

More than once after attending a school concert or play in which Katy took part, her mother would eventually get around to whispering, often cheerfully, "I hope people in the audience don't know you're up there on stage with stained underpants. What kind of mother would they think I was. How do you think I would feel if they knew?"

Katy learned to keep quiet during her mother's *sotto voce* diatribes, fearing an outright physical assault. But during her three years in high school at Cedar Mills, she grew to hate both her parents and their sanctimonious varnish of untouchable respectability. She started to daydream about running away, hitchhiking to Seattle and taking a Greyhound bus back to Iowa where her music teacher, Julia Howe, would take her in.

In Katy's senior year in high school her reputation as an accomplished pianist with the voice of an angel was well-established. Art Fletcher, now the assistant director of music and conductor of the swing chorus had promoted her to lead soloist and Katy was already thinking of a show business career, something she wouldn't dare discuss with her parents but talked about at length with her music teacher who was her biggest fan.

At home that year, there were more dark developments in the Owling's family life when Katy discovered a half-empty bottle of vodka hidden in the back of the cabinet under the kitchen sink. The liquor bottle helped explain her parents' late night raucous behavior. Katy would sit in her favorite place, an old easy chair on the upstairs landing, where she spent hours reading, listening into the night as Ron and Susan's voices got louder, sometimes arguing and sometimes having sex everywhere but in their bed.

"Jesus, that feels good, Ron" she heard her mother moan one night from somewhere in the living room.

"Don't take the name of the Lord in vain, even if it does," Ron drunkenly chortled.

Her father's voice sounded like it did that night in Nebraska and Katy ran to the bathroom to vomit. Later, she lay in bed sobbing. She was trapped in a madhouse.

❖ ❖ ❖ ❖ ❖ ❖ ❖ ❖ ❖ ❖ ❖

That spring, the Cedar Mills High School Good Time Swing Chorus took part in the annual all-state high school band and chorus festival in Tacoma, a four-day event held at Pacific Lutheran College. Art Fletcher was one of the co-directors of the annual gathering and he wasted no time in devising ways to get his favorite student plenty of stage time. He and Katy had been spending long hours together in the music room at school talking about her future. Their close teacher-student relationship had been borne from Katy's need for a parent-figure but it had grown into something beyond Platonic. There were long hugs, pecks on the cheek, and inadvertent body contact with a growing suggestion their relationship was developing into something sexual.

Then at the music festival, Katy met Johnny Herrera, an Hispanic Adonis, drum major, and lead singer of the Yakima High School Swinging Singers. He was a star, a beautiful star, and for the first time Katy was in love.

Art was director of the final event of the festival, the Saturday night all-school revue with the top chorus and band members from across the state selected by a jury of music teachers. Johnny Herrera and Katy Owling were chosen to close the show with two songs befitting the theme of the festival, "The Great American Songbook," Burt Bachrach's "Rain Drops Keep Fallin' On My Head," and Leonard Bernstein's "Somewhere."

On Friday, under Art's direction, Katy and Johnny rehearsed most of the day and well into the night until exhausted, the couple fell together on a sofa backstage after everyone else had left and Katy Owling lost her virginity without a moment's regret. They spent the next day together in more rehearsals and a few hours before the performance, snuck off to Johnny's dormitory room to be together one last time.

The Bachrach number opened the show's last act with Katy at the piano and Johnny walking on stage with his hands in his pockets and paper raindrops falling. Katy stopped playing the piano and handed him an umbrella and the two sang and danced together in a warm-hearted vaudevillian routine. Then they brought down the house with "Somewhere," wrought more heart-wrenching given Katy and Johnny's disparate ethnic backgrounds.

During rehearsals, when Art had made them prepare an encore number, both Katy and Johnny had laughed, telling the teacher there wouldn't be an encore. But there was. The audience was on their feet, clapping and shouting "Johnny, Johnny" and "Katy, Katy." Their encore number, Henry Mancini and Johnny Mercer's "Moon River" brought the audience back to their feet, when on the second time through, Johnny stepped out to the front of the stage and urged everyone to sing along. The show ended with the entire house singing with unabashed joy.

The next morning, Katy was one of the first to get on the Cedar Mills high school bus, part of a line of buses idling in front of the performing arts center, waiting to take everyone home. She sat on the aisle side of a seat near the back, away from the window so Johnny Herrera, who was walk-ing up and down on the sidewalk alongside the bus, couldn't see her. Half afraid he was going to climb on the bus looking for her, she kept low in the seat. Finally Johnny walked back to the Yakima High School bus and Katy whispered to herself "Goodbye Johnny, I love you."

It was early March when the festival in Tacoma ended. Katy returned home filled with thoughts of her future as a Broadway star and an adoring Art Fletcher telling her how it could happen. By the first week in June, with graduation only a week away, Katy knew she was pregnant, having missed three periods since the trip to Tacoma. She and Art had already put together their plan of escape from Cedar Mills the night of graduation. She had no idea what she'd do about the baby. There was no one to talk to and no doctor she could see. An abortion in that place at that time was out of the question. She just had to get out of town and escape from the crazy sickness of her family life.

Katy met Art after midnight when she ducked out of a graduation party at Sissy Palmer's house a few blocks from the high school and walked a block to the public library parking lot in the rear of the building where Art was waiting in his camper. He leaned over and tried to hug her when she got in the truck, but she pushed him away and said, "Let's get out of here."

Their third day on the road found Katy and Art crossing the Siskiyou Mountains into California on Interstate 5. Just south of Yreka, Katy told Art she was three months pregnant and that's why they weren't going to have sex. Art said nothing, he just turned up the radio and continued to drive. He kept driving for five more days, stopping only for brief naps at rest stops and for coffee and snacks when they needed gas. He never said another word to Katy. Finally, in Los Angeles, he pulled over somewhere on Sunset Boule-vard, walked to the back of the camper, took out Katy's suitcase, walked to the passenger-side door of the pickup and told Katy to get out. Handing her the suitcase, he got back in the truck and drove off.

Katy Owling's new life had just begun.

Friday Night Bridge

Every other Friday night, when the Cedar Mills Duplicate Bridge club met at the Trinity Episcopal Church parish hall, Larry Bradford left his apartment above the Madison Café at six-thirty and walked up the alley two blocks to Second Avenue and down a half a block to Maude Doud's, where she was waiting at the front door for their leisurely walk across Main Street and over to the parish hall, four blocks away.

His route took him past Katherine's back yard at the corner of the alley and Second Avenue. It was an early September evening, two days after Katherine had returned to work at the restaurant. As Larry started up the alley, he saw a short, stocky figure duck into Katherine's back yard. As he neared the backyard gate, the stranger darted out and pushed past him into the alley, running up to Second Avenue where he turned right toward Main Street. Larry yelled at him to stop but he disappeared into the night.

Larry walked over and closed the back yard gate. He stood on Second Avenue and listened to an idling diesel semi on Main Street get into gear and head east out of town. Then he walked over to Maude's.

✧ ✧ ✧ ✧ ✧ ✧ ✧ ✧ ✧ ✧ ✧ ✧

Larry didn't tell Maude about the incident in the alley. He was more interested in listening to her tell why Katherine hadn't come to work for two days. The older woman confessed that she'd probably caused the bout of hysteria that led to Katherine's not showing up for work. "I got nostalgic," Maude said. "I pulled out an old scrapbook with newspaper clippings about her time in high school, when she was Katy Owling. She went ballistic. Yelled that Katy Owling was dead, and walked out."

Maude told him about Katherine Baker nee Katy Owling's earlier life in Cedar Mills. How the Owlings brought a breath of fresh air to the community. They were the golden family from Iowa, she said. Then four years later, the family was broken apart and gone from Cedar Mills.

"Some people said that Katy caused the family breakup when she left town with the high school teacher the night she graduated," Maude said officiously. "But I didn't buy it. Katy's leaving was just the tip of the iceberg.

There was something else going on."

"Who cares? It was years ago." Larry said as they neared the parish hall.

"It doesn't matter, except that Katherine Baker had a conniption fit last Sunday when I mentioned her past as Katy Owling," Maude answered as they started into the hall. "Everyone knew who she was when she came back here and nobody really cared. She's just fooling herself. I can't figure why she ever came back in the first place."

At parish hall, they were greeted by Reverend Tom Flatte, the rector of Trinity Episcopal, and Reverend Bob Ericksen, the minister of St. Paul's Lutheran, a formidable team at the bridge table. They could be counted on to give Maude and Larry stiff competition for first place along with the couple standing behind the two clerics, Marty Birch and Len Biddle, partners in the clothing store Birch & Biddle's Main Street Toggery. The two nodded unsmilingly at Maude and Larry as they walked by. They were all friends, except on Friday nights at the bridge table.

Maude led Larry over to meet Anne Lindsay, a tall woman in her fifties with long blonde hair, who apologetically announced it was her first time playing duplicate bridge, that she had only come at Maude's urging.

"You two are Greeley Martin's aunt and uncle, but not related," she said with a smile. "I think that makes you shirt-tail relatives." They laughed as Maude asked Anne about her son Jack, a lawyer who had just moved from Chicago to Seattle.

There were ten tables that night and the competition was intense. The final round of the evening pitted Birch and Biddle against Maude and Larry. In his signature style of smiling while he eviscerated your game, Larry miraculously put the determined opposition down one on a three no-trump bid thus stopping them from taking the rubber and the match. This allowed Maude and Larry to regroup and eke out a small slam in a decisive *coup de grace*.

"I thought we might have a meager chance when you sloughed the jack of diamonds," Larry cheerfully told Marty Birch. "Well played gentlemen."

With that, Maude and Larry took the evening in first place followed by Birch and Biddle in second. Father Tom and Reverend Bob were a close third.

On the way home, Maude was bubbly with joy. "I love my nephew Greeley, but having you as my partner makes these Friday nights much more fun," she said. "Especially when we can take out the two Bs. Did you see how huffy they were when they marched out. Until you came along we had to raise merry Ned to even hope to beat them."

Then she gave Larry a detailed description of how the widow, and she stressed "widow," Anne Lindsay came back to town after a thirty-year absence. She told him about Anne's New Morning Farm where she bred quarter horses. She'd moved from Tennessee after her husband, the noted Episcopal theologian, Alan Lindsay, had suddenly died from a stroke. Her son Jack was a lawyer who'd been practicing in Chicago but had recently moved to Seattle to be closer to his mother.

As they reached Maude's front door, Larry laughed and patted Maude on the back "You're a great friend and bridge partner," he said. "But don't try to set me up with anyone. I'm not interested. And besides I'm an assistant cook in a restaurant, hardly a prime target for some high-powered horse breeder from Tennessee."

It was after ten when they said good-night on Maude's steps and Larry started down Second Avenue. As he approached Katherine's from across the street, he saw a dim light in the living room window. He turned down the alley and heard the soft sounds of a piano coming from the house. *Chopin nocturne*, he thought to himself as he walked home in the cool September night.

Larry is a Local Hero

"Katherine Baker" or "Katy Owling," Larry didn't understand what the big deal was and it didn't interest him. But Maude's story about Katherine's tantrum, had piqued his curiosity about her. From his first day on the job as her assistant cook, he'd been impressed with her business-like demeanor tempered by a sensitivity to the feelings of her co-workers. Now he began to watch her more closely and he was struck by how nothing in the restaurant got past her. No matter how busy she was, she was always aware of what was going on in the dining room, in the booths along the wall in the front, and where and what all the employees were doing.

Larry worked hard at breaking through Katherine's wall of no-nonsense, occasionally forcing her into a tight smile with some deadpan remark about an order or a customer. "Massive stroke up," he would say in a monotone, putting on the service counter a platter of pancakes smothered with sausage gravy with a side order of fried eggs. Or if someone they'd not seen before came in and sat in a booth in the front, he'd shout to Sadie, "Fresh fish in the front. You hook 'em, we'll cook 'em." Sometimes Katherine would respond with a tight smile or shake her head in amusement.

One morning not long after Maude and Larry's triumph at the bridge table, Roy and Hazel Willit came in and, like most new customers, sat at one of the booths along the wall in the front part of the restaurant, unaware of the large dining room around the corner in the rear. They were horse people from Tennessee, having reluctantly moved from the South to manage Anne Lindsay's quarter horse farm, something they'd done since Anne had started the farm in Sewanee nearly thirty years ago. They were on their way to the Marysville livestock auction and at Anne's recommendation, decided to have breakfast at the Madison Café.

The Willits were politely unassuming Southern folks in their early sixties who had the look of people who worked for a living. Sadie told Katherine and Larry they were so polite and soft-spoken she had to ask Roy to repeat their orders for breakfast. When Sadie brought their plates, both Hazel and Roy politely thanked her and then held hands while Roy whispered grace before they started to eat.

It was Katherine who yelled first when a few minutes later, she looked over at the Willits and saw Roy's face turning a bright reddish blue. He was choking. Hazel had leaned over the table and grabbed him by the shoulders, shaking him and saying "Roy, Roy." The noise from the dining room was loud and only Larry heard Katherine's shout. He was gone in two seconds, kicking his legs over the counter in a gymnastic sidebar move that seemed impossible for his six-foot frame. He managed to get Roy out of the booth, holding him from behind with the classic Heimlich maneuver and dislodging a fat chunk of sausage from his throat.

Larry turned Roy around and asked, "Are you ok?"

Then he said, "No he's not," and shouted, "Call 911."

The choking had caused a heart attack and Roy was slipping into unconsciousness when Larry gently laid him on the floor in front of the booths, telling Hazel to give him her coat to use as a pillow. Greeley was in the back of the kitchen standing in the storeroom door talking to Bert Peck, the bread truck driver, while Bobby was unloading the order of bread. He heard Larry's shouts and grabbed the phone on the wall but Sadie was already on the line calling for an ambulance.

"Good God," Larry yelled again, "Someone call 911" Then taking both Roy's hands he put his head down to Roy's and said over and over, "Stay with me partner, stay with me, you're going to be alright."

The volunteer fire department's emergency vehicle pulled up in front on Main Street. Larry shouted at Ray Kesecker and Chip Franklin as they ran in. With Larry directing the operation, they got Roy on the gurney, out the front door and into the ambulance. As he climbed into the back, Larry told Greeley to take care of Hazel and drive her to the hospital.

When Chip Franklin told him he couldn't be in back with Roy, Larry said "Try and stop me," and sat down next to the unconscious Roy.

The front page headline in the next morning's *Port Smith Herald* read "Local Hero: Restaurant Worker Saves Customer's Life." The story was short and to the point, and Greeley was pleased that in spite of the tragedy, the Madison Café was portrayed as a hometown place where people looked out for each other. A few Cedar Mills eyebrows were raised when, in response to the reporter's question about where he'd learned his lifesaving skills, Larry succinctly said "In federal prison when I was serving time for tax evasion."

A few days later, Larry learned from Maude, who had talked to Anne Lindsay, that Roy was home and doing well. The heart attack was mild and the problem had been resolved with a stint. He was already talking about getting back to work on the farm. Maude told Larry that Roy hoped he would pay a visit to New Morning Farm so that he and Hazel could properly thank him.

It went without saying the people at the Madison Café were proud of Larry. Many of the regulars at the restaurant stopped by the service counter and caught Larry's attention to give him a thumbs up or say, "Good job."

Greeley told him he was proud to be his nephew; Bobby snuck up and gave him a hug; Katherine and Sadie didn't say a whole lot about the incident except to tease him about his leap over the counter, asking where he learned a move like that, running from the law?

The following Monday morning just after nine, when the early morning crowd was gone and the café had quieted down, a stranger in his early thirties came in the front door. He was dressed in a dark blue business suit, button-down ecru oxford cloth shirt with a dark blue and yellow repp tie, and tassled loafers. Definitely an out-of-towner. His black hair was combed back and glistened with mousse. He tentatively stood at the end of the counter near the front door, looking into the long kitchen, his dark eyes staring with curiosity. When Katherine first caught a glimpse of him, she thought of Johnny Herrera.

"I'm looking for Larry Bradford," the stranger said. "Is this there where he works?"

Katherine nodded and looked down the kitchen for Larry who was quietly sidling down the kitchen toward the rear service door.

"Hey Larry," she called. "Someone wants to see you."

Sadie, who'd been standing at the service counter, poked her head into the kitchen and yelled at him too. They watched as Larry slowly walked back up the kitchen with a grave expression. He mutely stared at the stranger.

"I'm Jack Lindsay," the outsider said holding out his hand to Larry. "I stopped by to thank you for saving my Uncle Roy's life. He and Aunt Hazel mean the world to me. Thank you very much."

Larry shook his hand and said he was just glad to have been there.

Katherine and Sadie stood watching as Jack explained that Roy and Hazel weren't his blood relatives, but they'd raised him as much his parents. His father had been a theologian and preacher who was always writing books and his mother traveled all the time with her show horses, so he'd grown up on the farm with Roy and Hazel.

"Uncle Roy taught me how to work and Aunt Hazel taught me how to cook," he said with a winsome humility that contradicted his appearance. "Anyway, I've got to get back to Seattle. I just wanted to stop and say thanks."

When the front door closed and Jack Lindsay disappeared, Larry turned back to Katherine and Sadie who were still staring at him.

"Whew," Sadie said. "That guy is way above my pay grade."

"The tassled loafers and the mousse" Katherine huffed with a laugh. "Give me a break."

Then she looked at Larry mischievously, "Where were you headed when I called you?"

"Yeah," Sadie chimed in. "It looked like you were sneaking out the back door."

"I knew he wasn't the law, but he looked like he might be carrying paper," Larry said with a smile. "My lawyer in New York always said the first line of defense is never get served."

The three erupted in raucous laughter that rang through the restaurant, bringing Bobby in from the dining room and Greeley downstairs from his office. Then Katherine and Sadie retold the story, embellishing the details of Jack Lindsay's looks and Larry actions with Sadie doing an exaggerated imitation of Larry creeping out the back. The jokes about the citified stranger and Larry's attempted escape continued for the rest of the day and for the first time, a palpable bond was evident among the five co-workers when the restaurant closed that afternoon.

The Swarthy Foreigner's Quest

That same morning, around the time Jack Lindsay walked into the Madison Café in Cedar Mills, a tall, dark-skinned man was making his way north to south through the Pike Place Market in Seattle. He was wearing a blue blazer over an blue oxford cloth shirt, khaki trousers, and sockless cordovan loafers, all with the most expensive labels. When he reached the south end of the enclosed market, he took the walkway down two flights to the second underground floor of musty shops that lined both sides of a wide dark corridor. He passed shops selling used books, antiques, magic tricks, collectibles and finally came to the last shop on the water-side of the building which was called "Time Pieces."

Silas Peavey, the shop's owner, was a rotund elfin man in his early seventies, whose forehead, eyes, nose, and mouth were just visible through the mounds of curly white hair on his head and face. When the stranger came in, he was sitting at a large cluttered table with his back to the shop door, staring out a large plate glass window overlooking the Seattle waterfront. A telescope mounted on a small tripod was on his left and a pair of binoculars was on his right. A mirror hung above the window, giving him a reflected view of the shop's front door. Between him and the shop floor were two glass display cases set at a right angle and filled with watches, hourglasses, and any other piece of ephemera having to do with keeping time. The rest of the shop was crammed full of clocks of every description, many of which sounded the hour with chimes, bells, and cuckoos.

When the stranger announced himself as Paul Merrick, the man who had telephoned the day before, Peavey turned around in his chair and succinctly told him he was expecting an Englishman.

"You sound like one, but you don't look like one," he said.

Merrick told the shopkeeper that his father was English. His mother had been born in India but had grown up in England.

Then with a directness that could have been interpreted as impolite, the stranger got right to the point of his visit, telling Silas Peavey that he had been told by a professor at the university here in Seattle, a Dr. Edward Balfour, that Mr. Peavey had an encyclopedic knowledge of the city's maritime history and that he, the visitor, had an interest in one particular passenger vessel that had worked the Puget Sound trade from the late 1890s until sometime after the Great War, perhaps as late as the 1920s, a steam passenger ship named the *Arctic Maid*.

With an uncharacteristic modesty, Peavey professed to knowing a little about Puget Sound shipping and for what he didn't know, he had what he called *additional resources* at his disposal. He turned to a large book lying on the table, *Motherwell's Complete Mosquito Fleet: The Pride of Puget Sound*, and invited Merrick to come behind the glass display cases.

"Here's a picture of the *Arctic Maid*, not long before she was mothballed, which it says here was in 1922," he said. "I have no idea where she might be now and I don't think Eddie Balfour knows either. But let me bring to bear an additional resource who might be able to help."

Then he called to Will and Joey, announcing the pair, a twelve-year-old boy and an eleven-year-old girl, as his grandchildren. They stood silently assessing the dusky stranger with an English accent.

"Now go down and find Jim Underwood, you two rogues," Peavey instructed. "He's down in the weeds under the viaduct somewhere, this time of the morning he's probably still passed out. Bring him up post-haste."

While they waited, Merrick told the shopkeeper what he knew about the *Arctic Maid*. That in the 1890s, she'd been owned by his maternal grandfather, a Bombay merchant named Kumar Mahindra, and had originally been christened the *Arundhati Star*, which he said is the Hindu name for a star of some importance in the Indian firmament.

"Well, please sit down there sir, and tell me more," Peavey said with a sudden warmness, getting him a chair from the next room. "This is new information to all of us who ply the history trade and I want to know every detail. Bob, you knave! Where the heck is Bob? He can run up and get us some coffee. Bob, you blasted scoundrel!"

While they waited for Bob, Merrick continued with what he knew of the *Arundhati Star*, about his grandparents tragic murders in 1895, and how the ship had been sold to a San Francisco tycoon, Cyrus Milton. He told Peavey that after his mother died, he'd discovered a trove of his grandparents possessions, papers, and records, which had been shipped from India when his mother had been sent to London as a child. In one of his grandmother's diaries, she described how during the nationalist unrest in 1895, they'd moved many of their valuables to the *Arundhati Star* as they prepared to escape on the ship. This inspired his search for the remains of the ship, a quest that gained momentum when he'd joined the Vancouver office of Merrick & Son Imports the year before, thus bringing him conveniently close to Seattle which he believed was the vessel's final resting place.

As Paul Merrick ended his story, Will and Joey burst into the shop, shouting they had Jim Underwood halfway up the long iron stairs from Alaskan Way to the market, but he wouldn't budge and they couldn't carry him.

"Bob!" Peavey yelled. "Get in here, Bob, you roughneck."

Bob appeared. He was a tall thin fellow in his late thirties. His blond hair was cut in a crew cut that harkened back a generation and his deep blue eyes were slightly clouded. Peavey introduced him to Paul, explaining that Bob, a former University of Washington football star who had been in a coma for six months after a blow to the head, had lost his scholarship, been expelled from college and Peavey had no choice but to take him in as his gofer and chief of security.

Peavey told Bob, "Jim Underwood's down on the stairs, take Will and bring him up. Joey, here's a note for Myrna at the state store, you run and get two half-pints of scotch. We may as well get him some good stuff."

Joey was back from the state store before Bob and Will came dragging a barely conscious Jim Underwood into the shop, pushing him back behind the glass cases into a chair facing Silas Peavey and Paul Merrick. The disheveled Underwood, who was wearing a wrinkled, mud-spattered dark blue three-piece suit with the vest unbuttoned, sat staring at the floor in half-conscious state as Silas Peavey handed him a shot glass of scotch. He told Merrick that Jim Underwood was a history professor emeritus at the University of Washington who was an expert on Puget Sound shipping. Peavey said, "He knows more than me and Eddie Balfour combined. He was Eddie's mentor."

Jim Underwood downed the contents of the shot glass and his eyes opened. He held out the empty glass and it was refilled. After the second shot, Underwood said to Peavey, "To what sir, do I owe the honor?"

Peavey introduced Paul Merrick and told Underwood an abridged version of the Englishman's story, asking him about the disposition of the *Arctic Maid*. Underwood held out the shot glass again. For the third time, the glass was filled and emptied. The shop was silent as they watched Jim Underwood stare out the window at Elliott Bay.

Finally, the professor turned to Merrick. "Lake Union, sir. She's a hulk in Lake Union. Northeast end, near the Cut. Her hull was painted white with red trim. I believe she lies between the *City of Ilwaco* and the *Wee Laddie*."

Then standing, he said, "If that's all you need, I'll be on my way. And, by the way, have you considered any compensation for my assistance? I'd be much obliged."

Peavey and Merrick both stood. Peavey handed him the second half pint of scotch and Merrick reached into his wallet, handing him some twenty-dollar bills.

"We'd like you to stay here tonight, Jim," Peavey said. "We'll bring in some Chinese food, your favorite. There's a cot in the storeroom"

"Much obliged, Silas, but there's no fresh air," Jim said, walking past them to the shop door. "Perhaps another time."

After Underwood disappeared out the door and down the stairs to the waterfront, Merrick started to reach for his wallet, thanking Peavey for his help.

"No money for me, thank you," Peavey said. "You've paid me enough with your story. Priceless information heretofore unknown in these parts. It will be part of my *Complete Maritime History of Puget Sound As She Was Lived*." Then he shouted for Bob, "Where the devil is that cutthroat?"

When Bob came out of the next room, Peavey told him to get the car and take Mr. Merrick out to Lake Union, telling the Englishman he would never find the remains of the *Arctic Maid* on his own. But Merrick declined Peavey's offer, saying he had an appointment with Professor Balfour that afternoon and would impose on his good will to help him find the ship's remains. "Well, give Eddie my best," Peavey said. "You know he's a graduate of our academy here, a foundling whose parents died drunk, or disappeared, or were murdered down here on the waterfront, just like Will and Joey. Me and the others at the market did our best to raise the lad. We're all mighty proud of Eddie."

The Englishman and the shopkeeper parted with a hearty handshake with Merrick continuing to insist Peavey accept his offer of monetary compensation and Peavey declining. When Merrick was gone, Silas Peavey wondered to himself, *I wonder what he's really after?*

That afternoon, Paul Merrick and Edward Balfour, assistant professor of American history at the University of Washington, were standing on the northeast edge of Lake Union not far from the Montlake Cut, looking at what was left of the *Arctic Maid*. It wasn't much. Half the ship's hull, the half that rested on the lakeshore was still intact with the faded red lettering

"Arctic Maid" barely visible on the bow. Nothing was left of the wheelhouse or remaining superstructure and any hope of finding the baby grand piano or anything else aboard was lost.

But the undaunted Merrick would not give up. He was steadfast in his mission to find the Kimball baby grand piano that had graced the salon of the *Arctic Maid*. With Professor Balfour's help, he found Cyrus Milton III at the Arctic Hotel who took him to Cyrus Milton II who was residing at the Autumn Leaves Assisted Living Homes at Mukilteo. Cyrus Milton II was Luther Moody's old boss at the Northern Lights Club in the Arctic Hotel. He told Merrick that Moody had moved out of the Arctic Hotel when he went to work for Corky Carlsson and the All Stars and took the piano with him. If Corky was still around, he might know where the piano player had gone. But Corky Carlsson had died two years before.

Merrick combed the newspaper archives at the Seattle Public Library and interviewed anyone that might lead him to Luther Moody and the piano. Finally he found an advertisement in a 1962 *Seattle Post Intelligencer* announcing "Ron Lantz Presents Corky Carlsson and The All Star's at the Tiger Mountain Grange during the Issaquah Ragweed Festival."

Merrick located a Marvin Lantz on Mercer Island, Ron Lantz's younger brother who had taken over their father Sid's dental practice. The younger Lantz told the Englishman he was certain his brother Myron, now known as Buck McCready, would know what became of Luther Moody. He said his brother was living at Sekiu on the Olympic Peninsula and was the owner of a charter business, "Buck McCready's Salmon Adventures." In the off season he ran a tour guide service called "In Search of the Rain Forest Sasquatch."

Paul Merrick returned to Vancouver confident he was finally close to finding the baby grand piano. With the help of his cousin and business partner, Arthur Merrick, he began to formulate a plan to contact Buck McCready at Sekiu. He was determined to find the Kimball Compact Grand Piano, Serial No. 1891-9183 and the secret it held.

A Sunday Afternoon Picnic

The Saturday afternoon after Jack Lindsay's visit to the café, Larry saw Katherine outside in her front yard when he was driving home from Greeley's. Instead of turning down the alley toward his apartment, he drove around to Cedar Street and parked across the street in front of her house. He watched as she unloaded the square-back station wagon, carrying in plastic bags filled with clothes and paper bags filled with books. She didn't see him get out of the car and cross the street, and she was startled by his sudden offer to help.

"What are you doing here?" she gruffed. "No, I don't need any help, I'm done. But come in for a minute as long as you're here."

It was an awkward moment for both of them as Larry stood in the living room while Katherine lugged the plastic bags back to her bedroom. She told him to sit down while she put on some coffee. Larry demurred and told her tomorrow afternoon he was going out to the new piece of land he, Greeley, and Bert Peck were looking to develop and if she wasn't busy maybe she'd like to go along.

"Bert the bread truck driver?" she asked.

"Bert the bread truck driver. We're thinking about starting a new kind of vegetable farm. A place to grow produce for restaurants.

Katherine sounded interested. Larry said he'd stop by after church, around noon, and he'd bring a picnic lunch.

The next day, they drove north out of town on the Yarmouth Road for a couple of miles, then turned left onto the old Port Smith Road. After a mile, Larry turned onto an unmarked, overgrown dirt track that angled down a steep bluff which formed the north edge of Cedar Valley. The track ended at the bottom of the bluff in front of an abandoned farmhouse that had lost its paint years before. A hundred feet or so to the east of the house was a small barn facing twenty acres of what had been pasture land. From the small rise above the house where they parked, the town was just barely visible a few miles away and beyond that was a sweeping panorama of snow-capped mountains stretching from the eastern edge of the horizon to the western edge.

Katherine and Larry both felt uncomfortable being alone together outside the restaurant for the first time and they'd hardly talked on the twenty minute drive to the old farm. Now as they walked down the hill toward the old house, Larry broke the ice when he told her with some trepidation that Father Tom Flatte had told him at coffee hour after the service at Trinity Episcopal that morning they were looking for a temporary organist to fill in while Margie Parker was out for a couple of weeks.

"I hope you're not upset," he said thinking of her tantrum with Maude a few days before. "But I told Father Tom, that you might be interested in the job. It's only for a few weeks."

Katherine turned toward him and angrily asked, "What'd you do?"

"I knew you played the piano and figured you knew how play an organ," Larry said. "You don't need to overreact."

"Why is everyone so interested in my life? First Maude wants to shove the past in my face and now you want to sign me up to be a church organist."

They walked around the house and barn, then out through the fields as Larry explained it had been Roscoe Muhlenberg's goat farm and been abandoned when the old bachelor had died with no family. Bert Peck and Greeley had gone together and bought the place two years ago when it had been auctioned off for back taxes. A few months ago, when Larry started telling them about hydroponic farming, they suggested a partnership to develop part the land.

Greeley talked Lonnie into becoming a fourth partner with the plan that Larry's role in the partnership would be to design and oversee construction of the hydroponic infrastructure. Lonnie would contribute supplies from the building supply in exchange for his logging off the western red alder and big leaf maple that stood on the un-cleared twenty acres of the land which he and Walt Beaver would mill into hardwood flooring.

"Where'd you learn about hydroponic farming?" Katherine asked as they were finishing the hike around the property.

"At Allenwood," Larry answered. "They had a small hydroponic operation where I worked my last two years in prison."

"You're quitting at the restaurant then?"

"Not planning on it," Larry answered. "I'll be out here in my spare time."

They drove on to Salt Cliffs State Park along the Strait where they found a table overlooking the water for their picnic lunch. From their spot on the bluff, they could see the blue mountains of Vancouver Island eighteen miles across the Strait, a view that was populated with occasional ocean-going vessels, freighters, oil tankers, and container ships, standing in and out along the hundred-mile shipping lane between the Pacific Ocean and Puget Sound.

Katherine expressed amazement at the spread Larry laid out on the picnic table, fried chicken, potato salad, a tossed salad, and homemade rolls.

"I don't have a lot to do when I'm not working," he explained. "I like to cook and I learned a lot about cooking. . ."

Katherine laughed, "Don't tell me. You learned a lot about cooking in prison."

Pleased that her mood had changed, Larry told Katherine her laugh reminded him of his daughter, Emma.

"She's probably about your age," he said. "She turned twenty-seven this past June." Larry told her he hadn't seen Emma in over ten years and that he'd heard she'd changed her name from Emma Bradford to Emma Simmons, her mother's maiden name. He didn't know where she was.

"It was all part of the big family freeze-out when I got arrested."

"Don't you miss it, your life before prison?"

"I miss her. I miss Emma," he said. "But I don't miss the rest of it. I don't miss being Lawrence Adams Bradford the Fourth, only son of Federal Judge Lawrence Adams Bradford the Third and Margaret Bradley Bradford who makes it known within minutes of meeting her that they're the Waterbury, Connecticut Bradfords."

"What a life it must it have been," Katherine said, wanting to draw him out.

His life had all been a plan, he explained, a plan laid out by his father and by the Bradford family tradition. From private school at Groton, to Williams, to Harvard Law and then a Wall Street law firm.

"What's Groton and Williams?"

"Groton is a boys school in Massachusetts where over-bred kids are sent to learn their only calling is to attend Harvard or Yale. Williams College is an inbred little college in Western Massachusetts where they spend four years brainwashing you to believe how fortunate you were to be spared the horror of attending Harvard or Yale. I went there because my great-grandfather, my grandfather, and my father went there. All of them were on the board of trustees. I had no choice."

He went on to tell how he'd decided not to go to Harvard Law and went to The Wharton School in Philadelphia for an MBA, which sent shockwaves through the Waterbury Bradfords. All was forgiven, however, when he went to New York, made his first million as an investment banker, and married Ellen Simmons, a debutante from Greenwich whose family, although it was never definitively proven to the satisfaction of his mother, seemed to be on an equal standing with the Bradfords.

When he and Ellen were divorced five years later, Larry led the single life of a workaholic, amassing as much money as he could. This was when Greeley, the young GI from the West who was on temporary duty at Fort Monmouth, New Jersey, visited him in Manhattan. Then a few years later, after making more money than he'd ever thought possible, Larry found himself addicted to cocaine and booze.

After showing up drunk more than once to pick up Emma for the weekend, Ellen got a court order enjoining him from seeing his daughter. Not long afterward, his parents, who were tired of his angry phone calls, told him to stay away from Waterbury. His older sister Elizabeth was the only one in the family who would talk to him and all she said when she called from Cedar Mills was "Go to rehab."

Then everything changed when he was indicted on federal money laundering charges and tax evasion. The money laundering charges were eventually dropped, but he was convicted of tax evasion and sentenced to four years in federal prison. With his conviction, Larry Bradford ceased to exist to his family, his ex-wife, his daughter, and most of his friends.

"I was alone and broke when I went to prison," he said ending the story. "If it hadn't been for Greeley, I don't know what would have happened when I got out. He was there waiting when I walked out of Allenwood. It may sound corny, but he gave me a new start."

"I've never known anyone like you," Katherine said.

Larry laughed. "Well to be honest, I've never known anyone like you either," he said as they started to pack up the remains of their lunch.

It was quiet in the car as they started back to town until Katherine said, "You haven't finished the story. What happened after Greeley picked you up at the prison?"

"That's enough of Larry Bradford for one day," Larry answered with an avuncular air. "Way too much, in fact. What about Katherine Baker? I don't know anything about you. How did you learn to cook and run a restaurant?"

Katherine stared out the passenger side window and Larry's question hung in the air, ready to fall ignored, like the proverbial lead balloon.

"In jail," Katherine said, still looking out the window. Then she turned and look at Larry, laughing with a loud cathartic bellow. "I learned to cook in jail."

Larry hesitated and then started laughing with her, laughing so hard he pulled over on the side of the road.

"So I guess we're both just jailhouse cooks," Larry said as he pulled back onto the road.

Kaththerine said, "Let's take a long way home," suggesting they make a loop up into the foothills through Pleasant Valley and back around on the Cedar River Road. "I want to show you something."

Something had broken loose in Katherine. She was no longer tense, her mouth was relaxed, her brow was no longer knit. She told him part of her story as they skirted around town and up Pleasant Valley Road.

"I woke up in jail in California, Tulare County, doing six months to a year for drunk driving and attempted vehicular manslaughter," she began, and then with a grin said, "Maude Doud doesn't even know that part of the story.

"Just like you, it was all about cocaine and booze, only I didn't have any money, I had to hustle for what I could get. I arrived in LA alone and pregnant when I was eighteen.

After I had the baby and put it up for adoption, I worked as a backup singer for a skanky country-rock band called "Flaming Turtles." When they hit the road, I went along, married the bass player, Chauncey Baker, and hung out in every sleazy bar from San Bernadino to Barstow, coked up and drunk every night for two years. When I woke up in Tulare, the band, including Chauncey, was long gone."

She told Larry how started she working in the county jail's kitchen, then was offered an early out and commutation of her sentence if she completed a culinary arts course at the local community college and agreed to work at the Tulare high school cafeteria for a year after that.

"That's where I got my start," Katherine said wistfully. "As horrible as it all was, I ended up with my police record expunged and found a way to make a living."

"So what happened after that?"

"I got sober and decided to stay that way and with my trusty old station wagon, I worked my way up the San Joaquin Valley for eight years. I worked as a short-order cook in half the diners and truck stops along old U.S. 99 and I-5 from Bakersfield to Sacramento. I fought with dirty owners, covered for drunk managers, fired thieving waitresses, and fell in love with cowboy truck drivers. When I felt like moving on, I gave notice sometimes and sometimes I didn't."

By now they were driving through the Pleasant Valley farmland in the foothills south of town. Every now and then there was clear spot in the trees where they could see the town and six miles beyond the blue water of the Strait.

"I also learned how to take care of myself. Self-defense, judo, boxing, and firearms training, anything that would get me from the diner to my car at three in the morning. I loved that life. I was free. I just picked up and moved on when things weren't going my way or when I felt like it. Merle Haggard was my guru."

As they came down Mountain Road, Katherine told Larry to turn right onto Cedar River Road. After a mile she asked him to slow down as they approached a white farmhouse on the left. Years of neglect had taken its toll on the old house. The white paint was peeling, there were no curtains in the windows, the grass in the front yard was overgrown, and the picket fence was collapsing. A battered Ford pickup was in the driveway and a weather-beaten black Labrador paced on the front porch, barking as they went by.

"That's Katy Owling's old house," Katherine said. "She died years ago."

The Constable Stops Some Visitors

Will McCann was driving into town on U.S. 101 early one morning not long after Katherine and Larry's Sunday afternoon picnic, when a well-worn gray Lincoln Town Car suddenly pulled out from Cedar River Road, so abruptly that Will came close to rear-ending it. He was driving his unmarked constable's cruiser and the driver of the Lincoln was unaware that he'd almost caused an accident with the Cedar Mills chief of police and deputy sheriff for the east end of Cedar County.

Will suppressed his first impulse to pull the car over but instead followed the old car as it slowly moved down Main Street. When it braked at Third Avenue showing a burnt-out right tail-light and then turned left without signaling, Will followed the car around the corner, tapped his siren, turned on his flashers, and the town car immediately pulled over.

The driver's window was down when Will walked up to the Lincoln. He recognized Art Fletcher as the driver. Fletcher handed over his driver's license and the car's registration. Will told him he was driving with a burnt-out tail-light and didn't signal when he turned onto Third Avenue. He looked at the registration. "The car is registered to a Mitchell Lodong. Who's he?"

The rear driver's-side window went down and a voice boomed from the back seat, "I'm Bishop Mitchell Lodong. The car's mine. Mr. Fletcher is my driver." Lodong said. "We're just back from the Duckabush Hot Springs where I've been planning the annual Sanitarian Jubilee."

Will walked to the front of the car and told Fletcher to turn on the headlights and then work the turn signals. Then he walked to the rear and ordered him to do the same. He took the driver's license and registration to his cruiser. When he returned, he told Fletcher and Lodong to step out of the car.

In the years since Art Fletcher had left Cedar Mills, he'd gone from stocky to rotund. His blonde hair was thin and disheveled. The former teacher wore bright white sneakers, khaki trousers, and a tight blue sweatshirt that made him look like he'd swallowed a basketball.

Bishop Lodong was a foot taller than Fletcher. He was dressed in black, shiny black oxford shoes, black creased trousers with a matching shirt and sport coat. The shirt was unbuttoned at the top revealing a large silver cross on a silver chain around the prelate's neck. His straight black hair was parted in the middle.

Will told them the car was impounded until the left headlight, left rear turn-signal, and the right brake light were working. Additionally, Art Fletcher was going to be charged with negligent driving and operating an unsafe vehicle.

Will said they could get the work done that morning at Kesecker's Union 76. A tow truck was on the way. Lodong would ride to gas station in the truck. Fletcher was going with Will to the town hall for processing.

"After that you can meet Lodong at Kesecker's," Will said.

"*Bishop* Lodong," the prelate said. "It's *Bishop* Lodong, spiritual leader of the Western Washington Synod of Sanitarians Who are Washed in the Blood of the Lamb. And by the way, we stopped in your fair city at the request of one of my congregants, Mrs. Susan Owling. She recently received intelligence that her long-lost daughter has taken up residence in this dear little town. It is our blessed hope we will be able to bring good news back to the dear woman and assist her in arranging a joyful reunion with her daughter."

Thirty minutes later at the town hall, when Will finished with Art Fletcher, he asked how the ex-teacher had got mixed up with Lodong. Fletcher said he'd met the bishop in a bar in Gold Bar one morning after he'd finished a night run driving a produce truck from Wenatchee to Snohomish. One thing led to another and the bishop offered him a job as his driver. It was a coincidence that Susan Owling was living at the Sanitarian compound in Catchall.

Will drove Fletcher two blocks from the town hall out to Main Street and let him out. "I've got to be in Port Smith. You'll have to walk to Kesecker's. You know the way. You've made enough runs through here lately with that produce truck."

Fletcher thanked Will for the warning ticket, climbed out, and walked east down Main Street in the early morning sun with a short back-and-forth waddling gait.

Katherine spotted him as he continued down Main Street past Wilfong's Variety on the opposite side of the street. Her face flushed as she muttered,

"They're coming out of the woodwork."

Larry walked toward the front window of the café and stood next to Katherine. He recognized the rotund physique and the waddle of the man across the street. It was the stranger in the alley. Larry said, "I've got to tell you something. He was skulking around your house last Friday night when I walked up to get Maude for bridge."

Katherine shuddered and whispered "Good God. Tell me about it after work."

When Fletcher arrived at the Union 76, Ray's mechanic, Scooter Markham, was finishing up with the brake light of the bishop's car. Mitchell Lodong was standing in the service bay telling Scooter about his quest to find Katy Owling.

"She works at the Madison Café," Scooter said offhandedly as he put the brake light back together.

"Praise the Lord," Lodong intoned putting his hands together in prayer. "You've made this sojourn to your quaint village a success my good fellow. Bless you."

Scooter shrugged and yelled to Ray he was done. A few minutes later, Art Fletcher and Mitchell Lodong were back on the road, heading east, back to Catchall with the joyous news they'd found Susan Owling's long-lost daughter, Katy.

The One-Legged Shit Kicker

Katherine's solitary life of a vagabond short-cook started to change after her tantrum at Maude's. The outside world began to intrude on her self-created near-hermetic existence. The afternoon of the Mitchell Lodong and Art Fletcher's incident, Reverend Tom Flatte came into the café for lunch and asked Katherine if she'd be willing to fill in at the organ at Trinity Episcopal for a few weeks. Later, just before closing, Anne Lindsay and Hazel Willit arrived with a beautiful handmade invitation to Sunday afternoon dinner addressed to "Larry, Sadie, Bobby, Katherine, and Greeley" as a "small way to say thank you for what you all did for Roy."

After work, she and Larry stood outside in the alley as she was leaving the café. Larry told her about chasing Art Fletcher up the alley after he'd seen the fat man come out of Katherine's back yard. Katherine sneered, "I'll beat the crap out of him if he gets anywhere near my place again. The alley's a busy place. I see a couple of kids come by almost every night, poking around. Maude told me it's probably the Dolans. Parents live at Lou's Scenic Tavern."

When she got home, Ray Kesecker had driven the old Toyota station wagon back from the Union 76 after he'd installed a new battery. After a thorough going over, he and Scooter concluded the car was near the end of its life. Katherine could have a few things done now to keep it running, but it was worn-out after 230,000 miles and more repairs would be needed soon.

The next afternoon, after the restaurant was closed, she and Larry sat in the dining room talking about her car. Katherine wanted Larry's opinion. Should she put money into the old car, invest in new tires and have Ray replace the rear differential and the head casket, or should she buy a good used-car? Money was not the issue. After her time at the Madison Café with Greeley's generous salary, she had enough money in the bank to buy a decent car. But she was emotionally attached to the trusty old station wagon. The car had been her steadfast partner since she got out of jail a decade before.

"You'll need a reliable car when you're ready to get out of town," Larry said perfunctorily.

"Get out town?" Katherine asked. "What's that supposed to mean?"

Larry laughed, "You told me that's how you live. You pick up and hit the road when you decide it's time. If that's what you're going to do, you need a car you can count on."

He started talking about return on investment and Katherine said, "Now you sound like a banker."

"I am a banker, retired for the moment," he replied with a laugh. "You could put more money in the old Toyota but like Ray said, it's worn out. You do that and you're not going to get a decent return on your investment. It'll break down before the new tires are hardly worn and you'll be on the side of the road before you get back to Roseburg."

"Roseburg? Who said anything about Roseburg?"

Larry said, "You should get another car. I'll help you look for one if you want."

Lonnie, who'd let himself in the back door, asked "Who's getting a new car?"

"Larry says I shouldn't put any more money in my old Toyota," Katherine answered.

"Go see Andy Walnut. Walnut Ford in Port Smith," Lonnie said. "Some say he's a tough nut to crack, but he'll give you a good deal. I'll give him a call, let him know you're coming. Where's the boss man?"

Larry said Greeley was out with Tillie Foreman, looking at a house she'd just put on the market.

"Oh no, he's buying another house," Lonnie said. "The kid has got to stop this entreprenurski crap. He's gonna go out and buy some run down clap trap to fix up and rent out. Only it'll be me and Walt Beaver and his boys who'll do all the fixin' up. That's why he wanted me to stop by. My son never wants to just shoot the breeze. He never notices I'm busier than a one-legged shit kicker. So how's my favorite brother-in-law? You been working hard or hardly working?"

Larry hadn't known what to think of Lonnie years before when he'd come home from prep school for Lonnie and Elizabeth's wedding. Larry was in his second year at Groton and Lonnie was finishing his Ninety-day Wonder term at the Coast Guard Academy at New London just before the war ended. His older sister's dropping out of Connecticut College for Women in her junior year to marry this stranger from the West had stunned her family into acquiescence and they politely if begrudgingly hosted the modest marriage ceremony at the family home in Waterbury.

Larry, then a callow preppy with an air of omniscience, whispered to his father that Lonnie sounded like a nincompoop. The judge told him he tended to agree, but Lonnie was one of the shrewdest young men he'd ever met. And besides, Elizabeth was enchanted by him. He'd never seen her so enthralled about anyone or anything before.

For his part, Lonnie refused to be intimidated by the Bradford family which impressed the judge even more although it did little to endear him to his wife, who at their first meeting informed Lonnie that she would always be "Mrs. Bradford" and never "Margaret," her first name being reserved for those dearest to her.

Polite and respectful, Lonnie went along with the whole Waterbury program and by the time the newlyweds left for Lonnie's first duty station at Charleston, South Carolina, Judge Lawrence Bradford II and his wife Margaret, along with their son Lawrence III, had accepted Elizabeth's new husband into the family. As they watched the couple leave in a cab for the train station, Margaret Bradford said she hoped their lawyer was ready with the annulment papers.

"A lot of water's gone under the bridge since we first met in Waterbury compadre," Lonnie said to Larry. "Who would have thunk you'd be out here slinging hash in Greeley's restaurant after all you've been through, including a gazillion dollars."

Lonnie started telling Katherine how Larry had helped Greeley get started in business. Maude had told already told her some of the story, about Greeley's return to Cedar Mills with his wife, stricken with ALS and less than a year to live. How they'd both been teachers in Wenatchee for twenty years before Janis insisted she be taken home to die. After her death, Greeley had loaded up Lonnie's old pack horse Bill and headed into the mountains. They all wondered if he'd ever come back. When he returned a month later, he announced he was through being a high school English teacher. He was going to be an entrepreneur.

"I said an entre-manure sounds more like it," Lonnie said. "We all thought he was off his rocker. I told him, you want to go into business, then be my partner in the lumber yard. 'Oh hell no,' he said, he wanted to buy Lamar Kesecker's gas station. Everyone laughed behind his back. No one would loan him the money. No way, Jose. I sure as hell wouldn't. So he wrote to Larry back in New York City. Larry was old money bags then. I called him 'seven-figure Larry.' Larry says 'give me a business plan.' Hell, Greeley didn't know what a business plan was. But he found out and sent one back East to Uncle Larry who loaned him the money. Now Greeley's an *entrepreneur*, I guess, and everyone in town swears they knew he'd be a success."

"Everyone knew he was going to be a success but they wouldn't loan him the money," Larry said.

"Being called a fool, never stopped a Martin though." Greeley said as he walked in the back door. He stood behind Larry and put his hands on his uncle's shoulders. "I owe everything to this guy."

A Trip to Walnut Ford

Katherine and Larry drove to Walnut Ford in Port Smith the next day after work. On the way they talked about the upcoming Sunday afternoon dinner at the Willit's. Katherine told Larry how excited Bobby Carr had been when she'd offered him a ride to the farm. Greeley said he'd stop by and say hello, but couldn't stay for dinner. Sadie said she'd love to come but had to take a rain check. She was taking care of her two nephews now that her sister, Vicki St. John, was serving thirty days in the Cedar County jail for beating up her boyfriend, Tommy Lowry, in the Duchess Tavern parking lot.

Katherine told Larry about the Trinity Episcopal choir practice she'd attended the night before. She said Reverend Tom Flatte was a difficult man to turn down when he'd asked in his deferential, unassuming way if she could fill in at the organ on Sundays.

"Humble," Larry said. "I think the word is humble, when you're talking about Tom Flatte. He's even humble when he's cleaning your clock at the bridge table."

She hadn't said yes, but had agreed to come and take a look at the organ, talk to Margie Parker, who still had two more Sundays before she'd be in California helping her daughter with a new baby, and meet Brett Smallwood the choir director.

"The organ is small, like the one I played at my father's church," she told him. "I think I can handle it. But everything in the church seems so formal, so…I don't know what the word is."

"Ritual, it's all about ritual" Larry said as they drove into the Walnut Motors lot. "We Episcopalians love ritual. We're just Catholic wannabes, without the Pope."

Walnut Ford was the largest car dealer on the Peninsula. Andy Walnut was waiting for them when they arrived. He led them out to one side of the new car lot to the used cars. He said Lonnie had ordered him to take good care of Katherine. No shenanigans or Lonnie'd open a can of whoop-ass on him. Then he slapped Larry on the back as he ushered them to a row of station wagons and mini-vans. Andy said he'd read all about Larry in the paper, saving the poor fellow with the heart attack.

"Lonnie said you probably wanted to see something that could handle a hefty payload. So here's a few possibilities."

"She needs something big enough to haul a baby grand piano," Larry said dryly.

Katherine half-smiled at Larry and said, "Very funny," before she started walking around the cars as the two men watched.

Katherine was not a tire-kicker. She got into a three-year-old light blue Ford Taurus station wagon with 40,000 miles and asked Andy if she could take it out for a test drive. She was gone for five minutes. When she pulled back into the lot, she told Andy she'd take it. Andy told her he'd have it cleaned up and she could pick up in the morning. Thirty minutes after they'd arrived, they were in Larry's car and on their way back to Cedar Mills.

"That was easy," Larry said as they pulled back onto 101. "I'm impressed."

"I liked it, I have the money, and I figure if the car is a lemon, Andy has to answer to Lonnie, not me," Katherine said. "Let's take the Old Highway back, I want to see where the Willits live. On the way you can tell me about when you got out of prison, when Greeley picked you up."

But Larry said didn't want to talk about getting out of prison. There was nothing interesting in his descriptions of driving aimlessly around the country for six months until he landed in Cedar Mills and took Greeley up on his offer of a job at the Madison Café and a place to live.

"Things happened while I was on the road, but nothing I'd tell my daughter."

"I'm not your daughter," Katherine said matter-of-factly.

"I know, but a lot of times I feel like I'm talking to Emma when we're talking."

"I'll try to take that as a compliment," Katherine huffed.

"You should."

They drove in silence until they turned off the Old Highway onto Grade

Road, heading north toward Anne Lindsay's New Morning Farm, looking for Roy and Hazel Willit's farmhouse which they'd been told sat on the east side of the property.

"That must be it there," Larry said, pointing to a two-story white farmhouse with a rambling porch on three sides. "Now we know how to get here."

They continued on into town in silence. When Larry stopped at Katherine's, he told her he'd stop by in the morning to take her to pick up her new car.

"Thank you," Katherine said as she climbed out.

"See you tomorrow," he said, trying to sound upbeat.

But Katherine turned her back and walked away without a word.

Sunday Dinner at the Willit's

At two o'clock on Sunday afternoon, Katherine stopped to pick up Bobby Carr on the way out to New Morning Farm. She was wearing a billowy brown and yellow cotton print prairie skirt, a light yellow cashmere pullover sweater covered by a matching cardigan and a simple gold necklace. Her shoulder-length brown hair was pulled back on either side with gold barrettes. All of this combined with a light application makeup and the absence of her clear-frame tortoise shell glasses, made her look like an entirely different woman.

As she walked up to the Carr's front door, Bobby came out and shouted, "Gosh, Katherine, you're so beautiful."

"Now behave yourself, mister," Katherine teased, as they got into the car.

When they pulled into the Willit's drive, Katherine parked on the side of the house next to Larry's and Greeley's cars. They were greeted by a smiling Hazel Willit as they walked up to the side door that led through a wide hall into the kitchen. In the sprawling kitchen, Bobby handed Hazel the bouquet of zinnias his grandmother had picked from her garden. Katherine gave her a box of chocolate caramels she said was from everyone at the café.

Hazel gave them both a hug of thanks and ushered them through the dining room into the large living room which took up the entire front of the house. The room was bounded on three sides by six-foot high windows, offering a panoramic view of the mountains. The left side of the living room was sparsely furnished, with an oriental rug on the polished wood floor, six straight-back wooden chairs, three music stands, and an upright piano against the far wall. The right side of the room was the living room proper, where Larry and Roy sat next to each other in easy chairs and Greeley stood facing them in front of the windows. He was holding his jacket, looking like he was getting ready to leave, and was just finishing a story about Roy and an early encounter with Lonnie.

Greeley laughed as he talked, "Dad said he thought Roy was the nicest guy, a real Southern gentlemen, until he and Walt Beaver delivered lumber for the porch." He went on to describe to Lonnie's amazement at how Roy had told them to get "that crap out of here." He wasn't going to have porch made with second grade pine, he wanted the best they had. When a perturbed Lonnie asked him why the devil he wanted a porch that big anyway, Roy replied with disgust, "If you don't know what a porch is for, son, I'm not going to tell you," and then walked into the house.

Bobby walked in and sat on the sofa. Katherine stood in the doorway while the three men fell silent and stared at her. Finally Greeley said to Bobby, "You didn't tell us you were bringing your beautiful girlfriend. What's her name?" Then they erupted in laughter. Katherine quickly turned toward the kitchen, hoping they hadn't seen her blush. Greeley followed her into the kitchen to say goodbye to Hazel.

Hazel was glad to have Katherine's company. She handed her an apron and asked her to roll out the biscuit dough and cut the biscuits. Hazel had been to the Madison Café twice and both times she was quiet and withdrawn. But now she talked with an eagerness as the two women worked, telling Katherine how pleased she was they all could come for dinner and that except for the folks from church, they didn't have many visitors. They still were trying to adjust to life in the north, it was so different from back home in Tennessee. But they had to look after Annie. They'd been with her for thirty years and there was no way they'd have let her leave Sewanee for the North on her own. Especially after Alan had died so suddenly. It broke Annie's heart.

As the two women talked, the outside kitchen door opened and Jack Lindsay walked in. He was in his stocking feet, wearing jeans and red plaid shirt. His black hair was windblown and in contrast to the last time she'd seen him, he looked like a field hand.

Katherine exclaimed, "It's you!"

"And it's you too!" Jack replied with a smile. "Welcome to Aunt Hazel's kitchen. They're all fed and watered out there so Uncle Roy can take it easy this afternoon," he said to Hazel as he started for the living room.

Hazel told him that his mother had called while he was out feeding the animals. She was late getting out of Seattle. "She'll be here, but probably won't make it for dinner."

Katherine and Hazel could hear the men in the living room laughing as they finished up in the kitchen. When they walked into the living room, Hazel sat down next to Bobby and took his hand, telling him how glad she was he had come. Bobby told her he wouldn't have missed his date with the most beautiful woman in the world for anything. Katherine blushed again and trying to avoid everyone's stares, she walked over to the piano at the far side of the room, pulled back the keyboard cover and struck a few notes, middle C, then D, E, and F. "Ouch," she said in a whisper, a whisper that everyone heard.

"It's been out of tune since the move from Tennessee," Roy said. "I can't find anyone to tune it."

Katherine told him if he had a small pair of pliers she could get it to where it was playable. It would just take a minute. Then she could bring out her tuning kit sometime if they wanted and do a complete tuning.

Roy demurred saying that was nice but there was no way they were going to ask a guest to do such a thing, especially just before dinner. But Jack got up and said he'd get the pliers. "It's about time we got that thing back in shape."

Roy started telling Larry and Bobby how they'd remodeled the whole house when they first moved in, opening up the downstairs by taking out two bedrooms, adding the oversize windows, and putting on the porch. Jack returned with a small crescent wrench and was standing next to Katherine who had propped open the piano's upper panel. She struck middle C and ran up the keyboard to A. She asked Jack if they had an "A" tuning fork.

"How about a pitch pipe? I've got one right here," he answered, reaching into a cabinet on the wall next to the piano.

Katherine asked him for an A above middle C. She struck the A on the keyboard, adjusted the tuning pin and moved down to F, then each white to the C below middle C and up to the C above middle C. The white keys finished, she moved up and down from middle C adjusting the black keys, sharps and flats. She was finished in ten minutes. She put the front panel down and played a fast-tempo "Londonderry Air."

"It's not great, but it'll do until I can get back and do a full tuning," she said matter-of-factly, as she and Jack walked back to the other side of the room just as the timer went off in the kitchen which prompted Hazel to announce the biscuits were coming out and dinner was ready.

There were six for dinner and by the time everyone got seated, the dining room table was filled with food, baked ham with a honey-pineapple glaze, roasted chicken, mashed potatoes, glazed sweet potatoes, green beans, collard greens, biscuits, and gravy. Hazel and Roy sat at either end of the table. Katherine on Roy's right and Larry sat on Hazel's right. Bobby sat across from Larry, next to Katherine, and Jack sat across from Katherine next to Larry.

Roy asked everyone to bow their heads as he said grace, thanking God for their special guests who had helped give him a little more time on earth, after which Hazel apologized for not having fried chicken, but Roy was not going to get his hands on anything like that for a long time and no one was allowed to pass him the ham or the gravy, even if he insisted while she was in the kitchen.

Thanks to Roy and Hazel's natural, informal hospitality, the table conversation was easy and casual. Bobby wanted to know what collards were and said he'd never had sweet potatoes. Roy teased him, asking where he'd been living all his life. Larry told Hazel and Roy the meal reminded him of time he spent in North Carolina. Hazel smiled and allowed you might be able to get a good meal in North Carolina. Roy said he wasn't too sure about that. Jack didn't say much but he smiled a lot, obviously enjoying the company. Every time Katherine glanced at him, he was looking at her.

Roy asked Katherine where she'd learned to tune pianos. She told them about her music teacher in Iowa, Julia Howe, who had taught her not only voice and piano, but self-reliance in the true New England tradition of her forebears. "She told me when I became a concert pianist, I had to take care of myself and make sure the piano was tuned before a performance.

Roy chuckled and said he'd love to meet Julia Howe.

When they finished eating, Hazel asked Bobby to help clear and told Katherine she'd show her how to make a pecan pie, the pecan pie they were going to have for dessert.

"We'll have some music while we're waiting for the pie to bake," she said to Bobby.

When the dishes were washed and the pie was in the oven, Katherine walked back in the living room while Hazel and Bobby were finishing up. Jack and Roy were standing over near the piano, facing Larry, who was sitting on one of the straight-back wooden chairs near the front window acting as a one-man audience while Jack was tuning a mandolin and Roy was tuning a banjo.

Katherine took a seat next to Larry and with a hint of the third degree asked Jack, "Where'd you learn to play the mandolin."

Jack nodded at Roy and then at Hazel who had come in with a guitar and sat down as she started to tune it. He told Katherine, Hazel and Roy had taught him to play the guitar, banjo, and mandolin. They'd tried but finally gave up trying to get him to play the fiddle.

"He was the star of a bluegrass band when he was in college in Knoxville," Roy said proudly. "The Rainy Creek Boys. They opened for Dolly Parton once."

Hazel was clearly the leader of this trio. She told Larry, Katherine, and Bobby that back home they always played music after dinner, out on the porch if the weather allowed. Everybody where they came from played something or if they didn't, they sang, or "did something." Then she asked if anyone had a song they'd like to hear.

"Wabash Cannonball!" Bobby shouted.

"One of my favorites," Roy said, waiting for a nod from Hazel.

Roy sang the lead, with Jack and Hazel joining in with high and low harmony. Bobby joined in with gusto each time they got to the imitation train whistle, Roy Acuff-style, which brought a laugh from everyone in the room. This was followed by "Down Yonder," an old Doc Watson favorite. "He's from North Carolina," she said to Larry with a wink.

Then Hazel told them about living up in the far northeast corner of Tennessee, in Kingsport, a young woman from Clinch Mountain, Virginia working in a book factory when Roy came to town and stole her away, taking her south to Sewanee, almost to Alabama. She'd grown up around the Carter family and their music and one of the first songs she'd learned to play on the guitar was one of Mother Maybelle Carter's favorites. Roy and Jack stood silent, as she played and sang "Keep on the Sunny Side," in a plain, unembellished style that hushed every other sound in the house.

"Now let's have a couple hymns before that pie is ready," Hazel said looking at Katherine. "I've heard through the grapevine you're not only a piano player but you've got a beautiful voice. Come on and join us."

Katherine blushed and said she couldn't. She didn't know any hymns, or at least had forgotten any she knew. Hazel got up and lifted the top of the piano bench and pulled out a tattered songbook, *Hymns My Mother Taught Me*, and put it on a music stand. With Bobby and Larry clapping and saying "please, come on, sing," Katherine reluctantly got up and joined the trio.

We'll do "Sweet By and By," "Just A Closer Walk With Thee," and finish with "In the Garden," Hazel intoned with the authority of a drill sergeant.

As they started with the first hymn, Anne Lindsay came in through the kitchen and stood in the doorway between the dining room and living room. She nodded and smiled at Larry and Bobby, holding a forefinger to her mouth in a shushing motion. Larry later said it was a moment he'd never forget, seeing the tall, handsome Anne Lindsay, her windblown blonde hair tossed around her shoulders, standing in the doorway smiling.

By the time they'd finished "Sweet By and By," Katherine had figured out how her high harmony fit in with the rest of the group, and when they started in with "Just A Closer Walk With Thee," she was singing in a full soprano that Jack later said gave him goose bumps. Then Hazel announced she and Katherine would do "In the Garden" as a duet, telling Katherine to sing the verses and she would come in on the chorus. It was a song

Katherine remembered from her childhood, one she'd first learned from her grandmother, and one she'd learned to play on the piano when she was child.

Katherine's voice rang pure as an angel's, filling the room with the perfect integrity of her soul. *I come to the garden alone.* Her voice was filled with all the emotion and self-inflicted sorrow she'd felt for years after giving up her baby, now an eternal stranger in an unknown world. *While the dew is still on the roses.* Her voice held all her loneliness of the years she wound her way up the Great Valley, from diner to grill to truck stop to bus station cafeteria, fending off drunks, gagging on cigarette smoke in greasy spoons, and fighting the urge to drink again. *And He walks with me, and He talks with me.* Her voice embraced her longing when on Thanksgiving and Christmas she'd drive alone through the neighborhoods of whatever town she was in, gazing at homes filled with cars in the driveway, wondering what was on the table and yearning for the love and warmth of a family. *And He tells me I am his own.*

There are moments when a hushed stillness is more powerful than a loud ovation, when quiet reflection is more potent than clamorous praise. So it was when Katherine and Hazel finished their duet.

Roy and Jack wordlessly started packing up their instruments. Larry and Bobby walked across the room to Anne who told them to come into the kitchen and help get dessert ready. Hazel got up and put her arms around Katherine who returned her hug with an unexpected intensity. Katherine was trembling and softly sobbing. She held tight to the older woman as Hazel stroked the back of her head and whispered, "It's all right, it's all right, you're home now."

When they walked into the kitchen behind Jack and Roy, the pie was on plates, the ice cream was out of the freezer and Anne announced it was serve-your-self. The guys took their food into the dining room and sat at Roy's end of the table, watching football on a small television Roy had rolled out. Hazel, Anne, and Katherine sat at the kitchen table, eating as Anne told them about her trip to Seattle.

Larry was the first to get up and announce it was time to hit the road. He asked Jack when he was going back to Seattle and when Jack told him first thing in the morning, around six, Larry said, "Stop at the café, we'll have one of our power breakfast sandwiches and some hot coffee ready for you."

The women had started to clear the dishes when Larry came into the kitchen and offered his hand to Hazel, saying thanks wasn't enough. But Hazel rejected the offer of a handshake, holding out her arms and saying, "Come here and give me a hug." Larry reluctantly obeyed, hesitating like a shy schoolboy before he embraced Hazel. Then Anne walked him to the kitchen door.

She told him Maude had called and asked if she could sub as Larry's bridge partner on Friday night. "I told her I wouldn't dare say yes without your permission," she said taking his arm as they walked.

"I'd be honored. "I'll be looking forward to it all week."

After Katherine finished helping Hazel with the dishes, she told Bobby it was time to leave. Bobby and Roy were intently watching the football game and Jack was intently watching Katherine. He said, "Larry told me to stop in on my way out of town in the morning for a, what'd he call it. . .?"

"I heard him," Katherine replied with a forced smile. "For a power breakfast sandwich, a café specialty. I'll have one ready for you."

Then she and Bobby made the rounds, thanking everyone, hugging Roy, shaking hands with Jack, hugging Hazel and Anne. Hazel said they were so thankful they'd come and asked Katherine when she could come back and tune the piano. They agreed on Friday afternoon, and Hazel said with a wink, "Bring Bobby if he wants to come."

"Of course I want to come," Bobby answered loudly.

Then they were on their way home in early autumn twilight, with Bobby talking nonstop about what a great day it had been on his first date with the most beautiful girl in the world.

The Bishop Brings Someone To Town

Jack walked in the front door of the Madison Café the next morning five minutes after it opened at six. He was in his city lawyer clothes, the dark, striped suit, white shirt, repp stripe tie, and tasseled loafers, finished off with his black hair combed back and glistening with mousse. He stood at the counter near the door as Katherine walked up with a white paper bag in one hand and a large cup of coffee in the other.

"On the house," she said. "Anyone who plays the mandolin like you do, should get some bennies somewhere. I see you're got your power look on this morning," she teased.

"Power look for a power sandwich. Thanks very much," he said holding up the paper bag and coffee, nodding at Katherine and to Larry, who was standing in front of a grill, pretending not to watch.

Jack hesitated and then said, "I had such a great time yesterday. Would you like to go out sometime? I'll be back on the weekend."

Katherine stared at him for a moment and then whispered, "I not going out with you. Don't do this."

"Do what?"

"Don't reach down and try to be nice to me," she said. "I'm not part of your world. Don't shame me."

"What are you talking about," Jack replied. "Shaming you?"

By now, Larry had edged down the kitchen and Sadie was leaning through the service window, both trying to hear what was being said.

"You're better than this Jack. Don't be another chump trying to get me into bed because I was nice to you."

Jack was offended. "You really are something," he huffed. "You should climb down from that high horse and join me down here in the real world of regular people."

"You're not regular people and I'm not going out with you, period. Not now, not ever."

"Thanks for breakfast, I've got a ferry to catch," he said and walked out.

Katherine walked back into the kitchen and Sadie said, "Nice set of wheels," pointing out the front window to Jack's BMW, "What was that all about, anyway?"

Katherine walked past her, muttering, "Nothing, absolutely nothing." She walked past Larry and out the kitchen's back service door into the alley. A high wood partition shielded the area from the dining room's alley door and kept her out of sight from the café traffic moving in and out of the dining room. She stood in the cold morning air with her arms wrapped around her front, staring out at the mountains, now dark blue outlines in the early light of dawn.

Back when she was on the road, this morning's dust-up with Jack would have been enough to start her thinking about packing up and leaving. She could just keep walking up the alley, put a few things in her new car and drive away. She'd done that plenty of times. She'd start over, living in another cheap room on the side of the highway, working in another cheap diner where she could only hope her boss wouldn't keep grabbing her butt and she'd get paid at the end of the week.

But her life was different now. Things were more complicated. She didn't feel like leaving. She didn't want to abandon her little house, jettison her piano, and say goodbye to people who for the first time in her life felt like friends. Then there was Hazel. She'd told Hazel she'd tune their piano. She'd also told Reverend Flatte she'd play the organ at the upcoming Sunday service. And Larry expected her to decamp anytime. She'd prove him wrong, at least for now.

She was pulled from her reverie by the sound of footsteps in the gravel and then a young girl's "Good morning." The girl, who looked around ten or eleven years old and her companion, a boy who was probably twelve or thirteen, walked by without looking at her. *The Dolan kids*, Katherine thought. But they didn't look like street urchins. They were both scrubbed with neatly combed and brushed hair and clean clothes, carrying books, obviously on their way to school. But it seemed odd the boy was eating a candy bar at a little past six in the morning. *Is that his breakfast*, she thought. She started to call them back to offer them something for breakfast, but stopped and went back inside.

The café was starting to fill up with the early Monday morning crowd. There wasn't time for Sadie and Larry to pursue the most important question of the morning, what had happened between Katherine and Jack Lindsay. But, Bobby did take the time to sneak up and give her a hug, telling her she was still the most beautiful woman in the world, even in blue jeans and hiking boots and those crazy fake glasses.

When the breakfast rush was over and the morning slipped into early lunch time, Katherine ignored Sadie's plaintive looks of "tell me about it" and concentrated on her work. Monday's lunch special was always meatloaf with macaroni and cheese and green beans, something that attracted Will McCann and Charlie Sizemore like a magnet. The two law men liked to come in after the lunch crowd had cleared out. They'd sit in the dining room with Greeley talking well after closing, catching up on what had happened over the weekend: who'd wrecked their car, who threw her husband out of the house, who broke whose nose at the Duchess Tavern, what couple were spotted out steppin' on their respective spouses, and if anyone had seen Tommy Lowry, who had been lying low after his fight with Vicki St. John.

A half hour before closing that Monday, when the only people in the dining room were the aforementioned trio, a couple walked in the front door and sat in the first booth along the front wall of the original part of the café. The fleshy woman was wearing a bright yellow moo-moo with red polka dots, and Birkenstock sandals. A large gold cross hung low around her neck. Her hair sat on top of her head in a curly white ball, a golden-age Caucasian version of an Afro.

Bishop Mitchell Lodong was her escort, his straight black hair hanging was over his ears and parted in the middle. He wore a black and white clerical collar and black vest under his long black coat, all to make certain that everyone was aware of his venerable position as Bishop for the Western Washington Synod of Sanitarians Who are Washed in the Blood of the Lamb.

Larry was wiping down the counter facing the booths and gave them a cheerful "Hello folks. I'm sorry, the kitchen is closed. The café closes at two."

Lodong smiled and said, "Quite all right, kind sir. We are not seeking vittles this afternoon. We are on a more hallowed mission, a sacred journey, as it were, attempting to reunite a mother and daughter after years of separation. In short, my good man, we are in search of Katy Owling, who we understand is an employee of this fine establishment."

Lodong's partner, Susan Owling, sat across from him with her head bowed, her hands clasped, and her lips moving in prayer. The stench of cheap red wine swirled around them. She looked up and saw Katherine behind the counter standing next to Larry.

Suddenly Susan Owling threw up her hands and shouted "Praise the

Lord, thank you Jesus!" She squeezed herself out of the booth and walked to the counter, reaching for Katherine. "Is that you, my baby? My Katy? Oh how my heart has ached, how my soul has trembled night after night, wondering if you were safe, if you were thinking of me." Then she put her head on the counter and wept in loud uncontrollable sobs. Lodong came over and put his arm around her.

The bishop smiled at Katherine and Larry who were standing behind the counter mutely watching. "Such an emotional time my dear," he said to Susan. "But our Lord God has answered your prayers, you are washed in the blood of the lamb."

Susan lifted her head and held out her hands to Katherine, "Come here my Katy, come give mommy a hug. Tell me about my grandchild. I want to see my grandchild."

Katherine stepped closer to the edge of the counter and said, "I don't know who you are but you're not *my* mother."

Looking up toward the ceiling, Susan raised her arms and hysterically screamed, "What are you doing to me? Why do you punish me like this dear God? I want my grandchild. You can't just push me away!"

Greeley, Will, and Charlie had come around the corner from the dining room. They stood with Sadie and Bobby watching the rumpus. Katherine walked around the counter. She took the sobbing Susan by an elbow walked her to the front door, telling her to get out. Mitchell Lodong followed as Katherine pushed Susan out the front door and up against the ticket booth of the old theater, holding her there with an arm across her chest. Lodong started to protest, but Katherine told him to shut up. The little crowd inside moved to behind the counter just inside the front door which was open enough to hear Katherine's angry rebuke to the strangers.

"Don't you or your boyfriend ever show your face in this town again," she ordered, pushing hard against Susan's chest. "And get one thing straight, *you're* not my mother. You're nothing to me. You understand? You're nothing to me."

Lodong's car was parked front of the café with a terrified Art Fletcher at the wheel. Katherine said, "There is no grandchild. I gave the baby up for adoption when it was born. I don't even know if it was a girl or boy. And no matter what he told you, that fat dirtball in the car wasn't the father," she said pointing at Fletcher. "Now get out of here," she said, pushing Susan Owling toward the car,

Katherine marched over to Lodong who was watching the sobbing bovine battle-ax lumber toward the car. "What's that thing on your head? A dead skunk?" Katherine growled. "You look like a fool." She pulled the hairpiece off his head, spit on it and then stomped on it with her boot, rubbing it into the sidewalk. "Now get in that hearse and get out of here."

A bald Lodong started to protest as he picked up the toupee with two fingers like a dead mammal. Katherine turned him around and pushed him toward the car. "Go, get, leave, vamoose."

She stood on the sidewalk watching the car start down Main Street on its way out of town before going back inside where the group of onlookers had scattered. Greeley, Will, and Charlie were back at their table in the dining room, Larry was scraping down one of the grills, Bobby was loading the dishwasher, and Sadie was wiping down tables.

From the kitchen, Katherine shouted over the service counter to the guys in the dining room, "We're shutting everything down back here, anybody want anything before we do?"

"No, I think that about does it for today," Greeley shouted back. Both Will and Charlie nodded in agreement.

A Plan is Devised in the North

After his discovery that Myron Lantz aka Ron Lantz aka Buck McCready, the friend of Luther Moody, was living at Sekiu on the Olympic Peninsula, Paul Merrick spent hours in the Vancouver office of Merrick and Son Imports, thinking how the erstwhile cowboy singer turned charter captain and Sasquatch hunter could be approached and tell what he knew about the location of Luther Moody's baby grand piano. One thing was certain, however, Paul Merrick would not do the approaching. A dark-skinned man with the accoutrement's of a proper Englishman, turning up in a fishing village in the lily-white wilderness of the Olympic Peninsula, asking about the disposition of a deceased entertainer's beloved piano would not only cause suspicion, it could get him hauled in for questioning.

So Paul turned to his cousin and partner in the Vancouver office of Merrick & Son Imports, Arthur Merrick, Jr., for assistance in getting what he wanted from Buck McCready. Arthur, who was eleven years older than Paul, was a native Canadian who had been born and raised in Vancouver. His father, Arthur, Sr., was the older brother of Paul Merrick's father. He'd left England as a teen-ager aching for adventure, having caught the Yukon gold fever of the 1890s, and like many failed Stampeders, he landed penniless in Vancouver in 1900, where he eventually persuaded his family to set up a western outpost of Merrick & Son in British Columbia.

Vancouver has always been a valuable back entrance to North America for the East and South Asia trade and although the respectable businessmen of the city would vociferously but politely deny it, innumerable fortunes were built on undocumented trade, human and otherwise, in the financial and import offices along Hastings, Pender, and Granville Streets for generations, making the city a cousin to Marseilles, Naples, Hamburg, and Rotterdam.

The success of this robust, illicit and generations-old international trade, was founded on the carefully cultivated image of the harmless, cheery, and slightly eccentric British Columbian, smiling and shouting "tally ho," and "oot and aboot," while obsessed with hockey, scones, and firewood. Who would suspect such quaint folk were engaged in nefarious activities like the importation of countless thousands of undocumented Chinese, or trading in heroin, hashish, and opium from South Asia, and any other odious transaction the black market will bear?

The British Columbia office of Merrick & Son had not been immune to black-market activity. From the beginning, Arthur Merrick the elder had vigorously embraced the dark world of Vancouver's international commerce, particularly the transport of undocumented Chinese and South Asians into Canada and often, on to the United States. But by the time Arthur Merrick, Jr. became head of the Vancouver office after his father's death, Merrick & Son's import activities were all legitimate.

Paul Merrick, however, never tired of his cousin's stories about the dark underbelly of Vancouver's import business. He told Arthur he would have had a flair for the intrigue and secrecy that came with smuggling wealthy

Asians into Canada. It would have been a welcome change from the tedious London world of importing mango curry and balsamic chutney.

Influenced by the lore of the criminal netherworld, Paul proffered his ideas on how Buck McCready could be forced to divulge what he knew of Luther Moody's piano. He used terms like *force his hand; won't take no for an answer; twist his arm; in the dead of night; we'll stop at nothing; blackmail if we have to; put the screws to him; put him on the rack.*

Impressed as he was with Paul's imagination, Arthur said he had a better idea. He'd go to Seattle, rent a car and drive out to Sekiu, posing as a genial Canuck who was interested in using McCready's charter service. "I'll tell him about our new line of imported yoga wear and how we want to entertain some prospective American distributors with a salmon fishing expedition. Then I'll concoct a story about seeing him and Luther Moody perform years ago which will naturally lead to Luther Moody and his piano."

Paul liked the simplicity of his older cousin's proposal and the cousins agreed Arthur would make the trip to Buck McCready's lair in Sekiu the following week. Paul Merrick sighed with satisfaction, he was getting closer to his quarry, the secrets held by the Kimball Compact Grand Piano, Serial No. 1891-9183.

Sanctuary

When Katherine walked home after work on the day of her encounter with Jack Lindsay and the afternoon brouhaha with Susan Owling and Mitchell Lodong, she expected either Sadie or Larry to show up and see how she was doing. But Sadie had her nephews, Donny and Danny St. John, to take care of until her sister Vicki got out of jail, and Larry said he was going out to the Willit's after work. He'd told Roy at dinner the day before he'd help him haul some things out of the barn that Roy wanted to sell.

So Katherine sat at the piano in the late afternoon playing away the stress of another day at the café until she remembered she was supposed to meet Margie Parker at Trinity Episcopal to go over next Sunday's service when she'd make her debut as substitute organist.

She shed her hiking boots for a pair of light blue low-cut Chuck Taylors, left her clear-lens glasses on the dresser, donned a black-leather jacket she hadn't worn since Roseburg and decided to walk to the church. She never walked anywhere in town, except across the street to Maude's. But now she walked down Second Avenue not caring who saw her, then across Main Street two blocks to Elm Street and then up two blocks to Fourth Avenue where the white wood frame neo-Gothic Trinity Episcopal Church sat on the northwest corner of Elm and Fourth.

A square wooden sign with hand-painted block lettering that read, "Open for Prayer," hung to the right of the heavy eight-foot high double doors. She pushed a door open and stepped into the dimly lit empty church. The all-embracing quiet of the interior startled her. She sat in a pew on the left near the back waiting for Margie and then realized it was Tuesday, not today, they were supposed to meet. She got ready to leave but stopped. She sat in the dusky light, savoring the peaceful moment, while the six ten-foot stained glass windows, three on each side of the church, glowed with a pale luminescence in the late gray light of the autumn afternoon.

Katherine sat in a silent meditative state for over an hour, letting the peaceful ambience flow through her. She was brought back to consciousness by the sound of a door softly closing in the front of the church and then saw the outline of Father Tom Flatte kneeling in prayer at the altar. He rose and turned to leave through the side door that led to his office. Katherine called out, "Hello Father Tom, it's Katherine Baker."

He changed direction and walked down the aisle towards her, asking if she'd mind if he joined her for a moment. She patted her right hand on the pew and said she'd like that very much. She told him she'd thought she was supposed to meet Margie but then realized it was tomorrow, "I don't know what happened, it seems like ages since I sat down here."

The cleric smiled, "Prayer takes many forms, my dear. It isn't always supplication, you know. It can be contemplative."

"I don't think I believe in God anymore," Katherine said. "Maybe I never did. I've spent years believing I was the only one who was going to take care of me."

"I understand."

They talked about Katherine's debut at the organ on Sunday. Father Tom said he knew she'd do a great job and they were very thankful she'd agreed to do it.

"But what about your glasses? You're not wearing them." he said. "Do you have contacts now?"

Katherine shook her head and confessed they'd been fakes. She'd decided not to wear them anymore."I've deluded myself for a long time, Father Tom. I came back here thinking no one would know who I was. All this time I've been pretending no one knew about my past as Katy Owling. But everyone knew. What a fool," She said with a wry laugh.

Father Tom smiled. "I don't think it really mattered to anyone except you, Katherine. All I hear is how much you're admired. You're an extraordinary person."

Then he took her hand and led her to the back of the church. On the wall next to the baptismal font was a copper plaque with a black and white photo with a caption that read, "Bishop Stephen E. Bayne, 1908 – 1974" The plaque read, "On September 21, 1950, this church was consecrated by the Holy Bishop of Olympia, Stephen Bayne, to the glory of God and for the cultivation of faith in all the people."

"He was a great man. A prince of the church." Father Tom told her. He went on to tell Katherine about how, as a newly ordained minister on his first assignment at Trinity Church, he'd confided to the bishop that he was afraid he couldn't rise to the necessary level of grace to lead his congregation. Bishop Bayne had scoffed and said his congregation deserved more than his whining. "Then he said dismissively, 'Now pull up your socks and get to work.' And I'm still here after all these years. You see all of us have had our struggles."

They walked back up the church and through a side door that led to Father Tom's office. One wall of the large, welcoming space was covered with book shelves in front of which was a large library table and four chairs. Father Tom pulled a large album from a bottom shelf and opened it on the table, gesturing for Katherine to have a look. He turned the pages of what was the register of confirmations to *1951*.

"Here are some names you might recognize," he said with a smile, pointing to two entries, *Horace G. Martin* and *William H. McCann*. "Greeley and Will were both acolytes here at Trinity." Then he turned the page to

1952, saying "Here's another classmate a year later." He pointed to *Anne S. Oates*. "That's our Anne Lindsay, now."

Father Tom continued, "It was a joy to watch Bishop Bayne during their confirmation services. He always told the newly confirmed their faith was not a refuge but a responsibility and proudly told them that the words of the *Book of Common Prayer,* the words they repeat every Sunday, were the same words spoken by George Washington, Patrick Henry, James Monroe, James Madison and a host of other leaders of early America."

"Anne came back to be married here in the church not long after she graduated from the University of Washington," Father Tom said proudly. "None of us thought her new husband, this young divinity student named Alan Lindsay, would become one of the great philosophers of our church."

He told Katherine how he'd stayed in touch with Anne and Alan over the years and had made several trips to Sewanee, Tennessee where Alan was an associate dean at the divinity school. Alan Lindsay spent his life writing and teaching about the Nicene Creed and the relationship between faith and belief. Father Tom pulled out a slim, hardcover book from the bookshelf and handed it to Katherine. It was Alan Lindsay's, *The Platonic Ideal of Faith: There Isn't One*. He said it was still one of most widely read books on Anglican epistemology.

"You're starting to lose me," Katherine said. "But I'd like to read it sometime."

"Here, take this copy. "I've got several. I give them to people all the time."

It was getting dark now and Katherine told Father Tom she'd best be on her way home. "Thanks for the book, I'll start reading it tonight."

She held the book tightly as she walked home. The lights were out at Maude's when she went by. At home, she made herself a cup of coffee and sat on the sofa with Alan Lindsay's book. On the back panel of the dust jacket were blurbs praising his scholarship and provocative thinking, one by Bishop Stephen Bayne. On the bottom right, there was a small color headshot of the author, who Katherine had imagined to be a balding, dour, scholarly type with wire-rimmed glasses. Instead, Alan Lindsay was an older version of his son Jack, uncommonly handsome with flowing black hair and piercing dark eyes.

On the front inside endpaper was an inscription written in a bold hand, *For our dear Tom, a constant inspiration to Anne and me. Alan.* She thumbed through the front matter to the dedication page and read: *To Anne who has been my cherished partner in this journey and to whom I owe everything; to Jack, the prince of everything good in our future; and to Hazel and Roy, our guardian angels.*

A Crisis on Second Avenue

The next morning, Katherine went to work at five, a half hour earlier than usual. Tuesday's lunch special was chicken pot pie and she usually showed up early to help Larry put together the individual pies, the crusts of which were his special creation, something that made them a big hit with the café lunch crowd.

Tommy Lowry was sitting in the far corner of the dining room, eating a breakfast of bacon, eggs and toast. Katherine had bristled when she saw his pickup in the alley with the back bumper festooned with bumper stickers like, *I Love Animals, They're Good to Eat; Keep Honking, I'm Reloading;* and *I'm Going Nuckin Futs.* He was still sporting a black eye and a bruise on his right cheek, leftovers from his getting beaten up by Vicki St. John.

Greeley's rules for Tommy's free breakfast were that he show up sober before five-thirty and be gone before six. When he did show up, once or twice a week, Greeley told him who needed temporary help, bucking hay, splitting wood, or hauling trash, so he could earn a little money. Katherine didn't like the free breakfast deal, but he was Greeley's high school class-mate, who in Greeley's words was down on his luck, and Greeley was the boss. To Greeley and Will McCann, Tommy was the old "fireplug," a so-briquet leftover from when they were the "three musketeers" of the Cedar Mills high school football team and Tommy was the fullback who would put his head down and run through anything.

Larry and Katherine worked silently making pies. By the time the café opened at six, Tommy was gone and twenty-five pies were ready for the oven. Bobby would start baking them around ten o'clock, when things quieted down after the breakfast rush. It was one of the high points of Bobby's week. Every Tuesday morning, when he and Sadie arrived just before six, Bobby would go straight to the walk-in cooler and count the chicken pot pies ready for the oven.

There was none of the usual early morning banter that morning. Yesterday's incident with Susan Owling and Mitchell Lodong was still on everyone's mind, but no one wanted to talk about it. There were also no remarks about Katherine's new look. She wasn't wearing the clear-lens glasses. She had on a khaki skirt and yellow blouse instead of blue jeans and a plaid shirt. The hiking boots had been replaced with light blue Chuck Taylor's.

The most dramatic moment of the morning came when Bobby came out of the cooler and announced that there were five more chicken pot pies than the usual twenty as though it was a news headline of the highest import. Katherine told him two were for Sadie's nephews, Donny and Danny St. John, and one was for Maude Doud, who was under the weather.

"That leaves two more than normal," Bobby said solemnly.

"We'll figure it out," Katherine answered. "Maybe we'll sell the extras."

"Then I'm going to start baking earlier than I usually do," he answered with an approval-seeking determination.

"Good plan, Bobby."

She left the café in the afternoon with a chicken pot pie and a small tossed salad and stopped at Maude's on her way to meet Margie Parker at Trinity Church. The back door was unlocked and Katherine was struck by how cold it was inside. Maude was in a recliner in the darkened living room. The television was on but muted. Rascal was with Maude in the chair. The normally obnoxious Cairn Terrier was quiet, sitting on Maude's lap looking worried. Maude smiled and told Katherine to put the food on the kitchen counter. She'd get to it later. Katherine said she'd stop back again after her meeting with Margie.

An hour and a half later when Katherine returned to Maude's on her way home, she found Maude still in the recliner, nearly unconscious. In a hoarse whisper, she told Katherine she was burning up and was having trouble breathing. Katherine called 911 and in a couple of minutes heard the wail of the volunteer fire hall siren. Ten minutes later, Chip Franklin and Ray Kesecker pulled up beside Maude's house on Second Avenue in the fire department's emergency vehicle. Maude was going to the hospital in Port Smith.

As Chip and Ray wheeled her out on the gurney, Katherine started calling Greeley, Lonnie and Elizabeth, and Larry. She started cussing when no one she called picked up the phone so she left anxious sounding messages for everyone. Then she picked up a shaking Rascal and headed across the street to her house. She tried calling everyone again to no avail, and then headed to Port Smith.

Chip and Ray were just coming out of the emergency room with the empty gurney when Katherine arrived at the hospital. Chip told her it was acute appendicitis complicated by a secondary infection. Maude was already in surgery.

Katherine went inside and was curtly told that unless she was an immediate member of the family, she wouldn't be told anything about Mrs. Doud's condition. So she went back outside, got Rascal out of the car and walked him around the lawn in front of the emergency room. It was dark now and a chilly wind was blowing off the Strait. Rascal didn't want be outside and he stood shivering in the cold, looking up at Katherine.

She picked up the trembling little guy, put him inside her jacket, and told him it was going to be all right. When they walked back into the waiting room, Katherine noticed a bronze plaque just inside the door with a list of "The generous donors who had made building the new hospital possible." Herschel and Maude Doud, and Alonzo and Elizabeth Martin were near the top of the list.

Katherine stood at the front window watching for headlights pulling into the parking lot and started thinking about Chip Franklin. He'd been two years ahead of her in high school. He was a senior and she was a sophomore, the new girl from Iowa, and he'd wasted no time asking her out. They'd gone out a few times, but Katy Owling was more interested in music than boys, and Chip quickly took the hint.

Now over a decade later, they were strangers. Chip had taken over his father's insurance agency and lived in large house overlooking the valley with his gorgeous wife and two darling children. Katherine, by her own description, was a reformed drunk, an itinerant short-order cook in a small-town café, trying to maintain a modicum of equilibrium.

"Stop feeling sorry for yourself," she whispered into the night.

She heard Lonnie before she saw him. "Age before beauty," he chortled to his wife as they walked into the hospital followed by an out-of-breath Greeley. Rascal started whining and gave a little bark when he saw the Martins. They listened to Katherine's account of what happened and then Elizabeth took charge, telling Greeley to take Rascal to their car and ordering Lonnie to get the details of Maude's condition. She and Katherine would wait there.

Elizabeth Martin was as forceful as Katherine had been led to believe but she was much smaller than Katherine had imagined, about Katherine's height, and physically unintimidating. She took Katherine by the hand and squeezed it, telling her that in spite of the poor circumstances, she was so pleased they could finally meet. "I've heard so much about you from Greeley and Lonnie," she said with a surprising warmth. "Greeley's crazy idea of having a restaurant would be a bad memory by now if you hadn't stepped in and saved it. That place and the historical society make him the happiest I've seen him in years."

They sat on a sofa in the empty waiting room and like the well-bred woman she was, Elizabeth Martin talked with a pleasant self-confidence, asking questions and making observations that made Katherine feel as though she was one of the most important people in Elizabeth's Martin's life. The younger woman was charmed and unpredictably disarmed by her graciousness.

Lonnie came back with a report that Maude was having her appendix removed as he spoke, saying that her situation might have been fatal, if Katherine hadn't found her when she did. When Greeley returned, Lonnie asked if he'd got that "motorized bath mat" in the car.

"We'll take him home with us," Elizabeth said. "The cats hate him, but they'll all have to make do."

"I talked to Larry before I left town," Greeley said. "He's on his way."

"Why on earth would you call Larry?" Elizabeth asked.

"This should be good," Lonnie whispered to Katherine.

"Well, mother, the last time I checked he was a member of our family,"

Greeley said. "He's your brother and probably more importantly at the moment, Aunt Maude's favorite bridge partner."

"Don't be tedious," Elizabeth sighed. "You know how I feel."

"As though that's the only thing in the world, how you feel."

Then Lonnie chimed in, "Ok, put a lid on it. In case you've forgotten, my sister's in there getting cut open. Don't embarrass yourselves in front of Katherine. Remember your Waterbury Bradford blood."

"I never forget it," said Larry as he came up behind Lonnie and put his hands on his brother-in-law's shoulders. "In Waterbury, no one thinks it odd, that the elite speak only to Bradfords, and the Bradfords speak only to God." Larry turned and said, "Hello Elizabeth, how nice to see you."

Elizabeth rose from the sofa and extended her hand, "Likewise, Larry. You're looking fit. But I didn't know you're a wisenheimer now, where'd you pick that up? "

"Prison," he answered grimly as brother and sister shook hands.

It has been eight years since they'd last seen each other and this *ad hoc* reunion was about to become a full-blown internecine squabble when Dr. Terry Buzzby walked in and announced the appendectomy had been successful and that Maude's infection was being treated with an infusion of antibiotics. She was still in intensive care and couldn't have visitors until her condition had stabilized.

Lonnie said, "So she's still alive and kickin'. Thanks Buzz."

It was agreed that Greeley and Larry would stay until Maude was able to have visitors. Elizabeth and Lonnie would take Rascal home and wait for a call from Greeley.

"It's all over but the shoutin'" Lonnie with a sigh of relief.

Katherine said good night and turned to leave, but the four others surrounded her, thanking her for all she'd done. It wasn't easy for Katherine to accept anyone's gratitude. It made her uncomfortable. She finally broke free and walked out alone into the night.

The Piano Tuning

Larry gave her a full report on Maude's condition when Katherine got to work the next morning. Maude was conscious and already complaining by the time he'd left the hospital a little after midnight: *The room was too hot, there was no fresh air, she was thirsty, there weren't any nurses when she needed them, where the heck was Buzz, had he gone home already?* Larry said Maude would be there for a few days, until the infection was under control or until everyone got tired of her.

Katherine noticed Larry's shoes first thing, new low-cut black Chuck Taylors. She knew his penchant for understated monkeyshines, especially gags directed at her and Sadie after they'd made unending fun of his attempt to sneak out the back door when he thought Jack Lindsay was serving papers on him. So she figured this was some attempt at humor, his wearing the same style of shoe as hers. But she wasn't going to give him the satisfaction of letting him know she'd even noticed his new footwear.

He was still wearing his Chuck Taylors on Thursday morning when Sadie and Bobby came to work wearing new shoes. Sadie had on a pair of light-blue low-cut Chuck Taylors like Katherine's and Bobby's were black like Larry's. All three of them worked with an exaggerated air of seriousness, pretending that there was nothing strange about them suddenly wearing shoes identical to Katherine's.

But Katherine wouldn't break. She ignored them and worked with an amplified solemnity. Then, when she saw Greeley coming down the stairs from his office wearing a pair of brand new black Chuck Taylors, her stony detachment quickly dissolved and she started to laugh.

"Ok, ok," she said in a loud voice. "I guess you all think you're funny."

Sadie came over to the service counter, Bobby came out of the store room, Larry stood next to Katherine at his station near the back of the kitchen, and Greeley stood on the other side of her along the front counter. They all stared at her with expressions of mock perplexity as though they didn't understand why she was laughing. Then they all started to laugh. The racket spilled into the dining room prompting Carl Wilfong to tell the rest of The Table that Greeley's gang was having way too much fun.

On Friday morning, everyone came to work once again wearing their new Chuck Taylors, making them the official footwear of the Madison Café and when Katherine reminded Bobby they were going out to the Willits after work, he told her he'd have stop at home to get a pair of boots because he was going to help Roy in the barn and he didn't want to get his new work shoes dirty.

❖ ❖ ❖ ❖ ❖ ❖ ❖ ❖ ❖ ❖ ❖ ❖

The driveway into New Morning Farm first led to Roy and Hazel's house and then forked into two branches from the parking area at the side of their farmhouse. The left fork led up a rise a quarter mile to Anne's house, a low-lying cedar-sided, one-story dwelling which had been built when she'd moved from Tennessee two years before. The right fork ended five hundred feet beyond the Willit's house in a large yard filled with farm equipment beyond which was the horse barn and a hay barn beyond that. There were several outbuildings in the area, arranged in no particular order.

Roy was walking down the lane from the horse barn when Katherine and Bobby pulled into the drive. Hazel was standing in the kitchen door when they got out of the car. Bobby announced he was ready to go to work as Katherine pulled an oversize leather briefcase from the back of the station wagon. Hazel insisted that they all come in for a piece of cherry pie which she'd just pulled from the oven.

They all sat at the kitchen table eating warm pie topped with vanilla ice cream as Roy told Bobby he needed him to drive the tractor and trailer to the hay barn and bring up a load of hay to feed the horses. When Bobby told him he'd never driven a tractor and he'd never fed horses, Roy simply said "You'll learn, son."

Bobby finished his pie in a hurry and said, "Let's go. We've got work to do."

As the two men walked out the door, Hazel handed Bobby a cut-up apple, telling him it was for Major, the oldest horse on the farm. "Just hold your hand out flat and he'll take it. Tell him it's from me," she said.

Hazel said she'd give Katherine a tour of the house before she got started on the piano. Katherine put her tuning kit next to the piano and looked around the room. On the far end of the living room, opposite the music playing area, there was a brick fireplace with a platform rocker on either side. The one on the left was surrounded by brightly colored metal canisters which Hazel told her were filled with yarn.

"I knit all the time," she said. "Roy likes to sit and watch TV at night, but I've got to be doing something." She took a half-knit gray sweater off a low wooden rack next to the rocker and told Katherine she was working on something for Larry, something to keep him warm in the winter.

A long sofa at a right-angle to the rockers sat in front of a large television which was placed in front of the tall windows, so someone watching television on the sofa had a panoramic view of the mountains in the background. Two swiveling recliners faced the fireplace, finishing off the large open living area.

At the opposite end of the room where the piano was pushed against the far wall and the chairs and music stands stood, an entryway opened into a wide hallway which led to Hazel and Roy's bedroom. The room spread across the entire width of the house with the same six-foot windows on either end. Another doorway at the far end of the bedroom opened into another hallway, to the right was the farm office with two desks, file cabinets and assorted office equipment, straight ahead was an entry into the kitchen.

There were two large bedrooms on the second floor, each with bathrooms and front-facing windows with a view of the mountains. All the rooms were large with high ceilings but the house had a warm, comfortable feeling. Every room was furnished with antiques, the bedrooms had cozy sitting areas, and the beds were covered with handmade quilts.

Back downstairs, Hazel said she was going to clean up the kitchen and then sit and knit while Katherine worked on the piano. "I hope that won't bother you," she said.

"I'd like the company," Katherine said. "First though, help me push the piano out to where I can get behind it and I'll need to use your vacuum cleaner too."

The piano moved and the vacuum cleaner out, Hazel disappeared into the kitchen and Katherine got to work on the piano. It was a more complicated job than she first thought. Before she could get to the tuning, there was a good amount of preliminary work. Several of the hammers needed new felt. Most of the strings were showing a light coat of rust which she burnished off with steel wool and then applied a light coat of oil. Then she started adjusting the tuning pins. In a little over an hour, she was finishing up with the back panel down, vacuuming the inside.

Hazel was sitting in her rocker, knitting, when she closed up the piano. Katherine sat at the piano and played scales for a few minutes and then played a short Chopin polonaise. She went over and sat on the sofa, "That's that. It's back in shape."

"It doesn't sound like the same piano," Hazel said. "It sounds beautiful."

"If you have furniture oil, lemon oil or something, I'll get the outside looking like new."

"Not today, let's save that for another time. Let's just sit and talk for a few minutes before the guys show up," Hazel said putting down her knitting. "It's so much fun having you here, just the two of us."

She told Katherine she hoped they'd stay for dinner. She was going to see if Bobby would help her make a couple of pizzas. Katherine could make a salad if she wasn't too kitchen weary after a day at the restaurant. And by the way, she hoped that Katherine could come again for Sunday dinner. She and Roy wanted to hear all about her first Sunday at the Trinity Church organ.

Hazel said, "Larry's going to come. And probably Anne and Jack."

Katherine said she'd like to come on Sunday. She'd found some old sheet music in Luther Moody's boxes that Hazel and Roy might like. Then she told Hazel about Alan Lindsay's book that Reverend Tom had given her, *The Platonic Ideal of Faith: There Isn't One*. "I've read the whole thing, but I'm going to have to read it again, to really understand it. Oh, and I saw yours and Roy's name in the dedication."

Hazel smiled and said, "Well, I hope you understand more of it than I did." She told Katherine. "I didn't dare say a thing, but I thought it's just a bunch of gobbledygook. But after that book, Alan went from being an unknown professor at Sewanee to some bigwig philosopher. What'd they call him, a *seminal thinker*, whatever that means. People came from all over asking him sign their copy of the book. They wanted to talk to him for hours. One old fellow with a white beard, dressed all in black, talked with a foreign accent, showed up at our kitchen door looking for Alan. Scared the heck out of me. He'd come from Hungary to meet the great man."

She told Katherine none of the attention changed Alan though. He was still the same, unassuming, humble man he'd always been. And after the success of his book, he made an about face and started preaching, something he said he'd been called to do.

"He was a pied-piper, Alan was," Hazel continued. "He found a little abandoned Episcopal church at a country crossroads outside Sewanee. St. John's Episcopal chapel. All run down, windows broken out, floor rotting, everything inside had disappeared long before. After he got the ok from whoever he had to get the ok from, he started going out there alone on Saturdays. Started cleaning the place up. Never asked anyone for help, never talked much about it at all. Then Anne started going with him, then Jack started tagging along. They'd be out there on Saturdays, and when it was light enough in the evenings after dinner, fixing up the little church. Pretty soon, Roy and I were going with them. Then a few of his students from the seminary were pitching in. And all the time he never asked anyone for help. He was a pied-piper. People wanted to follow him."

The church was finished after two years of hard work. Alan asked Bishop Stephen Bayne, who came from New York, to officiate at the consecration, assisted by Reverend Tom Flatte from Anne's hometown of Cedar Mills. There were only a handful of people there that first Sunday, most of them from the divinity school. It was the same for several months. But slowly people in the area started to come and a little congregation started to grow.

"It was all about his preaching," Hazel mused. "Who would've thought this high falutin' professor, this philosopher, could preach like that. He had a gift unlike anything I've ever seen. Pretty soon so many people were coming to hear Alan preach on Sundays, you couldn't get in the church Then they wanted him to move to a bigger church, or build a bigger church there, but he just said no. This was his church, the place where he was called to preach."

"That's amazing," Katherine said, mesmerized by Hazel's story. "And the picture of him on the back of the book. He looks just like Jack."

"Jack looks just like him," Hazel said. "Two peas in a pod."

The sounds of Roy and Bobby coming in ended Hazel story. Bobby gave his report, describing his skills at the wheel of the John Deere tractor and how all the horses loved him, especially Major, who hadn't hesitated to take the apple when offered. It was settled that pizza and salad was on the menu for dinner. Roy went off to change his clothes while the other three went to work in the kitchen.

When Katherine finished the salad, she went out and sat in the living room with Roy. He'd lit the gas fireplace which gave off a gentle warmth and a soft orange glow that matched the dusky sky over the mountains.

"I don't much like this gas contraption. But no more wood after the heart attack. Too much for me to handle. Hazel said it was either this or nothing." Roy said with disdain. "And before I forget, I want to tell you how excited she's been that you were coming today. She's been talking about it all week."

"It's nice to be here," Katherine said. "You and Hazel make it easy for me to feel at home."

"Well, come any time you like. We love having you," Roy said as Hazel called from the kitchen that dinner was ready. "I hope we can hear how the piano sounds after dinner."

They ate pizza and tossed salad in the kitchen. Hazel made it clear that Roy could only have the pizza with ground turkey, not the one with pepperoni and sausage. As they ate, Roy pretended to reach over and take a piece of the pepperoni and sausage pizza with the "good stuff" as he called it. This prompted Hazel to take out a spatula next to her plate and whack him gently on the back of his outstretched hand, saying "Oh no you don't, I've got my eye on you." Bobby told Hazel he'd watch Roy too. He knew he couldn't be trusted.

After they finished, Katherine ordered everyone into the living room, saying she'd clean up and do the dishes. But Hazel wouldn't hear of it and stayed in the kitchen to help out. Katherine was standing at the kitchen sink looking out the window when she saw Larry's Suburban come down the lane from Anne's house and turn onto the main road toward town.

"That looked like Larry's car coming from Anne's," she said with surprise.

"Friday night bridge. Anne's filling in for Maude as Larry's partner," Hazel told her. "She invited Larry for dinner. She's been a nervous wreck all week, worrying about trying to keep up with him at the bridge table."

Katherine started to say, *Well, he didn't tell me*, but she didn't. She wasn't sure how she felt about Larry going out with Anne Lindsay. Anyway, it was none of her business.

When Katherine and Hazel came into the living room, Roy was sitting in his rocker by the fireplace and Bobby was across the room in one of the wing chairs facing the piano and music stands. Hazel sat at her knitting station opposite Roy while Katherine walked over to the piano, ready to demonstrate how it sounded properly tuned. She started with Scott Joplin's rag "The Entertainer." Then came "Raindrops Keep Falling On My Head," followed by "Somewhere," and "Moon River," the songs she and Johnny Hererra had done so many years ago at the high school chorus festival.

As she played and sang, she was transported back to that time. She didn't hear Bobby humming along. She wasn't aware of Hazel and Roy across the room. She was back in high school, when she was really just a little kid, self-hating, and scared. Those fleeting moments with Johnny had been the brightest thing in her life. Everything after that came from her pretending to be someone else. It was all a sham, she was a fake then and she was a fake now, trying to be somebody she wasn't.

She finished with "The Way We Were," and stood to the sound of applause from her small audience. Bobby was saying, "Encore, encore." All three of them gave her hug. She even saw a tear in Roy's eye as he kept telling her how beautifully she played. "It just doesn't sound like the same piano," he said with amazement.

Bobby told her he had to be home early because he was going to Puyallup to see his mother the next morning and Katherine told him they'd better hit the road. As they walked hand in hand to the car, Hazel told Katherine to come early on Sunday afternoon so they'd have some time together. As she was turning the car around in the parking area, Jack's BMW drove past, up the lane to his mother's house.

They drove back to town in the dark with Bobby talking nonstop about his afternoon with Roy, driving the tractor and feeding the horses, and laughing at how Roy tried to steal the pizza with the good stuff. Katherine was hardly listening, preoccupied with what she'd realized when she'd been at the piano. She really was the nasty troll her mother always said she was, a selfish little tramp. And now, back in Cedar Mills years later, she was living a phony life, putting on an act, thinking she was someone she wasn't.

She hadn't felt so alone since she could remember. Yes, she had people who claimed they liked her, that said they were her friend, even said they loved her. But they didn't know the real Katherine Baker, they didn't know what she really was. If they did, they'd be gone in a heartbeat.

Katherine dropped Bobby off and drove into town on Main Street. It was a few minutes before eight o'clock. She knew the state store would be open for another ten minutes. She continued on to the little strip mall on the east end of downtown. She'd never been to the state store. She hadn't had any booze for years. But anyone who's been a drunk always knows where to get the next shot of hooch when the time comes.

On a Friday night, just before closing, the place would be crowded. Who was seen in the state store mattered to folks in a small town and there'd probably be someone from the cafe who'd recognize her. But she didn't care. She'd be gone in a few days and they could take all their gossip and shove it. She walked out with two bottles of Grey Goose vodka and drove home with trembling hands.

The house was cold and dark. She put a bottle of vodka in the refrigerator and sat at the piano in the dark playing the same songs she'd played at Hazel and Roy's, lost in her memories of all that had gone before, from Johnny Hererra to her life on the road. She paced through the house with the lights out. She walked into the kitchen, opened the refrigerator and then closed it. She thought about calling Sadie. But she was too proud. She turned on the lamp next to the sofa and sat down.

Alan Lindsay's book lay on the coffee table. She opened the book to a bookmark and read out loud, *Some wander naked, alone in the wilderness of doubt, fearful of what they'll find if they reach for the light of understanding*. It sounded like a bunch of crap to her. She wouldn't be taking *that* book when she left.

She paced some more then stood staring out the living room window at the empty street, and finally went back into the kitchen, opened the refrigerator and took out the bottle of vodka. She took it and the other bottle out the back door to the small tool shed attached to the rear of the house. She put both bottles on the shelf at the back of the shed, came in and went to bed. She lay alone in the cold bedroom hugging herself, refusing to cry, wishing that Johnny Hererra was lying next to her.

Road to Recovery

Katherine planned to spend most of Saturday at Trinity Church, practicing on the organ for her debut at Sunday's ten o'clock service. But first, she decided to drive up to Port Smith and check on Maude. As she was driving by Maude's on Saturday morning, she saw a small wiry man wearing a black overcoat coming out the back door. The salt and pepper hair of his van dyke matched the small nest of hair on top of his head, making him look foreboding. He stood staring at her as she stopped the car, got out, and walked across the street toward him. When she asked what he was doing, he defiantly answered, "Who wants to know?" She guessed his accent was European, maybe Russian.

"I'm Maude's neighbor and I'm keeping an eye on her house while she's in the hospital."

"Congratulations. I'm Milos Grajek. Maude's in the hospital?"

"She's been there since Tuesday. Appendicitis with complications."

"Where's Rascal?

"At Lonnie and Elizabeth's."

Grajek shook his head. "That's no good. He hates their cats."

"Maude told me about you. How you used to stop and yell at Rascal, trying to teach him Polish."

"That would be me," Grajek said with a bow.

Katherine instinctively liked the man. "I'm on my way to the hospital. Why don't you come with me," she said.

"No." Grajek answered shaking his head. "No hospital."

"I'm not going to stay long. Maude would like to see you. Come with me."

That was enough for Grajek to nod his assent and they were off on the thirty-minute drive to Port Smith. Grajek sat stiffly in the passenger seat looking out the window. He didn't act like someone who took to small talk.

Finally Grajek said, "So you like Chopin. I hear you playing Chopin all the time when I pass by your house on my way to town."

Katherine said. "His music seems simple at first, but it's complicated to play correctly."

"A wise observation from a young person like you," Grajek answered.

"Why do they call you The Mad Polack?" she asked.

"Ha! Why, why, why!" he retorted with a sudden animation. "Because, I used to tramp back and forth to town with my garden cart, singing Polish songs, and doing crazy things like trying to teach Maude's dog Polish. Everyone thought I was mad. Maybe I am."

"Why?"

"Why!" he fired back. "Is that all you know, why? I stopped asking why when I watched the Nazi devils take my father away to be gassed at Treblinka. I was eleven."

Katherine drove in silence and Grajek asked, "You know Treblinka?"

"Yes, I know what it was. I'm very sorry."

"So am I. I'm very sorry every day. Thank you."

They finished the trip in silence.

Greeley was standing at Maude's bed when they walked into her hospital room. Maude was sitting up and looking perky. "Two of my favorite people!" she exclaimed when she saw Katherine and Grajek. She ordered "Milo," pronouncing it *my-low*, over to her saying, "Come here boyfriend, I'm so glad to see you." Grajek, with his black overcoat still buttoned, leaned over the bed awkwardly and pecked her on the cheek.

Maude held Katherine's hand as she stood next to the bed telling the older woman with a laugh about seeing Grajek coming out of her house thinking he was an intruder. Maude announced she was going home on Monday and it wouldn't be soon enough. They all stood around Maude's bed fawning over her as she basked in the attention.

Greely finally motioned for Katherine to come with him and they walked out to the waiting room.

"I just wanted to tell you how grateful we all are. You saved Maude's life," Greeley said. "Maude thinks the world of you and she's been upset since that brouhaha a little while back. She blames herself for getting you upset."

Katherine blushed. "Brouhaha. You mean when I had my little temper tantrum and stormed out of her house?"

"Well, yes. That's what I meant. She's been sorry ever since."

"I guess she meant well. Is that it?"

"That's it for now. Thanks. And good luck tomorrow at church. I'll be there."

When they got back to the room, Maude and Milo where laughing, talking about Rascal and the cats at Lonnie and Elizabeth's. Katherine gave her a hug goodbye and said she bring dinner over on Tuesday. Then she and Grajek were in the car headed home.

He was almost smiling as they drove, obviously cheered by the visit with Maude. "So tell me, how does a young woman, a chef at the Madison Café, know so much about Chopin?" He asked.

"I've been playing the piano all my life, since I was a little kid in Iowa. My piano teacher thought Stravinsky was too modern." she answered. "And I'm a cook, not a chef." Then she said, "What's more interesting is how you got from Treblinka to Cedar Mills. That's a long journey."

Milos Grajek pretended he hadn't heard Katherine's question but then he started talking nonstop, telling her how he'd come to live the life of a hermit in Cedar Mills.

He was thirteen when the war ended in Europe. He'd survived Treblinka, only to find himself alone and penniless in a displaced persons center in France. When a British aid worker, a fellow from the Cambridge Refugee Relief Fund, found he spoke English, he sponsored him for expatriation to England where he was placed with the Pembrokes, an older, childless couple at Cambridge who both worked at the university in service positions. He was eventually enrolled in Corpus Christi College at Cambridge, where he read Latin and Greek poetry and graduated with honors.

He took a position at a government-funded school for refugees in London where he taught English to European expatriates for very little money, lived in a one-room slum in Battersea, and began writing poetry. But he was restless. The vivid memories of the camps kept pushing him to move. He became an itinerant teacher of English, taking low-paying positions in second-rate institutes and academies, first in Stockholm, then Amsterdam, Brussels, and Paris. Some of his poetry was published in literary journals and he started to be known as a significant voice of the post-war Polish Jewish diaspora. After ten years of wandering through Europe, he landed in New York where he was surprised to learn he was a minor celebrity in the Jewish literary community.

I could be listening to a novel, Katherine thought as Grajek talked, with hardly a pause. She suddenly interrupted and said, "Let me buy you lunch on our way home. There's a place down on the water in Yarmouth I'd like to see. It's called the Blue Heron."

Predictably, he rejected the suggestion, "No. No lunch. No Blue Heron."

But Katherine saw through Grajek's rough exterior. *A pussycat,* she thought.

"It's not a fancy place," she said. "I've never been there, but everyone says it's good. Please let me buy you lunch."

Grajek begrudgingly said, "Ok."

By the time they drove through the old commercial center of Yarmouth, once a burgeoning nineteenth-century small-town seaport but now a collection of derelict buildings and decaying houses, and out to the beach at the end of the road where the Blue Heron sat at the edge of the Strait, Grajek was finishing the story of his wanderings.

In New York, he was a lecturer in classical poetry at Yeshiva University for two years. But the demons of his past haunted him and he hated New York, filled as it was with flocks of what he called literary charlatans.

So he ended up in Iowa City, at the University of Iowa, on the faculty of the Iowa Writers Workshop. But they wanted him to teach these dunderheads, as he called them, about the "creative process" and about how he himself wrote poetry. "It was a most miserable time," he mused. "I told them I took a pen and some paper and wrote. How else do you write poetry?"

He stayed in Iowa for three years. "They couldn't get enough of my nonsense. I told them how stupid they were, how they should leave and go work for a living before trying to write anything. Stop reading your precious 'creative' blather to each other and go learn something," he ordered. "But they loved my abuse. I couldn't shame them enough. They offered me an assistant professorship and promised me tenure, so I fled."

The Blue Heron was a modest one-story wood frame building with large windows in the front overlooking the water and separated from the seaweed-covered beach by a long row of driftwood. Atypically for this time of year, there was no wind and the water was a glassy calm. The sky was a bright, autumn blue, and across the Strait to northeast, the snowy tip of the 11,000-foot Mt. Baker could be seen in the distance, over a hundred miles away.

It was still early for the lunch crowd and the restaurant was empty except for one couple who sat at a table on the far side of the dining room next to the simmering stone fireplace. Katherine and Grajek sat at a window table staring out at the Strait. They both ordered the grilled salmon platter and Grajek continued his story.

"During that miserable time in Iowa, I kept thinking about Dvorak and how on earth he could have found inspiration in that god-forsaken land." he said. "You know Dvorak?"

"Of course I know Dvorak," Katherine said with a smile. She told him that when she lived in Cedar Rapids, her piano teacher, Julia Howe, had taken her to Spillville, where the composer had spent the summer of 1893. "There's a little museum with a tiny exhibition commemorating his time there. Miss Howe thought something might rub off on me by our pilgrimage."

Then Grajek told her how he had fled Iowa when he was offered a lecturer in poetry position in Seattle at the University of Washington. A distant cousin, Martin Grolman, who was a pulmonologist and professor at the university's medical school encouraged him to come west. He told Milos how great the air was in the Pacific Northwest.

"The university at Seattle was even worse than Iowa," Grajek told Katherine. When Grolman saw how his cousin was suffering, he told Grajek that he owned twenty acres of woodland on the Olympic Peninsula. He'd only seen the land once and all he did was pay taxes on it. "He said he'd sign it over to me for one dollar, and I could go live like the hermit I'd always wanted to be. And the air was even better there than in Seattle."

Grajek lived in a large army surplus mess tent his first year at Cedar

Mills while Walt Beaver and his boys, Harley and Matt, with the occasional help of Lonnie Martin, cleared some of his land and built him a house in exchange for logging off what hardwood there was along with a few of the older second-growth cedars.

"That was almost twenty years ago." he said finishing his story.

Their lunch came and they ate in silence. Katherine had no understanding of the worlds he'd just described and she was intimidated by his learning. Trying to say something halfway intelligent, she blurted, "I've been reading a book about Plato and the Platonic ideal."

Grajek put down his fork and chuckled. "My, my. You keep surprising me Miss Katherine. What's someone like you doing reading about Plato?"

She told him about Alan Lindsay's *The Platonic Ideal Of Faith: There Isn't One*, saying she really didn't understand much it but it made her look at things a little differently.

"It's a clever idea," Grajek said. "But I lost whatever 'faith' I had long ago. I stopped believing in God when I lost my family to the Nazis."

"I can't begin to understand what you've been through."

"No need to be patronizing. But tell me, you're a reader are you?"

"I was supposed to go to college but didn't. I've tried to make up for it by reading all the time. Mostly novels, especially English and American novels. I guess what they call the classics."

"So who are some of the novelists you like?" he asked with a genuine interest.

She listed all the usual suspects, the Bronte sisters, Jane Austen, George Eliot, Charles Dickens and Anthony Trollope among others. "Dickens is my all-time favorite. I'm reading *Little Dorrit* right now for the third time. If I could be like anyone, I'd be want to be like her, like Dorrit."

Grajek nodded and ate in silence until they finished. Katherine paid the check and they walked out into the gravel parking lot and over to the row of driftwood along the beach. Katherine pointed to a large old weathered driftwood log and told Grajek to come with her. Grajek started to say no, but didn't. He followed her to the driftwood where they sat and watched the seagulls glide in the air around them asking with their calls if there were scraps to be had.

"Let me be nosy," Grajek said. "Here you are a cook, as you call it, in a small-town café at the end of the earth who plays the piano with grace, loves Chopin, knows all about Dvorak, reads about Plato and is devoted to the novels of Charles Dickens. You know much more than all the dimwits I've tried to teach. There's a story, isn't there?"

"There's no story. I'm just a cook in a small town restaurant who plays the piano."

They got up and started walking toward the car. Grajek said, "Let me ask this with all due respect, Miss Katherine, and I do mean it respectfully. Are you running from something? Believe me, I'm an expert in running."

"Nothing of the sort," Katherine answered. "And with all due respect, even if what you say is true, it would be my business and no one else's."

Grajek laughed and said, "Well put, my dear. I've enjoyed this morning very much. Thank you for your kindness and thank you for lunch."

As they drove into town, Katherine asked him how to get to his house. He said no, she could drop him off at the Red & White Foodliner, he needed to get some things at the store. He'd walk home. But she insisted she drive him home, he shouldn't have to walk.

"That's all I do is walk," he said. "And besides, you don't need to know how to get to my house. Then you won't have to lie if someone stops at the café and asks if you know where I live. I hope we see each other soon. Best wishes on your journey."

It was early afternoon when Katherine got home. She sat at the piano and played for a while before she left for church to practice at the organ. When Milos Grajek walked by her house on his way home from the store, he heard strains of the Largo from Dvorak's "Symphony No. 9, From the New World" and Katherine's sweet voice singing the familiar words, *Going home, going home, I'm just going home. . .*

The First Sunday of the Rest of Your Life

After Sunday's ten o'clock service at Trinity Episcopal Church, all of Katherine's anxiety and fear of failure at the organ proved to be anticlimactic. In the words of choirmaster Brett Smallwood, she did a superlative job. Yes, there were some minor flaws in her work, a missed beat at the beginning of the procession and a brief hesitation with the hymn before The Collect, but that was easily ascribed to her unfamiliarity with the tempo of the worship service. She was complimented by several members of the choir on her selection of two Bach cantatas for the prelude and after the service, Reverend Tom Flatte was effusive in his thankful praise for her priceless contribution.

She'd enjoyed her solitary role in the midst of the collaborative effort of everyone else who took part in church service. She was an integral part of the goings on, but because she sat alone at the organ the entire time and played sporadically, she could spend the rest of the time surreptitiously watching everyone else without being obvious about it.

There were more people in the congregation this morning than she remembered from her first visit to Trinity the week before when she sang in the choir so she could watch Margie Parker at the organ. Anne and Jack Lindsay sat near the front in the left row of pews. Jack's lawyer power look was gone. He had on a navy blue blazer, charcoal gray slacks, the requisite blue oxford cloth shirt, and oh no, the tasseled loafers. Dry and combed to the side, his hair looked good without mousse. Greeley was sitting near the back on the right side between Will and Larry. She was amused to see them watching her like three judges at a talent show.

In the choir room after the service, Reverend Tom came in and handed her an envelope. "Jack Lindsay asked me to give you this," he said. "Now don't forget to join us in the parish hall for coffee." She put the envelope in her purse and started out the choir room door. She wasn't going to coffee in the parish hall. *I don't know them. These aren't my people,* she thought as she slipped out the back door of the church.

Then she laughed to herself, wondering just who "her people" were. She didn't have any people. She pulled the envelope out of her purse as she walked. In neat block letters on the front was, "Katherine Baker."

At home she sat on the sofa without taking her coat off and opened the envelope. The plain white note card read:

Dear Katherine,
I want you to know how embarrassed I am at my behavior last
Monday at the cafe when I asked you out. I was insensitive and
selfish. I'm sorry I offended you and I apologize for doing so. I
hope you'll be able to forgive me and that we can be friends.
   All the best from one of your admirers,
      Jack

Katherine read it a few more times, then put the note back in the envelope
and slipped it into Alan Lindsay's book at the dedication page. By now
she'd memorized the words on the page, but she read them again out loud,
rereading several times the phrase, *to Jack, the prince of everything good in*
our future. Then it was time to get ready to go out to Hazel and Roy's for
Sunday dinner.

❖ ❖ ❖ ❖ ❖ ❖ ❖ ❖ ❖ ❖ ❖ ❖

Katherine walked into the back door of Hazel and Roy's carrying a cardboard box filled with the sheet music from Luther Moody's collection. She
put the box on the dining room table, went into the living room and sat on
the sofa. Hazel was sitting in her chair next to the fireplace knitting. It was
only Katherine's third visit to the house, but coming in without knocking
and sitting down with Hazel seemed as natural as if she'd being doing it for
years.

"There you are," Hazel said smiling. "I've been waiting to hear how
things went this morning at church. Well, to tell the truth, I've already had
reports from Anne, Jack, and Larry. Everyone said you were great."

"It went ok," Katherine said. "Much better than I expected. I spent all
last week worrying about it. Episcopalians do an awful lot of kneeling,
standing, then sitting, then more kneeling and standing. It's hard to keep up.
Then they all line up and kneel at the altar to take communion. It's a lot of
up and down. You have to pay attention."

Hazel laughed and agreed with her. "It's simpler at our church. Just a lot
of singing, shouting, and praying. Then the minister tells us how we're all
going to hell if we don't behave, and we go home and eat a lot."

She said Jack was up at the barn feeing the horses and that Larry had taken Roy and Anne over to show them the land for the new vegetable farm.

"The turkey will be out of the oven in about an hour and we'll be ready to eat. What's in the box?"

"I brought some old sheet music from Luther Moody's collection. All country and western songs from the old days. I thought you and Roy might like to have it."

Hazel opened the box and started pulling out the sheet music that spanned the 1930s to the 1950s. "Oh, boy," she exclaimed. "Roy and I are going to have fun going through these." There were songs by Gid Tanner and the Skillet Lickers, Red Foley, Merle Travis, Patsy Cline, Roy Acuff, Wilma Lee and Stoney Cooper and a long list of others, a country music hall of fame.

Hazel carried the box into the living room and put it on the piano bench, saying she couldn't wait for Roy to see it. They went into the kitchen and finished getting dinner ready. By the time the turkey came out of the oven, Larry, Roy, and Anne had returned from their tour of the new farm and Jack had come in from feeding the horses. They were all in the living room going through the box of sheet music. Jack who was sitting at the piano, playing a few bars of the ones Roy handed him, saying "here play a little of this."

At the dining room table, Roy and Hazel in their usual places at each end. Anne and Katherine sat next to each other on one side of the table and Larry and Jack faced them on the other side. Jack had given Katherine a perfunctory "hello" when he'd come through kitchen from outside and now, sitting across the table from her, he looked a little shy. When Roy asked him to say grace, he hesitated a minute, but then as they held hands around the table and waited, he came through with some nice words about being thankful for having everyone gathered together. Katherine smiled and thought, *a B-minus*.

There was talk about Katherine's debut at church that morning. They all said she'd done an excellent job. Jack said he loved Reverend Tom but his sermons were always snoozers. Anne clucked that Father Tom was something of an expert on Paul's letters, especially those to the Corinthians, bless his heart, and he spoke with some authority, even though he might be a little tedious.

There was a discussion of the hydroponic growing of vegetables with Larry explaining how they'd done it at Allenwood and how, at the new farm, they planned to use the vegetables at the café and sell the surplus to other restaurants in the area. Roy was politely skeptical.

"Speaking of restaurants," he said, turning to Katherine. "Hazel and I've been wondering how you got started as a cook.

Katherine put her fork down and said, "In jail. I first learned about how to be a cook in jail. They let me out early if I took a culinary arts course."

Hazel said, "You were in jail?"

Katherine looked around the table. All eyes were on her. "I got six months in the county jail for attempted vehicular manslaughter while under the influence," she said. "But I got out in three when I finished a cooking course at the community college."

She continued in an even voice, "I was cocaine addict and a drunk after I ran away from Cedar Mills. Headed for Los Angeles with a high school teacher the night of my graduation. When he found out I was pregnant, he dumped me on the streets in LA. I gave the baby up for adoption and then spent the next two years as a backup singer and dancer for a sleazy rock band. Living on drugs and booze. It all finally ended at the Tulare County Jail. Or maybe it began there. Guess it depends on how you look at it."

She picked up her fork and started eating again, refusing to look around the table. Everyone followed suit except for Hazel, who asked, "Then what?"

"I spent a lot of years on the road, working in cheap restaurants, diners, and truck stops. First around Bakersfield, then gradually up through the San Joaquin Valley and into Oregon. Guess I can be proud that I haven't any booze or drugs since I left jail."

Hazel said, "You must have been lonely." Then dinner was finished in silence.

Hazel and Anne stood first and started to clear the table. Katherine stood and picked up her plate and silverware while the three men sat quietly. She told herself she was going to take her things out to the kitchen and then say goodnight, *for the last time in this house,* she thought with tears in her eyes. Hazel intercepted her as she walked into the kitchen, taking her plate and handing it to Anne.

"We're going for a walk," she told Anne. "Get the guys out here to help you."

Then she took Katherine by the arm and led her down the hall to the bedroom. She walked across the room to a six-foot long cedar chest and opened it. She took out a folded brown cable-knit sweater and held it up to Katherine. "I was going to give you this for Christmas," she said. "But now is a good time for you to have it. Try it on." Then she took out a matching brown stocking cap. The sweater was a perfect fit.

"Ok, let's go." Hazel said, putting her arm around Katherine's waist. They walked back out through the kitchen and got their coats. It was cold and windy as they walked. Hazel, who had brought a bag of cut-up apples said, "If you're going be a regular out here, you've got to meet the horses.

As they approached the horse barn, Roy came out of the house and shouted, "Hey!" as he walked up the lane toward them. "I saw the lights. What's going on?"

"We're out for a walk," Hazel said. "I'm going to introduce Katherine to the horses."

Hazel told him to go on back inside. Roy put a hand on Katherine's shoulder and said, "What's important now is you're here with us." He turned and went back to the house.

The horse barn was a one-story building with a wide walkway down the middle, and doors at either end. There were twelve stalls, six on each side of the barn. Only six of the twelve stalls were occupied. Hazel told Katherine that after Alan's death and the move from Tennessee, Anne's interest in showing and breeding her quarter horses had waned and she left the day-to-day management of the farm to Hazel and Roy.

Katherine said she'd never been around horses.

"Well, let's get started," Hazel said.

They heard movement in the six occupied stalls, hay rustling, nickering, and snuffling. They stopped at the first stall on the left and Hazel reached into her bag, brought out some cut up apple which she held outstretched to the eager horse who was pressing against the stall door. "Here's Major," she said. "He's our oldest and the daddy of everyone in here except Hannah, who's next to him. She's the mother of the other four."

They walked slowly down the row of stalls, stopping as Hazel gave each horse some apple and a gentle rub on the nose. Next to Hannah was Tommy, and then across from Major, Hannah, and Tommy were Jupiter, Sissy, and Plato. When they stopped at Sissy's stall, the horse started moving her head up and down with a soft whinny. "I think she wants to tell you something," Hazel said after Sissy had eaten her apple. "Here, take some more apple, hold your hand out flat like I did, and let her take from you."

Katherine hesitated but then she walked up to the horse, held out her palm with the apple and let Sissy take it. "Now give her a pat on the nose," Hazel said, and Katherine gingerly put her hand up to Sissy's nose. The horse responded with a big slurping lick on her hand and whinnied some more.

"I think she likes you," Hazel said. "I've never seen her so friendly with a stranger."

They walked back to the house with Hazel's arm around Katherine's waist. When they got to the back door, Katherine said, "I'm not going in, I'm just going on home. Thank you so much for the sweater and hat."

Hazel took her hand, "Come back in and say good-night to everyone before you go." It was a gentle order that would be obeyed.

The others were in the living room. Jack was at the piano and Roy had his fiddle out. They were playing pieces of songs from the sheet music and Roy was reminiscing about the old days in the Smoky Mountains. Anne and Larry were sitting on the sofa talking about last Friday night's duplicate bridge. Larry was saying "Don't worry about it, you did fine. Just remember, many a penniless man is walking the streets of London because he didn't get his trump out."

Katherine stood in the entryway from the dining room and said good-night. They all came over to tell her good-bye. Roy couldn't say enough about how tickled he was that she brought this sheet music. Larry told her he'd promised Jack another power sandwich on his way back to Seattle the next morning.

"On the house again?" she asked with a wan smile.

Hazel walked her out to the car and gave her a long hug before she got in, saying, "I'm glad you're part of our lives."

The drive home was like the drive home two nights before with the same voice telling her what a bad person she was. But at least she'd told the truth. Now she didn't have to live some phony life of pretending to be a decent person. She wouldn't be around much longer anyway. She should have been on the road already, heading for another nowheresville.

She sat at the piano in the dark, playing Dvorak and then the Mozart andante she loved, remembering Maude's first visit and thinking about Milos Grajek. She sat on the sofa and opened *Little Dorrit*. But she couldn't concentrate. She kept thinking about the vodka in the tool shed. She walked around the house, through the empty dining room and into the kitchen. There wasn't any ice in the refrigerator but the vodka would be cold from sitting outside. She went out the back door to the tool shed and opened the door. She turned on the hanging bare bulb and looked up to where she'd put the Grey Goose bottles. They were gone.

A Sortie From The North

Katherine woke up the next morning thinking about the tool shed and the missing bottles of vodka. The threat of someone skulking around her house and even breaking in while she was asleep was a cause for alarm. She could hold her own in a street fight and she'd done it more than once, but waking up to robber in the house scared her. And then she thought of the Dolan kids. But what would they do with two bottles of vodka? She'd talk to Will.

It was a typical Monday morning at the Madison Café. Everyone was talking at once, everyone except Katherine. Larry was telling Greeley about last Friday's duplicate bridge match with his new partner, Anne Lindsay, referring to their outing as the "Friday night massacre." Bobby was talking nonstop about his trip to Puyallup to visit his mother, telling Katherine that his mother had to be locked up because she was crazy. Sadie said she didn't know what to do with her nephews and she was counting the days until her sister Vicki got out of jail.

Katherine was only half listening while she worked, wondering if Jack would show up on his way to Seattle. She was sure he wouldn't, the people from Tennessee would keep their distance after her confession yesterday at the dinner table. She wasn't their kind of people. But Jack walked in a few minutes after Greeley unlocked the front door. Larry handed her a power breakfast sandwich wrapped in foil. She put it in a white paper bag, poured a cup of coffee to go, and walked up to the front counter where Jack stood smiling.

"Is this going to be a regular thing?" he asked. "You making me breakfast on Mondays."

"If you want," Katherine answered. "We may have to start charging you though. I'll talk it over with the owner."

When Jack offered to pay, Katherine told him no, it was on her, this time. Then she said, "Can I ask you something, Jack?"

"Shoot," he answered.

"I was wondering if you'd like to go out sometime."

"Is this some kind of joke?"

"No, I mean it," Katherine said. "If you're going to be back this weekend, I'll pick you up on Saturday and take you to lunch."

"You'll pick me up?"

"I'll pick you up."

"Ok, I'm game. Saturday it is. I'll call you later in the week."

"Sounds good. Now go catch your ferry."

On Monday mornings, Jack caught the seven-thirty boat for Seattle on Bainbridge Island which put him downtown at eight o'clock. From the ferry dock it was a short drive up to his office at Third and Pine where the law firm of Pushkin, McDonald, & Fishkin was housed. He lived a few blocks north in a condominium at Second Avenue and Blanchard in Belltown, but on Mondays he parked in the garage across from the office, not wanting to risk being late and incur any censure from boss, Hercules Pushkin, a founding partner in the firm.

As he drove off the ferry at Colman Dock, he passed a visitor from British Columbia who was sitting in a rental car waiting to board the boat for

Bainbridge Island. The Canadian was Arthur Merrick, Jr. who was on his way to Sekiu to meet with Buck McCready. According to the plan concocted with the help of his cousin Paul, he would use the red herring of being interested in McCready's salmon fishing charter service to put the cowboy troubadour at ease and then divert the conversation to Luther Moody. Paul had been unflinching in his orders, telling his cousin to come back with the goods, the goods being the location of the baby grand piano.

Paul had told him not to let McCready feed him a line of malarkey, "Make him give you the meat, not the potatoes," he'd implored. "Put the screws to him, if you have to. We'll put him on the rack if need be."

Arthur admired his cousin and was gratified he'd come to Canada to expand the Vancouver office of Merrick & Son, which had been languishing. He was impressed with Paul's development of the new line of goods from India that would be on the market in a few months, the Gandhi Yoga Mat and a line of yoga clothing they were calling Gandhiwear, "For the Yoga in You." But he was troubled by Paul's fixation on the piano and any other artifact related to the old passenger ship that now lay as the *Arctic Maid*, a broken hulk on the shore of Seattle's Lake Union. After his cousin's visit to Silas Peavey's, which led to finding the ship's remnants and the subsequent discovery of the possible disposition of the piano, he'd become obsessive, able only to talk of assembling "all the pieces of the puzzle."

To assuage his cousin's neurotic preoccupation with the boat, Arthur had agreed that after his visit with McCready, he'd go see Silas Peavey when he returned to Seattle and ask what he thought of Paul's idea of pulling what was left of the *Arctic Maid* out of the mud and transporting it to Vancouver by barge. It was a preposterous idea and a visit to Peavey meant another night in Seattle, but Arthur reluctantly played along, hoping that Paul would eventually come to his senses.

The drive from Bainbridge Island to Sekiu should have taken a little less than three hours, putting him at Buck McCready's close to noon, but once he was on Route 112 west of Port Smith, there was trouble, a rock slide which partially covered the road just before Pysht, fifteen miles from his destination. He finally arrived at Buck McCready's Salmon Adventures an hour late, but he found Buck to be a gracious host in spite of it.

"Happens all the time out here in West by Jesus. People are always late," Buck told him as he ushered Arthur into the large rustic lodge where a table had been set for lunch.

On the drive to Sekiu, Arthur had conjured an image of Buck McCready as a rangy, grizzled cowboy figure. But standing at five feet, nine inches, Buck bordered on the diminutive and with his soft pink skin and delicate hands, he wasn't at all what Arthur had imagined.

They sat at the table and a tall, thin, slightly stooped man with a brown, wind-blown complexion, brought out their lunch of poached salmon topped with a dill sauce, an arugula salad with cold beets and cucumbers, and warm sourdough bread. Buck introduced Roger Farnsworth, saying that during the off-season Roger was "the head cook and bottle washer," but during salmon season he was the best charter boat skipper on the Strait. Roger nodded sullenly and went back to the kitchen.

Buck apologized for not being able to show Arthur the *Wanda Jean* but she was in dry dock at Gosport for the winter. Arthur told him no matter, he was certain Buck's boat would be fine. The purpose of his trip was to see the location and meet Buck. Arthur said he was lining up a series of salmon fishing trips for prospective distributors of Merrick & Son's new line of yoga mats and yoga exercise clothing. Arthur bragged it was the brainchild of his cousin Paul. They were calling the mat the Gandhi Yoga Mat and the line of clothing Gandhiwear.

"It's all coming straight from India. Right now we're in the process of setting up a national network of distributors. We'll have small groups from Vancouver, Toronto, Chicago, Los Angeles, and New York coming out for meetings and a tour of the area, including a day on your charter boat," Arthur explained.

Buck said told him he'd be happy to work with him on a schedule of charter trips beginning in early summer. "It's always good to have something lined up for the new season. It helps with the credit line, if you catch my drift." Buck told him. "This time of year our only cash flow comes from the Sasquatch business."

Buck told Merrick about this other business, Bigfoot in the Rain Forest. People came from all over the country to spend a weekend on the trail of the

Sasquatch, hoping to see some sign of the legendary mountain wild man.

"We spend a couple of nights in the bush, along the Hoh River tracking the beast," Buck said whimsically. "Of course, we come across some warm ashes from a campfire. Just beyond that there's a couple of giant foot prints in the mud, and our guide, Augie Butts, regales the visitors with scary stories around the campfire. It's a lot of fun."

"Do they believe it?" Arthur asked. "Do they believe they're close to Bigfoot?"

"I've never asked," Buck said. "I used to be in show business. It's all shtick."

The two men laughed as they finished lunch and Roger brought out coffee and vanilla cheesecake with a warm raspberry drizzle.

Over dessert, Arthur asked Buck about his past in show business.

"I'm not from around here," Buck told him. "I worked in Seattle, in the music business for years. Managed my uncle's band, Corky Carlsson and the All Stars."

Arthur said, "You know, since we first talked on the phone, I thought something sounded familiar. I kept thinking I've heard that name, Buck McCready, before."

Buck told him that along with managing the band, he'd developed an act called Buck McCready's Cowboy Recitations Featuring His Sidekick Dallas Moody. "Dallas was the piano player. His real name was Luther, but I gave him the moniker 'Dallas' to fit in better with the cowboy stuff. Our stock in trade was the sentimental lonesome cowboy ballad. We'd finish our set with 'When The Work's All Done This Fall' and then all eleven verses of 'Little Joe, The Wrangler.' Never a dry eye in the house after that."

Arthur asked if the band had played in British Columbia and Buck told him they'd toured in Canada twice. Arthur told Buck about visiting his uncle in Chilliwack one summer, "He and his wife loved to polka," he said. "They took me to see you at the Chilliwack fire hall. I'll never forget it. I was just a city boy from Vancouver."

Buck was basking in the glow of old memories when Arthur asked him what happened to Luther Moody. Buck told him that Dallas had passed away a little over a year ago.

"When Corky retired and the band broke up, Dallas moved back home to Cedar Mills," Buck said. "We were best friends for years. His moving back to the Peninsula is the reason I ended up out here. We'd get together once a year on a Saturday night at the Shingle and Shake Festival in Cedar Mills and do the cowboy thing at the American Legion well into the night."

Before he left, Arthur found out that Luther Moody's baby grand piano was still somewhere in Cedar Mills, that it had been bequeathed to Greeley Martin, the owner of the Madison Café. Buck said he thought that Greeley Martin had given it to someone who worked at the café. He told Arthur about Greeley's biography of Dallas Moody in the Cedar County Historical Society's latest issue of *North Coast Passages*. He could probably get a copy from Greeley at the Madison Café.

After lunch, the two men agreed to meet again to plan the series of charter trips for the next summer. As he drove east on Route 112, Arthur decided to spend the night at Port Smith and stop at the Madison Café in the morning on his way to Seattle.

Café Visitors

On Monday afternoon after work, about the time Arthur Merrick was leaving Sekiu, Katherine stopped in to see Wally Berger at the Book Mart. Just as she opened the front door of the book store, the girl she'd seen in the alley came out of the store carrying a weathered canvas briefcase. Katherine held the door for her as she walked out, shouted a good-bye to Wally and said a soft "thank-you" to Katherine before purposefully starting down Main Street.

Katherine asked Wally, "Is that Clare Dolan?"

Wally smiled. "That's Clare. She's taking some things to Winifred Smith at the library for me."

Katherine wanted to say the little girl didn't look like a criminal but didn't. She asked Wally if there was a way he could find out if there were any books by or about Milos Grajek. Wally looked through *Books in Print* and found one book by Milos Grajek, a book of poetry entitled *The Lithuanian Septet* published by Princeton University Press. Katherine asked him to order it for her.

"It's twenty-eight dollars," Wally told her. "You sure you want it?"

"I want it. How long will it take to get here?"

Wally said, "Hard to say with a book like that. If Ingram, my distributor in Tennessee, has it, it'll take a week. Longer if I have to order it direct from the publisher."

She offered to pay in advance, but Wally said it wasn't necessary. She walked up Main Street thinking, *Tennessee, Tennessee. Every time I turn around, it's Tennessee.*

Will was waiting in his car in front of her house when she got home. They walked in the front door together and Katherine said she'd start a pot of coffee. Like every first-time visitor, Will's commented on the piano. "It looks like Luther's old piano belongs here."

"It does," Katherine said. "I love it. It's my best friend."

They drank coffee at the kitchen table while Katherine told Will about the two bottles of Grey Goose she'd stashed in the tool shed on Friday night and how they were gone on Sunday night. Will knew about Katherine's battle with alcohol and drugs and how proud she was of being sober for years. He was impressed by how she unapologetically told him about buying the vodka.

"The Dolan kids," Will said. "They probably took the booze and sold it. Any number people would have been glad to get a hold of it at a cut-rate price."

He told her their parents, Bud and Sophie Dolan, were two boozers who lived at Lou's Scenic Tavern and left the kids on their own. Bud was a busted up logger who got a disability check every month that mostly went to pay their tab at the Scenic. The kids were lucky to have anything to eat. They scavenged in the alleys of Cedar Mills for anything they could sell or barter.

"They hit the jackpot with two bottles of hooch, some good stuff too," Will said with a laugh.

"But how'd they know the booze was in the tool shed."

Will told her the pair made the rounds through town every night, checking for unlocked doors, looking for anything that wasn't tied down. "Little Clare is the brains of the operation. She scouts things out and then sends Curtis in to do the dirty work. They probably check your tool shed every night and finally, bingo, they found something. They're scavengers not burglars though. If they find your tool shed unlocked, they'll check it out, but I've never known them to break and enter. We keep trying to nab them, but they're wily little devils."

Katherine wondered how hard Will and his deputy were really trying to catch the two little bandits. "Well maybe I'll set a trap for them," Katherine mused. "Two little kids can't be that smart."

"I don't need any vigilantes around here," Will said. "Call me before you do anything rash. Now I've got to get of here, I told Greeley I'd help him with Maude. She's coming home this afternoon."

❖ ❖ ❖ ❖ ❖ ❖ ❖ ❖ ❖ ❖ ❖ ❖

Will had hardly been convincing about trying to catch the Dolans and Katherine walked to work the next morning determined to find a way to catch the two alley urchins.

It was Tuesday morning. Bobby came in and counted the chicken pot pies in the cooler first thing. When he found there were once again twenty-five pies instead of the usual twenty, he and Katherine had the same conversation they'd had the previous week. Katherine told him she was taking two to Maude's after work and two were going to Sadie's nephews. When Bobby challenged the count by telling her that last week, only one went to Maude, Katherine told him the other one was for Maude's friend Milo, who was taking care of her.

Just after the morning rush, around nine o'clock, a stranger came in the front door and headed straight for the dining room in the rear. It was Arthur Merrick. He walked past The Table, where Wally Berger, Homer Fisk, and Marilyn Smallwood were listening to Greeley's account of getting Maude home from the hospital, and took a table next to the picture window in front of the stone garden.

Merrick was buoyed by his meeting with Buck McCready the day before when he'd learned that the Moody piano, as he'd come to call it, was still in Cedar Mills and possibly in the possession of a worker at the Madison Café. He read the one-sided menu encased in a plastic sleeve and gazed around the café with an intensity that caught the attention of both Sadie and Katherine. He ordered black coffee and the Logger Sandwich, two fried eggs and three strips of bacon between two buttermilk pancakes.

Later, when he thought back on the episode at the Madison Café as he drove to Seattle, Arthur admitted that his trip to Sekiu had been a success but his stop at Cedar Mills was a disaster. He'd done everything he intended not to do, drawing attention to himself and arousing suspicion in everyone.

It all started when he asked for an extra plate as Sadie served his breakfast. Sadie watched as he separated the eggs and bacon from the pancakes, put the pancakes on the new plate, and cut them into fourths. Then he asked Sadie for some orange marmalade. Sadie laughed and told him he was in the wrong place if he wanted marmalade. All they had was grape jelly and strawberry jam. She walked back to get some strawberry jam and he heard her yell to Katherine, "He wants orange marmalade. I knew he was a Canuck."

It went downhill from there. When Sadie stopped to refill his coffee, he asked her if she was a musician which elicited a heated reaction from the waitress. She told him if that was a pick-up line, it was the weirdest one she'd ever heard and if he said anything about playing the piccolo, she'd call the police. When she brought the check, he asked if the owner was on the premises. Sadie told him if he had a complaint, he could talk to the head cook, and pointed to Katherine who was staring at them through the service window.

By the time he'd convinced Sadie that he wanted to talk to the owner about a personal matter and she'd pried Greeley away from The Table, Arthur had abandoned any plan to ask about the Moody piano, it was all too ridiculous. A slow, seething anger toward his cousin Paul started to grow. Suddenly Greeley was standing at his table. Arthur explained he'd just come from Sekiu where Buck McCready had told him about Greeley's article on the life of Luther Moody.

"What of it?" Greeley challenged.

Arthur stumbled through a disjointed story about seeing Buck and Luther perform in British Columbia when he was a kid and wanted to read Greeley's piece. Greeley told him he could get a copy of North Coast Passages at the Book Mart next door and walked away. Arthur paid the check, left Sadie a hefty tip, and walked out the front door while everyone stared.

Finally back on the road, Arthur consoled himself with the fact that at least he'd found a copy of the historical society journal which he'd bought from the officious clerk at the book store. He'd hoped to find out from her who at the Madison Café played the piano but when Wally's daughter, Nora Wineskin, explained she'd just moved from Brooklyn, Arthur decided it was pointless to ask about the Moody piano.

Back at the café, Sadie spent the rest of the day making wisecracks about orange marmalade and playing the piccolo until Katherine and Larry told her to clam up.

Sadie laughed, "You gotta watch those Canadians. They've all got a wild hair."

❖ ❖ ❖ ❖ ❖ ❖ ❖ ❖ ❖ ❖ ❖

Hazel came in the front door just after one o'clock. She sat in the same booth she and Roy had sat in when Roy had the heart attack. She waved at Katherine, who broke into a smile. Katherine went out around the counter and sat in the booth with Hazel.

"I came for one of those chicken pot pies, Bobby's been bragging about," she said. "And I wanted to see if you'd be home later this afternoon. I've got something for you."

Katherine asked Sadie to help Larry out in the kitchen and to ask Bobby to bring out the pot pie when it was ready. Larry poked his head around and said hello to Hazel just as Bobby, with intense concentration, started out from the service counter carrying a tray with the pot pie and tossed salad.

"So these are the pies you bake every Tuesday," she said to Bobby who proudly stood at the end of the booth nodding in the affirmative. "But, my gosh, I can't eat this whole thing. Can you get another plate so Katherine and I can share it."

While Katherine and Hazel ate, Bobby kept walking out to ask how Hazel liked her lunch. Sadie brought the coffee pot around for refills and

Hazel asked how her nephews were doing. Sadie sighed and said they were ok. But Donny, the oldest, needed a job. He'd lost his job as a milker for Jim Sorstrom after Jim had sold his herd the month before.

"He's sixteen, just got his license and now he wants a car," Sadie said. "I told him no job, no money, no car."

"We need help on the farm," Hazel said. "Bring him out to talk to Roy."

Hazel and Sadie agreed that she'd bring Donny out to the farm the next afternoon and Hazel told Katherine she was on her way to Port Smith. She'd stop by on her way home. Before she left, she told Larry that Anne had said to remind him about their bridge lesson at her place.

Katherine walked up to Maude's after work carrying a picnic basket with two chicken pot pies and a large bowl of tossed salad. The back door was unlocked. She walked in and left the basket in the kitchen. Maude and Milos Grajek were in sitting in the living room while Rascal dozed on the floor between them. Maude was in a wheelchair and Katherine was surprised at how frail she looked.

"There's my sweetheart," Maude said in a raspy voice. "Let's have a hug. Boyfriend is reading me some poetry. We're in the middle of Alfred Lord Tennyson's *The Charge of the Light Brigade*."

Katherine bent down and gave Maude a hug and a peck on the cheek. "I'm glad you're finally home," she said. "I put the food in the kitchen."

Katherine listened as Maude described her escape from the hospital and how she couldn't get any rest because everyone in town kept stopping in to check on her.

Then she said, "Milo told me you took him to lunch on Saturday after you left the hospital. That's good for him. To get out. He's got to socialize more."

Grajek blustered something at Maude and told Katherine he'd enjoyed their afternoon at the Blue Heron. He looked at Maude and said, "She was exceedingly gracious to take me to lunch."

Katherine blushed. "I've got to go. Enjoy your dinner." She left, disturbed at how weak Maude was."

Hazel pulled up just as Katherine was opening her front door. She was carrying a large clear plastic bag which contained a quilt and two embroidered pillowcases. Hazel told her were made by an old friend in Sewanee. The pattern was a favorite in the Smoky Mountains, a double Irish chain of large white diamond shapes outlined by chains of smaller blue and green diamonds. Hazel said "Let's try it on your bed," and marched into the bedroom.

"It's a queen and I can tell right now it's too big for this bed," Hazel said. "We'll have to do something about that. Which is why I came to talk to you. I can see you need some furniture."

Hazel saw the baby grand piano in the living room and exclaimed, "How beautiful." She walked around it, patting it like a baby and then sat down at the keyboard and asked, "My I?"

Katherine said "of course."

Hazel played some scales and then "Look for the Silver Lining," and "'Til the Clouds Roll By."

"What a wonderful sound. I can tell you keep this in shape."

They sat in the kitchen while Katherine started a pot of coffee. Hazel wasn't much for small-talk and she got right to the point, telling Katherine she was afraid that after Sunday night, Katherine might not come back to the farm again.

"You're right about that," Katherine said. "I figured you and Roy wouldn't want me around now that you know who I really am."

"Stop that nonsense," Hazel retorted. "You think Roy and I have lived some perfect life. Everyone's had problems. I told you I grew up in the Virginia mountains. Life was a struggle. I could tell you plenty of stories, girl. The most important thing is you have me and Roy now."

Katherine started telling Hazel things she hadn't told anyone. About the trip to the state store for vodka. How she hated herself for leading such a phony life after she'd come back to Cedar Mills which made her want to start drinking again, and how terribly alone and guilty she felt all those years on the road, and how she left Hazel and Roy's on Sunday night convinced she was a loser and all she wanted to do was start drinking and leave town, and how she'd slept with her new sweater on.

Hazel said, "I'm proud of you. You deserve a medal. Roy and I are blessed you're in our lives."

Katherine told her about how the bottles of vodka went missing and led Hazel out the back door. She opened the tool shed door and showed Hazel the shelf where she'd put the two bottles of Grey Goose. Back in the kitchen, Katherine told her Will's story about the Dolan kids and how she planned to catch them herself.

"Shouldn't be too hard," Hazel said. "Just like you catch a stray cat. Keep putting food out there until the cat gets used to coming around to eat every day. He lets his guard down, and bingo, you've got him."

As for the furniture, she said they wanted to get rid of a bunch of extra stuff they'd brought from Tennessee. Hazel wanted to make sure Katherine got whatever she wanted before Roy sold it.

Katherine said she'd come out after work the next day and take a look. Hazel told her she'd have Walt and his boys bring the furniture in to her place. "I've got the Beavers wrapped around my little finger," she said as she got ready to leave. "They'll do anything for me after I fed them all that pie when they were building our front porch."

The next afternoon, Katherine and Hazel were in the hay barn at New Morning farm looking through what amounted to enough furniture to fill three of Katherine's small houses. Katherine was supposed to be deciding what she wanted, but Hazel walked through the large storeroom, pointing to a round oak dining table with six chairs and a matching sideboard, a queen-size bed with an oak headboard taller than Katherine, and several other pieces she said Katherine should have.

"I've already talked to Walt," she told Katherine as they walked back to the house. "He says he and Matt and Harley will bring it over on Friday, if that's okay.

"I'm a little overwhelmed," Katherine said.

"Overwhelmed is a good thing," Hazel said with a smile. "I'm glad to know these things will have a good home."

Katherine stayed for dinner. This time it was just the three of them in the kitchen. It was warm and comfortable to be with Hazel and Roy, talking and laughing about Katherine's plan to catch the little Cedar Mills bandits. Before she left, they talked about Thanksgiving and invited Katherine if she didn't have other plans..

"It's only a few weeks away," Roy said. "We'd like you to be here. Hazel's sister May and her husband Archie are coming from Tennessee. Boy howdy, that'll be a time."

After dinner and the kitchen was cleaned up, the three walked arm-in-arm out to Katherine's car. She drove home eager to set a trap for the Dolan kids.

The View From the Hay Barn

The next afternoon, Larry was at Anne's for their second bridge lesson of the week. Larry had been patiently passive about Anne's lack of skill at the bridge table, telling her things went very well their first time as partners. But Anne was prideful enough not to accept his gracious fabrications, she knew how poorly she'd played. So she'd cajoled him into giving her lessons before the next duplicate bridge match. She didn't want to make a fool of herself again.

She'd set up a card table in the living room of her simply designed one-story cedar-sided rambler. Both ends of the living room which spread across the width of the house were all glass and from this elevation, a hundred or so feet up the hill from Hazel and Roy's, the waters of the Strait were visible to the north and the mountains could be seen to the south. There was a fire in the pass-through stone fireplace that separated the dining room and living room. Anne had brought out some homemade chocolate chip cookies and coffee before they started the lesson and Larry thought to himself he'd be happy to give Anne bridge lessons anytime she wanted.

Anne was having trouble counting cards, especially keeping track of how many trump were out, an original sin of the bridge player. So they spent a long time, interminable it seemed to her, doing memory exercises in counting cards. Next, Larry tried explain what an opening bid of one club meant, that she had eleven or twelve points but no strong suit. But it could also mean, that she had nothing at all. It depended on the situation. She rolled her eyes as he talked. Next he tried to show her why leading away from a king was the road to destruction. She was trying hard to understand and refused to admit she didn't.

After two hours with Larry acting as though he could continue for another two hours, Anne was ready for some fresh air. She ordered Larry up and outside for a walk. Enough bridge for one afternoon. They walked in the windy dusk out along the ridge where her house sat and then down to the hay barn. Anne said she wanted to show Larry a great view from the loft. On the second floor of the barn, they looked north out the open window toward the Strait. Anne pointed out Bert Peck's house in the distance. Beyond Bert's house they could see a loaded container ship, a lumbering overweight behemoth, standing out to the Pacific, another eighty miles to the west.

"We bought this land from Bert," she told him. "Eighty acres from his three hundred and twenty. It'd been in his family for four generations."

They stood at the window, chatting aimlessly until Anne turned and stumbled into Larry. He was as surprised as she was. It was an electrifying moment when they found each other entangled in one another's arms. Then they were hungrily kissing and tearing at each other's clothes. Anne pushed him toward the center of the barn away from the window and fell on top of him in the hay. It had been an eternity for both of them. They were primitive animals locked in an atavistic coupling, writhing naked, moaning *yeses,* and whispering *mores.* Both were equally enthusiastic in their union as they came together in a joyous celebration of the flesh.

Roy and Hazel were finishing up with the horses and getting ready to go in for dinner. Hazel said she wanted to show Roy the furniture she was giving to Katherine so they walked up to the hay barn and into the store room where above them they heard the creaking of floorboards and the thumping and moaning of two human animals locked together in passion. They heard "Oh, my God Anne," and "Larry, more…more…more." They fled from the barn and walked back down the hill to the house.

Hazel and Roy didn't talk much at dinner that night. Later they silently lay together in bed until Roy said, "I think Larry's over-mounted."

Hazel laughed and said, "You've got that right."

Then they fell asleep.

First Date

On Saturday morning, before Katherine left to pick up Jack, she called Sadie and told her Greeley had okayed her plan to hire a new waitress so Sadie could start training in the kitchen as a backup cook and how he'd kept her in his office after work the day before complaining about Buck McCready sending that weird Canadian to ask about Luther Moody which inspired Sadie to start in again about orange marmalade.

Katherine drove into New Morning farm at noon. It felt odd to drive up to Anne's house, past Hazel and Roy's. Jack was sitting on the front porch in the cold. Katherine sensed his male pride had been wounded by her picking him up and he didn't want to be further embarrassed by having her come to the front door for him. He'd called that morning and said he'd be ready earlier because Roy had a new hired hand, Donny St. John, so Jack was relieved of his weekend chores. But Katherine, enjoying the opportunity to tease him, had said she had things to do and couldn't pick him up until noon.

"You sure you don't want me to drive my car?" Jack asked as he got in Katherine's station wagon.

"I'm very sure I don't want you to drive your car," Katherine said with a smile. "It'll do you good to see how regular folks get around."

"I know all about regular folks," Jack said. "I is one."

Katherine laughed "My, my, how you talk. Next time you can squire me around in your BMW like the Queen of Sheba, but today it's just the meat and potatoes lifestyle in my used Taurus."

Gosport was thirty miles east of Cedar Mills. Katherine bypassed U.S. 101 and took the long way on the back roads through Pronoun, Point No Point, and Brumble, all little crossroads in the wilderness. They drove in silence for a while, both uncomfortable at being alone together. Except for two meetings at Hazel and Roy's and Jack's two stops for breakfast at the café, they were strangers.

Katherine told Jack she'd already heard Roy had hired Donny St. John to work on the farm. "He's the nephew of Sadie Nixon, the waitress at the café," she said. When Katherine told him about Donny's mother, Vicki, being in jail because she beat up Tommy Lowry in the Duchess Tavern parking lot, they both shared a muted laugh in spite of the sadness of it all.

Katherine said Tommy Lowry had got what he deserved.

She told Jack how she'd had Ray Kesecker take her old car down to the shop and get it in good enough shape for Donny to drive back and forth to work. She was going to give it to him if Roy said he was going to be hired on permanently and if Donny saved enough money for insurance. Jack was silent the rest of the way to Gosport and Katherine was sure he was already sorry he'd agreed to go out with her.

As they drove into Gosport, Katherine told Jack she was taking him to lunch at Harvey's Little Oyster, a seafood place on the water next to the Whidbey Island ferry dock. Jack told her he didn't want to be disagreeable, but if she was driving, he was buying lunch. They shared a laugh as they walked into the cozy little restaurant with white linen tablecloths and candles on the tables, only two of which were occupied. The restaurant sat on short pier. Its plate glass windows on three sides gave diners views of the ferry dock next door and the small Gosport harbor in front.

They stood waiting for someone to seat them when a tall, blonde man with blue eyes, looking close to forty, came out of the kitchen and exclaimed "Well, my God, look what the cat drug in." He rushed over and gave Katherine a full body hug. "Where in the world have you been girl friend?"

Katherine broke loose from the embrace and introduced Jack, "Harvey, this is my friend Jack Lindsay. Jack, this is my friend Harvey Pearson, the Harvey of the Little Oyster."

Jack and Harvey shook hands. Harvey put an arm around each of them and led them to a table overlooking the harbor. "Let me grab a couple menus and go get Adam," he said disappearing into the kitchen.

Katherine told Jack that she and Harvey had worked together years ago at a diner in California, the name of which she couldn't remember. They'd met again when she wandered into Harvey's Little Oyster one rainy Saturday afternoon not long after she'd come back to Cedar Mills.

Harvey and Adam came out of the kitchen smiling and laughing. Harvey introduced Adam to Jack, calling him "my little oyster." Adam gave Katherine a big hug and shook hands with Jack. Harvey complained that Katherine didn't come in enough and asked how the Madison Café was doing. He said he'd heard good things about the place so she must be doing something right. Then he told Jack about when he and Katherine worked together at Nestor's Northside Diner in Modesto.

Harvey said, "Let me tell you, this is who you want to be in the fox-hole with. Katherine and I were working the kitchen on second shift at this all-night greasy spoon. We're leaving late, around two in the morning and walking through the parking lot to our cars when some redneck cowboy staggers out of the shadows and grabs me. He says he doesn't want any fag fixing his food. Katherine turns around and says, 'Excuse me dirt bag.' He starts for Katherine who like out of nowhere, knees him in the crotch and gives him a karate kick in the face which puts him flat on his back. Then she says, 'Now get the hell out of here and leave us alone, you piece of garbage.' He was outta there. We never saw him again."

Adam took Harvey by the arm and led him toward the kitchen, saying Katherine and her beau probably wanted to be alone. As they looked at the menu, Jack said, "I have to hand it to you Katherine Baker, you know how to do it up right."

"Well, Jack Lindsay, it's only the beginning." she answered.

"What'd this whole production cost? Quite a bit, I bet. You get some people at a restaurant to put on a show, like you're old friends. If you wanted to impressed me, you've done it with flying colors."

Katherine laughed as Chloe, the waitress, came out to take their order. "Beware, Jack, I'm a woman of many strange and wonderful powers."

Chloe recommend the day's special, kelp-encrusted Bering Sea halibut baked in a reduction of sea cucumber butter and served with a crab and shrimp remoulade, steamed shitake and asparagus béarnaise, and an endive and dandelion salad with an aged Gravenstein apple vinaigrette.

They both nodded an affirmative and as Chloe left, Katherine said, "Harvey's come a long way from Nestor's Northside Diner, but I'm not so sure about me."

Katherine sat quietly looking out at the water until Jack said, "I'm glad we're doing this."

"Well, Jack, to tell the truth, I didn't ask you out to have a good time," she returned with a blush. "There's a purpose to all this. I'm on a fact-finding mission and I've got three questions."

"Okay. No problem Shoot."

"First question. What's Sewanee? All you Tennessee people talk about it like it was some sacred place."

Jack laughed, "That's it? That's your first question?"

Katherine nodded solemnly. Jack told her it was a town in southeastern Tennessee, the site of the University of the South. If you were an Episcopalian "Sewanee" also meant the University of the South's divinity school.

"It's the epicenter of Episcopal theology in the South. That's where my dad taught, at Sewanee's School of Theology. Lots of history and tradition, and lots of stuffy theology professors who are followed around by dutiful young Southerners who can't wait to be ordained and emulate them."

"Your father was stuffy?"

"My dad wasn't stuffy but he was reserved, until he took to the pulpit to preach. Everyone said he was a great preacher."

"Thank you," Katherine deadpanned as the salad was served. "More on that later. Now, my second question. What was it like for you growing up? You were probably pampered and spoiled, right?"

"You're making me laugh," Jack said. He told her about spending his early years in Sewanee as a "pretty regular kid" going to public school, until his parents decided to send him to boarding school when he started seventh grade. Alan and Anne wanted him to attend an Ivy League college so he was shipped off to St. Paul's, in New Hampshire.

"I hated every minute of it. I hated the people, I hated New England. I was mad at Anne and Alan, and I took it out on myself and everyone around me," Jack said.

"Kind of a Holden Caulfield deal?" Katherine asked, genuinely interested.

"Not really. I always thought Holden Caulfield was about angst. I was just pissed off big time, if you'll pardon the expression."

He made it through a year at St. Paul's without out getting thrown out, but in a polite letter to his parents when the year ended, the headmaster wrote that Jack might fare better in another academic setting. The next year, his hopes for staying home were dashed when he was packed off to New England again, this time to Choate, where he only lasted three months before Alan was asked to come and take him home.

"I was an obnoxious, angry, lout," Jack told her with some pride. "I was so glad to be home in Tennessee. To me everyone in New England was a self-absorbed, pretentious ass. They all acted like they were constipated. It's a ghastly place."

Katherine laughed. "So you were a bad boy, Jack. I'm surprised."

Jack told her he expected his parents to be angry when he told them he wanted to live at home, go to public school, and be a regular kid. His father had smiled and told him he hoped he would never be just a "regular kid." Then he meted out Jack's sentence: He was to come straight home from school every day and report to Roy who would put him work on the farm until dinner. After dinner, he'd study and go to bed. On Saturdays, he'd be expected to put in a full-day on the farm. He'd have Sundays off. This went on for two years, until Jack started high school, when the sanctions were lifted and he was free to take part in school activities. He was still expected to help Roy on the farm.

"I bet you were a football and basketball star," Katherine said.

"Far from it. I was a marginal nerd. The high school band and small parts in a couple of school plays. I studied a lot, got into the honor society, which made Alan proud. I had friends but I didn't do a lot of hanging out. I was a pretty serious guy for the most part. Then Roy and Hazel started teaching me to play the guitar and banjo and I was hooked."

They were so engrossed in their conversation that Katherine and Jack finished eating without remembering much about the food. Harvey was at the reception desk when they got up to leave. Jack asked him for the check.

"Not this time, Jack. It's on the house in honor of my old friend and her new friend."

But Jack refused to accept Harvey's hospitality and in a most lawyer-ly manner with a gentlemanly closing argument which greatly impressed Katherine, he talked Harvey into letting him pay for lunch. After hugs for Katherine and admonishments from Harvey and Adam to not stay away so long, the couple walked out into the gray November afternoon.

As they walked to the car, the Whidbey Island ferry was just coming into Gosport harbor. Katherine grabbed Jack's hand and started running to the car. "Come on," she ordered. "This is part two of today's adventure."

They were the last car to board the nearly empty ferry before the horn sounded and the crew started to cast off. When Jack asked where they were going, Katherine told him "nowhere." They were just taking a ferry ride. It was forty minutes over and forty minutes back. They'd be back in less than two hours.

"I did this all the time when I first came back to Cedar Mills," she told him. "It's liberating to me, just being out on the water with no real place to go. And besides, now I've got you trapped with no escape, unless you can swim in fifty-degree saltwater without succumbing to hypothermia in five minutes."

They walked around the passenger deck as the boat pulled out of the harbor and into the open water of the Strait at the head of Admiralty Inlet, the entrance to Puget Sound. A loaded oil tanker, low in the water, could be seen in the distance, making the turn south into the Sound. The wind was blowing hard and the little ferry was rolling with the waves. They went inside for coffee and sat side-by-side in an empty row of chairs in the gallery at the front of the boat, sipping their coffee, watching the whitecaps and feeling the unpredictable pitch of the boat as it labored its way toward Whidbey Island.

"Okay, I think I've got Jack Lindsay's early life down," Katherine said. "We're still on Question Two however and now it's Part Two. What about college?"

Jack feigned a disinterest in being interrogated but found himself savoring Katherine's affectionate curiosity. He told her that Alan and Anne had expected him to go to an Ivy League school. When he was admitted to Harvard and Princeton, Alan lobbied for Harvard, but Anne's choice was Princeton, it being the favored seat of higher learning for generations of young men from the South who wanted to taste life above, but not too far above, the Mason-Dixon Line.

"Something tells me you didn't go to either one," Katherine said.

"You're right. When I told Alan and Anne I was going to the University of Tennessee, you'd have thought I'd announced I was dying of leukemia," Jack said with a laugh. "They said if that's what I wanted, I'd have to pay my own way. They would pay for Harvard or Princeton but not Tennessee. I said fine. I was going to Knoxville, end of story. There were no loud arguments. We always fought about things with the greatest politeness. They eventually gave in."

"So you went to Tennessee."

Jack nodded and told Katherine a similar story about attending law school, how he'd rebuffed Alan and Anne's insistence of Harvard Law and went to Vanderbilt. By then his parents had become immune to his rejecting their ideas and didn't fight his decision to go to law school in Nashville.

Back at car as the ferry was pulling into the slip at Whidbey Island, Jack asked, "What do we do now?"

"We turn around and go back, Mr. Lindsay, unless you want a tour of Coupeville." Katherine said. "Now, if I can believe what you've told me so far, Jack Lindsay, you are a headstrong, even stubborn fellow."

The uncomfortable silence that filled the car when they drove to Gosport earlier was replaced by their nonstop conversation. On the ferry's return trip to Gosport, Katherine announced they were moving on to Question Three, but Jack said he was through talking about himself for a while. It was his turn to ask her some questions.

"Who's in charge here, Jack?" she asked.

"If I may approach the bench, your honor," he said. "I respectfully ask that I may be allowed to question you at will."

"In light of your headstrong nature, counselor, please proceed."

"Why'd you come back to Cedar Mills after all those years?" Jack asked as their eyes met and locked to each other for a minute.

She was surprised. She didn't know why and that's what she told him.

"God, I was a weird person back then when I drove into town in my old beat-up station wagon. Guess I still am. But I honestly don't know why I came back. Returning to the scene of the crime? I don't know."

Jack's silence encouraged her to continue. She told him what she'd told Reverend Tom, about creating a phony persona without a past, complete with the grunge garb, the plaid shirt, jeans, and hiking boots, topped off with fake glasses. She told him about her conniption fit when Maude Doud had shown her the newspaper clippings when she was the high school student Katy Owling. How she refused to acknowledge her Cedar Mills past to anyone, even though everyone in town knew who she really was. Now she laughed about it.

"Oh, and the hair. I forgot the hair," she said. "Do you know I'm a natural blonde? I'll never be a blonde again. But I really am Katherine Baker. Katy Owling's dead. It was a slow, painful death, but she's gone forever."

Jack couldn't tell whether or not she was joking. "You're a complicated woman, Katherine Baker."

"You've got that right, Jack Lindsay. I'm about as complicated as a bowl of tomato soup."

"I'd say more like minestrone," he said as they drove off the ferry in Gosport.

Katherine asked Jack if he had plans when they got back to Cedar Mills. Jack told her his only hope was the day wouldn't end. She suggested they'd go back through Pronoun and stop at Robby Marco's Grocery.

Katherine said, "Bert Peck told me it's only place around you can get real Italian pastry, even though the Marcos are Portuguese. But that's another story. Anyway, let's get some dessert and go back to my place. I'll make some coffee."

It was dark by the time they parked in front of Katherine's house. They went in the front door and awkwardly stood in the living room for a few minutes.

"We'll this is it," she said self-consciously. "I know it's not much, but it's the biggest place I've lived in since I was a kid. And, I just got a bunch of new furniture, thanks to Hazel and Roy."

"They told me about it yesterday," Jack said. Then he spotted the piano and whispered, "And Hazel told me about this beauty."

Katherine hung up their coats in the hall closet and went in to the kitchen to start the coffee while Jack walked over to one of the new pieces of furniture, a long walnut table that stretched the length of the living room's picture window next to the piano. It was covered with neatly stacked music books and sheet music from Luther Moody's endless trove. He picked up *Songs from Carousel* and sat at the piano, playing when Katherine came in from the kitchen.

"I was in a production of *Carousel* at Tennessee. One of the fair workers who was part of the chorus. What great songs."

Then he played and sang "When You Walk Through A Storm," and "If I Loved You," while Katherine sat on her new sofa and listened to his soft tenor voice ripple through the house.

"Talk about surprises," she said when he finished. "I didn't know you played piano."

"I'm a man of many talents," he laughed as he came over and sat next to her on the sofa.

If either of them were asked what precisely happened at Katherine's house that Saturday night, neither Katherine nor Jack could have recalled the details. But they both would have said there was a lot of talk, a lot of laughter, and a lot of music.

Jack remembered he asked Katherine to play some of her favorite music and Katherine played the Mozart andante from the Piano Concerto No. 23, and how it had the same effect it had on everyone who'd heard her play it, a slow welling of tears in the eyes of the listener.

Katherine remembered sitting at her new round oak dining room table, eating Robby Marco's Portuguese cheesecake Italiano while Jack told her how he wished he'd been around when she was working her way up the San Joaquin Valley. When she'd asked why, he'd said "Because I would have been with you."

Jack remembered that he'd never heard Katherine laugh until then and how beautiful she was when her loud infectious laugh rang through the house after she'd taken him out the back door to the tool shed to show him the bait she'd set out for the Dolan kids: a bag of Oreos and two bags of potato chips, one plain and one barbeque. "Or do you think they'd like rippled dippers?" she'd said, making them laugh some more.

Katherine remembered Jack's surprise when he found *The Platonic Model for Faith: There Isn't One* on the coffee table and how he started talking about his father and how he'd restored St. John's Chapel outside Sewanee and preached there every Sunday. Jack sat on the sofa staring into space and said, "Acceptance. He always came back to the same thing, how our biggest challenge was to accept ourselves, accept the love of others, and accept the love of God."

Jack remembered Katherine's surprise when he found *The Johnny Mercer Songbook* on the table next to the piano. He told her Johnny Mercer was one of his heroes, a Southern boy who'd gone north and made good. He said he'd visited Mercer's grave in Savannah to pay his respects a few years ago. Then Jack sat down and opened *The Johnny Mercer Songbook*. Katherine stood behind him as he played and they sang together, "Too Marvelous For Words," "Come Rain or Come Shine," "One For My Baby." The list went on and when they got to "Moon River," Katherine put her hands on his shoulders and sang the lyrics alone.

Katherine remembered sitting on the sofa afterward, telling Jack about Johnny Herrera and their starring moment in the high school chorus festival revue, and how she lost her virginity that weekend, and how she had to leave town when she found out she was pregnant, and how fat little Art Fletcher was a way to do it even though she hated herself for playing him along. It was the first time she'd told anyone the real story of how she left Cedar Mills.

It was two in the morning when Katherine said she had to play the organ at church in the morning and Jack said it was time to hit the road. They talked nonstop all the way to New Morning Farm. When Katherine pulled in to Anne's, they both fell silent, neither of them knew how to say goodbye. Jack told her he'd see her at church and hoped she'd be at Hazel and Roy's for dinner afterward. Katherine told him how much she liked the dedication in his father's book, and repeated the words, "And to Jack, the prince of everything good in the future."

He put his hand on hers and said, "I believe it says 'And to Jack, the prince of everything good in *our* future.' See you tomorrow."

Cars driving into New Morning Farm in the black stillness of early morning were unheard of unless there was trouble. Anne heard the car and jumped out of bed regretting she hadn't taken Roy up on his offer to give her a shotgun and teach her out to use it. She peeked around the curtain of her bedroom window and saw Jack getting out of Katherine's car and murmured, "Jack. Oh Jack."

Hazel and Roy heard the car too. Roy got his loaded shotgun out from under the bed. He and Hazel walked out to the kitchen window and saw Katherine's car up at Anne's. They both looked at the wall clock above the stove as they walked into the living room and out to the front porch, where they stood in the cold, watching Katherine drive through the gate and turn right onto Ridge Road, heading for town.

It was well after two o'clock by the time Katherine was driving down the deserted Main Street. *There's nothing lonelier than a small town in the middle of the night*, she thought. Charlie Sizemore was parked at his regular spot in the alley behind the Red and White Supermarket. Everyone knew he was always there on Saturday nights, so you either had to be blind drunk or completely sober to drive that way. He clucked when he saw Katherine's car go by, wondering if she was back on the sauce. She didn't drive like it, but it was a nice item for the gossip mill anyway.

Maude Doud was having trouble sleeping. She'd gotten out of bed and woke up Milos Grajek who was sleeping on the sofa, asking him to make her some tea. When she heard a car coming up Second Avenue from town, she involuntarily went to the living room window. Katherine drove slowly by, turned on Cedar Avenue and parked in front of her house. She shouted into the kitchen for Milos, "Look at this boyfriend," she said, "Katherine's just getting home."

"And we should care?" Grajek said with a sigh.

"Of course we should," Maude said. "Where's my tea?

As Katherine got out of the car and walked up to the front door, two pairs of eyes were watching her from across the street, hidden in the juniper hedge in front of Arne and Madge Swensen's. It was Curtis and Clare Dolan on their nightly rounds. Clare had a backpack over one shoulder which contained the night's loot. She'd told Curtis it'd been a good run.

Katherine was in a hurry for bed, but first she went out to the tool shed, opened the door and turned on the light. The shelf where she'd put the cookies and chips was bare. Back in the house, she climbed into bed with a smile and started plotting her next move to ensnare the Dolans.

Sunday Afternoon at the Bridge Table

When Katherine got to New Morning Farm the next afternoon, Hazel, Roy and Jack were in the living room ostensibly watching football, but she heard Jack say something about Harvey's Little Oyster. Hazel saw Katherine first as she walked into the living room and said in a stage whisper, "Shh! She's here." Then they all laughed while Roy told her Jack was giving them a detailed account of their date yesterday.

"Well let's hope he's not telling stories on me," Katherine said.

"Only good ones," Jack replied and patted the sofa, motioning for her to sit beside him.

But Katherine shook her head and took his hand to pull him up. She said she'd seen Donny out at the horse barn. She wanted to go out and say hello. Roy told her Donny was one of the best hands he'd had in the thirty years, even better than Jack. They all laughed as Katherine and Jack started out the back door.

They walked out into an uncommonly sunny November afternoon and started up the hill, toward the horse barn where Donny St. John was unloading bales of hay. Katherine asked him how he liked the new job. He said it was great. He loved working with the horses. Katherine told him if he stuck it out and made good with Roy, she had a surprise for him. Donny looked embarrassed and mumbled something about not wanting anyone to make a fuss.

They left Donny and walked up the hill past the hay barn into the open pasture. From there they could just see the Strait to the north and across it, the dark blue mountains of Vancouver Island. They walked for an hour, following a path worn by the horses that wound around the outer edges of the farm's eighty acres while Katherine told Jack about Donny's father, Johnny St. John.

Johnny had been a commercial salmon fisherman who took his purse seiner, the *Miss Vicki*, to Alaska every May for the Bristol Bay salmon season. At the end of May the year he died, he and his mate, Ralph Dalrymple were on their way north, a couple hours out of Gosport, in the Sound west of Bellingham, bound for the Georgia Strait when they passed a thirty-foot cabin cruiser, the *Lazy Girl* out of Camano Island, with smoke billowing from her stern. Johnny pulled alongside the stricken boat and jumped aboard, telling Ralph to take the *Miss Vicki* far enough away to avoid the risk of her catching fire.

A family of four was aboard the *Lazy Girl*, a young couple and their two daughters who were five and seven years old. The wife had managed to pull her unconscious husband from below deck where he'd been trying to put out a fire in the engine compartment. Johnny strapped life jackets on the two girls and threw them overboard one at a time. He put a life jacket on the wife, who by now was in shock, and told her to jump. She wouldn't, so he pushed her over the side and told her to swim to the *Miss Vicki*. A few minutes later, the *Lazy Girl's* fuel tank exploded, turning the cabin cruiser into a thousand pieces of smoking rubble.

The last thing Ralph Dalrymple saw before the explosion was Johnny staggering through the smoke toward the side of the *Lazy Girl* with the unconscious husband on his back. By the time Ralph had pulled the mother and daughters aboard the *Miss Vicki*, the Coast Guard cutter *Wolverine* out of Everett and a helicopter rescue team from Port Smith were on the scene, but the bodies of Johnny St. John and the husband were never found.

Everyone said it was just like Johnny St. John, who always went full throttle when someone needed help. He was lauded as a hero and Congressman Del Welker, now Governor Del Welker, made sure he was honored with the Coast Guard's Gold Lifesaving Medal and nominated for a Presidential Medal of Freedom.

In the aftermath, Vicki grew bitter, saying it was one thing to be a dead hero and another thing to be the widow of a dead hero with two boys to raise. It took a while for the acrimony to get her started on the road to self-destruction but it finally did. Then with the help of her old high school classmate, Tommy Lowry, Vicki St. John finally hit bottom.

Jack was silent as Katherine finished the story, he slipped his arm around her and pulled her close. Almost to the house, they stood by the barn watching Donny lead the horses out one-by-one. He rubbed each one on the nose and give them some sliced apple before letting run in the pasture. Katherine stopped and turned to Jack, giving him a punch on the shoulder, "You're not going to break my heart, Jack Lindsay, I mean it."

Surprised, Jack said, "That'll never happen, Katherine Baker. If I broke your heart, it would break mine."

It was just the four of them at dinner that Sunday. Larry and Anne were playing bridge at Maude's. Katherine asked why Donny didn't come in for dinner. Hazel shook her head and said he was a sweet boy and a hard worker, but he was very shy. She'd asked him to come in for dinner the day before, and dinner today, but he'd politely refused. He'd said his Aunt Sadie was coming to pick him up soon. Then Roy added he'd told Donny that after working all week before and after school, he could have the weekend off, but Donny said he'd rather be at the farm doing what needed to be done, if that was all right.

"Sadie says he's trying struggling to do the right thing," Katherine said. "His dad's gone and mom's turned into a drunk. He's trying to support the family the best he can."

"I hope he decides to stay on," Roy said.

The talk switched to Katherine's tool shed. Katherine smugly announced the cookie and chips she'd put on the shelf on Saturday were gone. She was sure it was the little Dolan bandits. Roy told her to wait a couple days before baiting the trap again. "Make 'em fret a little, wondering if there'll be more," he said with a chuckle.

Hazel asked Katherine how Maude was doing. "Annie said she's got someone there with her. Her boyfriend?"

Katherine told them all she knew about Milos Grajek, how he and Maude met when he tried to teach Maude's dog Rascal Polish and Maude had to call Will because The Mad Polack, as he used to be called, was scaring the wits out of Maude and her dog, and then afterwards, when Grajek had apologized, they'd become friends. She told them about taking him to lunch at the Blue Heron after they'd gone to see Maude at the hospital. How he'd told her about Treblinka, then his relocation to England after the war and how, after his move to New York, he'd ended up on the Peninsula.

❖ ❖ ❖ ❖ ❖ ❖ ❖ ❖ ❖ ❖ ❖ ❖

While Milos Grajek was being talked about at the Willit's, the man himself was sitting across from Maude at the bridge table in Maude's living room where they were locked in combat with Larry and Anne. Maude's health had improved enough to rejuvenate her feisty personality but her physical condition was another matter. She could walk around the house unassisted but she had to have a wheelchair for walking Rascal and for that, she needed her boyfriend Milo.

The opposing sides at the card table were evenly matched. With Anne as Larry's partner and Grajek as Maude's, they gave a neutralizing handicap to Larry and Maude's blood thirsty approach to the game. Milos wasn't a complete novice when it came to bridge, he'd played a little in New York City and Iowa City, but he found the whole thing rather simplistic, the bidding, the counting cards, and the childlike emotion over winning or losing a bid. Anne's determination to improve her skills at the bridge table was impressive but any real improvement in her game was moving at a glacially slow rate. She couldn't count cards and never knew if all the trump was out so Larry found it difficult to be sanguine when playing as her partner.

Near the end of the match, as both teams were locked in a tie for the rubber and Larry and Anne were vulnerable, Anne was playing the hand, a bid of three hearts. Certain she'd played out all the trump, she led with the ace of clubs. Everyone but Anne knew one trump card was still out. It was Milos' turn to play and he looked at Maude with a twinkle in his eye while Larry put his head in his hands and stared at down at the table waiting for the guillotine to fall. Maude gave Milos a kick in the shins and glared at him. He shrugged with a smile and threw out the last trump, the three of hearts, which took the hand and put Larry and Anne down one. It was all over the next hand when Maude and Milos took the match with a three no-trump bid.

"I was sure I had all the trump out," Anne sighed.

"Many a man is walking the streets of London in rags because he didn't get his trump out," Larry said, trying to sound good-natured.

Anne laughed and said, "Yes Larry, I do believe you've said that before."

The card game finished, they sat at the card table drinking coffee and eating dessert, Anne's homemade apricot-mocha oatmeal bars with a marionberry glaze. Maude asked how Katherine was doing on the organ at church. Larry said she was a natural, like she's been doing it for years. Anne seconded the opinion saying that not only Reverend Tom was relieved but even the fussy choir director, Brett Smallwood, was happy.

"Katherine's such a talented young woman, in spite being a bit of a waif and all," Anne said.

Maude said sharply, "Waif? Katherine a waif? You should have seen her in high school, met her family. Waif? What are you talking about?"

"Well maybe I didn't mean a waif. Maybe more like a gypsy, bless her heart. She's been such a godsend for Hazel and Roy."

"And to me," Maude said, raising her voice. "She saved my life. She's no waif. She's no gypsy. You're way off base, Anne."

"Be that as it may, she's doing a great job at church." Anne said with a smile.

They finished eating in silence. Larry got up from the table, cleared the dishes, and with Anne's help, cleaned up in the kitchen before saying he had to get going. He went over to Maude's wheel chair and kissed her on the cheek. She whispered in his ear, "Don't worry, I'll be back at duplicate bridge in no time." He said goodnight to Anne and Milos. They stood on either side of Maude at her living room window and watched him walk down the alley toward his apartment.

Anne left soon after Larry. Maude sat in her wheel chair at the living room window and waved as Anne's black Audi sedan drove off and turned left on Cedar Street, past Katherine's and down to Yarmouth Avenue. She turned left again on Yarmouth Avenue and then left again into the alley. She drove up to the rear of the Madison Café and parked beside Larry's Suburban in the small area that was reserved for employees.

Larry was standing on the landing as she started up the stairs to his apartment. They embraced before he led her in through the back door into the kitchen. The apartment was nearly dark, a single lamp was on in the living room. Larry followed Anne as she briskly walked through the apartment, complimenting him on how simple but tasteful it was. She found the bedroom in no time. Then they were on the bed, kissing, moaning, and pulling at each other's clothes in a reprise of their afternoon in the barn.

This time they were familiar with each other. The furtiveness of their first encounter was gone. When Anne finally arched her back and yelled, "Larry, Larry, Larry," he responded in kind with what Anne later laughingly called the force of Niagara Falls. Then they lay together in bed, Larry holding Anne and stroking her soft, blonde hair, both of them feeling things each thought had died inside them long ago.

Later, on the sofa in the dimly lit living room sipping brandy, Anne pointed to three small oil paintings on the far wall. She walked over to the sideboard and turned on the lamp above the paintings.

Larry sat on the sofa watching her inspect the oils. "Those are my savings account, my life insurance, my get-out-of- town fund," he said.

"Are they the real thing?" Anne asked.

"Yes, of course they're real. Art can be a great investment. The IRS took everything: my co-op on the Upper East Side, my Jag, all my investments, and most of my art. But my tax debt was settled. I didn't owe anything when I got out of the slammer. And they didn't get what you're looking at there. One George Caleb Bingham, one Winslow Homer, and one Edward Hopper."

"How'd you get them here?" Anne asked.

"When I heard the Feds were nosing around I took three small paintings that could be easily transported to a vaulted storage firm under an assumed name. Not long before they put me in handcuffs, a close friend, who shall remain nameless, transported them to Cedar Mills for safe keeping."

Larry got up and poured them another brandy. "There's something I have to tell you, Anne."

"Oh boy. Is this the other shoe about to drop?"

Larry put a hand on hers, "I'm in no position to get seriously involved with someone. I love what's happened with us, but I'm still trying to put my life back together."

Anne smiled, "I'm relieved Larry. I feel the same way. I'm still trying to figure things out too. I like our bed buddy thing and we'll leave it at that. It's fun and you're fun. I like you a lot."

Larry sighed, "I think the world of you, Anne."

"Well let's get back to bed then," she said, putting down her drink and pulling him up from the sofa.

As Anne and Larry were falling back into bed, Milos was pushing Maude down Second Avenue on their nightly walk with Rascal. They continued down Cedar Street to the vacant lot, five houses down from Katherine's, which gave a unobstructed view of the back of the Madison Café.

Maude suddenly said, "For Pete's sake, look over in the alley." Rascal stopped and cocked his head. "What on earth? That's Anne's car parked next to Larry's, boyfriend. What the Sam hell's going on? Those scalawags."

"Maybe they're practicing their bridge game," Milos said with a laugh.

"They're practicing all right and it isn't bridge," Maude said shaking her head. "Just like a couple of teenagers."

When Jack stopped at the Madison Café the next morning at six, Katherine was standing at the end of the counter waiting with a power breakfast sandwich and black coffee. Jack told her he'd be back on Friday night, "If you're going to be home, I'd like to stop by. "I can bring dinner if you want," he said.

"I'll be looking forward to it, Mr. Lindsay," Katherine said. "If you're free on Saturday, I'll take you to one of my favorite places. You can drive this time and I'll be the Queen of Sheba."

Sadie was eavesdropping at her listening post just outside the service window. She looked at Larry and said in a low voice, "So I guess the lovebirds are getting serious."

Larry huffed, "Lovebirds? What lovebirds?"

Unrest in the North

Paul Merrick and his cousin Arthur sat having drinks before dinner at the Fraser River Club on Hastings Street in downtown Vancouver. Their perch on the twenty-seventh floor of the Cathay-Pacific Building, gave them a full view of the harbor. They watched the lights across the water in West Van start to twinkle in the gray dusk while the commercial seaplanes swept in out of the inlet on their way to and from the British Columbia bush.

But all was not well with the cousins. Their relationship was strained after Arthur's sortie to the States in search of information about the baby grand piano. That combined with the growing pressure of bringing to market their new line of yoga gear, the Gandhi Yoga Mat and Gandhiwear, which was scheduled to launch in selected college towns south of the border in the first quarter of the new year, had both men on edge.

Arthur had come back to Vancouver upset with himself for even making the trip south. It had been an unequivocal failure except for the trip to Sekiu and his meeting with Buck McCready where he'd found out the Moody piano was probably in the possession of a restaurant worker in Cedar Mills. But he'd made a fool of himself at the café in Cedar Mills and later at Silas Peavey's clock shop in Seattle when he'd told the shopkeeper about his cousin's plan to salvage the *Arctic Maid* from the Lake Union mud and transport it by barge to Vancouver.

Peavey had been in no mood for a visit from another Merrick from Canada, one whose skin tone was the opposite of his cousin's. It confused the old man and his churlishness was anything but hospitable. Peavey said the proposal to salvage what was left of the *Arctic Maid* sounded like a confidence game and accused the cousins of playing the old "Mutt and Jeff." But he gave Arthur the business card of a local lawyer, Hercules Pushkin and with a gruff, "Go see Pushkin," he threw Arthur out of his shop.

Back in Vancouver, Paul had been less than pleased with Arthur's report on the Moody piano's whereabouts, without reason, in Arthur's opinion. He had found out it was in Cedar Mills, after all. Upset by Paul's petulance, Arthur put his foot down and said he was out of the game unless Paul told him the truth, why was the piano so important? The whole Gandhiwear project was being threatened by Paul's obsession with it.

But Paul put him off, saying that keeping Arthur in the dark could save him from danger if their quest went awry.

Arthur laughed and shook his head, "I'm through with this foolishness. You're on your own. My time will be spent with Gandiwear."

Paul shrugged and said he'd make one more trip to Seattle to meet with Hercules Pushkin and if that didn't bear fruit, he'd suspend his hunt for the

Moody piano. Arthur nodded a tentative assent, certain his cousin was flirting with madness.

Together Again

A week after their Saturday outing at Gosport, Katherine and Jack were together again, driving west on U.S. 101 headed for the Pacific Ocean. Jack drove this time. The night before when he'd come back from Seattle, he'd stopped at Katherine's with a pizza from Robby Marco's Pronoun Grocery. He also had two matching backpacks he'd bought at Eddie Bauer. Jack acted embarrassed when Katherine laughed in jest at their new "his and her" outdoor gear.

Like many people from other parts of the country, Jack had thought Seattle, which was a major Pacific seaport, was actually on the Pacific Ocean instead of 150 miles inland. He told Katherine that even after six months in the city he still was getting used to the fact that seagoing traffic had to travel the 100-mile long Strait of Juan de Fuca which fed into Puget Sound to get to Elliott Bay.

It was almost 90 miles from Cedar Mills to their destination, Third Beach, a remote half-moon shaped ocean beach south of La Push. On his first trip to Cedar Mills, he was struck by how wild and undeveloped the country was. Now, heading west on U.S. 101 into the part of the Peninsula the locals called the West End where the largest settlement was the garish rain-soaked town of Forks with a population of barely 1,000, the area around Cedar Mills seemed highly developed in comparison. Beyond Port Smith, the highway cut through a towering second-growth forest of Douglas fir occasionally punctuated by a clearing which might be home to a gas station, restaurant, or small grocery store.

Katherine did most of the talking as Jack concentrated on the narrow two-lane road. She told him about Hazel and Roy coming for dinner on Wednesday night and how nervous she'd been because it was the first time she'd ever had "people over for dinner." She described the dinner of cod filets baked in a bed of Swiss chard, macaroni and cheese, and a lime Jell-o salad embedded with shredded carrots and celery, each square served with a dollop of mayonnaise on top. Hazel and Roy were gracious with their compliments, telling her how wonderful it was have such unique food.

After dinner, Roy had brought two chairs from the dining room and placed them beside the piano. Hazel got out her guitar and Roy got out his banjo. Katherine sat at the piano and leafed through the *Songs From the Grand Ole Opry* songbook while they tuned up. Katherine had to read the music but Hazel and Roy didn't, all they needed to know was the key, and the three of them sang and played like they'd been a family trio for years.

The music had attracted Maude and Milos who were out with Rascal. Maude knocked on the front door and then marched in with Milos, who was holding Rascal with one hand and helping her walk with the other. She apologized for barging in but she just had to finally meet Hazel and Roy.

Katherine skipped telling Jack that the first thing Maude had wanted to know was what Hazel and Roy thought about this "Anne and Larry thing." Katherine was hearing about the "Anne and Larry thing" for the first time. Hazel said she thought that Annie was just trying to figure things out, bless her heart. Roy repeated what he'd told Hazel earlier, that he thought Larry was a little over-mounted. Then they'd all shared a laugh.

Before she'd left, Maude told Katherine that Clare and Curtis Dolan were usually in the alley between one and two a.m. and that they were always looking for something to eat. She'd seen them checking Katherine's tool shed the night before. Hazel didn't let them go before they accepted her invitation to dinner on Sunday afternoon. Katherine offered to drive.

But that wasn't the most interesting thing that happened that evening, Katherine told Jack as he navigated the twisting road where U.S. 101 narrowed for fifteen miles around Lake Crescent. Earlier in the evening, before dinner, Roy had noticed the claw feet of the baby grand piano's front legs and said, "That piano is old. Kimball stopped making those claw feet before World War One. She probably came out of Chicago in the 1890s." Roy said his father had owned a music store in Knoxville, the Dixie Bandbox, and he was raised with the lore of musical instruments, especially pianos.

Katherine told Jack that Roy crawled under the piano inspecting every inch of its underside while she and Hazel were in the kitchen cleaning up. He'd yelled "Come in here. "Look at this." Lying on his back, he pulled on a wooden lever along the front underside of the piano next to the left leg.

As he brought the lever slowly down, another square leg came down behind the original leg, gently raising the piano enough so the front leg was slightly elevated, allowing it to swing out to the side of the piano. Then he slid over to the other side of the piano and repeated the action with the right leg.

Roy pulled himself up and pointed to the left leg, a copper cylinder was embedded inside. Roy gently pulled the tube out of the leg. The cylinder, now a patina-green, was approximately two-feet long and four inches wide. He unscrewed the lid, which didn't turn easily. The cylinder was empty. He put the lid back on and inserted the tube back into the piano leg. They walked over to the piano's right leg. The hollowed out leg was empty. There was no copper cylinder.

Thirty miles after rounding Lake Crescent, as they turned west onto Route 110 toward La Push, Katherine said, "I'm sorry, I've been yaking all the way."

"Hasn't bothered me," Jack said. "What a great story. You've got to show me the piano legs when we get home."

A few miles before La Push, they pulled off the road into parking area and hiked a mile and a half through the woods to Third Beach. It was quiet as they started down the wide trail, the towering firs on either side hid most of the gray sky. Everything was damp, the dirt trail bed, the giant ferns that covered the forest floor, and the salal bushes that bravely tried to crowd in between the trees. They walked in silence, both wondering when a bear or Bigfoot would leap out at them. They started to hear the distant roar of the ocean surf as the trail began a steep descent. The trees started to thin out. The wind was blowing hard. Gray stratus clouds were sailing low on the horizon when they came out of the woods and onto the beach.

Katherine told Jack it was a perfect time for an introduction to the North Pacific Coast, on the cusp of winter, with the wind gusting to over thirty miles per hour, the slow rolling surf pounding on the beach in ten foot waves, the spray from the white caps combining with the low lying clouds to form an eerie mist over the tall rock formations offshore, and the exhilarating wind-whipped salty air that blew around them with an intimidating force.

Jack murmured. "What is this place?"

Katherine took his hand as they walked through the piles of driftwood down toward the water to where the sand was still wet from the now-ebbed high tide. They turned south toward a tall-cliffed small point of land that jutted out into the water from one end of the inlet. By the time they walked a mile, they were close enough to the point to be in the lee of the wind. They walked back up to the row of driftwood that spanned the length of the beach, huge weather beaten logs, ocean-worn tree root formations, and an endless assortment of small logs and lumber that had washed ashore years ago and were still washing up as they watched.

Katherine started to assemble a rude shelter out of the smaller pieces of wood while Jack stood and stared at the ocean and then turned to help. Before long they'd assembled a windbreak where they sat, leaning against a giant saltwater-aged log.

It was pointless to have a conversation. Any attempt to talk would require shouting over the howling wind and the roaring surf. So they sat huddled together and silently watched the dazzling chaos. Katherine pulled out a pair of binoculars and started scanning the beach to the north. She handed them to Jack and raised her hand toward to the point of land that formed the north boundary of the beach. A solitary fir tree, with a few limbs on top and bent by years of unforgiving wind, hung out over the cliff at a forty-five degree angle. A bald eagle was perched midway down the trunk, scanning the waves.

It was difficult to say how long they sat there in the sand in a semi-hypnotic state, an hour, two hours, each pushing closer to the other, trying to keep warm, each of them occasionally pointing to something in the sky or on the water, each thinking that this was how eternity was meant to be. Jack put his arm around Katherine and she put her head on his shoulder and thought, *I love you Jack, but I'll never let you know. You're not going to break my heart,* and Jack silently sang to himself, *If I loved you, time and again I would try to say. . . .*

They walked back up the beach to the trailhead in silence. By the time they were in the woods and halfway back to the car, everything was soundlessly still again. No wind, no pounding surf, no windblown Pacific Ocean coastline. The door had closed to an ethereal primitive world which had held eternity.

Back on 101, Katherine suggested they take Route 113 through the woods to Sekiu. She told Jack she wanted to see if Buck McCready was around. She wanted to meet him after reading Greeley's piece about Luther Moody in *North Coast Passages*. Jack was happy to do whatever she asked.

Just beyond Beaver, at Sappho Junction, they stopped for gas at Jake's Forest Diner and went in for coffee. They sat at a table in the front window across from a long, chipped white Formica counter of twenty stools with chrome pedestals and red vinyl seats. The place was empty except for two men who sat at the far end of the counter talking to a sweaty, unshaven man with greasy black hair. He was wearing a soiled white smock and pushing a toothpick back and forth in his mouth. "Probably Jake," Katherine said. When they told the waitress, a short middle-aged woman with stringy blonde hair, that they just wanted coffee, she looked surprised and told them there was still some wild blackberry pie left, last of the season. They ordered a piece to share.

Typical of many city dwellers, Jack loved to stop in places like this, places that supposedly exuded local color and always boasted specialties created in a cauldron of hot cooking oil. He started to say as much. But then he watched Katherine peer around the grubby place with the concentration of a health inspector. She examined the plastic-encased four-page menu, reading it line by line. She peered past the counter at the service window, trying to see beyond into the kitchen. She got up and went to the restroom, taking her time walking through the diner. Back at the table, Katherine said nothing.

"Can I tell you something," Jack said as they alternately took bites of the blackberry pie.

"Oh brother, is this the other shoe about to drop?" Katherine said, signaling the waitress for a coffee refill.

Jack looked serious and said, "Remember the first time I saw you? At the café when I came in looking for Larry?"

"Of course I remember."

"You were so serious and so pretty."

"Yes, I have that effect on men when I'm in my whites, sweating in the kitchen, mixing pancake batter and frying eggs."

"What I'm saying is, you're different now. You're not so intense."

"Not so uptight? Yes I am. Just not around you."

"I like this you. This beautiful you."

Katherine blushed and said, "You make me think that things might be all right some time. Let's get out of here."

The ten-mile trip on the gravel roadbed of Route 113 through the forest from Sappho to Route 112 took nearly an hour. It was late afternoon by the time they got to Sekiu and found Buck McCready's place, a large one-story log lodge that served as both McCready's living quarters and the office for Salmon Adventures. They walked up a set of stairs onto the long porch that ran the length of the building and was filled with a row of Adirondack-style chairs fashioned out of logs. A rectangular hand-painted wooden sign hung by a rope on the front door read, "Gone Sasquatchin'"

Jack pointed to another sign that read "Doorbell." He took a long cedar handle inlaid with carved figures of salmon, which was cradled under the sign, and tapped a metal tube which was hanging from the roof of the porch, producing a soft reverberating gong.

Katherine walked to the end of the porch and peered around the side. A gray-bearded man was staring back at her from the rear of the building. He stepped off the back steps. It was the chief cook and bottle washer, Roger Farnsworth. He yelled, "If you're looking for McCready, he's not here," and then disappeared behind the building. They left, both a little spooked by the wild-eyed string bean of a man who was anything but friendly.

They headed east toward Port Smith on Route 112, the same route Arthur Merrick had traveled on his visit to Sekiu. Jack wanted to hear the rest of the piano story. Katherine told him the next day, the day after Hazel and Roy had been there for dinner, Roy called her at the café. He'd been talking to Lonnie about the movable piano legs when he'd been at the building supply that morning. An excited Lonnie, who couldn't resist anything having to do with wood and carpentry, asked Roy to see if Katherine would mind if he came over to take a look.

That afternoon after work, when Katherine got home, Roy, Lonnie, and Walt Beaver were sitting outside the front of her house, each in their own truck, waiting for her. She told Jack, the three of them acted more like excited teenagers than grown men. They headed straight for the piano when she let them in. She came out of the kitchen after starting a pot of coffee and saw three pairs of legs sticking out from under the piano. The three men were all on their back, their hands up in the underside of piano, talking in low tones. She could hear words like "a masterpiece," "a stroke of genius," and "beautiful workmanship."

Later, when she was pouring coffee as they sat around the dining room table, Lonnie and Walt agreed, this was the work of a master craftsman. And who would even come up with such a confounded original idea? They all asked what the Sam hell had been in the legs of the piano?

Walt asked her if he could shave off a tiny sample of the wood. When she said he could, he went out to his truck and brought in a small hand plane. The three men all climbed back under the piano to discuss where to take the sample. When they resurfaced and were getting ready to leave, Lonnie showed her a plastic bag containing a tiny sliver of wood Walt had planed off a corner of one of the secondary legs. The original wood used for the piano was maple but no one could identify the wood used for the secondary legs. "If Walt doesn't know, no one knows. And Walt doesn't know," Lonnie had told her.

Lonnie was going to send the sliver over to Randy Weaver, a professor of forestry at the University of Washington. With Katherine's permission, of course. Weaver would nuke it or whatever they do with an electron microscope and hopefully tell them what the wood was. Elizabeth was going to take the sample to Seattle next week when she took Maude to Swedish Hospital for a biopsy.

It was dark by the time Katherine and Jack got back to Cedar Mills. Jack said the first order of business was to see the piano's secret compartments. He and Katherine both crawled under the piano and Katherine showed him how the lever mechanism worked to slightly elevate the original leg and lower the secondary leg. Then she did the same with the other leg while Jack crawled out to look down the hollowed out legs. When they were done, Katherine told him she had always had a feeling about the piano, that it had something to tell her, and this was it, spooky as it was.

They sat together on the sofa, pushing their shoulders against each other like they had at the ocean, and talked non-stop, then ordered dinner from Chicken in a Basket. After they ate, they took turns playing the piano and singing for a couple hours. It was a little after one a.m. when Katherine walked Jack out to the car. They stood in the cold beside his car, each wondering what would happen next. Katherine settled the matter when she put her arms around Jack and kissed him lightly on the cheek and said goodnight. A few minutes later, Jack was back at her front door.

"Can you come with me for a sec? I want you to see something." he said.

They drove down Cedar Street and then turned into the alley with the headlights off. Jack stopped behind the Madison Café, where Anne's Audi was parked next to Larry's Suburban in the employee parking area.

"That's Anne's car," Jack said. "What's it doing here in the middle of the night?"

Katherine told him it was the back of the café and Larry's apartment was upstairs. "Those are the stairs to his place," she said pointing to the wooden staircase that led up to the small deck attached to the apartment.

They sat in the car staring up at Larry's dark apartment. "What do you think I should do," Jack said.

"Probably nothing," Katherine said, embarrassed for him. "What are you going to do, run up the stairs, pound on the door, and tell your mother to get home?"

They both laughed. Jack said "Good God, what's got into her?" and then started slowly up the alley.

They were halfway up the alley with the headlights still off when they saw two shadows dart out of Katherine's back gate and run across Second Avenue and up the alley behind Maude's.

"The Dolan's!" Katherine exclaimed.

Jack turned on the lights and stepped on the gas. By the time they got up the alley behind Maude's, the little bandits were gone. Jack stopped the car and Katherine got out. She shouted in a loud whisper, "Clare! Curtis! It's all right. We want to help." But there was only silence. They slowly drove around the block and back to Katherine's looking for the two little scavengers who had disappeared into the night.

For years Katherine had trained herself to not think about it, but tonight she lay in bed wondering about the baby she'd given up to the nuns in Los Angeles. She'd lied to her mother. She knew the child was a girl, a girl she refused to name even though the nuns urged her to call her something. Naming the baby would be a form of possession. The little girl would be a bit older than Clare Dolan now. Katherine hoped she wasn't running through an alley in the middle of the night looking for something to eat.

Maude and Milos at New Morning Farm

After all their years together in Tennessee, the Lindsays and the Willits were more family than employer and employee. Roy and Hazel had built the Lindsay's horse farm into a force in the quarter horse world. The couple had helped raise Jack. They'd been the rock Anne leaned on when Alan died. Then they'd stoically moved to the Northwest because they couldn't let their Annie move without them. But two thousand miles away from family and friends, Hazel and Roy were lonely and regretted they'd left Tennessee. Then Katherine, Bobby, and Larry came into their lives and inspired a revival of a Sewanee tradition, Sunday afternoon at the Willit's.

The family-style custom was being played out in full-force on Sunday afternoon when Katherine took Maude, Milos, and Rascal out to New Morning Farm. Maude's health was slowly improving. She could walk a little on her own but Milos insisted they bring her wheelchair over Maude's protestations.

Maude and Milos sat in the back seat. Rascal curled up on Milos' lap which prompted Katherine to remark that the once feisty little dog seemed to have taken to him. Milos said he was finally able to teach Rascal some Polish and joked the dog liked being bilingual. Maude shook her head and groused that Milo had become a real comedian. But she didn't feel like laughing. She was worried about her biopsy in Seattle next week. Terry Buzzby, the surgeon who'd removed her appendix said he didn't like the look of her liver and insisted she have what was supposed to be a routine procedure.

At the farm, Katherine was pleased to see her old Toyota station wagon parked beside Roy's truck. Katherine had wanted to give it to Donny St. John, but Sadie said no, he should have to pay something for it. So she'd sold it to Donny for fifty dollars and taken a $250 loss after she'd paid Ray Kesecker for getting it in good enough shape for Donny to drive back and forth to the farm.

"So I see Donny finally got your old car," Maude said as they parked. "Ray Kesecker told me he and Scooter had got it going good enough to get him to work. Chip Franklin told me he paid the full insurance premium for him. Donny's paying him back so much a week. Good for you, Katherine."

Maude held Katherine's arm as they walked into the kitchen where Hazel greeted them with hugs. Milos followed, carrying Rascal and his little bed. He put the bed and Rascal on the far side of the kitchen, saying something to the dog in Polish. The little guy laid down, shaking in fright.

Katherine was certain Milos would be as uncomfortable as Rascal. She remembered his gruff exterior on their Saturday afternoon together and was surprised when he politely introduced himself to Hazel, taking her hand and bowing with a European formality unknown to Americans.

Maude stayed in the kitchen gabbing with Hazel while Katherine took Milos in to meet Roy, who was in the living room watching football. Roy told her Jack was up at the horse barn with Donny. Katherine said she'd go find him and Milos went with her. When they started out the kitchen door, Rascal jumped out of his bed and started barking. Milos said something in Polish, but Rascal didn't want Milos to leave. Roy came in the kitchen when he heard the commotion. He scooped Rascal up and gently told him to come sit with him. The dog went quiet and the two disappeared into the living room.

Up at the horse barn, Katherine and Jack watched Donny lead Milos through the barn as Donny eagerly told him about each horse as though he'd known them for years. When they started back to the house, Donny told them, "no," he wasn't coming in for dinner. He had work to do.

At the dinner table where the conversation was constant, Katherine watched Milos as he sat politely listening, smiling and watching everyone with a friendly inquisitiveness. He was enjoying Maude's holding forth as they ate, barely allowing anyone else to get a word in. She asked Jack if he'd been out to his grandparents old place, where his mother grew up and then clucked when Jack said his mother never talked about her parents. Whenever he'd asked about his grandparents, she'd always said, "not now, it doesn't matter anyway."

"So she probably didn't tell you she was the state champion barrel racer either," Maude said. "We all called her Little Annie Oates back then. The whole town was proud of her."

"Annie never talks about growing up here in Cedar Mills," Hazel said.

Maude went on tell them about Anne's father, Jack's grandfather, Carl Oates, the only veterinarian in the county for years. "He was a legend around here, a saint to the dairy farmers who fought tooth and nail to survive." Maude said. "Sometimes he'd hear through the grapevine that so-and-so had a dauncy cow down and there he'd be. He'd show up casually, like he was just stopping by to chat. Before he left, he'd have the cow back on the road to recovery, telling the farmer to pay him when he could. They were always bringing him milk, butter, chickens, and vegetables in payment. Jack, your grandmother Edna always said they'd have to invite Coxey's Army for dinner every night unless she gave most of it away to people who needed it."

All eyes were focused on Maude as she continued. "And she probably never told you about how she and Alan were married here at Trinity Episcopal by Father Tom. My my, what a day that was. Anne just out of the UW bringing this handsome, black-haired, divinity student home to marry. He was so polite, so thoughtful. It was obvious Anne was head-over-heels in love. What a time that was."

When Maude finished, Roy said, "We're hearing all this for the first time."

Jack said, "I never knew anything about Cedar Mills. Anne and Alan never talked about their past."

"Whenever I asked about her growing up, she'd said she didn't want to talk about it," Hazel said, getting up to start clearing the table.

"By the way, where is Anne? And Larry told me he'd probably be here today," Maude said with a wink.

Hazel said "Anne said she was going to Seattle to one of her alumni board meetings. Larry called and said something had come up and he couldn't make it."

After dinner, Hazel, Roy, and Jack got out their guitar, fiddle, and mandolin, and played before the apple pie came out of the oven. Hazel enjoined Katherine to come up and sing high harmony with her on three hymns to finish the set. When they were done, Maude clapped loudly. Milos stood and bowed to her with a smile.

With everyone back in the dining room for dessert, Milos told Jack his mandolin reminded him of an instrument someone had at Treblinka. "It was called a Jewish dulcimer," he said. "Every evening the fellow would play the same mournful tune over and over, plucking each note on a single string. Years later when I was teaching at Yeshiva in New York, I saw my first western movie. It was an old one with Gene, Gene Aw..., Gene Aw..."

Roy broke in, "Gene Autry."

Milos continued, "Gene Autry. He was playing a guitar and singing this song, the same one from the camp. 'Red River Valley.' The saddest tune I'd ever heard. I didn't know it had words. I bought a recording and listened to it for months. One phrase, *Do not hasten to bid me adieu*. So oddly formal for a cowboy. I never forgot it, this cowboy singing, *Come and sit by my side if you love me, Do not hasten to bid me adieu*. It made me smile."

Roy raised his hand holding an imaginary glass and said, "I propose a toast to 'The Red River Valley.'"

Jack raised his hand and answered, "Here, here," and everyone followed with "To the Red River Valley."

At the end of the afternoon, Hazel and Roy walked Maude and Milos outside while Katherine brought the car around. Hazel told Maude she hoped to hear more about Annie's family. Maude said there was plenty more to tell. Hazel would have to come by for coffee one afternoon.

On the way back to town, Maude asked Katherine if she'd go with her to Seattle on Thursday when Elizabeth took her for the biopsy. She'd already talked to Elizabeth who liked the idea, saying Katherine would be a much needed help. They'd be there two nights, Thursday and Friday, and be home on Saturday morning. Katherine said of course she'd go.

A Trip to the City

On Thursday, shortly after noon, Katherine was at Maude's helping Elizabeth get Maude ready for the trip to Seattle. When she asked where Rascal was, Maude told her Milo had taken him to his place. Elizabeth said "Well at least our cats won't have to put up with him." Not long after, they were on their way out of town with Katherine and Maude in the back seat of Elizabeth's Mercedes 350SL sedan. Maude was supposed to be at Swedish Hospital between three and four that afternoon to check-in. The biopsy was scheduled for Friday morning at eight o'clock.

Maude was atypically silent as they left town. Except for the radio softly tuned to the classical music of KING-FM the inside of the car was quiet. Maude dozed. Elizabeth was happy to be alone in the front and Katherine was thinking how liberating it felt to be leaving for a trip out of town on a weekday.

She'd left the restaurant that morning after the breakfast rush. The new waitress, Muriel McClune, had started on Monday and fit in perfectly. Muriel was a seasoned "hash slinger" as she called herself when Katherine interviewed her. She knew Sadie. They'd worked together at the Tomahawk One Stop and at the Brumble Mill Diner. Sadie had said Muriel would be perfect for the job and Sadie was right. The perky, redhead in her late forties, knew half of the café's customers. On her first day, it was like she'd been there for months. Sadie assumed the second cook's position with no trouble and by the time Katherine left on Thursday she knew Sadie was going to do a good job while she was gone.

But Bobby, who fretted over any change in the routine, was upset. On Monday when Muriel had shown up, Katherine sat with him on the steps leading up to the second floor, explaining she wasn't quitting and more importantly, he wasn't going to lose his job. By Thursday morning, he was still pouting when she left.

Just past Big Eddie's Burger Shack, when they turned off U.S. 101 onto Route 104, the road to the Hood Canal bridge, the sleeping Maude woke up when she nodded onto Katherine's shoulder. A few minutes later, she took a folded newspaper out of her bag and handed it to Katherine, saying "I thought you might like to see this."

It was the "Regional News" section of the morning's *Seattle P-I*. Maude pointed to the "Local News Briefs" where the lead story was headlined: "Local Cult Leader Jailed for Assault." Katherine read:

> *The leader of a religious cult based in Catchall and his*
> *common-law wife were arrested on Wednesday night for*
> *aggravated assault and public drunkenness in Gold Bar.*
> *According to the Snohomish County Sheriff's office, Mitchell*
> *Lodong, the self-described "Bishop" of the Western Washington*
> *Synod of Sanitarians and his companion, Susan Owling, were*
> *taken into custody outside the Minnow Lake Inn in downtown*
> *Gold Bar, where deputies found them beating a man with their*
> *shoes. The victim, Arthur Fletcher of no known address, had*
> *been tied to a utility pole while Lodong, 61, and Owling, 59,*
> *were chanting "We shall smite the devil," as they pummeled*
> *him with their footwear. When the handcuffed Lodong was led*
> *to police car, he shouted: "Leviticus 28:12. You shall smote he*
> *who curses the Lord with thy left foot." Bail had not been set at*
> *press time.*

Katherine handed the paper back to Maude, "She's finally locked up where she belongs."

As they passed Poulsbo, crossing the bridge onto Bainbridge Island, a few miles from the Seattle ferry, Katherine told Maude about last Saturday night when Jack discovered his mother's car at Larry's and how they'd chased the Dolan kids up the alley in the middle of the night, describing her plan to catch them in the tool shed.

"I heard you out there yelling at them," Maude said. "But what are you going to do if you catch them, have them hauled off to the calaboose? It's their folks, those deadbeats Bud and Sophie, who should be locked up for child neglect." She told Katherine a lot of people in town left food out for them and said she was perturbed at Will McCann for not doing something about Bud and Sophie.

They caught the two forty-five boat at Winslow for the thirty-minute ride to Seattle. Katherine stayed in the car with Maude while Elizabeth went up to the passenger deck to get coffee for everyone. Maude said, "I'm glad you're going to spend some time with Elizabeth. I know you've heard about her shunning Larry since he came to Cedar Mills, but she's embarrassed about her brother. She's really not the harridan some people make her out to be."

Once they landed at Colman Dock in Seattle, it was a quick drive up Marion Street to Boren and one block over to Madison and the hospital, which sat on First Hill, the west side of Capitol Hill, overlooking downtown. They had Maude registered and in her room by four o'clock. Elizabeth left for the University District with the wood sample from Katherine's piano Lonnie had given her to drop off at Randy Weaver's office. She told Katherine she'd get them checked in at the hotel on the way back.

Maude fussed for a while, refusing to get into bed at four in the afternoon, calling nurses in to give them instructions, and in general, making a pest of herself. When Katherine observed the small suite definitely wasn't a regular hospital room, Maude replied of course it wasn't. She said her late husband Herschel, known as "King," was not only mayor of Cedar Mills for a generation but was a potentate in the Democratic Party, serving as state chairman for eight years. "He knew every politician that mattered, Democrat and Republican, and any power broker who even pretended to have clout," she said. "When there was opposition to Swedish expanding on First Hill, he was part of a group that made it happen. They'll never forget King Doud at this hospital."

They sat in two wing chairs in front of a window on the hospital's eighth floor with a sliver of a view of Elliott Bay through the buildings on Boren Avenue, just enough to see the yellow-orange sunset over the Olympic Mountains while Maude talked about Elizabeth. How everyone had thought how odd it was when Lonnie had married her, a society girl from the East.

"We all said it wouldn't last a year. But they've been together forty years now," Maude said. "Lonnie acts like a dipstick sometimes, but it's a front. My brother is as sly as they come. He and Walt Beaver have made a fortune exporting hardwood lumber to Japan and they couldn't have done it without Elizabeth. She keeps the books."

Elizabeth returned to the hospital a little after six o'clock and told Katherine they were checked in at the Westminster Mews hotel, a block down Boren Avenue at Spring Street. Not long after, Maude kicked them out, saying she wanted to be alone, she had to make some phone calls. They could come back later if they wanted.

It was a short walk to the Westminster Mews, which had been a landmark First Hill apartment building, built between the wars, and recently renovated into a boutique hotel. The doorman greeted them with a "good evening again, Mrs. Martin and this must be Ms. Baker."

The doting concierge ushered them to the elevator, telling them Presto, the restaurant on the top floor, served for another two hours. He highly recommended it.

Thirty minutes later, Katherine walked into Presto and saw Elizabeth at a banquette across the room, nursing a martini. The restaurant was surprisingly informal compared to the rest of the hotel, a small, well-lit place with rows of banquettes along two walls and a few tables in the middle. The tables were covered with blue and white checked tablecloths to match the rest of the restaurant's décor. The soft yellow light from ceiling lamps that hung low throughout the room, gave it a warm, intimate atmosphere. In the background, Linda Ronstadt sang old standards backed by the Nelson Riddle orchestra.

Katherine ordered an iced tea. When the waiter returned with her drink, he told them about the evening's special. "We have Chicken Fried Steak ala Bakersfield," he officiously announced. "Accompanied by Idaho russet potatoes fried in seasoned Crisco, and fresh canned beans Del Monte." As he finished, a short bald-headed man in chef's whites came up behind Katherine and said, "Sound like the old days?"

Katherine stood and turned around. "Oscar Mendes, Oscar, Oscar," she said wrapping him in a bear hug.

They stood side by side with their arms around each other as Katherine introduced Oscar to Elizabeth, telling her how Oscar had hired her years ago in Bakersfield. She had walked into the Battista Diner, Steaks and Chops, Open Twenty-four Hours, looking for a job, her first real job after getting out of jail and finishing the culinary course at the community college.

"He taught me everything I know," she said patting his shoulder.

"Not everything," he told Elizabeth. "This was one tough cookie when she walked into the Battista. Quiet, never said a word. Sullen. See seemed perpetually angry. But she worked like no one I'd ever seen. Did everything I asked without question." Oscar continued with a story of how a drunk cowboy grabbed Katherine's rear end a few days after she'd started. "He ended up in the parking lot with a face full of gravel. She had a rep after that. No one touched her again."

After a few more stories about the old days, Oscar recommended the Crab Louie salad with sourdough crostini and a shared plate of clams casino, oysters Rockefeller, and shrimp scampi. Before he left, he told Katherine a job was waiting at Presto anytime she wanted. After dinner, they walked back to the hospital to say goodnight to Maude. She was sitting with Jack, who looked like he'd just come from the office.

Maude pointed to a bouquet of flowers and a box of candy. She chirped, "Look at what this dear old fashioned boy brought me."

Katherine beamed when she saw Jack, who stood and offered Elizabeth his chair. He walked over to Katherine and took her hand. Katherine whispered to him, "You didn't tell me you were coming to the hospital," and he whispered back, "You're here aren't you? My boss told me Maude was here and that you'd come with her. So of course, I'm here."

When Katherine asked with a smile, "So how does your boss know these things?" Jack just shrugged.

When Katherine thought back on that time in Seattle with Maude, she always remembered how she felt when she'd walked into Maude's hospital room and saw Jack, the embodiment of what she came to call the Professional Jack, the city lawyer whose natural sophistication made her uncomfortable because in her mind, she was everything the opposite. His personality hadn't changed. He was still the same kind, interested, and caring person she'd come to know. But he exuded poise and sophistication in this metropolitan milieu. He was part of a world that would never include her and whatever kind of love they might pretend to share was pointless.

The three women were back in Cedar Mills on Saturday morning after leaving the city as the sun was coming up over the Cascades. Maude had called each of them that morning at five, announcing she was checking out and the car needed to be downstairs in an hour. They were on the eight o'clock boat at Edmonds, because Maude insisted it was a shorter drive home than going to Bainbridge Island. Elizabeth had offered no argument, she just wanted to get home.

When Katherine got home, the house was cold and dark after two days of sitting empty. She was overcome with ennui. She unpacked and started the oil stove in the dining room. When she called the farm, she told Hazel it was good to be home. *Good to be home*. The first time she'd ever thought that.

Hazel talked excitedly about Thanksgiving, now just a few days away. The number of people coming to dinner kept growing and she couldn't wait to see her sister May, who would be arriving on Tuesday. After they hung up, Katherine brought a blanket and pillow out to living room, laid down on the sofa, and tried to sleep.

While Katherine Was Away

If Katherine had looked down the alley on Saturday morning when she'd got home from Seattle, she'd have seen a platoon of pickups parked at the back of the Madison Café. Greeley's Ford F150, the same model as Lonnie's, but an off-white instead of black, was parked next to Larry's Suburban. Lonnie's truck as well as three pickups belonging to the Beavers, Walt, Matt, and Harley, were also in the parking area along with Roy's.

The men were working on a remodeling project they'd started after the café closed the day before, an office for Katherine. An office off the kitchen had been laid out in the original blueprints when Greeley started renovating the café, but because he'd decided to put his office upstairs, the one on the first floor had never been built. The wiring for it had been installed and was in the ceiling ready to be dropped. So it was a fairly simple matter of clearing out the ten-by-twelve foot area in the front corner of the storeroom and putting up two walls of studs and drywall, a task that was no challenge for Lonnie and the Beavers.

By late Saturday afternoon, Larry and Roy were painting the interior walls, Lonnie and Walt were hanging shelves on the outside walls, Greeley was running a new phone line, and Matt and Harley were installing an old walnut door with a large oval of clear beveled glass and a transom they'd found on the second floor of the theater. It didn't go with the stark surroundings of the restaurant storeroom, but everyone agreed the door was a touch of class and had to be used. They'd also found, a large walnut desk with brass hardware that Lonnie said he'd give his left you-know-what for.

By five o'clock, the office was finished and everyone was packed up and gone. Katherine had missed the hubbub down the alley. She'd stayed inside, alternately lying on the sofa and then playing the piano. She was exhausted after the Seattle trip but couldn't sleep. She kept thinking about her time with Maude and Elizabeth. Whenever she'd been alone with one of them, they'd eagerly unloaded family gossip in an unending stream. It had gone on for two days and she was worn out. And then there was seeing Jack in his big-city surroundings. It bothered her.

Over dinner at Presto on Thursday night, Elizabeth, in the wake of three martinis, told Katherine how she'd met Lonnie during the last year of World War II, when he was a ninety-day wonder midshipman at the Coast Guard academy at New London and she was a junior at Connecticut College for Women. They met at a mixer sponsored by the college to entertain the lonely ensigns-to-be. Elizabeth Bradford was a sassy, outspoken, spoiled twenty-year old and many of the men at New London were small-town boys from the Midwest and West who were easily intimidated by the sophisticated co-eds. Alonzo Martin wasn't. Elizabeth said he was the same cheeky and never shy Lonnie Martin he is today. But she also saw how smart and respectful he was and she fell in love.

She'd always been a rebel. She refused to follow the plan her parents had laid out, going to New York City after graduation and finding a job until she met a stock broker, or lawyer, or doctor to marry with the goal of ending up a dutiful housewife in Greenwich, Fairfield, or Rye, drinking a glass or two of wine before picking up the kids from school and hoping her husband would be home from the city. Just like the horrible little Ellen that Larry had married. No, she told her parents, she was marrying Lonnie and going out West.

Greeley was born a year later at Charleston, South Carolina, and Judge Lawrence Adams Bradford III and his wife Margaret ventured south of the Mason-Dixon Line for the first time to see their new, yet to be named grandson. In an uncharacteristic display of levity, the judge said if they were taking the baby west after the war, they should name him Horace Greeley Martin. "Do you understand?" he asked to the couple. "Horace Greeley. Go west young man."

Katherine heard more Martin family lore from Maude on Friday afternoon, after she'd recovered from the anesthesia and Elizabeth had gone shopping. Maude talked at length about her long marriage to King. They'd met at the University of Washington where he'd been a callow farm boy from east of the mountains whose only interest seemed to be rowing on the crew with his best friend and fraternity brother, Hercules Pushkin. Maude married him and took him back to Cedar Mills where he'd made a fortune in timber leases and real estate before he got involved in politics. Lonnie and Elizabeth spent years nagging them to build a big new house up on the hill near them. But she and King were happy to stay in the little house on Second Avenue where they'd started their life together. They were right in the middle of everything, just where Maude had to be.

Maude told her Greeley had opened the café as more of a hobby than anything, never thinking it would be as successful as it was. Then *sotto voce* she said Greeley had told her a few weeks ago he was hoping Katherine would eventually take over the business. He wanted to devote his time to the historical society and getting back to writing westerns.

Their stay in Seattle culminated with Katherine and Elizabeth's Friday night dinner at Jack's apartment. They'd both told Maude they weren't going to go because they wanted to be with her at the hospital. Maude said "balderdash." She was tired of both of them and besides, they had to find out as much as they could about Jack's life in the city. She expected a full report.

Late Friday afternoon, before Jack picked them up, Elizabeth returned to Maude's room loaded down with shopping bags from Frederick & Nelson and the Bon Marche. She told Katherine that she and Maude wanted to do something in return for her help. She'd bought three different outfits, a skirt, blouse and hounds tooth jacket with a gold necklace, a black cocktail dress with a faux pearl necklace, and a black business suit with a pencil skirt, ivory blouse, and black jacket with a silver rope chain necklace.

The two women watched with glee as Katherine opened each box and said, "oh no, you can't do this." Maude said "oh, pshaw." Neither of them had a daughter and they'd both always wanted a little girl to dress up. They made her try on everything, ordering her into the bathroom to change and come out for a viewing. Everything fit perfectly, although Katherine said she thought the blouses were a bit tight.

They both said she had a beautiful body and didn't understand why she worked so hard to hide it. She'd moved her hands across her front and asked if it wasn't a little too form fitting. Maude said, "You've got beautiful breasts. Don't you want Jack to see a little bit of that?" Then the two elderly women laughed, giggling like two schoolgirls.

Early Friday evening, Elizabeth and Katherine sat in the lobby of the Westminster Mews waiting for Jack. Elizabeth wouldn't stop talking about Larry and how bad she felt that she'd shunned her brother when he'd turned up Cedar Mills. Larry had been the golden boy, the one who was supposed to make good in recompense for her messing up by marrying Lonnie and moving out West. He didn't disappoint. There were a few little forks in the road, business school instead of law school, Wharton of all places. He'd married that little twerp Ellen, who divorced him after three years, walking away with a small fortune. But he'd made big money, he was generous, and considerate. He had given Greeley a new start when he needed it. Then he'd screwed up and went to jail. Elizabeth didn't know how to forgive him. She wanted to reconcile but she didn't know how.

Katherine suggested she just be honest with him. Tell him she wanted to patch things up. Elizabeth clucked and said that was out of the question. She told Katherine she was worried about him though. When she saw him at the hospital for the first time in years, he wasn't the same Larry she remembered. He wasn't the dynamic, take-charge guy she'd known and his new constant kidding around was just a front.

The conversation ended with Katherine saying, "Larry's been a good friend. He's helped me more than once. He's like an uncle to me. You should tell him how you feel."

Jack's condo was on the eighth floor of a high rise at Second Avenue and Blanchard, an easy walk to his office at Third and Pine. Elizabeth reported to Maude the two-bedroom apartment was immaculate and that Jack had fixed a elegantly simple dinner of grilled salmon with a lemon dill sauce, brown rice with sweet and sour pearl onions, and steamed haricot vert with herbed butter.

As Jack gave them a tour, Elizabeth forwardly said the place must have set him back quite a bit, what with the view of Elliott Bay and the mountains. Jack told her the apartment was part of the package he'd been offered by Pushkin, McDonald & Fishkin. It was owned by the law firm. They'd taken it as part of a lawsuit settlement and now the partners wanted to unload it. It was his free and clear if he stayed with the firm for two years. All he paid were the condo fees and the taxes, which amounted to a lot less than rent for a similar place.

Katherine didn't say much while they were there. While Jack worked in the kitchen and Elizabeth watched the evening news, she walked through the apartment quietly examining everything in a way that would have made Maude proud. Except for the three instrument stands in the living room which held Jack's mandolin, guitar, and banjo, there was nothing personal about the place. It was nicely but coldly furnished and decorated like any decent American hotel.

She came back to the kitchen and watched him fix dinner, asking if she could help. It was then she'd realized how naïve she'd been to think their time together on the weekends, at her house, at the ocean, at Gosport, and at the farm, were part of Jack's world. She now saw how he really lived, impersonal and professional, a man handcuffed to his career. He'd come to Cedar Mills on the weekends for amusement because he had nothing better to do.

In the category of reporting to Maude however, the headline of the evening was what happened when Elizabeth asked for a glass of wine before dinner. He apologized and said he didn't have any, he was a recovering alcoholic. But he would call down to the doorman and have a bottle delivered. He went on to tell them how he'd started drinking heavily in law school at Vanderbilt and how it continued when he spent a year in New Orleans on a fellowship at Tulane, studying maritime law.

"I ruined someone's life because of my drinking," he said. "Thankfully he wasn't killed, but for all intents and purposes, his life was over. I live with it every day."

The subject of wine was dropped. Over dinner, inspired by Maude's orders, Elizabeth asked Jack how such a died-in-the-wool Southern boy had landed in Chicago, of all places. Jack told her after the accident, a friend had talked him into a change of scene. They decided to move north to Chicago.

"Was he a lawyer too?" Elizabeth had asked.

Jack said the friend was a she and yes, she was a lawyer. They'd met at Vanderbilt. After a couple of years together in Chicago, their relationship wasn't working and he decided to move on. Seattle seemed like a logical place, he specialized in maritime law and his mother and Roy and Hazel were nearby. As luck would have it, he'd received an offer from Hercules Pushkin just when he'd started looking for a job in Seattle.

After that, he'd kept them laughing with stories of a Southern boy adjusting to life in the Northwest. Then he proudly announced that after weeks of being nothing more than an intern, his boss had just given him a real case, a salvage case involving an old passenger ship from the Alaska gold rush days named the *Arctic Maid*.

Greeley Makes An Announcement

Katherine walked to Trinity Episcopal on Sunday morning, feeling a little sorry this would be her last time at the organ. She'd started to enjoy the weekly ritual, in spite of Reverend Tom's tedious sermons on St. Paul's letters to the Corinthians. Brett Smallwood told her now that Margie Parker would be back at the organ next week, he'd like her to join the choir. Father Tom heartily seconded the motion. She'd told them she'd think about it.

She sat at the organ, sneaking looks at the congregation and was surprised to see Elizabeth and Lonnie, who hadn't been to a ten o'clock service since Larry moved to Cedar Mills. They'd been going to the eight o'clock service so Elizabeth could avoid her brother. "The Express Lane," Lonnie called it. "You get your wine and wafer, no letters to anybody, and get out in time to enjoy the rest of Sunday."

Elizabeth had told her in Seattle how the Martins and Douds kept Trinity alive during the late 1960s into the 1970s when the congregation was dwindling and everyone was debating whether or not God was dead. Not only had they poured money into the church treasury but King and Lonnie had gone to Seattle to tell Bishop Seymour that the diocesan board could not close the church and they'd do whatever it took to keep Trinity alive. The Bishop acquiesced and sent Reverend Tom Flatte into the breach with orders to save the church.

She saw Jack in his regular place, sitting with his mother, and was surprised at how, after two days of trying to dislike him, she felt her heart skip and her cheeks flush. After seeing him in Seattle, she knew they shared a bond. He was a lone rider, like her. Someone who kept their pain inside and never forgave themselves.

After the service, Greeley caught up with Katherine as she was walking out the back door of the church and asked if he could walk with her. Would she mind stopping at the café on her way home, he asked. Out on Fourth Avenue in front of the church, Elizabeth was talking to Larry. She had a hand on her brother's arm. It looked like an emotional conversation. Greeley whispered, "Well, if doesn't that beat all. She's talking to him."

Greeley talked nervously as they walked over to Main Street and east toward the café. "I asked Elizabeth to put together a report on the café's results for the first three quarters this year and I've decided to make some changes."

"Oh boy," Katherine said. "The other shoe's going to drop."

"After a fashion," Greeley said with a grim expression. "We need to make some adjustments. First of all, I never envisioned this place to be a money maker. I just thought it would a nice friendly place for folks to schmooze and have a decent meal, something they'd never get down the street at Jill's Grill."

He told her, much to his surprise, the café had made a profit beyond anything he could have imagined, mainly because Katherine was running the place.

Katherine interrupted and said, "It's about *all* the people who work here."

Greeley agreed, "We've got a great gang and you hit a home run when you hired Muriel." Then he said, "As of today, I'm officially making you manager of the Madison Café. That means a lot more responsibility and of course an increase in salary. I'll have Elizabeth teach you how to keep the daily books and make the bank deposits. There'll be a lot of other things to learn, but you're pretty much running the place now. What do you say, do you want the job?"

Katherine tried to catch her breath and said "Yes, yes, yes."

Greeley unlocked the café's front door and entered first, motioning for her to follow him down the kitchen. He stopped at the store room and swept an arm toward the interior, motioning for her to walk in. Just inside to the right was the old walnut door to her new office. On the wall to the left of the door was a small white sign with black lettering that read, "Katherine Baker, Manager." Katherine opened the door and walked inside. She turned to Greeley in tears, who was proudly standing behind her beaming like a Cheshire cat.

"I don't know what to say," she said, hugging him.

"I'm expecting a lot of you. But I know you can handle it," he said returning her embrace.

Katherine walked around the office, touching the antique walnut desk, noting with surprise there was even a phone so she wouldn't have to stand in the hall to place orders over the noise of the kitchen. She sat in the walnut high-back swivel captain's chair that came with the desk and turned around. On the wall, above two four-foot high walnut bookcases were two large framed black and white photos that Hazel had hung as the office was being finished the day before. One was of a spindly little colt standing next to its mother, trying to look brave. The caption read, *Sissy at Two Weeks With Her mother Hannah*. The other photo was a full head shot of Sissy staring directly into the camera over the door of her stall. The caption read, *Sissy at New Morning Farm*.

Greeley left Katherine alone in the office, where she couldn't stop blubbering. She heard people coming into the dining room. The coffee hour after the Trinity Church service had been moved from the parish hall to the café dining room. When she finally came out of her office, Katherine was greeted by a crowd of well-wishers. Everyone was there, people from the church, everyone from the café, and folks who saw the cafe was open and wandered in.

After Greeley made the formal announcement of Katherine's promotion to café manager, Hazel and Anne started cutting the cakes and pies they'd baked the day before. It was mid-afternoon by the time it was all over and Katherine was sitting at a table with Lonnie and Walt who were telling her that Randy Weaver had identified the wood from her piano. Lonnie handed her a fax from the forestry professor declaring it to be *Chloroxylon Swietenia*, East Indian Satinwood, native to southern India. Katherine read through the description, "yellowish brown…hard and durable…even more dense than the very dense East Indian Rosewood." Lonnie told her Randy wanted to see the piano himself, maybe take some photographs for the School of Forestry's library.

"I told him that was up to you" Lonnie said. "So he said he'd call and see if you'll let him come over to take a look at those gizmos under your piano."

Walt chimed in, "Randy's a good boy. You'll be safe."

Lonnie laughed, "He's a nice boy. He only hugs trees." Then they both laughed.

Maude rounded the table and stood behind Katherine. "Randy's a fine boy. These two jokers helped him through the UW after his dad was killed in the woods."

"We thought he'd be finished when he got his degree at the UDub, but then there was Montana and Wisconsin, then Yale. He wouldn't stop. He's got enough sheepskin to paper an outhouse."

Walt said laughing, "I asked him, you're a doctor but you don't make house calls?

Lonnie bragged that Randy used their lumber operation as a case study in his Ph.D. dissertation: *In Pursuit of the Rising Sun: Modalities in the Export of Lumber to Japan.* "Walt said we'd be famous, be on *Sixty Minutes* or *Johnny Carson*, but it didn't work out." They burst out laughing again.

It was late afternoon when Katherine and Jack left the café and walked up the alley with Milos and Maude. Jack pushed Maude in her wheelchair. Katherine and Milos walked behind. She asked Milos how Rascal had got along at his house while Maude was in Seattle. Milos told her he had a good time, he loved chasing the chickens who easily out-ran him.

"You've got chickens?" Katherine asked with surprise.

"He's got chickens, two goats, and a burro," Maude said. "Is that it, boyfriend?"

"Except for a cat who lives in the woods," Milos answered.

"Walt and the boys keep bringing him strays and he can't say no," Maude said. "But *I've* never seen them. He's never asked me to his place."

Milos chuckled. "For good reason, I don't want you moving in. I've got enough problems."

They all laughed as Katherine and Jack said goodbye at Katherine's back gate.

Later that night at the Blue Heron, where Jack insisted he take Katherine to celebrate her promotion, they sat looking out at the Strait as the water started to disappear in the darkening dusk. They talked quietly over dinner, Jack's grilled salmon and Katherine's crab cakes. She made Jack laugh when she told him about the missing bottles of vodka and felt relieved that her confession seemed to him more of a joke than a transgression.

On their way out, Katherine spotted Bert Peck and his wife Ina sitting next to the fireplace. She pulled Jack over to their table to say hello. Bert looked different in his civilian clothes, without his Bateman's Bread uniform, and his wife, a small woman with short, black curly hair and darting eyes, made Katherine curious. Bert stood and shook hands with Jack, telling him how happy he was that his mother had bought that eighty acres from them, now it was being put to use.

As Katherine and Jack walked out, Ina said, "It's fun to see a couple so much in love."

Bert nodded in agreement. "You know who she is don't you? She's the girl who ran away with the high school teacher years ago. Doesn't seem possible."

"I don't remember," Ina said.

Thanksgiving at New Morning Farm

The three days before Thanksgiving were chaotic at the Madison Café partly because Katherine Baker, Manager didn't know what to do. She didn't feel comfortable sitting in her new office all day and when she was there, it became a magnet. People would wander in and want to talk.

It started on Monday morning when Bert Peck made his bread delivery just as the café opened at six o'clock. Bert got Bobby to check in the delivery and then walked into Katherine's office. He told her how nice it was to see her at the Blue Heron. "Ina said you and Jack fit together like two pieces of a puzzle," he said and then without asking, took a seat in the chair at the end of her desk. He wanted to tell her about a new line of pastries Sig Bateman wanted to sell. He said if she was willing, the Madison Café would be a test market for daily deliveries of bear claws, maple bars, and butter horns from a Norwegian bakery in Poulsbo owned by a cousin of Sig's.

Bert explained in exhaustive detail how they would provide the display case and give them the first delivery at no cost, just to see how the goods would sell. He carefully outlined Sig's marketing ploy that was more complex than Katherine thought possible for selling pastry in a restaurant. While Bert was still yakking, Jack stopped for his sandwich and coffee on the way to the ferry. Sadie had given him the power breakfast sandwich and coffee, telling him with a teasing, artificial formality that the manager was in a meeting.

Later in the morning, she got a full report from Larry and Sadie about how things went on Friday when she was in Seattle with Maude and Elizabeth. Larry said that Sadie had only two or three complaints about her pancakes. Then she'd had two long conversations with an emotional Bobby about how they would get the store room straightened out again so he could do his inventory just like he had before the new office had disrupted things. Then Muriel, the new waitress, wandered in to her office to announce that Randy Weaver was her first cousin. Finally Jack called and she closed the office door.

Jack told her he was doing some leg work for Hercules Pushkin in advance of their meeting with a potential client from British Columbia who was interested in salvaging what remained of an old passenger ship that was buried in the mud on the north end of Lake Union. He was on his way to the Pike Place Market to talk to Silas Peavey, the owner of a clock shop and a friend of Hercules, who had referred the Canadian, Paul Merrick, to Pushkin. Then on Wednesday he was meeting with a professor at the University of Washington, Dr. Edward Balfour, who had taken Merrick to the remains of the old ship named the *Arctic Maid*. The meeting with Professor Balfour late Wednesday afternoon meant he wouldn't leave the city for Cedar Mills until Thanksgiving morning.

There was a knock at the office door as Katherine hung up, feeling disappointed that Jack wouldn't be at her house on Wednesday night. Will came in, looked around, and sat down.

"Congratulations on your promotion.

He asked if she'd heard about Lodong and her mother. She bristled when he said "her mother." She couldn't accept the fact that the white-haired bovine boozer who'd had invaded the café dressed in a polka-dot muumuu and Birkenstocks a few weeks ago, was her mother. Katherine told him she'd seen the news clip in the *P-I* about their arrest in Gold Bar for being drunk in public and beating up Art Fletcher.

Will told her Marty Wamback, the Snohomish County sheriff, had called. Lodong and Owling had jumped bail and disappeared over the weekend. Lodong's followers at Catchall said the pair had packed up Lodong's Town Car and left on Saturday night with Art Fletcher driving. Marty said they might head over to the Peninsula again.

By Wednesday morning, she was trying to avoid the office altogether. She kept moving, helping Muriel in the dining room when it was busy, bussing tables with Bobby and helping him with the dishwasher when he was overwhelmed, and wandering around with a coffee pot, refilling cups. She knew about the social requirements of a restaurant manager which include chatting with customers, especially the gang at The Table. But she was accustomed to being safely in the kitchen and would have to learn the art of schmoozing.

On Wednesday afternoon, Katherine drove out to Hazel and Roy's to meet May and Archie Castile, Hazel's sister and her husband, who'd arrived from Bristol, Tennessee the day before. It had been three years since Hazel had seen her younger sister, younger by twenty months, and she had been talking about her visit for weeks. In Tennessee, it had been a family tradition that the Willits and Castiles spent Thanksgiving together at the farm in Sewanee.

Hazel and May were walking down from the horse barn when Katherine got out of her car. She leaned against the front of her car, watching them approach, talking and laughing. She was struck by how much they looked alike, so much so they might be twins. May was a little shorter than Hazel and her chestnut hair didn't billow down to her shoulders like Hazel's, but she had the same deep green eyes, sharp nose, and fair complexion as her sister.

They each took her by an arm and led her into the house, talking non-stop. This was a Hazel she had not seen, laughing, joking, and trading stories with her sister. They sat in the kitchen over coffee as Katherine watched and listened to the two of them carry on.

Roy and Archie had gone into to town to the lumber yard and then at Archie's request, to visit a couple of grocery stores. Archie and May owned a small chain of supermarkets in the tri-cities of Kingsport, Bristol, and Johnson City, and whenever he traveled, Archie wanted to see how the retail grocery trade was conducted elsewhere. Later, Roy said who would have thought that going through the meat cases piece by piece, checking the expiration date on dairy products, and taking careful note of what fresh fruits and vegetables were available could be of such intense interest. But it was to Archie and when they returned, he gave a full report to May.

As the sisters continued to chatter, Katherine said she was going to run up to the barn and say hello to Donny and the horses. When she got back, Roy and Archie had returned and everyone was sitting in the kitchen talking and laughing. Archie jumped up and said, "So this is Katherine!" He shook her hand and put an arm around her shoulder like they were old pals.

With his short, wavy, reddish blonde hair combed straight back, his flashing brown eyes and his ready smile which displayed the whitest teeth Katherine had ever seen, there was nothing to dislike about Archie Castile. He was an ardent apostle of Will Rodgers' maxim of never meeting a man he didn't like. He was a storyteller and, like his yarn-spinning brethren in the best tradition of the South, he could turn a mundane happening into a laugh-filled tale that would bring a smile to even the most cynical listener. But he also liked to listen and he questioned everyone he met for the first time with a warm and genuine curiosity. May always said he should have been a politician. Archie always said he wasn't dumb enough.

Katherine stood behind Hazel with a hand on her shoulder as they listened to Archie tell the saga of his and May's first trip out West, having driven from Bristol to Charlotte and taking the red-eye to Sea-Tac, where praise God, Roy and Hazel were there to pick them up. Archie's telling was punctuated with jokes, asides, and observations that had everyone laughing. The stories were ones that had been told a thousand times before by anyone who traveled by air, but in Archie's telling, they all were all hilariously fresh and new.

Finally, over everyone's protests, Katherine said she was heading home. She was bringing a salad for Thanksgiving dinner and had to make it that night if, as Hazel had ordered, she was to be back early in the morning. When Hazel asked if she was going to make that lime Jell-o salad they'd had at her house, Archie chimed in, asking if it was that salad with shredded carrots and celery like his mother used to make.

"I love that stuff," he said. "Why don't you bring that."

Katherine said, "I wasn't planning on it but I'll make you a little batch for you, if you promise not to put it on the table."

Before she left, they told her about tomorrow's after-dinner musical entertainment: A reunion concert of Clinch Mountain music by the Dunn Sisters, with each of them playing their acoustic guitars and accompanied by Roy on the banjo and Archie on the fiddle. Katherine asked with a laugh, "Does everyone in Tennessee play a musical instrument?" Archie told her in an affected east Tennessee accent, "Everyone except them that don't."

❖ ❖ ❖ ❖ ❖ ❖ ❖ ❖ ❖ ❖ ❖

When she got to the Willit's the next morning, Roy came out and helped Katherine carry in two large bowls of her special layered salad and a square glass dish of lime Jell-o salad. Archie was in the kitchen finishing what he called his award winning sausage and cornbread dressing. He told Katherine he'd kicked May and Hazel out of the kitchen because they wouldn't stop chattering and he couldn't concentrate.

There was something about his easy manner that neutralized Katherine's defenses and she found herself making teasing comments as she watched him, first crumble the cornbread into a large bowl, and then chop an onion and some celery as the sausage simmered in a frying pan. She soon discovered that Archie was as competitive as he was funny when she said with a little laugh, "That isn't how to chop an onion. Where'd you learn that?"

Archie retorted, "Oh it isn't is it? You're the chef, you show me."

Hazel, May, and Roy came into the kitchen when they heard the goings on. Katherine and Archie were standing side by side at the large butcher block table in the middle of the kitchen. Both were armed with chef's knifes and both had an unpeeled medium-size yellow onion on a cutting board in front of them. Archie ordered Roy over to start the countdown for the onion chopping contest. Roy shouted, "On your mark, get set, chop!"

Katherine and Archie went to work, reducing their onion to a finely chopped mound ready to be sautéed. They both insisted they'd won and debated whose chopped onion was more suitable for the cornbread dressing. But the panel of three judges who had carefully monitored the competition, declared it a tie, much to the mock chagrin of both contestants.

Larry arrived later in the morning with a football for what he called the traditional Thanksgiving touch football game before dinner. He'd told Katherine and Sadie the day before that with all the people who'd be there, fourteen in all, they should be able to put together two teams. Hazel had invited Sadie and her nephews, who surprisingly had accepted. Bobby and his grandparents, Winona and George Carr would be there. And of course, Anne and Jack were coming.

Not long after Larry arrived, Sadie, Danny, and Donny came in, looking ill at ease and uncomfortable until Archie ushered them into the living room and started telling them about the trip from Tennessee and politely but probingly, asking all three about themselves with a keen interest. Soon, Sadie and Archie were talking and laughing like old friends while the two boys kept interrupting, eagerly trying to tell Archie about themselves.

Katherine hadn't met Bobby's grandparents. Bobby carefully took them around and formally introduced them to everyone, saving Katherine for the last. "Here, she is," he told them proudly. "The one, the only, Katherine Baker, the prettiest girl in the world." Everyone laughed when he added, "Oh, oh, I probably shouldn't say that about my boss."

Hazel and May kicked everyone out of the kitchen so they could finish getting dinner ready. Winona and Bobby helped George, who at 81, didn't move very fast, into the living room and into Hazel's recliner next to Roy. George told Roy he'd worked for the post office for forty years and how, even though he didn't get around too well, he hadn't lost his talent for remembering zip codes. A few minutes later, Roy was saying the name of a city and George was shouting back the zip code. "Boston." "02109." "Atlanta." "30303." "Baton Rouge." "70802." George interrupted, "Come on, those are too easy." "OK, Pittsburgh."

"Which one, Pennsylvania or Kansas?" "Both." "Pennsylvania, 15219. Kansas, 66762."

Katherine, Sadie, and Winona were sitting at the dining room table talking about how well Bobby was after starting to work at the cafe when they heard George shouting out numbers. Winona told them George had competed in the Western States Postal Competition several times. She said "He almost won the whole thing just before he retired, but he lost the speed competition. Reversed the zip codes for Texarkana, Texas, 75501, and Texarkana, Arkansas, 71854. It nearly broke his heart to lose."

Danny, Donny, and Bobby took the football down to the front lawn to throw it around. Archie and Larry sat in the living room while Archie grilled Larry about life on Wall Street and then about prison life. Their conversation drifted to fighting the effects of late middle age. Larry told Archie that he'd started meditating and yoga exercises in prison, including standing on his head for five minutes every other day. "It's supposed to help prevent dementia, floods the brain with blood," Larry told him.

"Well, brother, you don't have to tell me," Archie said. "I am a big believer in head stands. Do it regularly myself."

With that, the gauntlet was thrown down and a head-standing competition was declared. Both men removed their shoes and moved to the middle of the living room. Once again, Roy was recruited to start another contest and act as timekeeper. The winner would be the one who lasted ten minutes on his head, or if both men failed, it would be the one who stood the longest.

As Katherine, Sadie, and Winona stood in the doorway between the dining room and living room watching, Roy shouted, "On your mark, get set, stand on your head!" Both men effortlessly put their hands on the floor and raised their legs upward in smooth, practiced movements, their heads barely touching the floor.

Then there was a commotion in the kitchen as Anne walked in, followed by a tall, blonde, blue-eyed woman, with Jack behind her.

Hazel held out her arms and exclaimed, "Why Sheila, Sheila Costigan. Anne called yesterday and told me she was bringing a surprise guest, but I'd never guessed it was you, come all the way from Chicago."

The two women embraced as the newcomer said, "Dear, dear Hazel, it's been so long. And look at you, still the same, working, working, working." Then she turned to May and said, "My goodness May, it's been years," and hugged her.

Jack stood in the background, quiet and unsmiling, as Anne explained she'd talked Sheila into flying out from Chicago for the holiday. She'd arrived yesterday afternoon. "Jack's been so lonely since he moved out here," she said. "I wanted to surprise him."

Sadie and Katherine, turned and stared into the kitchen. Sheila, who was thin and fit, was dressed in a svelte black outfit of a knee-length skirt and jacket which she wore over a ruffled light pink blouse. Her lipstick was a bright red. Her jewelry, the necklace and bracelets, were gold.

Sadie whispered to Katherine, "What on earth is that?"

Katherine, who felt light-headed as her heart pounded and her stomach churned, said, "That's the other shoe. It just dropped." Then she said, "She's beautiful."

Sadie told her, "Honey, it's amazing what a bunch of makeup can do."

Anne took Sheila into the dining room, where she took Sadie's hand and said "You must be Katherine."

"Nope. I'm Sadie. Here's Katherine," Sadie said with a smile as she pulled Katherine toward Sheila.

They shook hands while Sheila told Katherine it was a honor to finally meet her. *Whatever that means*, thought Katherine as she smiled and told her she was so happy to finally meet her. As she said it, Katherine stared at Jack, who in return, grimaced with a shrug.

Sheila and Anne walked into the living room and stopped. They stared at Archie and Larry standing on their heads while Roy jumped up and embraced Sheila, saying it was a great surprise to have her come for Thanksgiving. Larry finally threw in the towel and lowered his feet and stood to greet the two women. Archie stayed on his head for another minute and then righted himself, proudly declaring himself the winner. After hugging Anne and shaking hands with Jack, he took Sheila in a warm embrace.

"Say it isn't so," he told her. "Sheila Costigan, my favorite girlfriend."

"Oh, Archie, you haven't changed a bit" she gushed, giving him a peck on the cheek. "You sly old fox, you."

Katherine didn't remember much after that until dinner. She did remember Larry declaring it was time for the football game. There were just enough draftees for two teams When they assembled on the front lawn it was Jack, Danny, Sadie, and Archie on one team. Larry, Katherine, Donny, and Bobby were on the other. Roy was the neutral, non-playing center, who hiked the ball to both sides.

The front lawn, which was bounded by rhododendron and salal bushes, was twenty feet wide and extended well beyond the house on both ends. It was a warm afternoon for November, the sun was out and just over the tops of the shrubs, the snow-capped Olympics were visible. After thirty minutes of intense play, the score was tied at twelve to twelve. It was third down and Katherine, who had emerged as a formidable quarterback and play caller, told Larry and Donny to run to the right and she would feign a pass to one of them. She told Bobby to run to the left, just past the scrimmage line, and then turn and stand still. She'd throw it to him.

"When you catch the ball, turn around and, pardon my French, run like hell," she told Bobby as they broke the huddle.

Roy hiked the ball and the defense followed Larry and Donny to the right. Katherine threw the ball to Bobby. Just as she did, Jack, who had decided to blitz the quarterback, came running at her fast, stumbled and fell into her. He managed to keep his balance and grabbed Katherine in a hard embrace to keep her from falling. She felt his warm breath against her cheek. Her breasts pushed against him and she felt her nipples harden as they were momentarily locked together. Then she pushed him back and walked away without a word.

Bobby caught the ball, turned and ran like hell. And he kept running, well past the goal line and into the rhododendron bushes. Everyone started yelling, "Stop Bobby, stop." He finally emerged from the bushes smiling. Everyone cheered and gave him high fives as Hazel came out on the porch and announced dinner would be ready in ten minutes. Archie insisted they should have a chance to tie the score, but Larry and Katherine adamantly said "no way." They'd won fair and square, thanks to Bobby, and the game was over.

When Sadie talked about Thanksgiving dinner, which she did for days afterward, she talked mostly about Sheila Costigan and what an obnoxious bitch she was. But Katherine disagreed. She was impressed with Sheila, who'd come unannounced into a unknown environment and handled it with aplomb. Sheila had been trained to navigate such situations with a self-possessed confidence and good manners, and she did. And when Sadie called Sheila a two-bit, disingenuous little twit with the syrupy accent, who wanted everyone to think she was helpless, Katherine disagreed again. She said Sheila didn't get where she was by playing the sweet little Southern dumb belle. She might be two-faced and devious, but a twit she was not. She wouldn't be a high-paid corporate lawyer who'd graduated with honors from law school if she was.

It was Anne who Katherine found irritating at dinner that day, prattling on about how wonderful it was to have Sheila there, how pleased Jack had been to see her, how great it was in the old days when Jack would bring Sheila home to Sewanee when they were both at Vanderbilt law. Jack was silent and looked sullen as Anne outlined the agenda for Sheila's weekend stay. Jack and Sheila were going back to Seattle that night so they'd have time alone to catch up after months of being apart. Then Anne was going to Seattle on Friday morning to take Sheila shopping while Jack went to work.

"We'll be downtown and maybe we can get Jack to go to lunch with us," Anne said. "His office isn't far from the original Nordstrom store, and we've got to go there."

"Be still my heart," Sheila gushed. "We're going to the mother ship!"

Katherine and Sadie smirked at each other across the table, while Sadie rolled her eyes.

"Then on Saturday, Jack and Sheila are going skiing at Snoqualmie while I go to my alumni board meeting at the UW."

Jack finally spoke. "I don't ski, remember," he said in a near growl. "Sheila's going skiing. I'm taking her."

Sheila laughed and said, "Is somebody a bit grumpy? Does Action Jackson need a nap?"

Anne and Sheila laughed with glee while Jack glowered. Sadie and Katherine continued to stare at each with looks of undisguised amusement. Larry caught Katherine's eye. He shook his head with an expression of disdain as the listened to Anne's manic banter. It was a side of Anne he hadn't seen.

When dinner was over, Katherine and Sadie ushered everyone into the living room. They started clearing the table and cleaning up the kitchen, while the Kingsport Bluegrass Squad, as Jack had named them on the spur-of-the moment, tuned up. Sheila came into the kitchen, grabbed an apron, and pitched in with the dishes. She chatted easily with Katherine and Sadie asking them about the Madison Café and what it was like to live in a place like Cedar Mills.

Later, Sadie insisted it was all part Sheila's fake front, but Katherine liked her. She liked the way Sheila was disarmingly down-to-earth and seemed genuine when she insisted on helping. When they finished up in the kitchen, Katherine thought maybe Sheila Costigan was all right, even if she'd probably stab you in the back in your sleep if she had to. It was Jack she thought of with a disparaging disappointment. She knew whatever feelings she thought she had for him were misplaced. She'd been right all along, she'd been a weekend diversion for him, someone to temporarily occupy his otherwise empty life.

Roy's Flat Tire and the Four Aces

After dinner, everyone gathered in the living room as Jack introduced the members of the Kingsport Bluegrass Squad: the amazing Dunn Sisters from Clinch Mountain, Virginia; the Knoxville wonder, Mr. Roy Willit, and a special guest Archie Castile, born and bred in Bristol, Tennessee, the birthplace of country music and Tennessee Ernie Ford. As Jack said each town, Bobby's grandfather George, who was sitting in the front, echoed the name of the town and its zip code, "Clinch Mountain, 24245." "Knoxville, 37902." "Bristol, Tennessee, 37620."

Archie asked with a smile, "What about the other Bristol?"

George proudly responded, "Bristol, Virginia, 24201," and everyone clapped. Winona finally told him to be quiet and stop showing off.

When Hazel said they'd start off with requests from the audience, Bobby jumped up and shouted, "Wabash Cannonball." What followed was a rousing thirty minutes of acoustic bluegrass and old-time country music that should have been recorded for the ages. When it was over, everyone reassembled in the dining room for dessert.

Katherine, Sadie, and Sheila took orders and served everyone from the pies Sadie had brought. While they ate, Katherine asked Archie how they all met, he and May, and Hazel and Roy.

"Well let me tell you the story of Hazel and Roy. That's more interesting, because May just fell for me right away and I had to marry her. She wouldn't leave me alone." Archie said.

"In your dreams," May retorted, looking at Hazel and Roy, who were both shaking their heads.

Archie began his story, "It all started in 1954 on a cold Thursday afternoon in February. All of us except Roy were working at the book plant in Kingsport, the Kingsport Press. It was a big place, over a million square feet in the main press building. There was another plant over in Hawkins County. At that time there were almost three thousand people working at the press. It pretty much supported the town. They used to brag then that half the bestsellers in the country came out of Kingsport.

"May and I worked in the shipping department. She drove a fork truck loading and unloading trucks. I worked in the traffic office, scheduling trucks in and out. Hazel was working in what we called the bible bindery, running a Smyth sewing machine, stitching bibles, hymnals, and the like. I already knew the Dunn sisters pretty well by then and May and I were kind of soft on each other."

"So you say, Casanova," May interrupted. "Stick with story, don't start making stuff up."

Archie continued, telling everyone how Roy had backed into Loading Dock 31 late that Thursday afternoon, after the snow had been falling for a couple of hours. It was one of those ugly early spring snowstorms that could easily dump a foot or two of heavy wet snow overnight, and it did. Fresh out of the Navy not long after the Korean War ended, Roy was driving truck for Montfort Haulers, out of Knoxville. He was in Kingsport for the first time, there to pick up two loads, a pallet of prayer books for the Episcopal seminary at Sewanee and a pallet of hymnals for the Baptist Sunday School Board in Nashville.

Roy was already running late and worried about getting back on the road before the snow got too bad. He was a little short with May, telling her he needed those books on the truck now. Things didn't get any better when Archie came down out of the traffic office and told Roy he had a flat tire on the front driver's side.

"It was a new truck, too," Roy chimed in. "My boss gave me holy hell when I got back, saying he couldn't believe a new tire like that would go flat. He thought I'd made it up so I wouldn't have to get back on the road in the storm."

Roy was fuming and started yelling at Archie, telling him the Baptists wanted those hymnals in Nashville by Monday, which would have been easy without the flat tire and the snowstorm. He told Archie he didn't know what it was like to have a bunch of angry Baptists on your tail. So Archie called his cousin Ike who had a truck shop over in Johnson City. Ike said he had the tire Roy needed and would be over in the morning to put it on. No way was he coming over in the snowstorm.

"I told Roy to relax, there was nothing he could do," Archie continued. "He'd be on the road first thing in the morning. I said he could bunk at my place. I shared a house with two other guys and he could sleep on the sofa, it was better than sleeping in his truck."

Anne interrupted Archie, "Don't forget about the Four Aces, Archie."

Jack followed suit, "Yeah, Uncle Archie. Let's hear about the Four Aces."

"Hold your horses," Archie said. "I'm getting there."

Roy didn't have a choice but to spend the night. Archie let him use the phone in the traffic office to call his boss and give him the bad news. It was quitting time by then and as they walked through the shipping area, Archie made sure that May heard him telling Roy he'd take him over to the Four Aces for a burger and a couple of cold ones.

"Oh for Pete's sake, stop making things up," May said. "Next you'll be saying Hazel and I went the Four Aces because we knew you'd be there."

Archie laughed, "Why else would you've gone? But wait a minute, let me back up for a second and say something about the Dunn sisters.

"You know what they say about the whole being more than the sum of its parts? Well that was them, the Dunn sisters. There was May Dunn, quite a woman in her own right. And there was Hazel Dunn, another extraordinary gal to boot. But when you put the two together, it was the *Dunn sisters*, a force to be reckoned with. Just step back and get out of the way. They'd come down off Clinch Mountain a couple of years before, went to work at the Press, and Kingsport was never the same. Everyone used to say, 'the Dunn sisters, my, oh, my.' They did as they pleased and got what they wanted. They could talk the socks off a shoe salesman."

Hazel finally said, "Come on Archie, don't exaggerate. We were just a couple of country girls working in a factory, trying to make a living."

"Oh you were that, all right," Archie chortled.

The Four Aces was a downtown bar and grill a few blocks from the book plant's main gate. It was a popular hangout for Press people and crowded every night of the week. That Thursday night when Archie and Roy walked in was no exception. Roy was still in a sour mood as they worked their way through the crowded bar, grumbling about having to spend the night in Kingsport.

May and Hazel were sitting in a booth on the other side of the room, drinking beer. A silver-haired man in a shiny sharkskin suit sat across from them. It was Will McPhee, a salesman from the New York sales office who'd brought some customers down from the city, cooped up production editors from a publishing house who wouldn't hesitate to take a junket to Tennessee for a tour of the Kingsport Press. He'd dumped them on some customer service lackeys so he could go slumming alone in Kingsport.

Roy broke in, "Archie pointed and told me, there's May and her sister Hazel. I saw Hazel and my life changed then and there. She was the most beautiful woman I'd ever seen. And there was this little soft white cloud-like thing floating just above her head, like a halo telling me she was the one."

Hazel sat at the other end of the Thanksgiving table blushing and said, "Oh, Roy, you big old fool you, you're crazier than a Missouri mule. But you were mighty handsome yourself, you know."

"So when the sisters saw us walk up to the booth, May says to Will McPhee, 'time's up big guy. We've got a couple new patients coming in. We'll send you the bill.' Then they both starting laughing while Will slid out of the booth, nodded with a smile at Archie and Roy and walked away. Then Hazel shouts, "Write when you get work,' and we sat down while the sisters giggled like schoolgirls.

"I've never seen anyone change so fast as Roy did when he met Hazel. The flat tire and the Baptists were all forgotten, everything was sunshine and roses for Roy after he met Hazel. And then we couldn't get rid of him. He was back in Kingsport every chance he got, even when he wasn't working. He'd make the two-hour trip from Knoxville, up Route 11 in his old 1940 Chevy coupe every weekend to see Hazel. And the rest, as we all know, is history. They got married a year later and moved to Sewanee."

The story of Hazel and Roy. It was a fitting end to what Katherine thought was the best Thanksgiving she'd spent. It was early evening as Bobby and his grandparents said goodbye. Larry gave Bobby the football to commemorate his being named the football game's MVP. Bobby proudly held it up as he stood in the kitchen door and bowed to everyone. Then

Anne, Sheila, and Jack got ready to leave. They stood around in the kitchen talking to Hazel and May. From the dining room, Katherine, Sadie, and Larry could hear Anne gushing about her upcoming two-week Christmas trip to Florida to see her cousin in Fort Myers and how they were going to spend several days in Key West after Christmas.

Sheila had already said her goodbyes, but she came back into dining room. She took Katherine's hand and walked her back through the kitchen, telling her that when she came back, she'd come to the Madison Café for breakfast. Katherine hugged her and said with a smile, "I'd like that. I hope you come back soon."

When she drifted back to the dining room, Sadie said, "What the heck was that all about? You two girlfriends now?"

Katherine walked past her into the living room, saying, "Anne and Jack aren't going to have the pleasure of thinking they can hurt me." She drifted over to the piano and sat absent-mindedly playing the melody line of "Raindrops Keep Falling on My Head," with one finger.

Danny came over to watch. He told her that Sadie had an old keyboard at home and he was trying to learn how to play it. Katherine's expression brightened. "Would you like some lessons? I can teach you a few basics if you want." But Danny told her he'd already asked Sadie about piano lessons and she'd said there was no money. Katherine said, "They'll be free. I'll talk to Sadie about it if you're interested. Maybe one day a week after school." Danny's broad smile answered her back.

Soon after, Sadie and the boys were gone and Katherine was in the kitchen helping Hazel and May, who were carrying on like the Dunn sisters.

"I'm furious at Anne for what she did," Hazel said. "How embarrassing for everyone, even poor Sheila, who I've never liked, by the way. She's a selfish spoiled brat who was always manipulating Jack. And Anne had no business sticking her nose into Jack's business, trying to get them back together. Sheila's the reason Jack left Chicago, to be rid of that, that, you know what."

May said, "Jack should have more backbone. Why doesn't he tell Anne to lay off? Mind her own business."

"Jack's mixed up in a lot of ways. He was ok until the car wreck in New

Orleans. He came home to Sewanee and lived with us for a year until Sheila talked him into moving to Chicago. Anyway, you're right sister, Anne needs to mind her own business and Jack needs to tell her."

Katherine was glad she'd accepted Hazel's invitation to spend the night. It was a cold, windy November night and the thought of driving home alone to her chilly, empty house was hardly inviting. She and Hazel walked Larry out to his car. Katherine said she'd take him to lunch at the Blue Heron on Saturday. Back inside she and Hazel went up to her room where a pair of flannel pajamas were laid out on the bed and a pair of slippers were on the floor. Hazel told Katherine there were some clothes in the closet and some more things in the dresser.

"I've never had a daughter to dress up," she said. "So you've been elected."

Katherine laughed to herself, wondering why everyone was so intent on dressing her in new clothes.

The next morning Katherine was awake at her usual time of 4:30. Hazel was already in the kitchen pouring her first cup of coffee. They sat in the kitchen, talking softly, enjoying the peace of the predawn morning. Katherine asked about the books in the two bookcases in her bedroom, they were all bibles, hymnals, missals, and prayer books.

"They're books I bound when I worked in the bindery at Kingsport. Mementoes of the old days," Hazel told her. "I love to hear Archie's stories of those times, but don't get the impression that it was all fun and games when we were coming up. May and I never had a thing. We fought and scrapped for everything we got."

She told Katherine how they'd left Clinch Mountain not long after high school, when their mother died of tuberculosis. Their father had been killed on a beach in France during the D-Day invasion, they'd never even been told which one, and the family had survived on a monthly government check.

"When Mama died, our Uncle Merle, gave us an old black satchel. It looked like a doctor's bag," Hazel said. "He told us there was no point staying around there unless we both wanted to be baby factories for the rest of our lives."

Soon after, Hazel and May walked out of the old house in Dante, Virginia and down the Clinchfield Railroad tracks a few miles to a place called Brill Switch, where the coal trains always stopped until the brakeman made sure the switch was correctly set.

"Everything we owned was in that satchel. We sat on a log in the dark for hours waiting for a train. May was sobbing. I was freezing. I told her we were walking to Kingsport if a train didn't show up by daylight," Hazel said.

Just before dawn, a ten-car coal train came rattling down the mountain and stopped at Brill Switch. The girls hopped on and left Clinch Mountain forever.

"That was our grand entrance into Kingsport," Hazel laughed. "Two scared hillbilly girls, standing between the coal cars on the Clinchfield Railroad."

As Hazel finished, May, Archie, and Roy had come into the kitchen for coffee. By a unanimous vote, it was decided Katherine would fix blueberry pancakes for breakfast, while Hazel and May fried eggs and bacon. When it was all over, Katherine was on her way to town after exchanging tearful goodbyes with May and Archie. It seemed like a week since she'd been home.

Before she left, Hazel took her back up to the bedroom. She said it was Katherine's room now. She could stay any time she wanted. Then she took a red-leather copy of *The Book of Common Prayer* out of one of the book cases and handed it Katherine. It was the Episcopal prayer book and holy bible in one volume.

"I want you to have something from Kingsport. Something I made," she said, giving Katherine a hug.

When she got home on Friday morning, Katherine put *The Book of Common Prayer* on the coffee table next to Milos Grajek's *Lithuanian Septet*, started the stove, and sat down at the piano. She played her favorites for a couple hours, Mozart, Chopin, Schubert, and Dvorak, and thought of all that had happened the week before, her promotion and new office, the Sunday reception at the café, Thanksgiving Day. And before that, there was that odd trip to Seattle with Elizabeth and Maude.

But she kept returning to thoughts of Jack. She had already written him off as a deceitful fraud, maybe a good-hearted deceitful fraud, but still a duplicitous skunk. Yet she couldn't stop smiling when she thought back on their Saturday at Gosport. The lunch at Harvey's Little Oyster and the ferry ride to nowhere; and then the trip to Third Beach where they'd spent eternity. Jack seemed to love being with her. She knew she loved being with him because she felt a new way, a new complete way when they were together. His double-dealing was a poison arrow to her heart.

PART II

The Only Constant is Change

On that Friday morning after Thanksgiving, Jack was in his office in Seattle finishing a report on Paul Merrick which Hercules Pushkin wanted in his hands that afternoon. Merrick was coming from Vancouver on Monday and they had to decide whether or not the firm would take him on as a client. If they did, Jack would be the lead attorney.

Pushkin was cautious about the proposed salvaging of the *Arctic Maid*, after his old friend Silas Peavey had called and said he'd referred Merrick to Pushkin, McDonald, & Fishkin, because there was something squirrely about the brown-skinned Indian Englishman that didn't add up. Peavey told Pushkin he'd become even more suspicious after Arthur Merrick, a white-skinned Canadian who claimed to be Paul Merrick's cousin, paid a visit to the clock shop asking for advice on the far-fetched salvaging scheme. Hercules Pushkin wasn't opposed to billing a client for services rendered in a harebrained scheme, but he wanted to have all the bases covered if they did.

In the three days before Thanksgiving, Jack had met with Silas Peavey, who, when Jack ventured into the depths of the market to visit the clock shop, had proved to be a gracious host, regaling him with stories about when he and Hercules were best friends, growing up on Queen Anne Hill. Peavey gave Jack an unabridged account of Paul Merrick's visit, complete with a detailed narrative of how they fished Professor Jim Underwood out of the weeds under the viaduct so he could tell them the location of the *Arctic Maid*, and how Merrick had told him he'd been in touch with Eddie

Balfour at the university.

Jack had gone out to see Professor Balfour who had taken him on a tour of the northern end of Lake Union and pointed out the remains of the *Arctic Maid*, which had been half-buried in the mud for years. Balfour had told him the Cyrus Milton family might still hold the title to the wreck.

Jack tracked down Cyrus Milton III at the Arctic Hotel on Second Avenue, where he found out that indeed the Miltons still held title to the hulk. The younger Milton told him about Paul Merrick's visit and how he'd taken the Englishman out to Mukilteo to see his father, Cyrus Milton II, who afterwards wondered why Merrick had been so interested in the whereabouts of a piano that had been aboard the ship.

When Jack met with Hercules Friday afternoon, Pushkin told him he was impressed with Jack's diligence and asked if Merrick's scheme was as crazy as it sounded? Jack said given the cost of the salvage operation, let alone what the Miltons would ask for title to the wreck, and the international complications of towing the remains of the ship to Vancouver, made him believe the proposal was a red herring. But for what? It had to do with the Merrick's fixation on the piano. They agreed to put the screws to Merrick on Monday.

Katherine fidgeted around the house on Friday. It was quiet. The café was closed. She sat on the sofa and looked at the books on the coffee table, *The Platonic Ideal of Faith*, *The Lithuanian Septet*, *The Book of Common Prayer*. Wally Berger had been right, she was wading in some pretty deep water with her reading.

Maude called to say she saw Katherine was finally home and wanted to know how Thanksgiving went out on the farm. She'd had her traditional quiet Thanksgiving at Lonnie and Elizabeth's. Greeley and Milos were there for dinner. But she really wanted to talk about Larry and find out what time he'd left the Willit's last night because she'd seen Anne drive up the alley around midnight and she was pretty sure Larry wasn't home then.

Anne driving around at midnight on Thanksgiving night looking for Larry, unseemly or what?

Katherine tried to sound interested but she wasn't and it showed.

"You sound a little down in the dumps, sweetheart," Maude said. "Something happen yesterday. Is it Jack?"

"It's nothing. Jack is nothing. Is Milos over there?" she asked.

"He's home," Maude told her. "I think he's tired of me. Anyway, I'm doing fine by myself now. What'd you say about Jack?"

Katherine told her she might drive up to see Milos. Maude told her to do so at her peril. Milos didn't take to unannounced visitors. He'd told her his shotgun was always ready at the door. When Katherine said she'd call him first, Maude laughed and said he didn't have a phone.

Katherine put *The Lithuanian Septet* in a canvas shoulder bag and drove up Pleasant Valley Road in search of Milos Grajek's house. She knew it was set back in the trees, not far past the lumberyard. As she started up the hill, past Lonnie and Elizabeth's, she started looking for a driveway through the trees on the opposite side of the road. By the time she passed Greeley's mailbox on the other side of the road, she knew she'd gone too far. She'd never been to Greeley's and as she passed, she looked down the long gravel drive through the fields but couldn't see his house.

She turned around at the top of the hill where the road ended at a T, and started slowly back down the hill. Toward the bottom of the hill she spotted a narrow dirt track that ran through the trees. There was no mailbox on the main road. She turned in and drove a quarter mile through the dense, tall firs, to a large clearing in the middle of which was a log house, the kind built from a kit of pre-cut lumber. Smoke was drifting up from a chimney at the back of the house.

Katherine felt a small sense of security knowing that if this was his place, Milos might recognize her car before starting to shoot. She pulled up to the front of the house which was surrounded on three sides by a wide, covered porch. A flock of chickens started pecking their way toward her from the barnyard, which consisted of a small barn surrounded by a barbed wire fence. She could see a shaggy gray burro and two tall white goats inside the fence staring at her.

She sat for a moment, ready to leave. Then she saw the front door open a crack, then open wide. Milos walked out on the porch sans shotgun, looked down at Katherine in the car and smiled. He came down the porch. Katherine got out of the car.

"What a surprise," Milos said. "Not a complete a surprise. I half-suspected my refusal to tell you where I lived would be taken as a challenge."

They shook hands and Milos told her to come in. He'd brew some tea. On the inside, the house was deceptively large. The downstairs was one spacious area separated in half by a row of five load-bearing posts that supported the main beam of the house. The logs were exposed on the inside as they were on the outside, giving the interior the woodsy atmosphere of a hunting lodge. On the left side of the great room, a kitchen area was defined by a long counter that divided it from a dining area which was furnished with a rough-hewn fir table and six matching chairs. The living area on the right was a hodgepodge of easy chairs, tables, and bookcases. A drafting table and chair sat in the front corner of the area and afforded a view of the driveway and front yard. An open stairway at the back of the room led to a landing which ran across the rear part of the house, leading to bedrooms on either end.

Milos ordered her into one of the overstuffed easy chairs in front of the fireplace and started water for tea. In the background she could hear the music of Handel, an oratorio she recognized, *Judas Maccabaeus*. Waiting for the water to boil, Milos returned and sat down in the chair beside hers. Before he could say anything, Katherine pulled her copy of *The Lithuanian Septet* out of the canvas bag and handed it to him. She said, "I can't stay long. I just wondered if you would sign it for me."

He took the book and slowly turned it over and over. "Where did you get this," he asked in a harsh, low voice. "Where in God's name did you get this?"

Katherine told him Wally had ordered it for her, They'd found it listed in *Books in Print*. She said proudly that Wally had got it in on Wednesday, before Thanksgiving, and she'd read the entire book that same night.

"Why, why should I sign it?" Milos asked coldly, staring into the fire. "What would that signify? What's the point?"

Katherine sat up in her chair, wounded by his brusqueness. She said, "Because it's something special to me. Because knowing you, even the little bit I do, has been special to me."

Milos got up, put the book on the end table between their chairs, and walked into the kitchen. He returned carrying a tray with the teapot and two cups. He poured and tea and asked, "You know that music?"

"Of course I know that music. Any schoolgirl who's studied piano knows that music. It's Handel's *Judas Maccabeus*."

As she spoke, they could hear the great choral refrain of "See, The Conquering Hero Comes."

Now perturbed and sorry she had come, she prattled on, "And I can play Beethoven's *Twelve Variations on See, The Conquering Hero Comes for Piano and Cello*, the piano part, from memory. You mention Judas Maccabeus in the third poem." She took the book back and opened it, "Here, here it is, *Our paean to the hero, their redeemer, The flesh of our faithful ones, There was no one to bury them.*"

"I borrowed those last lines from what you call the Old Testament," Milos said vacantly. "Hanukkah is soon, when we celebrate Judas Maccabaeus saving Jerusalem."

Katherine put the book back in her bag and stood to leave. "I'm sorry I bothered you," she said, and started for the front door.

Milos sat staring at the fire. "Don't be a baby. Give me the book. I'll sign it with some profound inscription, some wisdom for the ages. You'll have to leave it with me though, such priceless words don't easily come to the Jew poet sage of Lithuania."

Winston Finds A Home

Katherine drove down the hill toward town wondering whether she'd see her copy of *The Lithuanian Septet* again. He' probably throw it in the fire. She kept thinking of Handel on the stereo. She needed music. She had the piano but it suddenly wasn't enough. She had no stereo, no radio, no television.

She drove straight to Nils Holmgren's Cedar Country Appliances with its "We've Got What You Want" neon sign flashing in the front window, parked in the alley and walked in the back door. Thirty minutes later, she and Nils were carrying boxes out to her car, a stereo receiver with CD changer and matching speakers, a tabletop radio for the kitchen, and an old turntable that Nils said was free if she'd just take it. She'd also bought a television, which Nils' son Andy was going to deliver when he got back from a service call.

"He'll be there in a couple hours and get it all set up for you," an ebullient Nils told her as they put the last carton in the back of her station wagon.

On her way home, she stopped at the Book Mart where Wally's daughter Nora Wineskin, told her she was expanding the store's music department. She ushered Katherine to a room in the rear of the store and proudly showed her several new racks of CDs, including Enya's latest, which she highly recommended.

Armed with a large bag of CDs, Katherine got home exhausted. She unloaded the car and stacked the cartons in the living room. In advance of Andy's arrival, she thought she'd see if she could figure out how to get some of the equipment hooked up. But once she got the radio out of its carton, plugged in and tuned to the classical music of KING-FM, she laid down on the sofa where she stayed, half asleep until she heard a light knock at the back door.

She turned off the radio, walked through the kitchen and opened the back door. A brown-haired girl wearing black pea-coat and watch cap stood holding a large gray and white cat that looked like it was dead. It was Clare Dolan.

"Is this your cat," the girl asked solemnly, her big brown eyes looking a little misty. "I found it in the alley. Looks like it's been hit by a car."

"No it's not my cat," Katherine brusquely answered. "But bring it in so we can take a look at it. You sure it's not dead?"

Clare walked into the kitchen carrying the cat, which looked like it weighed thirty pounds. It hadn't been going hungry. But the right side of its head was torn open and its right ear was bloody and bent. It was unconscious.

"We've got to find a soft place for it," Clare said. "Do you have something we could use for a bed?"

Katherine pulled an old pillow out of the hall closet and put it on the floor in the dining room next to the stove. Clare gently laid the cat down on the pillow. It's head flopped off onto the floor. They stood staring at it. Clare bent down and felt the cat's chest.

"It's still breathing. We need a box or something so the cat stays on the pillow," she said with authority. "I'll run over to the Red & White to see what Nell and Ned have." Then she was gone, out the back door.

Katherine stood blankly staring at the comatose cat until the front doorbell rang. It was Andy Holmgren with a hand truck loaded with her new television. They got it in the living room and positioned in the far front corner. Katherine cleared the sheet music off the side board in front of the picture window next to the piano and they moved it to the wall behind the sofa where Andy started setting up the stereo system.

Clare returned with a large, shallow cardboard carton which easily held the pillow and the cat. She saw Andy in the living room and shouted "Hi Andy," as though she it was routine to meet Andy at Katherine's house on a Friday afternoon.

Andy turned and waved, saying "Hey Clare," and went back to work.

Clare sat at the dining table with Katherine who had the bag of CDs on the floor. She pulled each CD out separately and removed the plastic wrap while Clare talked.

"I should have got some food while I was at the store," Clare told her.

"We'll see," Katherine answered noncommittally. "I'm going to make some coffee. Do you want something to drink?"

"I don't drink coffee, thank you." Clare said. "But I like orange juice or grape juice, if you have some and it's not too much trouble."

Clare sat alternately staring at the cat and at Andy in the living room. When Katherine returned with a cup of coffee and a glass of orange juice, Clare said, "Thank you Miss Baker."

"I'm Katherine. You're Clare, right?"

"Yes. I'm Clare Dolan. What do you go by, Kathy, Kate?"

"No Kathy, no Kate, no Katy, no Kat, no Katherino. Just Katherine. Always Katherine."

"Yes, Katherine, I understand," Clare solemnly answered. "That's one big piano. It takes up half the living room. I hear you playing it all the time. You play beautifully, Katherine. Unfortunately, I'm not musically inclined."

"Who on earth told you that?" Katherine asked still pulling CDs out of the bag, wondering when Andy was going to be finished.

"I'm just not. One of my teachers somewhere told me that. Somewhere where we lived, I don't remember. I do have an artistic bent, though. I like to draw."

When Andy finished, Katherine took a new CD into the living room so he could demonstrate how to operate the changer and Clare followed. During the demonstration, Andy proudly announced the changer, or in his words, "this bad boy," held five CDs at a time with an auto restart feature, so it would play continuously. Katherine and Clare helped him load the empty boxes in the van and Andy was gone, leaving Katherine and Clare standing on the sidewalk.

"Why don't you come back inside so we can talk about the cat for a minute," she told Clare.

They sat down on the sofa and Clare said, "What do think we should name him?"

"I didn't know we were that far along in deciding what to do with him."

"Well, whatever happens to him, he should have a name."

Katherine smiled. "Any ideas?

Clare sat thinking for a minute and then said, "I like Winston. We just studied World War Two in school. How Winston Churchill saved England. I like Winston."

"Winston it shall be," Katherine said.

"Hooray," Clare said. "Now, we really should think about getting him some food, and probably a litter box and some kitty litter."

Katherine acquiesced with a smile and a shake of her head. They walked over to the Red & White Foodliner where, under Clare's direction, Katherine bought the food Winston would probably like if he woke up, which was canned tuna fish in water, not oil and definitely not plain canned cat food. Then they walked to Wilfong's Variety where Carl Wilfong showed them the latest in litter boxes, the most expensive of which, the one with a removable top, came with a free bag of litter and a plastic scoop.

When they were at the counter checking out, Carl said, "Looks like somebody has a new cat."

"I found a hurt cat in the alley," Clare said. "Katherine's going to help me get him well."

Katherine rolled her eyes at Carl.

"Is it Len Carper's cat, the big gray and white one?" Carl asked. He's been living in the alley since Len's kids put him in the nursing home."

"I think that's the one, Carl," Clare answered.

"Katherine's going to have her hands full then. All Len talked about was how he loves to eat. Haven't seen Curtis for a while. How's he doing?

"Curtis is doing very well, Carl. Thank you for asking," Clare said as they turned to leave.

It was five o'clock by the time they got back to Katherine's and had everything unpacked. Clare methodically put the litter box on the enclosed back porch and filled it with litter. She stacked the cans of tuna on the kitchen counter and put the two new cat bowls, one for food, and one for water, next to Winston's bed, and filled the water bowl. Katherine offered to help, but Clare told her no, she'd take care of it. Katherine sat in the dining room and watched her work.

When Clare had everything arranged, she told Katherine it might perk up Winston if they put a little bit of tuna in the food bowl so he'd smell it if he woke up. Katherine dutifully opened a can of tuna and handed it to Clare who put some in the bowl.

"Anything else," she asked.

"No, Katherine. I believe we're all set," Clare said. "Winston and I both are thankful for your help."

Katherine said she going to Chicken in a Basket to get something for dinner and if she wanted, Clare could come along and get something too. Clare said she had no plans for dinner and she would like that very much. So they walked down Main Street to Jerry Zampini's Chicken in a Basket where they both ordered the two-piece white meat basket with Texas fries. Katherine also ordered a large side of coleslaw and two jumbo chocolate chip cookies.

"Where's Karen tonight," Clare asked Jerry as he brought out their order and handed them two large grease-stained brown paper bags.

"I gave her the day off," Jerry said. "She went skiing with her boyfriend."

Katherine bristled. *Went skiing with her boyfriend.* She thought of Jack and that wench Sheila. Her cheeks flushed.

"How's Curt? Tell him I said hello," Jerry said.

"Curtis is very well, thank you Jerry. I'll tell him you asked after him," Clare said as they left.

At home, Katherine got out plates and silverware, and unpacked their dinner. They sat in the dining room eating while Clare did most of the talking. She said they'd moved to Cedar Mills two years before, after her father had been hurt in the woods. He was setting chokers when a log rolled on him and broke his back. They'd moved around a lot. This was the longest they'd been in one town. Her mom and dad drank all the time and were gone a lot. Clare said it was better when they were gone, then she and Curtis didn't have to hide out.

As they finished, Katherine said, "So you knew all along the cat wasn't mine."

Clare unapologetically replied, "Yes Katherine, I was pretty sure it was Len Carper's cat. Len's house is empty now and I knew it was homeless. I'd seen it in the alley looking for food for a couple of weeks. Then it got hurt and I didn't know how to ask if you'd take it in."

After dinner, Clare cleared the table and washed the dishes. Katherine dried. When they were done, Clare announced it was time to be going. She sat for a moment on the floor next to Winston, petting him and telling him to get better. Then she had her coat and cap on, shook hands with Katherine and thanked her. "I couldn't have done it without you," she said and went out into the night.

❖ ❖ ❖ ❖ ❖ ❖ ❖ ❖ ❖ ❖ ❖

About the time Katherine and Clare were walking to Jerry Zampini's Chicken in the Basket, Jack was leaving Pushkin, McDonald & Fishkin. He was buoyed by the meeting with his boss and was looking forward to the Monday meeting with Paul Merrick. He felt good as he walked up Third Avenue toward his apartment until he remembered he was supposed to meet his mother and Sheila Costigan for dinner after their shopping trip to

Nordstrom.

Anne would normally have spent the night at Jack's. But tonight she was staying at the Westminster Mews hotel on First Hill on the recommendation of Maude. Anne had been particularly obnoxious when she kept telling him and Sheila with a wink, that she wouldn't think of barging in on their few precious nights together.

Instead of going straight to the hotel, Jack walked home. He was late by the time he walked into Presto, where the week before, Katherine had met her old friend Oscar Mendes, the owner of the restaurant. Anne and Sheila were sitting at a table in the bar. Sheila was drinking white wine and Anne was drinking scotch. It was clear when Jack arrived, they'd had more than one. They greeted him with an obnoxious effusiveness. He stared at them with a look of disdain.

He handed Sheila a key to a room at the hotel and told her he'd packed her things and brought them to the hotel. The concierge had supervised their transport to her room which was paid for in advance for two nights.

"I'm sorry you had to be a pawn in my mother's adolescent conniving," he told Sheila. "It was unfair to you. But I'm not going to be part of it. You and Anne can decide how to spend the rest of your time in Seattle. I wish you well."

Sheila said nothing as Jack turned and walked away. But Anne jumped up and followed him out to the restaurant's reception area. She grabbed him by an elbow and said, "Just a minute. You stop and explain yourself."

Jack pulled his arm loose. "Explain myself…You have your nerve," he said in a loud voice. "Go back in there and apologize to Sheila for what you've done. What planet are you living on?"

"Don't talk to me like that. I'm your mother," Anne snarled.

"My mother! What the hell is wrong with you? First you're running around town like a floozy with people laughing behind your back. And now this. Go take care of Sheila."

Fueled by the scotch, Anne's cheeks were scarlet and her hands were shaking. "Be careful Jack. You'll could find yourself out in the cold."

Jack shook his head and smiled. "Don't lower yourself to start talking about money. I don't want anything from you." He turned and walked away.

Larry Hits a Speed Bump

Katherine had just finished her first cup of coffee on Saturday morning, when Archie and May called to say they were on their way to the airport. They were talking simultaneously on two phones and it was difficult to sort out what they were saying except that she'd better get Hazel and Roy to bring her to Bristol soon. Archie would to teach her how to make real sausage gravy and biscuits, the Tennessee way. She hung up with a warm longing inside, glad she knew the Dunn sisters and their husbands, and crazily wishing she'd grown up as Hazel and Roy's daughter.

Over her second cup of coffee, with Schubert playing on her new stereo, she thought about Clare Dolan, a tall, thin, and pretty in a little-girl way with a round face, a small nose, bright brown eyes, straight brown hair cut in a Prince Valiant, and a mouth that didn't smile. She carried herself with an air of cautious confidence that made her all the more enigmatic.

After breakfast, she sat on the sofa and read the preface to *The Book of Common Prayer*, which was dated "Philadelphia, 1789." She read out loud with a stentorian air, "The Church of England, to which the Protestant Episcopal Church in these States is indebted, under God, for her first foundation...declares in her said Preface, to do that which, according to her best understanding, might most tend to the preservation of peace and unity in the Church; the procuring of reverence, and the exciting of piety..." She called Father Tom and left a message on his answering machine saying she'd join the Trinity Church choir.

Then she left for Maude's where they sat in the kitchen drinking coffee while Maude grilled her about her statement on the phone that "Jack is nothing." Katherine told her the whole story of Anne luring Sheila Costigan from Chicago under the guise of reuniting her with Jack and how Jack gave the impression of stoically accepting his mother's machinations.

"I'm not surprised. Hazel told me she's always meddling in Jack's life. Anne knew Jack left Chicago to get away from Sheila Costigan. She's just afraid of what you'll do to her poor little boy." Maude said"

"What I'll do to her little boy?" Katherine said with a scowl. "I thought Jack was a grown up. Anyway, he was just using me for entertainment on the weekends because he had nothing better to do."

"Look at it this way, you're better off without a guy who can't stand up for himself," Maude said. "If Jack's a wimp, then goodbye Charlie."

She told Katherine she'd seen Andy Holmgren bringing in the new television and Clare Dolan bringing in the cat. "You've been busy, girl. I'm glad Len Carper's cat's found a home."

"The cat has a temporary home," Katherine corrected her.

Maude asked about Larry. Both she and Elizabeth had been calling him for two days without success. His car was in its regular spot. It looked like he was home, but he wasn't answering his phone and the answering machine wasn't working. Greeley hadn't heard from him. Maude was concerned. Katherine told her she was on her way down to his place and would find out what was going on. They were going to lunch at the Blue Heron.

Katherine ran into Clare halfway down the alley to Larry's. The girl asked about Winston and Katherine walked her back to the house so she could see the cat.

"I'm on my way out now but if you're not doing anything tomorrow, come over in the afternoon for an early dinner." Katherine told her.

"Thank you, Katherine, I'd like that very much." Clare said.

"How about hamburgers?"

"My favorite. And tater tots?" Clare asked.

"And tater tots. I'll be home all day."

Katherine patted Clare on the shoulder as they said goodbye. "See you tomorrow," she said, and started down the alley toward Larry's apartment. But she took a detour. She turned into the narrow walkway from the alley to Main Street between Wally Berger's Book Mart and Marilyn Smallwood's Cedar Mountain Cleaners. She crossed the street and went to Wilfong's Variety. She bought a Scrabble game, a Monopoly game, a combination chess and checkers set, two decks of playing cards, a sketch pad in a folding carrying case, and a set of drawing pencils.

At the counter Carl said, "So you've adopted a cat. Has someone adopted you?

Katherine laughed. "Something like that."

"Clare's a good girl." Carl said. "It's her brother Curtis we're all worried about. He's going to end up in the slammer if he's not careful."

Katherine took the her new purchases home and then went on to Larry's. The living room of Larry's apartment fronted on the alley. His Suburban was parked in its usual place. When Larry was home, the shades were never drawn during the day, but now they were. Katherine walked up the outside stairs and knocked on the back door. Silence. She went back down the stairs and let herself into the café's service door, walked through the dimly lit kitchen and up the front stairs to the second floor. The hallway was dimly lit with a bare, overhead bulb. On the right was the door to Greeley's office and on the left, the door to Larry's apartment. She knocked on the Larry's door. Silence. She turned the doorknob. The door was unlocked. She slowly pushed it open and whispered, "Larry, are you home?" She walked into apartment, down the short hallway past the bedrooms. In the living room, the muted light through the brown translucent window shades filled the room with an eerie, funereal glow.

Larry was sprawled on his stomach in his underwear on the living room floor. An empty bottle of Old Grand-Dad was next to him. Another empty bottle of Old Grand-Dad lay on the coffee table. "You son of a bitch," Katherine muttered as she tried to turn him over to see if he was still breathing. But she couldn't. He was 220 pounds of deadweight. Finally, she heard a muffled snore, telling her he was still among the living.

She sat at the table in the dining area staring at the middle-aged drunk in his underwear, passed-out on the living room floor. It gave her the willies. She went into Larry's bedroom, pulled the bedspread from the bed, brought it out and covered him up. Then she called Sadie.

❖ ❖ ❖ ❖ ❖ ❖ ❖ ❖ ❖ ❖ ❖ ❖

Just after noon, Greeley was on the way to his office to drop off some papers. He parked behind the café between Larry's Suburban and Sadie's Buick sedan. *What the devil is Larry up to? First Anne Lindsay and now Sadie*, he thought.

As he walked through the kitchen and started up the front stairs, he heard noises from Larry's apartment. It was Sadie groaning "Come on, you big moose, come on." He stopped and listened. He heard Larry groan and then Katherine say, "Move over, so I can get a hold of him." *What in God's name goes on around here on the weekends*, he thought as he crept up the stairs.

On the second floor landing he saw Larry's door was open. Sadie and Katherine were still moaning and groaning, sounding like they were straining hard. He walked down the hall into the apartment. "Hello," he called with a tentative voice. "Hello."

"Thank, God, it's Greeley," Sadie said.

Katherine ordered him to give them a hand. She told him Larry was dead drunk, probably been on the sauce since Thanksgiving. They were trying to get him dressed and take him to Sadie's. When Greeley saw Larry comatose on the living room floor, he muttered, "You son of a bitch." Then he pitched in, helping them get him dressed in a sweatshirt and jeans.

Sadie had a spare room attached to the back of her house where her mother stayed when she came down from Sitka. They were going to stick Larry in there until he sobered up. Sadie said when he came to, she was going to beat his ass with a big stick.

The three of them managed to get the unconscious, bare-foot Larry down the outside stairs and into the back of his Suburban. Sadie led the convoy up the alley, followed by Katherine at the wheel of Larry's Suburban, and Greeley in the rear. They turned right on Second Avenue, passing Maude's house, and turned left on Main, heading west toward Sadie's.

Sadie's house was a surprise to Katherine. She didn't live in a trailer. Her house on Cedar River Road, was about a mile past the old farmhouse where Katherine had lived as Katy Owling. The new modular house was a cozy little place, with an open living and dining area, and a kitchen with a right-angled counter dividing it from the dining area. A hallway from the living room led to three bedrooms and a bathroom. Skylights over the kitchen and dining areas added a soft, uniform light to the interior.

An addition to the house, which was attached to the carport at the back of the house, consisted of one large room and bathroom. The room was furnished with a bed, a desk and chair, and a recliner which sat in front of a large console television. The room was cold and damp when they dragged

Larry in and wrestled him onto the bed. Sadie opened the curtains and turned on the baseboard heater.

With the still unconscious Larry on the bed covered with a comforter, Sadie, Katherine and Greeley stood in the kitchen talking. Greeley refused Sadie's offer of coffee, saying he had to get back to town. Katherine asked where the boys were. Sadie told her she'd taken Danny to a friend's house for the night and as usual, Donny was out at New Morning Farm with his new best friends, the horses.

"I'm trying to get custody of the boys," she said. "Harry Stamp is filing the documents for me to be their legal guardian on Monday. Vicki's life's in the toilet. Since she's been in county jail, she's been charged with assault and battery and drug possession. They're shipping her off to the big house at Gig Harbor until she goes to trial."

Greeley asked if she knew where Tommy Lowry was. No one had seen him for a few weeks. Sadie said she'd heard Tommy was over east of the mountains, working in the orchards and hop fields, pruning. "Hopefully he won't be back, now that his drinking buddy Vicki is in the hoosegow for a while."

"I'm sure the Presbyterians would love to get Tommy out of that old farmhouse.," Greeley said. "They've let him live there as a charity case, all he had to pay were the utilities and half the time, I paid those for him."

As Katherine and Greeley walked out into the carport, Sadie told them not to worry, she knew how to handle Larry. "I'll beat the crap out of him, if he doesn't behave," she said with a laugh. "We won't see him on Monday morning."

Back on the road to town, as they passed the dilapidated old farmhouse where she'd lived, Katherine almost said something about Tommy's place being the house where she'd lived when she was in high school. But what was the point?

Greeley said he was surprised about Larry. "He seemed pretty stable," he said, shaking his head.

"He didn't do so well at Thanksgiving after Anne's shenanigans," Katherine said.

It was late afternoon when Greeley dropped Katherine off at her house.

She went straight into the dining room to take a look at Winston. He hadn't moved. Then she remembered Clare Dolan was coming for dinner the next day and went out the back door, heading for the Red & White Foodliner where she bought hamburger, buns, frozen tater tots, and two boxes of lime Jello.

Clare Comes to Dinner

Sunday morning, Katherine stood in the doorway between her kitchen and the dining room with a cup of coffee staring down at Winston. It had been forty-eight hours since Clare had carried the unconscious cat into the house. He was still breathing but he hadn't moved an inch. Not much different than Larry when she'd found him the day before. She sighed. She figured it was fifty-fifty that Larry would come back to work at the café.

She'd just got off the phone with Hazel and had a full report on the trip to Sea-Tac with May and Archie. Hazel had started to blubber when she described saying good-bye to her sister. Then she said Donny was trying to talk Roy into letting him make the storeroom in the hay barn into a room where he could live. He'd told Hazel and Roy he'd lived in a outbuilding at Jim Sorstrom's when he milked cows. But Roy was skeptical and said he wanted to talk to Sadie. Katherine told her about Clare showing up with the injured Winston but she didn't say anything about finding Larry dead drunk the day before.

Clare knocked on the back door a little after one o'clock. Katherine wasn't sure what you did when an eleven-year-old girl came alone for dinner on Sunday afternoon. But the first order of business for Clare was fussing over Winston. She changed the water in his water bowl, replaced yesterday's tuna with some fresh, and then sat stroking his back and talking softly to him, telling him he was going to be up and around in no time.

Katherine sat at the piano, playing from the Johnny Mercer songbook and watching Clare. When Clare came in the living room and sat down on the sofa, Katherine went over and sat beside her.

"Winston is making good progress," Clare said. "I'm sure he's going to be fine. It just takes time."

"We'll see," Katherine said. "He hasn't moved since he got here.."

"He's big and strong," Clare answered. "He'll be up in no time. And by the way, I'm pretty sure he's an American Shorthair, not a tabby. Winifred Smith at the library helped me do some research yesterday. At first she said he might be a Maine Coon when I described him, but then I saw a picture of an American Shorthair in one of the cat books. It was Winston. Do you know Winifred, she's the town librarian."

Katherine said no, she didn't know many people in town. She said was sorry she forgot to tell Clare to bring Curtis. Clare told her that she didn't see Curtis all that much anymore. He'd starting hanging around with some older guys, one of whom had a car. In fact she'd hadn't seen him since Thanksgiving Day. Katherine asked what they'd done for Thanksgiving. Clare told her, that her mom and dad hadn't been there, they'd gone off with Uncle Tim a few days before. So she and Curtis bought two large-size frozen turkey dinners at the Red & White for Thanksgiving.

"It was good," Clare said. "Lots of stuffing and gravy. We had a very nice holiday. Thank you for asking."

When Katherine asked where her parents had gone and who was Uncle Tim, Clare told her that Uncle Tim was her mother's brother. He came to town now and then they all went off together. Uncle Tim said they had to go see a man about some money. Katherine asked how she got along by herself when Curtis was gone and her folks weren't around.

Clare said, "I don't want to be impolite Katherine, but you're starting to sound like a social worker, just like the social worker I had once, after Dad got hurt. If you want to be friends, please don't interrogate me. Let's just talk about what friends talk about."

Katherine was embarrassed, "I'm sorry for sounding like a social worker."

"That's all right, Katherine. I believe you. There's just one thing I want to say about my family. My mom and dad are good people. They've had some trouble since Dad got hurt in the woods. That's when they both started drinking. But they've always meant well. They're sick right now and I need to do the best I can by them. I need to help them get well. That goes for Curtis too. He's always watched out for me. He's a good boy who's just confused at the moment."

"Good for you Clare," Katherine said. "Let's go fix something to eat."

In the kitchen, Katherine told Clare she had been appointed second cook, which meant while Katherine fried the burgers, steamed the green beans, and monitored the tater tots in the oven, Clare was to set the table, get the mayonnaise, mustard, and ketchup out of the refrigerator, warm the buns in the toaster oven, and pour the drinks, sparkling water for the first cook and whatever the second cook wanted. Clare went to work without a word.

As they sat down to eat, Katherine said, "I forgot the salad," and went back to the kitchen. She brought in two salad plates each with a square of lime Jell-o salad with shredded carrots and celery and topped with a dollop of mayonnaise. "One of my specialties," she told Clare.

"That looks interesting," Clare said.

They ate in silence at first and then Clare started telling Katherine about Winifred and the library. She went to the library every day after school for an hour or so to do her homework. Winifred helped her when she needed it. She'd also referred Clare to Beata Holmgren, who'd wanted someone to read to her in the evening.

"Beata's Nils Holmgren's mother, Andy's grandmother," Clare told her. "She's eighty-six and doesn't see too well. So I go over three times a week and read to her for an hour. We're in the middle of *The Caine Mutiny* now."

She told Katherine that Nils gave her ten dollars a week in one dollar bills. She wasn't supposed to tell anyone about the money. "But, since we're going to be friends, I'm telling you," Clare said.

Clare had been suspiciously eyeing the lime Jell-o salad. She asked Katherine what the white stuff on top was.

"Mayonnaise," Katherine said. "It's a garnish. Supposed to make it look inviting."

"I'll remember that. Mayonnaise is a garnish that is supposed to make something look inviting," Clare said. "I've always put it on sandwiches."

Katherine laughed and Clare said, "I was trying to make a joke. I'm glad you laughed." She sampled the salad. "This is good, Katherine, Really good. Better without the garnish though."

When they were done with dinner and the dishes were washed,

Katherine got out the new Scrabble game which was still wrapped in plastic, and asked Clare if she played.

"My three favorite games are Hearts, Scrabble, and Parcheesi," she said. "Let's play."

But before they could start, Clare insisted they do, in her words, "an audit of the tiles," to make sure the set was complete. When Katherine protested, saying it was a brand new game, the tiles were certainly all there, Clare countered, saying there might have been an mistake at the factory, that whoever packed the boxes might have missed one or two tiles. It never hurt to double check.

"You can't always assume things like that, Katherine," she said with authority. "We'll feel better if we know we have all the tiles."

As Clare sat at the dining table, sorting the tiles into letter groups, lining up the A's in one line, the B's in another line, Katherine put some new CDs in her new changer. When she sat at the table, Clare told her to read the number of tiles per letter from the list on the Scrabble board. As Katherine read, "A, 6 tiles," Clare responded, "A, 6 tiles here," until they went through the alphabet and all the tiles were accounted for. Then Clare asked Katherine if she would mind keeping score, because she concentrated so hard, she sometimes forgot to record the score of each play.

"Anything else before we begin?" Katherine asked.

"No, I believe that's it, Katherine," Clare answered. "I assume you know the rules. Anyway, we have the rule book right there to check if we get into an argument."

"No arguments at this table," Katherine said. "We're friends, remember."

It was a close game. Clare was an aggressive player who knew how to play the double letter and triple letter squares as well as the double word and triple word squares with skill. She didn't give Katherine the opportunity to play to a triple word score. In spite of her assumed advantage of a larger vocabulary, Katherine worked hard to keep up.

While they played, Clare asked, "What's that music you have on, it sounds familiar."

"The New World Symphony," Katherine answered. "Or more formally, 'The Symphony Number 9 in E Minor, From the New World, Opus 95' by

Antonin Dvorak. He wrote it after he spent a summer in Iowa after he'd come from Czechoslovakia to live in America."

"How do you know all that?"

"I've studied music since I was a kid. Since when Miss Howe taught me piano and voice in Cedar Rapids, Iowa." Katherine said. "That music reminds me of Iowa, when I was about your age.

"What was Iowa like?" Clare asked.

"It was a fairy tale world. I had everything a little girl could want. Everything was perfect just like it is supposed be in Iowa. I thought my happy life would never change."

"Iowa is a long way away," Clare mused.

"This music also reminds me of a new friend that's mad at me right now," Katherine added.

"Why's your new friend mad at you?"

"I'm not sure," Katherine said. "I think it has something to do with reminding him of part of his past he didn't want me to know about, when he was somebody he didn't think he should be. Anyway, let's play Scrabble."

As the end of the game approached, Katherine had held the Q most of the match and hadn't drawn a U. Clare had played three of the four U tiles and with only four tiles in her rack with no more to draw, it was obvious she had the last U. She looked at Katherine with a smile and played on the I in the vertical word P R A I S E with the horizontal word M U F T I. The F was on a triple letter tile and the M was on a double word tile. Clare finished with a final play worth thirty-six points.

"I'm out," she said with a sigh. "You get one more turn. Oh, in case you don't know what it means, *mufti* is a soldier's civilian clothes."

"I know what it means," Katherine said, trying not to sound testy. She had three tiles left, played two and had to eat the Q for a minus ten points. The final tally was Clare Dolan 203, Katherine Baker, 199.

"I'm glad you didn't play down to me," Clare said. "I like to win fair and square."

As they ate their post-game vanilla ice cream topped with caramel syrup, Clare asked, "Ok, what's that playing now? That piano music."

"That's the Piano Concerto Number 2 in C Minor, Opus 18, by Sergei

Rachmaninoff."

"Wow. That's neat you know all that," Clare said.

"Tell me what Miss Howe, was like. Your music teacher in Iowa."

"She was strict and demanding like anyone who'd studied music at Oberlin. She said I wasn't going to get to Julliard without years of hard work in spite of my talent."

"What's Julliard?" Clare asked.

"It's a music school in New York," Katherine answered.

"What was it like. What was Julliard like?"

"I didn't go."

"Why not?"

"We left Iowa and moved here. I gave up my piano and voice lessons," Katherine. "Now who's interrogating whom? Let's change the subject."

Clare laughed and took the dishes into the kitchen. She told Katherine she had to leave as soon as she finished cleaning up. It was close to six o'clock when she was supposed to be at Beata Holmgren's.

"I like to get there a little early because Beata likes to chat for a while. She loves the company," Clare said. "After I read for about an hour, she starts to doze off. Then I call Nils or his wife Maida, and one of them comes over from next door and gets her to bed." She walked into the dining room and sat with Winston and then she hugged Katherine, thanking her and telling her how much she enjoyed their Sunday afternoon. "I'll see you later," she said as she turned and walked out the back door.

A Weekend Alone

On Friday night after Thanksgiving, when he'd walked out on his mother and Sheila Costigan at the Westminster Mews hotel, Jack felt like he'd finally cut himself loose from a part of his past that had been weighing him down like a proverbial albatross. Early the next morning as he drove north on Interstate 5 with no set destination, he realized what a hollow life he lived. Like an automaton, he'd walked back and forth to work during the week, spending the workday half-convinced he'd made a mistake by moving west, and dutifully driving to Cedar Mills on the weekends. He'd made no friends in the city and the stark reality of his empty life was painfully apparent.

On top of that, he'd alienated the only woman he'd ever loved by passively accepting his mother's moronic machinations of staging a reunion with Sheila. He'd thought of calling Katherine on Friday night when he got home. He wanted to tell her what he'd done, that he'd told the two half-drunk harpies where to go. But then he'd sound like the proud little boy, eager to brag about what a good job he'd done. He wanted to hear Katherine's voice. He wanted to tell her how he felt. But he didn't call.

An hour north of Seattle, he left the interstate at Mount Vernon and drove northwest on Route 20, through the now-barren tulip fields of the Skagit River delta toward Anacortes. He'd seen a sign for the San Juan Island ferry and it made him think of his Saturday afternoon ferry ride to nowhere with Katherine. It was a good time for another ferry ride to nowhere.

At Anacortes, a dreary blue-collar town supported by a large Shell Oil refinery he'd passed on the way to the ferry dock, he caught the 9:30 boat for Friday Harbor, a trip that took a little over an hour. It was a gray overcast morning. With no wind, the water was a smooth glassy surface, broken only by the wake of the ferry as it crossed Rosario Strait and wound past Orcas and Lopez Islands to the small island village of Friday Harbor. As he drove off the ferry, he smiled when he remembered asking Katherine what they did now when the ferry had landed at Whidbey Island. *We turn around and go back, unless you want a tour of Coupeville*, she'd said with a comic brusqueness.

Once off the boat, he parked the car and walked aimlessly around the village, stopping and staring into souvenir and gift shop windows. He wandered into the Bell Bottom Trouser, a waterside restaurant which had a cozy bar on one side with a roaring fireplace overlooking the harbor. He overcame the urge to sit in one of the overstuffed chairs at the window and order a Jameson's on the rocks.

He picked at his the fried halibut sandwich Monte Carlo and beer battered Walla Walla onion rings, thinking about Katherine, wishing she was sitting across the table making him feel there was no better place to be than together. Back outside, the ferry from Anacortes was just rounding the point, a few minutes away from docking.

On the return trip, Jack sat at a window-side table on the ferry's passenger deck and wrote a postcard to Katherine. On the front of the card was a photo of the ferry he was on, the *M/V Nooksack*, leaving the landing at Friday Harbor. He started to write something mushy but stopped. He didn't know who read postcards at the Cedar Mills post office and who they gossiped with.

Jack got back to Seattle in the late afternoon and called Hazel and Roy. When Roy answered, saying Hazel was up at the barn giving Donny a riding lesson, Jack overcame the urge to tell him about the dust-up with his mother and Sheila. He started to ask about Katherine but didn't. He only half-listened to Roy's story about their trip to Sea-Tac with May and Archie and how afterward, they'd thought about driving into the city to visit him but remembered he was skiing with Sheila. He started to ask again about Katherine, but caught himself and said good-bye.

✧ ✧ ✧ ✧ ✧ ✧ ✧ ✧ ✧ ✧ ✧ ✧

Sunday afternoon, Jack wandered down to Pike Place to Silas Peavey's shop. He had a question about Paul Merrick's visit to Time Pieces, something he'd forgotten to ask on his first visit. When he walked into the shop as the bell tied to the door jangled, Joey came out of a door at the rear of the shop, next to Peavey's large work table in front of the window, looked at him, and yelled back "It's the guy from Uncle Herk's office."

"Send him back," came the reply from Silas Peavey.

Joey, who had a napkin tucked in the top of her blouse, hooked her arm with a "come on," motion and said, "Follow me, please."

The "back room" as the shop denizens called it, ran parallel to the shop proper and was equal in size. In front of the waterfront window which extended the width of the room was a dining table where Peavey was presiding over plates of chocolate cake and ice cream. He was joined by the two kids, Will and Joey, his gofer Bob, and Professor Edward Balfour who had taken Jack to Lake Union to see the remains of the *Arctic Maid*.

"Have a seat son," Peavey said, motioning to an empty place at the table. "My sister just left. She tries hard, but she can only stand so much of us hooligans. She decamped before dessert. Bob, you scoundrel, get Mr. Jack some cake and ice cream. And bring us more coffee if you would please."

Jack said, "Good to see you again, Professor Balfour. Thanks again for taking me to see the *Arctic Maid*."

"Eddie. It's Eddie down here," Peavey said. "He gets to be Professor muckety muck at the UW."

The two kids looked at each other and chanted, "Eddie it was, Eddie it is, and Eddie it always shall be."

Eddie laughed and said, "My fan club," while Peavey shouted, "Pipe down you Huns or you'll walk the plank at sundown."

Jack told them he and Hercules were meeting with Paul Merrick the next afternoon.

Peavey said, "We've just been talking about that whole stinking business. Eddie's brought us some more news about that ship. Tell him Eddie."

Eddie told Jack that he'd been searching the Suzzallo Library's Mosquito Fleet microfilm archives for any references to the *Arctic Maid*. He explained the Mosquito Fleet was the flotilla of small and medium sized passenger and freight steamers that plied the waters of Puget Sound in the late nineteenth and early twentieth centuries. He'd found a reel of film that contained photographs of the metal plates that were often on a bulkhead of a ship, sometimes in the wheel house, sometimes in a public area, which described where the ship's keel had been laid and other facts about its history.

Peavey interrupted as Bob brought Jack's cake and ice cream, "Come on Eddie, get to the point. You're not lecturing your undergraduates."

Eddie said, "Too make a long story short, one of the photographs, which by the way were all taken by my mentor, Dr. James Underwood, was the plate from the *Arctic Maid*, which states her keel was laid in 1890 at the Martineau Shipyards in New Orleans. How she got from there to India, who knows, but this is something Paul Merrick isn't even aware of."

Jack said it was interesting, but he didn't see how it was relevant.

Peavey half-shouted, "Relevance be damned, Jack. It's information. it's another fact we add to our arsenal of history. What Eddie calls our precious repository of maritime knowledge. Now let's change the subject. Herk told me you came from Chicago."

Jack nodded, "I worked in Chicago."

"Well, that accent isn't Chicago, unless they moved the city south across the Ohio River."

Jack laughed. "You're right. What do you think it is?"

"Well, it isn't that deep, syrupy South. I spent four years in the Coast Guard along the Gulf Coast and I know all about the Alabama accent and Mississippi for that matter. That's not yours. I'm guessing Kentucky."

Eddie broke in, "I'm saying North Carolina, maybe Virginia."

"You're both wrong," Jack said, enjoying their little game.

Then Bob spoke up, "Tennessee. "I say Tennessee."

"Bob wins," Jack said.

"Bob, you sharper, how'd you know that?" Peavey asked, obviously pleased.

"Triangulation," Bob said with a smile and got up to clear the table.

While Bob, Will, and Joey were clearing the table and washing the dishes, Jack asked why Paul Merrick was so curious about what had been on board the *Arctic Maid*.

In the other room they could hear Will and Joey singing, "Bob said see, it's Tennessee, he's got the key, it's Tennessee, glory be, it's Tennessee." Peavey roared, "Pipe down in there you vandals or it'll be bread and water for a week!"

Peavey said, "He told me that back in India, when the ship was still the *Arundhati Star* and his grandparents were afraid of some native uprising, they moved most of their personal effects to the boat in anticipation of fleeing before they were captured."

Eddie said. "He thinks there's a stash of valuables somewhere in that hulk."

"He's a wily one," Peavey said. "He'll never admit it. You and Herk will have to put the screws to him tomorrow, Jack. Put him on the rack and make him talk."

It was late afternoon and the sun was starting to set over the Olympic Mountains across Elliott Bay. Jack thought, *She's over there on the other side of those mountains*, as he watched the snow-capped Olympics turn a darkening blue in the growing dusk. *What's she doing right now?*

His reverie was broken when Peavey shouted, "Bob, you blackguard, we're closing up. Let's go home."

Eddie said he'd go get the car and meet them out at the market's main entrance on First Avenue. Jack promised Peavey a full report on the meeting with Merrick. Then he and Eddie walked up the wide, dimly lit walkway with its switchbacks at each floor, to the street level. Eddie told Jack he was going up in the mountains to his uncle's birthday party on Saturday.

"They're all from North Carolina up there," Eddie said. "Why don't you come along. Bring your guitar. You might find it interesting."

They stood on First Avenue at the market entrance waiting for Peavey and the others. Across the street, a small crowd of women, mostly teen-age girls, were gathering in front of an all-night donut shop.

Jack asked, "What's that all about?"

"The nightly street trade's starting up. Seattle's a magnet for every run-away kid from here to Bozeman, Montana and beyond," Eddie said. "They pour into town every day. A lot of them end up down here. If you go down Second Avenue a few blocks, you'll find the boys preening in the alley behind the Arctic Hotel. Seattle's a dirty little town in a lot of ways. It's attracted the lost souls of the Northwest for generations. I grew up down here. I'll take you on a tour of the underbelly sometime. I need to find Jim Underwood before Christmas. He's drunk around here somewhere."

"Sounds like fun," Jack said as Peavey and his entourage appeared. Peavey, in his black wool overcoat and stocking cap, looked like Santa in mufti with two overgrown elves. He held the hands of Will and Joey as they walked, while Bob followed, on the lookout for any threats spawned by the First Avenue night.

Silas lived on Queen Anne Hill. Jack's place was on the way. Eddie offered Jack a ride home. But Jack declined. He went up Pike Street across the street from the whores, turned left on Second Avenue and walked home with a cold winter wind at his back, wishing he and Katherine were feeling that freezing wind, sitting close together in their lean-to at Third Beach while the ocean roared.

Monday Monday

On Monday morning, Bobby came to work with the football from the Thanksgiving Day game. He put it on a shelf in the storeroom after giving Bert Peck detailed description of how he'd caught Katherine's pass and run for the game winning touchdown.

Bert listened patiently to Bobby's blow-by-blow account of the game while they unpacked the morning's delivery of bread and then he eagerly updated Katherine on the upcoming test marketing of Bateman's new line of pastries. The first delivery would most likely be in two weeks, as soon as the display case was ready, which, Bert reminded her again, was being provided to the café at no cost. Bert told her they were going to start with six each of maple bars, butter horns and bear claws.

"What do you think?" Bert asked Katherine. "Are you on board?"

"I think it's very exciting Bert," she said. "I'm sure Sid Bateman appreciates your dedication to this."

Katherine was working as second cook in Larry's absence, something she told herself she'd be doing for a while. He'd called the night before to ask for some time off, saying he'd probably be back in a few days. But she didn't believe him. He was heading for the bottom. She kept looking down the kitchen as she worked, half expecting Jack to come in for his Monday morning breakfast for the road. But no Jack. *Thank God, that's over,* she thought.

The rest of the day went by in a blur. When Greeley came downstairs and asked about Larry, Katherine told him Larry was taking some time off.

"What if he starts drinking again?" Greeley asked. "What do we do?"

"He'll have to figure that out for himself," Sadie answered. "They're his demons, not ours."

Just before closing, Randy Weaver, the forestry professor from the University of Washington called and asked Katherine if he could, in his words, make a field trip to her house to examine the piano and it's modifications made with *Chloroxylon Swietenia*. He'd sounded more excited about seeing the East Indian Satinwood than Katherine thought normal. She agreed to a visit the coming Saturday morning but curtly told him that was it. No more exotic wood enthusiasts lining up at her front door to swoon over contraptions made from *Chloroxylon Swietenia*, which was beginning to sound as sacred as water from the Ganges.

Katherine walked home up the alley laughing at herself, thinking how when the phone rang in her office, she thought it was Jack. How strange. Jack is nothing, she thought. She walked into the kitchen and looked into the dining room at Winston's bed by the stove. It was empty. The food bowl was empty. The water bowl was empty. She spotted Winston in the living room, sitting under the piano staring at her. He was as big as a bobcat. The wounds on his face still looked gruesome, but were starting to heal. His right ear, which had been bent, was now straight. She stared at him and he stared back.

Meanwhile in Seattle, Jack and Hercules Pushkin were meeting with Paul Merrick who'd arrived at the office of Pushkin, McDonald & Fishkin promptly at three o'clock. Merrick was impeccably dressed in a brown worsted three-piece suit, a blue spread-collar shirt, yellow hounds tooth tie, and gleaming brown wing-tip brogues. His Etonian accent was just as impeccable.

The Englishman told them he was on a sales trip, visiting stores in Seattle and Portland to generate interest in Merrick & Son's new line of yoga gear called Ghandiwear.

But Pushkin brushed aside the small talk with a curt, "So Mr. Merrick, please tell us why you're here, surely not to sell us yoga paraphernalia."

Merrick said he wanted to explore the possibility of salvaging the remains of *Arctic Maid*, the old hulk that Silas Peavey and Professor Balfour had helped him locate. He wanted to take what was left of the ship, which was originally named the *Arundhati Star*, back to Vancouver as a memorial to his Indian heritage.

"With all due respect to your family background, sir, and in no way do I mean to degrade the honor of your forebears, but what you propose is preposterous," Pushkin said. "Pushkin, McDonald & Fishkin has a sterling reputation and getting involved in that kettle of poppycock would make us a laughing stock."

Merrick's convivial countenance changed. His smile became a frown and his eyes narrowed. His hands were white knuckled around the arm of his chair.

"By God sir, what the deuce are you really after? My colleague here, Mr. Lindsay, has done some research into what your game might be. We've had other operatives on your trail as well. None of what you say adds up. So I'll ask again, what the deuce are you really after?"

Merrick rose slowly. "I was expecting a more welcoming reception but unfortunately I was wrong. I'm insulted that a law firm with such a sterling reputation as you call it, would stoop to having me followed, an honest businessman wishing to pay homage to his family. Thank you for your time," he said glowering at Pushkin and Jack before starting for the door.

Pushkin stood and said, "For the third time, sir. What the deuce are you really after?"

Merrick stopped at the door and turned with a sneer, "The Moody piano. The Moody piano that is rightfully mine." And then he was gone.

Pushkin asked Jack, "What the deuce! Does this have something to do with Cedar Mills? One of our gumshoes found out that nut log's cousin was over on the Peninsula nosing around."

Jack said, "The so-called Moody piano is in Cedar Mills. I've played it. I know the person who owns it. "

"Katherine Baker? The woman Maude Doud told me about. The one you went to see when Maude was at Swedish?"

Jack nodded and told Pushkin about the piano's hollowed out front legs.

"So this crackpot thinks there's something in those hollow legs. That's not difficult to figure out. Was there?"

"They were empty. Whatever they held had been long gone by the time Katherine found out about them."

"What the deuce Jack, we've got more to deal with than a dark-skinned Englishman who's off his rocker," Pushkin said. "But you did a fine job lad. You passed my bullshit test. I put you onto Merrick to see what you'd do and you saw what I did. The guy's a harebrain. Now I know I can trust you. Pack your bag tonight, you're going to Kodiak in the morning to help Bart

Ladderback buy a crab boat."

❖ ❖ ❖ ❖ ❖ ❖ ❖ ❖ ❖ ❖ ❖ ❖

Like Paul Merrick, Buck McCready also had a three o'clock meeting in Seattle on Monday afternoon. His was with Alfred Lightwell at Dryad Appraisals on the second floor of the Smith Tower where he hoped to resituate his languishing bank account with a sale of what he liked to call the family jewels.

Buck had spent the Thanksgiving holiday in a funk, being as Roger called him, a big lummox. But Buck had every reason to be grouchy. Not only was there a problem with his cash flow, not to mention the unending diet of salmon because of it, but Buck had been on edge since the Canadian, Arthur Merrick, had paid them a visit. Buck had been suspicious when Merrick had shifted the conversation from scheduling charter trips for the yoga gear distributors to Dallas Moody.

Afterward, he'd gone through his journals from the Corky Carlsson years which listed every venue the band played. Merrick said he'd seen them in B.C. at the Chilliwack fire hall. But they were never in Chilliwack. They'd played Kamloops, Penticton, Coquitlam, and Squamish, but never Chilliwack. The Canuck was lying.

Then there was the surprise appearance of the couple from Cedar Mills. The woman, who Buck assumed had been that Katherine Baker from Greeley's café, had also said something about Luther Moody. Two visits by strangers. Two mentions of Dallas Moody. Buck was nervous.

But now he was in Seattle, anxious to get through his meeting with Alfred Lightwell and hopefully come away with a sizable addition to his dwindling bank account. And it came with a price. It didn't matter how many years had passed since he'd become Ron Lantz, impresario extraordinaire, the man who had put Corky Carlsson on the map. It mattered even less that he had carved out a modest career as Buck McCready, the cowboy troubadour, who with his sidekick Dallas Moody, was a favorite at every Grange dance from the Methow Valley to Enumclaw. To people he met from his Mercer Island days like Alfred Lightwell, Buck McCready was always Myron Lantz, son of the famed dentist Sid Lantz.

A Card From Nowhere

On Tuesday afternoon after work, Katherine found Jack's postcard buried in the junk mail piled on the living room floor under the front door mail slot. Tears filled her eyes when she read: *Hello Katherine, Am writing this on a ferry trip to nowhere wishing you were by my side. Missing you. Love Jack.* She carried the card around the house, looking at the photo of the *M/V Nooksack* leaving Friday Harbor, then turning it over and reading Jack's note.

Damn you, Jack, you fool, she thought. The card was the first piece of personal mail she'd ever received.

When she finally stopped blubbering, she walked down to Cedar Country Appliances to tell Nils Holmgren her new television didn't work, there was snow on every channel. When he asked about the antenna, she said she didn't have one. He hemmed and hawed, saying Andy should have checked all that before he'd left on Saturday. Then he remembered that Greeley had torn down the old antenna when he'd bought the house. To make up for Andy's oversight, he said he'd sell her a top-of-the line rotating antenna at cost and waive the installation charge.

"You'll be able to get all the channels with that puppy," Nils said. "Seattle, Tacoma, Bellingham. Even the Canadian stations." Katherine started to pay for the antenna and Nils asked her if she wanted a new VCR to go with the TV. "I've got a demo unit I can let you have for almost nothing. Then you can rent movies from Solly's Video Den. Just stay out of the back room," he added with a laugh.

Katherine asked if he'd seen Clare lately. She told him Clare's cat Winston was awake and getting better.

"She was just here a little while ago," Nils said. "She comes by every Tuesday afternoon for her reader's fee. She told me she told you about the ten dollars I give her every week."

"Let her know about her cat if you see her," Katherine said.

"Sure. But she told me Winston was your cat," Nils chuckled. "So I hear you might need to brush up a little on your Scrabble game."

Katherine smiled, "Tell Andy, I'll see him on Friday."

On her way home, she stopped at the Red & White and stood in the tuna fish aisle in a quandary. If the cat was recovering, did he really need a top flight diet of tuna fish? Wouldn't plain old canned cat food suffice? It was a third the price and given the way he ate, the difference was considerable. But she put a pile of canned tuna fish in her basket and went to the front to checkout.

"I see your cat's going to be eating high on the hog for a while," Nell said with a smile as she bagged the cans. "Unless you're on some new diet."

"Clare's cat is getting much better," Katherine said. "By the way, have you seen Clare lately?"

"She was here just a little while ago, getting some things for George Sizemore, Charlie's dad," Nell answered. "Clare picks up groceries for several of the older folks who can't get out. She's always in and out of here. She also told us you were a little rusty with your Scrabble game."

At home, Winston was sitting on top of the television staring at her, and for the first time, she smiled when she saw him. "Hello, Winston. How was your day?" she said. "Come on, I'll get you some of this gourmet tuna fish."

By the time she'd changed her clothes, made a cup of coffee, and worked her way through the beginning of the Rachmaninoff Piano Concerto, there was a knock on the front door. She could hear Maude saying in a loud voice, "Just open it up, boyfriend. We know she's home. She's playing the piano."

Katherine opened the front door to Milos and Maude. Maude's wheel chair was parked at the bottom of the front steps and she was walking with a cane. Milos helped Maude into the house and onto the sofa, and then handed Katherine a square package severely wrapped in butcher paper.

"Milo wanted to bring that over to you," Maude said. "The old cuss won't tell me what it is. Said it's none of my business. But, everything's my business, boyfriend, everything."

Katherine caught sight of Winston peering around the corner from the dining room when she put the package on the dining table. Milos sat in the wing chair across from the sofa while Katherine sat next to Maude and heard the story of her unfortunate relapse. The results from the biopsy on her liver were positive, or negative, she said. Whichever meant that nothing was wrong. But she'd started feeling light-headed a couple days ago and the doctors said the swelling in her legs might be phlebitis.

"Those doctors get their meat hooks into you and they won't let go," Maude said. "But enough of that. Milo and I've made up. He's back taking care of me."

Milos watched Winston cautiously inch his way into the living room.

"You've got a cat," he said with surprise.

"It's Clare Dolan's," Katherine said. "I'm taking care of it for her until it's better. It was hit by a car."

Maude said. "Clare told me this morning the cat was yours."

"You saw Clare this morning?"

"She stopped by on her way to school to see how I was doing."

Winston disappeared around the sofa and reappeared on the side of the wing chair where Milos sat. He jumped up over the side of the chair and on to Grajek's lap. Milos smiled and petted the purring cat who stared at Katherine.

Maude said she'd heard Katherine was trying to watch television with no antenna. "Pretty funny, sweetie. Guess Andy's going to put one in on Friday. That's what I heard." Maude said. "Oh and what's this I hear about the scrabble game, you losing to Clare."

Katherine got up to make coffee, but Maude said they couldn't stay. Milos picked up Winston, put him on the floor, and got up to steady Maude, who was making her way to the front door.

"Keep working on the Rachmaninoff. You'll get it," she said going down the steps. "I want to hear all about Randy Weaver's visit this weekend."

Katherine walked back into the house and closed the door. Winston was perched under the piano watching her unwrap the package from Milos. She was surprised he'd returned the book and amused by the heavy-duty wrapping, double protection from Maude's prying eyes. She read his inscription, carefully written in block letters, on the front inside endpaper:

For Katherine Baker: One of the brightest stars From The New World that I now live in. May you keep shining, helping me on my way. Gratefully, Your Friend, Milos Grajek, Cedar Mills, Washington.

For the second time that day, Katherine walked around the house blubbering.

Before she went to bed, Hazel called to say Anne had phoned the night before from Los Angeles, saying she wouldn't be home for awhile. She was on her way to spend a week with an old friend from the UW who had a time share at Cabo San Lucas. She needed to get away after a dust-up with Jack in Seattle. Anne had given Hazel a blow-by-blow description of the incident at Pesto. Sheila had found an early flight back to Chicago the next day and left without even saying goodbye to Anne.

"This isn't the first time Jack and his mother have had it out," Hazel said. "I made the mistake of getting in the middle once, and I'm not doing it again."

Katherine went to bed night with the Lindsays on her mind. She knew all about the mirage of familial perfection. The Owlings had lived with an impenetrable veneer of a perfect family which successfully hid a secret macabre world. She laughed to herself, *The Platonic ideal of family, there isn't one.*

She couldn't stop thinking about Jack, growing up in that recondite world of Sewanee, Tennessee. There was something inextricably poignant about him, as if all the supposed love and caring from his family was illusory. She remembered how he'd described Hazel and Roy as his "Aunt Hazel" and "Uncle Roy," on his first visit to the café, and how he'd called Archie, "Uncle Archie," at the Thanksgiving table, as though he had cobbled together his own extended family out of a deep-seated need to belong. He was alone and he was lonely.

The Family Jewels

On Tuesday morning, after a night in Seattle following his visit to Dryad Appraisals, Buck McCready was on the Edmonds-Kingston ferry heading back across the Sound, glad to be returning to Sekiu, where the intemperate Roger's companionship and cuisine were waiting, and relieved that the Myron Lantz persona was dormant once again. He'd bristled each time Alfred Lightwell called him Myron, telling himself it was the cost of doing business. But it'd been worth it, he'd got what he'd come for, money.

Lightwell hadn't changed since the last time they'd met under similar circumstances. He was a thin, elegant man with a thick shock of gray hair which hung slightly over his forehead. His inquisitive green eyes focused on Buck with an unrelenting, unnerving intensity. Buck endured a rehashing of the old Mercer Island days and Lightwell's laudatory comments about Sid Lantz, the best dentist in the Northwest and then Lightwell got to the point, "So Myron, what do you have for us today?"

Buck handed him a small cedar jewel box which contained a gold oval pendant inlaid with rubies and diamond chips in the shape of a nine-pointed star. Nine tear-drop shaped rubies encircled a small diamond center piece. Each ruby was encased by a thin circle of diamond chips which intensified the deep color of the red gemstones.

If Buck or Lightwell had been privy to a worn four-inch by seven-inch brown leather notebook, now owned by Paul Merrick, which was a catalog, handwritten in English, of all the items the Mahindra's had hidden in the Kimball baby grand piano before they were murdered, they would have known the exquisite ruby pendant was the *Arundhati Star*, which was purchased in a Goa gem bazaar by Kumar Mahindra in 1867 for his new wife, Amrapahli, Paul Merrick's grandmother. Years later, when the Mahindra's flagship came out of the Martineau shipyards in New Orleans, they named the boat after the singular pendant.

Buck had waited with bated breath as Lightwell took the pendant to his light table and pored over it with his loupe. Lightwell reached for a yellow legal pad at the edge of the table. He wrote "$200,000" and handed it to Buck, saying, "I've never seen anything quite like it, Myron. It's a stunning work of art."

"I agree," Buck had said, writing "$300,000" on the pad and handing it back to Lightwell.

Lightwell knew the pendant would go at auction for five times what Buck was asking. He hesitated, then drew lines through the "$200,000" and "$300,000" and wrote, "$250,000." He handed the pad back to Buck, who wrote "Sold," under the figure.

"Very good Myron," Lightwell said, putting one hand on Buck's shoulder and shaking his hand with the other, "The money will be wired your account at Glacier Trust today."

Now as Buck watched the Edmonds ferry dock fade in the distance and the oil tanks at Point Wells become hazy white orbs, he sunk into the same reverie he'd had the last time and the time before when he'd sold a piece of the family jewels to Alfred Lightwell. Did he get the better part of the deal when he and Luther had split the piano's hidden loot? He'd never know.

It was when Luther had first moved back to Cedar Mills those many years ago that they discovered the piano's secret. The underside of the piano had been sealed with thin hopsack cloth which had been stapled to the bottom to keep out dust and dirt. When the movers wrestled the piano into Luther's new house in Cedar Mills, the hopsack was torn loose in front and hung down to the floor.

Luther and Buck crawled under the piano to tack the cloth back up and found the wooden levers that lowered the hidden supplementary legs and allowed the front legs to swing to the side. Each hollow leg contained a copper tube sealed at the top with a copper lid. It was the first time Buck had heard Luther raise his voice, "Jiminy Crickets," he'd gasped.

Buck reached for the left side tube's handle to pull the copper vessel from the leg, but Luther stopped him, saying they had to have a plan. Luther said he didn't want their friendship jeopardized by this bizarre discovery. He told Buck each of them would take a tube. They'd open them privately. The contents would never be discussed with the other. They flipped a coin to decide who would take the copper cylinder in the piano's left leg. Luther won. Buck removed the container from the right leg and carried it unopened to his car. Nothing was ever said about the piano's secret again.

There were five pieces of rare jewelry in Buck's piano leg, each carefully wrapped in oilskin. He'd put them in five separate safe deposit boxes in five different banks around Seattle. Now three of the boxes were empty. Buck never found out what Luther's share was or what he'd done with it. The secret had gone with him to the grave.

❖ ❖ ❖ ❖ ❖ ❖ ❖ ❖ ❖ ❖ ❖ ❖

It was late afternoon by the time Buck cleared Port Smith and was on Route 112, the last leg of his trip home. The heebie jeebies he'd had since his visit to Dryad Appraisals were beginning to abate the closer he got to home. He'd stopped in Gosport at Porky Pataca's Four Seasons Marina and Dry Dock where he freed the *Wanda Jean* from her bondage of an unpaid dry dock bill and refitting charges. He wrote Porky a check and told the sour-faced Portuguese yard master to put her back in the water, that Roger would be down in a few days to take her back to Sekiu.

Porky's eyes fixed on him with an analytical, unnerving stare as he showed him the remodeled cabin of the thirty-two foot charter boat, the new fish finding sonar equipment, and the latest in GPS communications. He said Buck could take that bad girl to South America if he wanted. *Who knows, we may have to*, Buck said to himself as he waved goodbye to Porky and headed for Cedar Mills, where on a whim, he stopped at the Madison Café for lunch, hoping to get a look at this Katherine Baker and maybe run into Greeley.

It had been a bad decision. Greeley was still sore about Buck sending the snoopy Canadian, Arthur Merrick to town, looking for information about Luther Moody. Buck's heebie jeebies returned when Greeley invited Katherine Baker to join them for lunch. Katherine demurred but sat with them for a moment, her eyes trained on Buck with a sharp, unnerving intensity.

Buck had been surprised by two things, Katherine's firm handshake and her good looks. The handshake meant business and so did her demeanor. With her shoulder length light brown hair in a flip with light brown eyes to match, her small, sharp nose, and a well-proportioned mouth that looked like smiling was not a regular occurrence, she was a handsome woman who was not easily forgotten.

But Buck didn't like the way the two of them kept looking at him and he was glad to get on the road. Finally back home at Buck McCready's Salmon Adventures, he was profoundly happy to have some money in the bank. He walked up the wooden steps to the sprawling front porch overlooking the marina. He paused at the front doorbell. He took the long cedar handle inlaid with carved figures of salmon and struck the hanging three-foot, light green copper cylinder with a resounding force. The low bass metallic ring reverberated down the hill and across the deserted marina. Buck McCready, cowboy troubadour, was home.

In Invitation

Greeley was still sitting in the dining room writing in his notebook when Katherine walked through on her way home. "Buck McCready was a surprise. He didn't look at all like I imagined."

Greeley laughed. "What were you expecting? The Marlboro Man?"

"Well, I wasn't expecting someone barely taller than me with a pinkish complexion and hands that look like they've never done a day's work. Then that hair with a bald spot in the back and a comb-over that looks like it's a scalp disorder. I kept staring at it, fighting the urge to reach up and pour something on it."

Greeley laughed again. "Buck's okay. When he met Luther, he concocted a cowboy minstrel universe inhabited by Buck McCready and Dallas Moody. They were devoted to each other for years."

As she started out the door, Greeley asked with a snicker, "When's Andy Holmgren coming over to get that snow out of your TV?"

"Very funny," Katherine said, "Everyone in town's a comedian."

She went up the street to Wally Berger's Book Mart to pick up another book she'd ordered, Alan Lindsay's first book, *Voyage from Nicaea: Faith in the Modern World*. She thought it might help her understand *The Platonic Ideal of Faith: There Isn't One,* which she was still struggling to decipher after two readings. But reading it, with its exhaustive exegesis of the Nicene Creed, had inspired her to open the *Book of Common Prayer* every morning and read the profession of faith out loud. She liked the sound of the words and she liked opening the book because it made her think of Hazel and her days at the Kingsport Press.

This new book by Jack's father would be another reminder of him, however. Now only a week after the Thanksgiving debacle, she could openly admit she missed him. She missed him hard. As hackneyed as it was, Jack felt like the missing half to her life. He brought out a Katherine Baker that had long been buried, the whimsical one who was facetiously funny, the antic one who loved to laugh, the one who made her think it might be possible to love someone.

Wally was behind the counter when she walked in. He handed her the new book and asked with a laugh, "You planning to study for the ministry?"

She smiled and then saw with alarm copies of *The Lithuanian Septet* on a small table to the right of the counter. A sign on a pedestal above the books said, "Poems by Milos Grajek, Noted Local Poet." Wally looked confused when she asked what he thought he was doing, selling Grajek's book.

"That's what I do. I sell books. I have you to thank for letting me know just who he is. Lonnie's always said he knew Grajek was something, he just didn't know what. Nora's at Maude's right now, trying to talk Grajek into letting us have a book signing and a poetry reading here at the store."

Katherine left clutching her new book, fearful of how Milos would take the news that his book was on sale at the Book Mart. She walked past Maude's half expecting Milos to come out of the house and yell at her. By the time she was home, she'd decided to stay out of it. His fear that people would find out he was a noted poet of the Holocaust was his problem.

When she came through the back gate, Clare Dolan was sitting on the back porch steps reading a book. Two more books were on the step next to her.

"What are you reading?" Katherine asked as she sat down next to Clare.

"The Black Stallion Returns," Clare said. It's the book after *The Black Stallion*, where he gets taken to Arabia and Alec goes after him. Winifred says there are seventeen or eighteen books in the series. Maybe I can get through them all, I don't know. I've already read *Black Beauty* and the three Flicka books."

"So you like horses," Katherine said, picking up the two books on the step.

"I like stories about horses," Clare said. "I don't know if I'd like a real horse, I've never been around one. Anyway, I came by to see how Winston's doing and I brought you a couple of books from the library."

"Your cat's doing great. He's up and around. He eats all the time and his wounds are healing. Doesn't look like there's any infection. Come on, let's go take a look."

Winston was perched on the kitchen table, staring at them. Clare walked over to pet him, "Winston, you look great," but the cat jumped off the table and sauntered into the dining room. When Clare walked toward him, he moved out of reach, repeating the move each time she tried to get near him. "What's the matter, Winston? You mad at me?"

"He's that way with me too," Katherine said. Putting the two books from the library on the dining room table. "You brought *me* these books? *Caring for Your Cat*, and *How to Live With Cats?*"

"I didn't think you'd ever had a cat before. Those might help," Clare said.

Katherine said she was taking care of Winston for Clare until he got better. But Clare pointed out she couldn't take him home and they couldn't just let him loose in the alley again, so Katherine had to care for him. Katherine sighed and said Winston could stay until Clare was able find a good home for him. Clare said she knew Katherine would see it her way.

Clare said. "Now I need to tell you what happened the other night."

They went into the living room and sat on the sofa. Winston stationed himself under the piano and stared at them. Clare told her the night before she was walking up the alley past Katherine's house around nine o'clock when she saw someone on the side of the house at her bedroom window. "He was trying to peek through a crack in one side of the curtain," Clare said. "I snuck in the yard and threw rocks at him. I hit him a couple times. It was that short, fat guy who was hanging around a while back."

Clare said he ran after her out the back gate but didn't catch her. "I'm surprised he could run at all."

Katherine made some hot chocolate and they sat at the kitchen table while Clare told her about her mother coming home alone on Monday after Thanksgiving because her dad had a new job at a mill in Kelso. Katherine asked her if they were going to move to Kelso.

"Mom says not right away." Clare said. "She wants to see if Dad can keep his job. And she started working at the tavern this week, so I think things are going to get better. It's just Curtis who's the problem now. He's never around."

"I just remembered I've got to go to choir practice tonight," Katherine said. "You want to have supper here before I go?"

Clare said "I can't stay long, I'm reading at Beata's tonight, but I guess I have time to eat. Thank you for inviting me, Katherine."

Katherine said they'd have hot dogs, hash brown potatoes, and steamed green beans. As second cook, Clare would take care of boiling the hot dogs and steaming the green beans while Katherine fried the hash browns. Clare asked if it would be ok if she had two hot dogs. Katherine felt a tear well up and said of course, she could have as many as she wanted. While they ate at the kitchen table, Clare talked about how different things were now that Curtis was never around and her dad was gone, and her mom was working at the tavern.

"So you're not out every night, checking my tool shed for food?" Katherine asked with a smile. "If you are, you've noticed there's been nothing there. I like you in here, eating with me."

Clare's face turned red. "We don't make our runs anymore. And now that Mom's got some money for food, we seem to be doing ok."

Katherine said, "I know some horses, six of them to be exact. Would you like to meet them?"

Clare just stared.

"They live out at New Morning Farm with my friends Hazel and Roy Willit. If you have the time sometime, I could take you out to see them."

"Are you serious?" Clare asked, still smiling. "I could be around real horses?"

"If you want to go."

There was no doubt Clare wanted to go and they decided on Saturday afternoon for a trip to the farm.

"Some professor from Seattle, Randy Weaver, is coming at nine on Saturday morning to look at my piano. We'll go after I get rid of him. But you'll have to ask your mom if it's ok."

"Randy's coming here on Saturday?" Clare said. "I go to the store for his mom. Can I come over when Randy's here? I haven't seen him in ages."

"Sure," Katherine said. "Why don't you come over early for breakfast. I'll teach you how to make pancakes."

They walked out the back door just before six o'clock.

"Don't forget to talk to your mother about Saturday," Katherine said.

"Maybe I should come over to your house to meet her."

"No, don't do that," Clare said. "I'll tell her. She won't care."

Katherine watched Clare turn right and head down the alley for Beata Holmgren's, a little girl alone in the night.

❖ ❖ ❖ ❖ ❖ ❖ ❖ ❖ ❖ ❖ ❖

When she came home from work on Friday afternoon, Andy Holmgren on the side of the house stringing cable from new television antenna, which was perched atop a thick aluminum pole several feet above the peak of the roof, around to the front of the house, under the front porch to the small window next to the front door where he'd drilled a hole through the sash.

"Perfect timing," he said when Katherine opened the front door. "We're almost ready to blast off."

By the time Katherine had changed her clothes, made a pot of coffee, and filled Winston's food bowl, Andy had the antenna plugged in and the rotation control installed on top of the television. He stood in front of the TV, changing channels and rotating the antenna until a channel was tuned in. He wrote the settings on the back of the antenna's instruction manual. Then he motioned for Katherine to sit on the sofa and handed her the remote control.

"That's state-of-the-art stuff you've got in your hand, my friend," he boasted. "You change a channel and the antenna will automatically rotate to where it should be for optimum reception. Not too shabby, huh? Dad said you deserved the best."

"Very nice," Katherine said. "Great job Andy. Now all I have to do is figure out what to watch."

"Well, you've got the whole shootin' match with this gizmo. Everything around the Sound, from Bellingham to Seattle to Tacoma, and the all the Canadian channels to boot. The list is right there on the back of the manual."

"What's on the Canadian channels?" Katherine asked.

"I don't know. Never watch them myself. But everyone brags about being able to tune 'em in."

After Andy left, Winston left his perch on the dining room table where he'd been closely monitoring the goings on, and sat on the living room floor in front of the sofa, just out of reach of Katherine as she played with changing channels on the television. He jumped up and hid in the dining room when he heard Hazel knock on the front door, then open it and shout "hello."

They sat at the dining room table drinking coffee while Katherine told her about her plan to bring Clare Dolan out to the farm on Saturday.

"Sound like a great idea," Hazel said as Winston, who'd made his way to the side of her chair unnoticed, jumped up on her lap. Hazel gasped with surprise. "What are you doing, you big lug. You must weigh fifty pounds."

"You've been ambushed," Katherine said. "He won't let me touch him. He did the same thing to Milos. Snuck around and jumped on his lap when he and Maud were here yesterday."

Hazel said Maude had called to tell her about Larry's Thanksgiving holiday binge. She shook her head, "I'm not surprised. It's this whole thing with Anne. They were both in way over their heads. What a disaster."

"There's more to it than that," Katherine said. "My old boss from the Log Cabin Restaurant in Oregon called this morning. Said a guy named Larry Bradford had come in the day before looking for a job."

Katherine recounted the conversation with Nolan Beane in Roseburg.

"This Larry fella said he'd worked as second cook for you in that little one-horse operation you're running up there," Nolan had said with a laugh. "Don't you miss the big time sweetheart?"

"You mean the big time in Roseburg, Oregon where log rolling, arm wrestling, and chainsaw sculpture are the big attractions?" Katherine retorted.

"That's the place," Nolan chortled. "Anyway, so Larry Bradford wanted a job. I said no. He didn't look the type. Not down and out enough to be a short order jockey. No hint of destitution and desperation."

"Did he say where he was headed?"

"Nope."

"Thanks for letting me know, Nolan. Call me again when you can't talk so long."

Nolan laughed. "Hey, how 'bout I sell this place, come up there, we'll get married, buy a ritzy, four-star hash house, and have a lot of babies."

"We'll have a lot babies?" Katherine laughed. "Always the charmer. Give me ten years to think it about. I've got to go."

Katherine told Hazel that Maude had told her about Margaret Woolley's sister, Joyce, who'd just moved down from Alaska where she'd been a cook for the last twenty years. Katherine hadn't hesitated to call Joyce Woolley after she found out Larry was on the road. Joyce was coming in for an interview on Monday morning.

Hazel was getting ready to leave when there was a knock at the front door. Katherine opened the door to Clare who was standing next to her mother, holding her hand.

"Katherine Baker, this is my mom, Sophie Dolan," Clare said with a formality, which coming from the eleven-year-old girl, was heartbreakingly poignant. "Mom, this is my friend, Katherine Baker."

Katherine and Sophie Dolan shook hands and Katherine ushered them in. Sophie saw Hazel at the dining room table, "Oh, you have company. I'm sorry." She turned to leave.

"No, no. Come in and meet Hazel," Katherine said. "She owns the horses I was telling Clare about. Please sit down. I'll get some coffee. How about you Clare?"

"Nothing for me, thanks," said Clare who solemnly sat with folded hands on the table.

Sophie said she was on her way to work and thought she'd stop by to say hello. Clare had told her about going out to the horse farm on Saturday. "Are you sure it's all right?" she asked.

"We'd love to have Clare come out to the farm," Hazel said.

Sophie Dolan didn't look like Katherine had imagined. She was younger, probably in her late thirties or early forties. She was pretty with streaked brown hair to her shoulders and a self-deprecatingly polite manner. There was a soft, plaintive look in her brown eyes. Her face told the story of a hard-lived life. She was nervously uncomfortable until Hazel starting talking about New Morning Farm and how she and Roy had moved from Tennessee a few years back.

"Where are your people?" Hazel asked. "Arkansas maybe?"

Sophie looked at the floor, "Southern Missouri. Might as well be

Arkansas." she said apologetically. "I met Bud when he was stationed at Fort Leonard Wood. That's how I ended up out here."

"I knew we had something in common," Hazel said with a laugh. "Two Southern girls trying to figure out these Yankees. Where Roy and I come from, we call 'em damn Yankees when they move to the South and don't go home."

Everyone at the table laughed. Sophie smiled apologetically and nodded to Clare, saying she had to go to work. She thanked Katherine and Hazel again and said she hoped Clare wouldn't be too much trouble at the farm. As they were headed out the front door, Clare told Katherine she'd be over early in the morning for breakfast.

"What a darling little girl," Hazel said, getting up to clear the table. "I've got to get home. Roy will be looking for his supper."

Hazel told her not to worry about Jack coming over for the weekend. "He won't be around for a while. He'll be thinking his mother's home."

Then she said Anne had called from Palm Springs the night before after leaving Baja sooner than she'd planned. She told Hazel when she got home next week, she wanted to talk to Roy and Hazel about the farm. "I can't wait to hear what that's about," Hazel said. "At least Roy and I own part of the land out there. And we still have a place in Tennessee. I think she's starting to go off her rocker."

As Hazel walked to the front door, Winston walked beside her. She bent down and gave him a pet, "Tell Katherine to bring you out to the farm. The horses would love having you around. But you have to be a mouser."

She told Katherine about Tiger and Matilda, two stray cats Jack had brought home when he was in sixth grade. "Alan and Anne said absolutely not, there'd be no cats in their house. They didn't care how much Jack loved them. Of course he was heartbroken. But we took them out to the barn where they lived for years. The horses loved the company."

After hugging Hazel goodbye on the front steps while Winston sat in the doorway watching, Katherine sat at the piano with the Johnny Mercer Songbook, playing and singing the songs Jack loved. She laughed when she sang with a growl, "I'm gonna love you, like nobody's loved you, come rain or come shine." Then she saw the pile of mail she'd dumped on the coffee table when she let Andy in to hook up the antenna. The corner of a postcard was sticking out of the middle of the pile. It was from Jack. On the front was a photo of the *M/V Hoquiam* leaving the dock at Bremerton. On the other side, Jack had written *Taking the ferry to nowhere is nowheresville without you. Missing you. Love Jack.*

She walked around the house with the card, reading it again and again as she paced. *Go ahead and stay away for while. Go ahead and run, she thought. Just not for too long and not too far.*

A New Day at New Morning Farm

Clare knocked on Katherine's back door at eight o'clock on Saturday morning and they got right to work in the kitchen making pancakes and sausage for breakfast. Katherine stood watching as she told Clare how to make the pancake batter and then showed her how much batter to spoon onto the griddle for a perfect pancake.

"This isn't something I show to just anybody," Katherine said. "You have to be in the inner circle to learn how to make Katherine Baker's pancakes."

"So I guess I'm in the inner circle," Clare said.

"You're the second cook of the inner circle," Katherine told her. "And while you're doing the pancakes, you've got to get your sausage started in the frying pan."

Once she'd made the sausage patties and had them in the pan, while at the same time tending to the growing stack of pancakes which were keeping warm in the oven, Clare said, "It seems like the second cook of the inner circle does a lot of the work."

"That's how a second cook of the inner circle learns to be first cook," Katherine said with a smile. "You've got to work hard."

While Clare concentrated on the sausage and pancakes, Katherine set the table, got out the butter and warmed the syrup. Winston lay in his bed next to the oil stove in the dining room squinting into the kitchen, watching them work. Clare shouted to him, "You're not fooling us, you old goat. You're not asleep. You're just waiting for some sausage."

They were in the dining room, just starting to eat, when Randy Weaver knocked on the front door. He was an hour early. Clare asked if she could get the door and Katherine nodded her head. Clare ran through the living room, opened the door and shouted, "Randy!" and gave him a hug, the top of her head just reaching above his waist. He patted her head and smiled, "What a surprise. How are you Clare?"

Dr. Randy Weaver was tall and thin and loomed large in the doorway. He peered tentatively into the house and started through the front door, led by Clare. Katherine walked into the living room. The professor was carrying a briefcase with his right hand. A curved black pipe was in his left. A camera was slung over his left shoulder.

"Stop. You're not bringing a pipe in here," Katherine scolded. "Take that thing back to your car. No pipe."

Dr. Randy Weaver shrugged, turned around and went back out to his car. Katherine watched him with amusement, an oversized version of the rumbled professor, with his light brown corduroy jacket, red and yellow checked shirt, blue jeans, and brown hiking boots. The crowning piece of his outfit, however, was the crumpled tweed walking hat which looked like it doubled as a seat cushion.

He apologized as Katherine led him into the living room, apologized for being early, apologized for not calling before he came, and apologized for the pipe. Katherine curtly told him he may as well join them for breakfast. She set another place at the table and poured him a cup of coffee.

Winston sat on the coffee table in the living room, watching as they ate in silence. Clare kept looking nervously at Katherine, who did nothing to hide her irritation with Dr. Weaver.

"I'm the second cook of the inner circle, Randy. So I got to make the pancakes and sausage. Under the direction of the first cook of the inner circle, of course," Clare said, pointing to Katherine.

"Well, they're mighty good," Randy Weaver said. "I thank you for inviting me to breakfast unannounced. A hearty thanks to the first and second cooks of the inner circle from the first nitwit of outer circle."

Clare and Katherine laughed. Katherine said, "I'll get over it, Dr. Weaver. Just keep that smelly pipe out of the house."

When they finished eating, Randy was up from his chair and clearing the table. "The least I can do is the dishes," he said. "The cooks of the inner circle probably need a break."

But they all ended up in the kitchen including Winston, who had settled on the kitchen floor peering at the counter where two leftover sausage patties sat on a plate like unsuspecting mice soon to be set upon. While Randy washed and Clare dried, Katherine fussed around putting things away. She crumbled a sausage patty, put it in Winston's food bowl, and officiously said, "I read in one of those books you brought from the library that a cat should only be fed in his food bowl. Never off a plate and never off the floor."

Clare nodded, "I'm so glad you're reading the books I brought you, Katherine. They should be a big help with Winston."

As Randy and Clare were finishing up, Katherine went to the small writing desk in the dining room and retrieved two copies of an agreement she'd had Harry Stamp prepare for Randy to sign before he looked at the piano.

Randy came in from the kitchen and said, "Now I forget why I'm here. It wasn't just to barge in and have breakfast with two wonderful ladies was it?"

"Very funny," Katherine said, handing him the agreement. "Read this, sign both copies, and then you can take a look at the piano."

Randy read the agreement, took a ballpoint pen out of his front pocket, and signed both copies. As he took a notebook from his briefcase and unpacked his camera, Katherine told him, "You're the last one to come in here to examine my piano. No more samples, no more investigations, no more anything. If you talk about or write about this, the owner of the piano or its location cannot be divulged."

"I hear you loud and clear. I'm the last of the chosen few. Now where's the piano?" Randy said, looking into the living room.

"You're just a barrel of laughs," Katherine said. "Come on, I'll show you what you've come to see."

They all crawled under the piano and laid on their backs as Katherine demonstrated how, by pulling down on the hidden wooden lever, the supplementary piano leg lowered to support the piano while the original hollow leg swung out to the side.

Clare said, "Wow," and Randy Weaver said "Jumpin' Jehosaphat!" as

Katherine pulled the lever connected to the right leg and then the lever connected to the left leg. Then they all crawled out from under the piano and watched as Katherine pulled the empty copper cylinder out of the left leg to the wonderment of Clare and Randy.

Katherine and Clare set up the Scrabble board in the dining room while Randy went to work examining the piano. He took photos of the front, then crawled back under the piano and took more photos. He laid on the floor and wrote in his notebook, then rolled back under the piano and took more pictures. He was done in an hour and walked into the dining room as Katherine and Clare were finishing their Scrabble game. Randy sat and watched as Katherine played six of her remaining seven tiles on a V for BREVITY with the Y on a triple letter score for 23 points. With only five tiles left, Clare played on an H with GHOUL on a double word score for 18 points and turned in a J for minus 8 points. Katherine turned in her a U for a minus 1 point and ended the game losing once again, this time 205 to Clare's 209.

"Now I'm really in a bad mood," she said with mock irritation as she looked at Clare whose wide smile spread across her face. "I guess in a couple of days everyone in town will know about my latest defeat."

Clare's face turned red. Then she laughed, "It might be sooner than that Katherine. News gets around fast."

"She's a vicious competitor," Randy said to Katherine. "Don't ever get her in a game of Hearts. She's a shark."

"Hey, we've got three here now. That's enough to play Hearts," Clare said. "Do you have a deck of cards, Katherine?"

But Randy said he couldn't stay and Katherine said they had to get going to the farm. After Randy packed up his things as Katherine and Clare put away the Scrabble game, he sat down at the dining table and said, "Hey, I was thinking. I should do something in return for you two feeding me breakfast. Do you want to go on a field trip with me tomorrow? I'm going to meet the Beaver brothers down near Quilcene to look at some strange fungus they found on a bunch of downed Doug fir. On the way back, we could stop and get something to eat."

Katherine and Clare both laughed. Katherine said, "How chivalrous of you, Dr. Weaver, taking us to the woods to see some fungus. It sounds like a lot of fun."

Clare said she couldn't go, she was going to Kelso with her mom and Curtis to see her father. Katherine said she had church in the morning and couldn't go. Maybe she'd take a rain check.

Clare gave Randy a hug as he stood in the front doorway, thanking Katherine and telling Clare he hoped they could play Hearts the next time he was back in Cedar Mills. They waved to him from the front steps as he drove off.

"He's a real character, " Katherine mused.

"He's a very nice guy," Clare added.

Clare talked all the way to New Morning Farm. She said was looking forward to the trip to Kelso to see her father, but she didn't want to move there. She was worried that Curtis was turning into a juvenile delinquent. She hated the guys he was hanging around with. She was glad her mother had a job, but working until two in the morning at a tavern wasn't the best thing for her right now. Katherine tried listen as she drove but all she could think about was Jack. She wondered where he was and suddenly wanted to hear his voice.

Clare was quiet as they drove through the farm's main gate and up the drive to Hazel and Roy's. They saw Roy, Hazel, and Donny talking and laughing as they walked through the field past the horse barn. Katherine sat watching as Roy patted Donny on the shoulder and laughed. Like Jack years before, Donny had fast become something of a surrogate son to Hazel and Roy.

Clare said she was nervous as they walked up to the horse barn holding hands. The stalls in the horse barn were empty. They walked through the barn and out the rear door while Clare silently and solemnly took note of everything. They caught up with Hazel, who was waiting for them at the other end of the barn. Katherine asked where the horses were.

"We've been letting them out for most of the day when the weather's okay now that Donny's here," Hazel said, pointing out across the field to the band of six horses grazing in the distance. "They'd much rather be out of their stalls."

Hazel gave Clare a big smile and took her hand, "Come on, we'll go find the guys and then get the horses."

As they neared the hay barn, Katherine saw one of the horses in the distance raise its head and then start cantering their way. It was Sissy and she'd recognized Katherine. They stopped while the horse approached, raising her head and snuffling hello.

"She's been waiting for you," Hazel said.

Katherine walked to Sissy and rubbed her white nose and the horse nickered a greeting in return. "I'm glad to see you too," Katherine said putting her head on Sissy's neck. "Here's a friend of mine," she said motioning for Clare to come over.

Clare hesitated, but Hazel walked her over to the horse. Katherine introduced the two girls while Hazel pulled a plastic bag of cut-up apples out of her coat pocket and handed it to Katherine who pulled out a couple pieces and laid them in the palm of her right hand. Clare watched as the horse walked up and took the apple out of Katherine's hand with a big slurp. She asked Clare if she wanted to give the horse some apple, but Clare said not yet, she needed to get used to things first.

They turned and started into the hay barn looking for Roy and Danny. Hazel and Clare walked together holding hands as Hazel explained all about taking care of horses. Katherine and Sissy followed. They found Roy and Donny in the front corner of the barn, looking at the storage room that was still filled with furniture. Roy hugged Katherine and then he spotted Clare. His face beamed as she held out her hand and introduced herself as Clare Dolan who'd come with Katherine for a visit to see the horses.

"Thank you for having me, Mr. Willit," she said. "I'm already having a good time."

Roy said, "Well, we're honored to have you here, Clare Dolan. Just remember, I'm Roy and she's Hazel. No mister or missus anybody, please."

Clare replied, "Okay Roy, I'll try my best." Then she saw Donny and said, "Hi. I didn't know you worked here."

"Over a month now," Donny said. "How's Curtis, I haven't seen him for a while."

"He's doing fine," Clare said. "We're all doing fine. Thank you for asking Donny."

Roy told Katherine that Donny had finally talked them into letting him fix up the storage room into a place where he could stay. But only if his Aunt Sadie agreed.

It would have been difficult to decide who most enjoyed that Saturday afternoon in December. Was it Clare Dolan, whose experience with horses until now had only been vicarious? Or was it Katherine, Hazel, and Roy who watched with pleasure as Clare grew more and more comfortable with the animals? It wasn't long before Clare held out a palm filled with cut-up apple for Sissy and reached up to pat her nose. The other horses, whose curiosity was piqued by the goings on at the hay barn, ambled over. They stood in a circle while Roy led Clare went to each one and told her its name.

When he was done, Clare said, "I'll do my best to remember their names, Roy." She took a step toward Major and said, "This is Major." And continued around the circle, stopping at each one and saying their name. Then she turned to Roy and said, "I have a question, Roy. Something I've wondered about in the horse books I've read. What's the difference between a bridle and a halter?"

Roy nodded to Donny who went into the barn and brought out one of each, after which Roy asked him to tell Clare what the difference was. Clare looked like she was committing to memory everything Donny said. When he was finished, Roy took the halter and handed it to Katherine, asking if she remembered how to put it on Sissy. When Katherine had the halter on Sissy, she motioned to Clare to come along for a walk while Hazel and Donny started brushing the other horses and Roy began checking their hooves.

By the time Katherine and Clare and made the turn at the far end of the field, Clare had taken the reins and was leading the docile Sissy back to the barn. Donny was putting a saddle on Major when they returned and Hazel was putting on his bridle. Roy had brought out a step stool.

"Would you like to take a ride on Major?" Hazel asked Clare.

Clare shook her head. "Oh no thank you, Hazel. I'm not ready for that. I don't know how to hold the reins."

Hazel told all she had to do was sit in the saddle. Roy and Donny would walk along either side of Major while Hazel led him. When Clare was finally up on the horse, grasping the saddle horn and looking down at her with a pure, unassailable delight, Katherine felt a wave of heartrending love for the little girl. After Major had circled the barn several times, Hazel stopped while Roy brought out a camera from the barn and told Katherine to stand next to Major while he took pictures of Major, Clare, and Katherine, then the three of them with Hazel and Donny. Then Donny took the final shots with Clare on Major, with Roy and Hazel on either side of Katherine.

Donny started ushering the horses back into their stalls, something he did without having to lead with a halter, while everyone else headed for the house. Hazel told Clare she'd made lasagna for dinner which they were going to have with two different salads and garlic bread. By the time the table was set and the lasagna was warm, Donny joined them in the kitchen where the food had been put out buffet style. Katherine laughed when she saw a dish of lime Jell-o salad on the counter.

After dinner, Hazel and Clare cleared the table and did the dishes while Katherine and Roy sat talking in the living room, mostly about Clare. Then Hazel got out her guitar and Katherine sat the piano, while Roy and Clare sat in the two wing chairs waiting for the music to begin. Roy reminded Katherine of the first time she had visited and sang "He Walks With Me" with Hazel and asked them to do it again. Katherine sang with the same pure angelic voice, filling the room with an overpowering feeling of happiness, making everyone feel thankful they were there together.

By seven o'clock, Katherine and Clare were saying goodbye and starting out the back door for the car. Clare shook hands with both Hazel and Roy, telling them not only thank you very much for dinner, but that today had been the very best day of her life, without a doubt. As they drove back to town, Clare talked about horses all the way. She said the afternoon had been beyond anything she could have imagined and couldn't thank Katherine enough for taking her to the farm.

In town, Katherine drove down Second Avenue past her house, across Cedar Street and down two blocks to Madrona where she turned left and drove to the middle of the block. She stopped across the street from Clare's house which was two doors up the block from Luther Moody's now empty house.

"How'd you know where I live?" Clare asked with a note of consternation.

"I've got my sources," Katherine said. "You're not the only one who knows everything about this town."

Clare laughed and reached across the front seat to give Katherine a hug. She said her mom was getting off work early and they were going to drive to Kelso as soon as she got home. Then she hopped out of the car, ran across the street and up the front porch steps just as the front door opened and a lanky boy in a T-shirt walked out onto front porch. He patted Clare on the back as she ran in the house and then stood at one end of the porch hunched over from the cold smoking a cigarette. She couldn't make out his face in the dark. But it was probably Curtis, who stood shivering and staring into the December night. He took a final drag, flicked the lit cigarette into the middle of street, and walked back into the house.

Katherine drove off slowly wondering what kind of life Clare led behind that closed door.

Tennessee Jack Lindsay

On Saturday, while Katherine and Clare were at New Morning Farm, Jack was on Interstate 5 driving north to the Burnt Volunteer Fire Hall with Eddie Balfour to attend a birthday celebration for Eddie's uncle, George Neeley. Burnt is a wide spot in the road on State Route 530 which runs through the mountains along the Sauk River between Darrington and Concrete. Originally a logging camp that had been named for Otto Burnt, the president of Big Marsh Pulp and Paper, the settlement had evolved into a small village populated mostly by loggers who'd migrated from North Carolina to work in the woods during the Depression.

Eddie had jokingly warned Jack he wasn't sure how folks up at Burnt would take to a newcomer from Tennessee and suggested Jack bring his guitar and mandolin for protection. Eddie said it might soften any of the North Carolinians' suspicion of someone from the Volunteer State if Jack could play some decent bluegrass licks because when it came to entertainment in Burnt, bluegrass music was the coin of the realm. Jack had laughed and said he be happy to show some Tarheels a few things about bluegrass.

He was looking forward to playing some music with folks who had roots south of the Mason-Dixon Line.

On the trip into mountains, Eddie told him about his sister Leah, who'd be there, and how they'd been taken in by their Uncle George Neeley when they were kids. They'd spent most of their early childhood in the back seat of a car in the parking lot of whatever bar their parents had picked for their temporary headquarters until their mother's older brother George and his wife, Gladys, got temporary custody of the two children, when they were seven and five years old. But the Balfours returned a year later, absconded with the kids, and headed for Seattle where six months later, they drunkenly disappeared into the miasmic world of the waterfront slums.

Back then, Jim Underwood was a newly tenured associate professor of history at the University of Washington who was making a name for himself in Puget Sound maritime history circles with the publication of his first book, *Bearing the Burden: Piling Usage On the Seattle Waterfront*. On a chilly Saturday morning in April, he and Silas Peavey had just crossed Alaskan Way and were starting up Columbia Street when they found the cold and hungry Eddie and Leah Balfour huddled together against a concrete pier below the Alaskan Way viaduct.

They weren't the first children Silas Peavey had pulled from the grisly cryptozoic world of the waterfront but they were two of his favorites. With Jim Underwood's assistance, who used his position as a member of the university faculty to recommend Silas Peavey and his sister Beatrice as foster parents, and with the approval of George and Gladys Neeley, Eddie and Leah Balfour grew up in the Peavey home on Queen Anne Hill.

When they weren't in school or occupied with after-school activities, Eddie and Leah spent their time hanging around the clock shop in the market, running errands for Peavey and other tenants at Pike Place, in the same way Will and Joey did now. By the time they got to high school, Leah stopped going to the market regularly but Eddie was there every day. On the weekends, he'd be at Jim Underwood's side on some investigative ramble along the waterfront, gathering material for the professor's next book.

By the time the Balfour kids were out of high school and attending college, most of those at the market who had contributed something to their success felt a proprietary sense of pride in their achievements. It explained why Eddie had been greeted with the fanfare of a returning prince by Dimitri Pappas the owner of Café Knossos when he and Jack had came in for lunch earlier in the week and why so many of the people in the stalls yelled to Eddie when he and Jack had walked through the market. The young professor was a local hero.

Now on Saturday afternoon, as they took the Arlington exit off Interstate 5 onto State Road 530 and headed into the mountains toward Darrington, Jack was interested to see Professor Edward Balfour among a bunch of loggers from North Carolina, and to meet his sister Leah, who Eddie compared to a female tiger, beautiful from a distance and dangerous up close.

The business district of Burnt consisted of Sonny's Grocery and Hardware, a sprawling false front wood-frame emporium with a wide front porch, the post office, which was a small, unpainted wood-frame building that had once been the logging camp's cookhouse, and the two-story brick volunteer fire hall, the largest building in town.

It was three o'clock when Eddie and Jack parked in the fire hall parking lot and walked upstairs to the crowded second-floor social hall. The hall was filled with long rows of tables. In the front was a foot-high raised platform that spanned the width of the building and at the rear was a row of several sinks and a long counter where covered dishes of casseroles and salads were being set out for a potluck dinner. Uncle George was sitting with a group of men in a circle of chairs near the platform and when he saw Eddie and Jack walk in, he waved them over with a shout. The circle of men, most with their arms crossed, sat silently staring as they walked over.

It was Uncle George's seventy-fifth birthday. He stood and hugged Eddie and shook hands with Jack. Eddie told him he didn't look a day over eighty which brought out a round of guffaws from the others who were all taking a good long look at Jack. Uncle George introduced Jack to the rest of the group, three of which, Bob Taylor, Charlie "Ozone" Hall, and Cousin Tut Burwell were part of his band, the Skagit River Ramblers, which had been together since the end of World War II.

There was an awkward moment of silence and then Cousin Tut Burwell brusquely asked Jack where his guitar was, saying George had told them

Eddie was bringing a boy from Tennessee who claimed he could play the bluegrass guitar. Jack nodded without a word and went out to the car to get his guitar and mandolin. Uncle George stood on the stage and shouted everyone to silence, announcing the music was about to begin. When Jack walked back in with his instruments, he heard George tell the crowd that before the Skagit River Ramblers took the stage to play a set before dinner, they had a special guest from Tennessee by way of Seattle, Tennessee Jack Lindsay, who was going to start the musical proceedings.

Jack gave Eddie a hard questioning look as he stepped up onto the stage. Eddie replied with a smile and a shrug. While Jack tuned his guitar, the Skagit River Ramblers gathered at the back of the stage with their instruments. Uncle George told Jack to do three songs to "show us what you got, son." He could hear the four of them laughing and talking softly, enjoying having a newcomer in the hot seat.

It had been a few years since Jack had played in public with the Rainy Creek Boys in Knoxville but he immediately felt the old adrenaline rush when he took the stage and faced the questioning crowd. He didn't say much, no one expected him to. He started with the "The Wreck on the C & O Road," but cut it down from the original eleven verses to six. The hall was silent when he finished. Then he did a fast-paced rendition of "Footprints in the Snow," a song no one could dislike. The hall was silent when he finished. For his final number, he got out the mandolin and introduced the next song, "The Darkest Hour is Just Before Dawn," by saying it was his Aunt Hazel's favorite hymn and had been written by a neighbor of hers when she was growing up on Clinch Mountain, Ralph Stanley. On the chorus, he put the mandolin down at his side and sang a cappella in a high lonesome voice that hardly matched Ralph Stanley's, but moved the audience enough to give him a round of applause when he finished.

When the Skagit River Ramblers walked up to the front of the stage, Uncle George slapped him on the back, "Not bad son, not bad at all." Cousin Tut Burwell told him to take a stool and he could join them in a few minutes to finish the set with a couple of gospel tunes. Jack sat in the back and watched the Ramblers, who after forty years together, played like a well-oiled machine. From Cousin Tut's orders, he assumed he had passed a preliminary test of acceptance. At the end of the set, they motioned him up front and told him to choose and introduce the gospel numbers with the only stipulation being that he play the mandolin. They finished the set with "I'm Using My Bible for a Roadmap," and "Heaven's Bright Shore," which brought the audience to their feet with a standing ovation.

After that, the rest of the afternoon seemed anti-climactic. The potluck supper where the food was Southern and the talk drifted aimlessly from story to story about hard work, family, and music made him nostalgic for Tennessee. It also made him acutely aware of how much he missed Katherine. He couldn't stop thinking about her all afternoon. He thought of her while he said yes, the Rainy Creek Boys had played in Boone at Spanky's Red Hat Lounge. He thought of her when he asked if any of the Ramblers had been part of the Tennessee Barn Dance on WNOX in Knoxville. And when he and Eddie were finally getting ready to leave, making the rounds, saying goodbye to everyone, Jack wished she was there beside him, making him feel that the other half of his life that had been missing had finally been found.

Just before they left, Uncle George and Cousin Tut Burwell stood alone talking in earnest and looking over at Jack. Finally they came over to tell him the Ramblers were coming to Seattle in a few days to play at the annual Northwest Folklore Society fundraiser, something they'd been doing for ten years, and they wanted Jack to join them on stage for a set.

"The show's on Friday night someplace at the university," Uncle George said. "Eddie'll know where. We can get together at his place the night before and work out some songs. But you've got to play your mandolin."

"We got nobody in these parts who can play the mandolin like you, son," Cousin Tut Burwell added.

Jack said he'd be honored to join them at the fundraiser and thanked them for inviting him. After a round of handshakes, he and Eddie headed for the door when someone poked him hard in the back and said, "Hey there, Tennessee Jack, I like your music." It was Leah Balfour, dressed in a plaid shirt, jeans, and cowboy boots. Eddie was right, she was a pretty woman, with flowing black hair down to her shoulders and a twinkle in her dark eyes. She held out her hand and shook his with the grip of an arm wrestler.

Leah said she was sorry they hadn't had a chance to talk but Silas had told her Jack was coming for dinner at the clock shop the next day. Maybe they'd have time to get acquainted then. Jack was taken with Leah Balfour's good looks and her sassiness. On the drive back to Seattle, he told Eddie his sister wasn't what he'd expected. Eddie said he didn't know what Jack had expected but to keep his guard up.

❖ ❖ ❖ ❖ ❖ ❖ ❖ ❖ ❖ ❖ ❖ ❖

Earlier in the week, after Jack and Eddie had lunch at the Café Knossos, Jack had stopped at Time Pieces to say hello to Silas Peavey and look for a gift for Katherine. Silas showed him some small porcelain clocks from nineteenth-century Austria that were tucked in the back of a display case. When Silas pulled a delicate white figure of a brown-haired angel holding a small round clock at her mid-section, Jack knew it was what he wanted and didn't flinch when Peavey told him the price. Peavey threw in a complete cleaning and overhaul of the mechanism at no charge. He invited Jack to dinner on Sunday afternoon, saying he'd have the clock ready by then.

It was a big crowd that Sunday afternoon at Time Pieces. Jack got to meet some of the people Eddie had told him about at lunch, including Beatrice Peavey, Silas' older sister as well as Professor Jim Underwood, who with the help of Eddie and Silas had ended his drunken jag down on the waterfront not long before. With Will and Joey, Bob, Eddie and Leah Balfour, along with Silas and Jack, there were nine people around the big table in front of the waterfront window in the back room enjoying a Nooksack River ham, steamed asparagus, buttered red potatoes with parsley, and a Waldorf salad, all courtesy of Beatrice and Bob.

Silas cackled, Beatrice chortled, Jim Underwood smiled, Bob clapped his hands, and Will and Joey sat at rapt attention while Eddie and Leah told the story, with far too much dramatic flair in Jack's opinion, of Jack's foray into the mountain wilds of Burnt the day before, where he'd confronted a hostile crowd of Tarheels only to emerge victorious with mandolin in hand and the sobriquet of Tennessee Jack Lindsay as his legacy.

Will and Joey spent the rest of the afternoon making up chants about

Tennessee Jack, who didn't look back, and had a duck that went quack, quack, quack, until Silas silenced them with a threat to limit their grog to a half portion and make them walk the plank at sundown if they didn't shut up.

Jack didn't say much to Leah, who spent most of the time talking with Beatrice. But before he left, she handed him her business card which identified her as a managing partner of the accounting firm of Balfour, Warburg, & Blister whose offices were at Third Avenue and Bell Street, just around the corner from Jack's apartment. She told him maybe they could have dinner sometime.

When Jack got up to leave, Silas went into shop and came back with an ornately decorated box which contained the Austrian angel clock. He proudly said Bob had thoroughly cleaned the mechanism and it kept perfect time. There were no secrets among the extended family at Time Pieces and everyone at the table started clamoring to see what was in the box. Jack's face turned red. He knew he wasn't going to win this one. He opened the box and handed it to Beatrice who passed it around the table while everyone gushed over the delicate antique time piece. When Leah handed it back to him with a smile and said it must be for someone very special, Jack blushed again.

As he walked through the shop and opened the door to leave, he could hear Will and Joey chanting, "Tennessee Jack has a very special girl, tick tock, tick tock, a very special girl who's got a new clock," while Silas was shouting, "Pipe down you lubbers, pipe down or you'll spend the rest of your days swabbing the deck!"

Jack was halfway up the ramp to the market's main floor when Leah Balfour caught up with him.

"I thought you might need an escort with that antique clock you're carrying," she said, out of breath. "I've got to stop at my office on the way home. I'll walk with you. I want to hear all about the pissing contest up at Kodiak."

"I just got back on Friday. How'd you hear about that?"

Leah told him she'd been at Pushkin, McDonald & Fishkin on Thursday afternoon. "We do work for Uncle Herk now and then. It was all he could talk about. You and the Samson brothers facing off over Bart Ladderback buying their crab boat." She said Ladderback had called Hercules from Kodiak and told him the whole story. How Jack forced the Samsons into taking half-price for the boat after he'd inspected it and put together a lengthy list of repairs that were needed.

"It wasn't that complicated," Jack said as they walked through the market up to Pine Street. "Shysters like that pair fold like a two-dollar suitcase when they get caught. It didn't take much."

Leah laughed. "So did you really tell them you hadn't come to Kodiak for a pissing contest and start to walk out? Uncle Herk wouldn't stop talking about it."

"I guess I did. But Hercules never said a thing to me about it when I got back to the office on Friday afternoon. All he said was he'd heard things worked out and Ladderback was happy."

"That's high praise for one of his new lawyers," Leah said.

They walked up Pine to Third Avenue and turned north in the gray December dusk. Jack told Leah about running into Hercules and Max Fishkin in the lobby as they were leaving for lunch when he just come in from Sea-Tac on Friday afternoon. It was only the second time Jack had seen Fishkin, who spent most of his time in San Franciso, New York, or Washington, D.C. arguing admiralty cases.

Hercules had reintroduced Jack to Fishkin, calling Jack one of their bright young men but said nothing about Kodiak. Fishkin, with his closely cropped white hair and his tailored suit, stood in marked contrast to Pushkin, whose eclectric dress and demeanor made him seem like a country cousin. Fishkin gave Jack a firm handshake, inspecting him like he was looking for mold on a loaf of French bread.

Leah laughed. "So you met the elusive Fishkin. He and Uncle Herk go all the way back to high school on Queen Anne with Uncle Silas. Now tell me about your girl, Jack."

Jack shook his head. Leah Balfour was anything about shy. He told her 'his girl' lived over on the Peninsula. Her name was Katherine.

At Third and Bell, Leah stopped in front of a three-story office building and pointed to the third floor where the lights were on. "This is it Jack. Thanks for the company," she said.

He asked how she was going to get home and offered her a ride.

"Nope. I've got a ride. My partner Maggie's up there working. We've got a house on Capitol Hill near the park. I'm fine," she said, punching him on the shoulder. "And by the way, Tennessee Jack, it's a tough crowd out there at Burnt. You managed to bring tears to some eyes with that last song of yours."

Jack laughed. "That's me. Pissing contests and bluegrass gospel. I can do it all. Thanks for the company."

Leah laughed and punched him on the shoulder again. "See you around, I hope," she said and waved before she disappeared inside.

Warnings

Katherine went to work an hour early on Monday morning because now that she was officially the café manager, Greeley no longer showed up before five to turn on the grills and start the first round of coffee. As she turned on the lights in dark café, she remembered Joyce Woolley was coming in at nine for an interview. Unless Joyce Woolley was a complete troglodyte, Katherine was going to offer her the job of second cook on the spot.

Fifteen minutes before nine o'clock, Joyce Woolley was sitting in the middle booth in the old part of the café. She was a big, friendly woman with streaks of gray in her short black hair. When she stood and introduced herself, she gave Katherine a strong, firm handshake and talked with a low raspy tone that old-timers called a "whiskey voice."

They sat in Katherine's office as Joyce unaffectedly told her about working as a short order cook in beaneries around the Gulf of Alaska, in fishing villages like Homer, Kodiak and Cordova. She was plain spoken and likable. When Katherine said the Madison Café was a small place and fitting in might be a challenge, Joyce said she'd fit in.

"I can get along with anybody. Just show me where things are and tell me what I'm supposed to do. I'll be fine." she said.

Katherine asked if she could start the next morning and Joyce said of course, she'd be there early. She didn't ask about the pay. But she looked confused when Katherine asked her shoe size. She laughed and said she'd never had a job interview where they asked her shoe size. Katherine laughed and explained how the wearing of Chuck Taylors by the café staff got started. She said the shoes weren't mandatory. Joyce told her it wasn't a problem, she'd wear sneakers along with everyone else.

They shook hands again and Katherine showed her around the café, introducing her to Sadie, Bobby, and Muriel. At the front door, Joyce thanked Katherine with the promise she wouldn't be disappointed. When Joyce turned toward the door, Katherine saw a long scar on the left side of her neck that ran from just below her ear to her shoulder, a long, wide wound of disconcerting proportions that made Katherine shiver. She walked back to the dining room and told everyone she'd hired Joyce as second cook.

"Now I'm completely surrounded by women," Bobby moaned in mock irritation.

"You poor boy," Sadie said, mussing his hair. She turned to Katherine, "I'm so glad you took care of that in a hurry boss, I don't know how long we could have survived with you as second cook."

❖ ❖ ❖ ❖ ❖ ❖ ❖ ❖ ❖ ❖ ❖ ❖

When the morning rush subsided, Katherine sat in her office with the door closed, relieved she'd found a replacement for Larry but glum when she looked at Jack's latest postcard of the *M/V Hoquiam* leaving the dock at Bremerton. The week ahead promised to be frenetic. It had already started that way when Sadie, Bobby and Muriel had burst in first thing, demanding to know whether or not Larry was coming back and were only halfway mollified when she told them about hiring Joyce Woolley to replace him.

Then came an animated Bert Peck who, before he'd even brought the bread delivery in, had eagerly told her there were some new developments in the new pastry sales campaign, something to do with doughnuts added to the offering of maple bars, bear claws, and butter horns. She wasn't interested. She called Bobby in and told Bert that Bobby would be managing the new pastry program under her supervision. Bert and Bobby could work out all the details and keep her updated. She'd escorted them to the door telling an excited Bobby, she knew he could handle it. Later that afternoon, Elizabeth was coming in for another tutorial on keeping the café's books, a task Greeley had gladly relinquished when he'd promoted her to manager.

But now she sat in the quiet office thinking about the past weekend, how fun it had been to take Clare out to the farm, and the peaceful feeling she'd felt the next morning returning to church, this time as part of the Trinity Episcopal choir.

She'd stopped at Maude's on her way to church, ready to confront Milos about *The Lithuanian Septet* being on sale at the Book Mart, but he'd gone home for the morning and taken Rascal with him. Maude said it something about his burro having a bad leg, or some of his chickens were missing, or one of the goats was ailing. She couldn't remember and anyway, she was pretty sure he just wanted to get away from her for a while.

When Katherine asked about Nora Wineskin's visit on Friday with a proposal for a poetry reading and book signing, Maude told her he'd pranced around the house taking Katherine's name in vain for a while until she told him to shut up and stop acting like a baby. He settled down after that and told Nora he'd think about it. Maude couldn't understand why he was ashamed of being a noted poet, published by the Princeton University Press no less, but that was his business.

As part of the church choir, Katherine had the same advantage of surreptitiously watching the congregation as she did when she was at the organ. In her absence, the congregation had changed. Anne and Jack were gone but they'd had been replaced by Elizabeth and Lonnie. And Will sat by himself in the back, no longer flanked by Greeley and Larry. Maude told her that Greeley was going to the 8:30 service now that his folks were back at the ten o'clock. But some things hadn't changed, most notably Father Tom's interminable sermon, which this morning was on Paul's first letter to the Corinthians. She caught herself starting to doze and laughed to herself thinking about Jack saying Father Tom's sermons were better than prescription sleeping pills.

Something else had changed on Sunday's. Rather than sidling out the back door and walking home immediately after the service, Katherine went to coffee hour in the parish hall, a venerable Episcopalian tradition that many devout members of the Anglican Communion claimed Thomas Cranmer himself had started.

Will came over to her as soon as she walked in. He wanted to talk to her about Clare. Katherine told him about their trip to New Morning Farm the day before and how for the first time, she'd seen Clare really smile. She said Clare had told her things might be looking up for the Dolans now that her father had a job in Kelso and her mother was working. Will said that's what he wanted to talk to her about. The only job Bud Dolan was going to have was breaking rocks at Walla Walla. He was in the Cowlitz County Jail on armed robbery charges.

❖ ❖ ❖ ❖ ❖ ❖ ❖ ❖ ❖ ❖ ❖ ❖

Sadie interrupted Katherine's Monday morning reverie when she barged into the office to tell Katherine about her Sunday with the boys at Hazel and Roy's and how she'd given her okay for Donny to stay out at the farm. She said she'd been awarded custody of the boys with her sister Vicki's blessing. Vicki was facing three-to-five at Gig Harbor.

Randy Weaver's voice boomed out of the dining room and they went into kitchen for a look through the service window. Katherine smiled as she watched how Randy, who was younger by at least a generation than everyone at The Table, felt at ease among them. Carl Wilfong said they'd heard Doctor Weaver had been making house calls. Randy just smiled as they all laughed. Lamar Kesecker told him he had a bad headache and wondered what the doctor could prescribe. Randy said he had a baseball bat out in the car. He'd be happy to give Lamar a couple whacks alongside the head. Lamar said, hell, he got that at home. Everyone laughed and beamed at Randy, clearly proud of their hometown boy.

Not long after, Randy poked his head in the service window and said good-bye before he went out the front door. Katherine threatened him with mock seriousness about breaking the agreement he signed. "So put that in your pipe and smoke it, professor," Katherine teased.

Randy laughed out loud, "Touché. And don't forget your rain check to look for fungus."

After he left, Sadie said, "That ain't Jack honey."

Still smiling, Katherine said, "I know, but he's a nice guy."

Looking For Clare

Katherine left the café at four o'clock and walked home up the alley in the chilly December dusk after a day of trying to double as second cook and restaurant manager, relieved that Joyce Woolley would be starting work in the morning. She expected to see Clare sitting on the back steps when she came through the back gate but the steps were empty.

Was she expecting to see Clare or wanting to see Clare? Expecting or wanting? Supposing or yearning? It was a question Alan Lindsay posed about belief and faith in *Voyage from Nicaea: Faith in the Modern World,* which she was finding just as difficult to understand as *The Platonic Ideal of Faith: There Isn't One.* She was ready to end her quest to unlock the mysteries of the theologian's philosophy of faith.

She fed Winston. She was glad to see his wounds were almost healed and he was showing an interest in the outdoors by cautiously peering out the back door when it was open. She changed her clothes and sat at the piano with a musty book she'd found in a box of Luther Moody's old music, *Schreiber & Schumacher's Big Book of Lieder,* when Will McCann knocked on the front door. Franz Schubert's songs would have to wait.

Will was out of uniform. He had on a brown hounds tooth sport coat, light brown slacks, brown loafers with brown socks, and an ecru oxford cloth shirt with a button down collar under a camel-hair v-neck sweater. Katherine asked facetiously if he was working undercover, saying she hardly recognized him in mufti.

"That's a good Scrabble word," he said dryly.

"Everyone in town's a comedian," Katherine answered.

While she was in the kitchen making coffee, Winston jumped on an arm of the sofa and stared at Will. He ignored the cat and thumbed through the books on the coffee table, Alan Lindsay's two books, and Milos Grajek's *The Lithuanian Septet.* With a raised eyebrow, he read Grajek's inscription

for Katherine on the inside front end sheet. Then, turning to the brief biography of the poet on the back flap of the dust jacket, he read out loud as
Katherine came in with the coffee:

"Born to Jewish parents in a Lithuanian village…Treblinka at age sev-
en…father gassed in the death camp…made his way to England after the
war…read Latin and Greek poetry at Corpus Christi College, Cambridge…
lecturer at Yeshiva University…instructor at the Iowa Writers Workshop…
Vernon Watkins Lecturer in Poetry at the University of Washington…"

Will shook his head and whisper whistled, "I knew there was more to
Milos than people thought."

Katherine laughed and said, "You always knew he was something, you
just didn't know what."

"Exactly."

Will said he was on his way to Gosport for an opening at his ex-wife
Rhonda's art gallery, Periwinkle. Afterwards, he was taking her to dinner at
The Little Oyster which Rhonda had described as an upscale bistro with a
sensitive, eclectic menu. He was hoping she would go easy on the Chardon-
nay and avoid getting into the *where did we go wrong?* mode which would
end up with her in tears and him wishing he'd never let his guard down
enough to think this time would be different.

He'd stopped by to talk about Clare but also wanted her to know that
Susan Owling and Mitchell Lodong had been spotted in town with Art
Fletcher as their chauffer. They'd all been at the Duchess Tavern on Saturday night. Susan Owling had on a blonde shoulder length wig. The muumuu
and sandals had been replaced by blue jeans, Icelandic ski sweater, and shoe
boots. Mel Connor, the bartender, told Will he didn't know they made jeans
with a rear end that big. Lodong had exchanged his black bishop's garb for
blue jeans, a hooded sweatshirt, and a denim jacket, making him look like
an over-the-hill reprobate.

Fletcher had left them at the Duchess and disappeared while they sat at
the bar swilling red wine. Susan Owling kept blubbering about her grandchild until Mel asked her to quiet down. She lit into him, bellowing that he
didn't know what a real family was and that her daughter was a no account
tramp. Art Fletcher returned just as Mel was getting ready to throw them out

and they drove off in a brown Ford conversion van.

Will said the assault charges for their shoe attack on Art Fletcher had been dropped but Lodong and Owling were still wanted for jumping bail on the public drunkenness charge. It was hardly an offense that was going to prompt a statewide dragnet, but Will's point to Katherine was the hapless trio was hanging around because of Susan Owling's fixation on Katherine and her imagined grandchild. It could lead to a risky situation.

"What makes the drunken screwballs dangerous is they might do anything," Will said. "I know you can take care of yourself, but don't be a posse of one. Call me if they show up here."

"You're right about one thing," Katherine said. "I can take care of myself."

Will changed the subject to Clare Dolan. A lot of people in town wanted to help her, but Katherine had become her real friend. Clare had told everyone about her visits at Katherine's, describing their Scrabble games, how Katherine had made her second cook of the inner circle, and about Katherine's caring for Winston.

"In a few weeks, you've become her idol and her pal," Will said. "I might need your help when the Dolan train goes completely off the tracks."

"Off the tracks?" Katherine asked.

Will said what was left of the Dolan family was a train wreck waiting to happen. Bud Dolan was still in the Cowlitz County Jail. He'd been denied bail on the armed robbery charges. He'd also been charged with attempted manslaughter, unlawful possession of a firearm, and wanton and reckless endangerment, after his brother-in-law, Tim Jessup, had pled down to lesser charges and named Bud as the trigger man who wounded the desk clerk in the shoulder during their holdup of the Starlight Budget Motel in Kelso the day after Thanksgiving.

Then Curtis was missing. He'd disappeared after Sophie and the kids had visited Bud in jail. He hadn't been in school today. When the school principal had called to ask about his absence, Sophie sounded drunk, saying Curtis was staying with his father in Kelso for the week.

Clare had been in school, but no one had seen her afterward. She usually went to the library after school to do her homework, but Winifred Smith said she hadn't been there today. But at the "What I Did Last Weekend" story time that morning, Clare couldn't stop talking about Saturday with her friend Katherine and the horses at New Morning Farm. It was the first time all year Clare had spoken up in class.

"So how exactly do you know all these little details of what's going on in town, like what Clare did at school today?" Katherine asked.

"It's my job to know," Will said. "I've got resources."

Sophie Dolan was the other part of the train wreck, according to Will. Her working at Lou's Scenic Tavern was already a disaster. She'd was drinking more than ever and slipping around with everyone.

"She'll have been in bed with every barfly at the Scenic before New Year's," Will said. "It's only a matter of time before Sophie goes gunnysack and Clare ends up in foster care."

"So what do we do?"

"I don't know," Will answered. "I can't just say Clare's in a bad situation and take her out of there without cause. Neither can the welfare folks. Things have to get worse and in the meantime, Clare's going to bear the brunt of it. I'm not asking you to do anything. I just want you to know. Things are going to get worse, much worse, sooner rather than later."

They stood on the front porch as Will got ready to leave and watched Winston cautiously poke his head out the front door. Katherine told him the restaurant where he and Rhonda were going was *Harvey's* Little Oyster. The owner, Harvey Pearson, was an old friend from her San Joaquin Valley days. She told him to say hello to Harvey if he had the chance, before he had to carry his wife out. As she watched Will drive off, she thought of that Saturday with Jack in Gosport, their lunch at Harvey's and the ferry ride to nowhere. *God, I miss you, Jack,* she thought as she closed the door.

She sat at the piano skipping through the book of Schubert lieder for a couple hours, remembering her painful lessons with Julia Howe in Cedar Rapids when her teacher kept trying to make her sing in German, which would have been an affront to anyone with even the slightest understanding of the language.

Then she thought of what Will said about Clare. She closed the music book, got up and went into the bedroom where she changed her clothes, putting on her old uniform of jeans, flannel shirt, and hiking boots. She pulled on the sweater Hazel had knit and zipped up the new anorak she'd bought at Eddie Bauer when she was in Seattle with Maude and Elizabeth. She filled Winston's food bowl a second time and told him to behave. It was ten o'clock when she walked out the back door.

The original town of Cedar Mills was platted in the center of a 640-acre section of land. On each side of Main Street, which runs east and west, are four streets that run parallel. Yarmouth Avenue is the principal north-south thoroughfare and has four avenues on each side. The junction of Main Street and Yarmouth Avenue is the town's central intersection which boasts a three-light stoplight, the only one in the east end of Cedar County. The town's central business district occupies two blocks on either side of the stoplight along Main Street.

Katherine walked up her alley between Main Street and Cedar Street to Fourth Avenue, the western edge of the original town, and then over to the alley behind Madrona Street, the last street on the south side of Main. She had no plan except to walk the streets of town for a while, thinking she might see Clare. She hadn't worn a hat because she wanted to be easily recognized if Clare saw her. A chilly wind blew out of the west and swirled the loose hair around her face. She walked east, down the dark alley eight blocks, then west, up Madrona Street which was dimly lit with incandescent streetlights, creating a shadowy atmosphere suitable for a village in Transylvania.

An occasional house sported outdoor Christmas lights and she could see lit-up Christmas trees in the living room windows of a few others. Halfway up the block between First and Second Avenues, she stopped in front of the dark Dolan house and stared at the front windows looking for a sign that Clare was inside. She walked up the steps and knocked on the front door with trepidation. Only trouble would be coming to call after ten-thirty on a dark night like this. Even if Clare was home, Katherine wasn't surprised that the house was silent. In a high whisper, she called, "Clare, it's Katherine. Are you home?" But there was no sound.

Katherine continued on, walking up each street and down each alley. No sign of Clare. No fleeting shadow of a little girl, no greeting of "Katherine, what are you doing out here in the middle of the night?" Nothing. The town was zipped up tight. She thought of the eleven-year-old girl, slipping through the cold darkness alone and afraid. Alone and afraid, a solitary little soldier in the night. *Where are you little friend?* Katherine thought as she walked the deserted streets.

When she got home and went through the back door a little after midnight, her frosty cheeks were wet with tears. She felt helpless. "Where did everyone go?" she sobbed as she undressed and got into bed still crying. Her tears were for Clare and for Jack and for Larry and all the others who wandered through the night thinking they were alone. She couldn't recite it in German, but she knew the English translation of Wilhelm Müller's poem that Schubert set to music: *Some frozen tears, Cling to my face, Have I really been crying, And not noticed them flow?*

The New Cook

The next morning Joyce Woolley arrived at the café early, ahead of everyone else. By the time Sadie, Muriel, and Bobby got there, Joyce was making oatmeal and starting a second round of coffee. Katherine smiled as she listened to Sadie officiously explain to Joyce what she needed from her second cook while Joyce silently nodded. An hour later, at the height of the morning rush, it was as though Joyce had been there for months. Katherine breathed a sigh of relief and Sadie whispered, "I think you got us a winner."

Elizabeth and Lonnie came in shortly after nine o'clock. Elizabeth came to show Katherine how to fill out the paperwork for a new employee but before they got started, Will poked his head into Katherine's office and said "Still no sign of where Clare Dolan's staying, but she's at school today. Also Harvey Pearson says I should hire you as my enforcer. Anyway, Rhonda loved Harvey and Adam. She's got two new friends to keep her occupied for a while. Thanks."

Elizabeth shook her head, "Will and Rhonda. What a pair."

They could hear Lonnie in the kitchen, talking to Sadie and then introducing himself to Joyce. "My brother-in-law was second cook here, but he's on the lam. Drunk and running from a woman," Lonnie said.

Joyce smiled politely and went back to work, but Lonnie wanted to talk.

He said he'd heard she'd just come down from Alaska, "You ever hear of Alvin Berry up there, red headed character with freckles. We called him Strawberry in school. He's supposed to have a restaurant in Homer."

"The Thoroughbred Grill," Joyce answered. "I worked there for a while."

Lonnie asked how she got the scar on her neck, a question that might have offended some, but Joyce didn't flinch. She said she'd broke up a fight when she was tending bar in a dive at Dutch Harbor and got on the wrong end of a switch blade. "Flew me down to Seattle. Spent two months in Virginia Mason before I could get back up north."

"Remind me to keep on your good side," Lonnie said with a laugh. He looked down at her feet. She wasn't wearing Chuck Taylors. "Aren't you going to play basketball with the rest of them?"

Joyce laughed and said she'd given Katherine her shoe size.

Lonnie wished her luck and wandered into the office as Elizabeth and Katherine were finishing up. Elizabeth was putting papers in her briefcase and Katherine was putting some forms in the file cabinet when they both simultaneously said, "I'm sorry about Larry." Lonnie laughed first and then they all erupted in laughter that spilled out into the kitchen.

Sadie shook her head and looked at Joyce, "I never thought a middle-aged boozer running away from his job and a woman could be so much fun."

Joyce laughed. "Don't worry, I don't go for booze or women."

Then they both laughed.

As soon as Elizabeth and Lonnie were gone, Bobby barged in without knocking. He wanted to talk about the new pastry program. Bert had suggested that they add a line of doughnuts to the pastry offerings, but Bobby had told him no, it was too complicated. He told Bert they should just stick with maple bars, bear claws, and butter horns to start.

"Good going, Bobby. I agree with you," Katherine said patting him on the shoulder. "Your first executive decision. I'm proud of you."

A few minutes later, Hazel and Roy were standing in the office door. It was the first time they'd been back to the café since the Sunday afternoon celebration of Katherine's promotion to manager. Roy said they were on their way to look at Milos Grajek's ailing burro and couldn't stay for lunch.

They sat in Katherine's office while Hazel and Roy told her about Anne, who had returned from Palm Springs on Sunday night. She was at their house first thing Monday morning for breakfast and stayed most of the day. She'd made some major decisions after the Thanksgiving debacle and her ensuing epiphany in the desert sun of California. She was going to give up the horse farm and travel.

Katherine whispered, "You've got to be kidding."

Hazel said Anne was going to divide the eighty acres of New Morning Farm between them. She'd take ten acres around her house and Hazel and Roy would get the remaining seventy acres. The deed would be transferred to the Willit's for one dollar.

"I knew she was going off her rocker," Hazel said. "She's been driving left of center for a good while. Even before the Larry thing."

They'd said it didn't sound right to them but Anne said it would be done. She'd made up her mind. Money wasn't the issue. She had more than she needed and they all knew she'd lost interest in the horses since the move to Cedar Mills. She was never at the barn. She hadn't been on a horse in months. Hazel and Roy couldn't argue with that.

Anne had already been at Stamp & Grubb. Harry Stamp was drawing up the papers for the deed transfer. When Hazel had asked Anne about Jack, what would he think about losing most of the farm, Anne had said he had his own money, part of Alan's trust. She'd also split the money from the sale of the Tennessee farm with him. Plus he'd have Anne's house and land when she was gone.

"She wants all this done by the end of the week, before she leaves for Florida," Roy said. "After Florida, she says she's going to Europe for a few months and then who knows."

"Roy says let her go ahead and do it," Hazel said. "We all know Annie does what she wants. It's better than her selling it to someone else and we can get back to working a real horse farm."

As they got up to leave, Hazel said, "You've got to bring Clare back out to the farm. We couldn't stop talking about your visit on Saturday. She's such a sweetheart."

Katherine started to tell them about what had happened with Clare, but they were already out the door.

That night, Katherine left the house again at ten and walked the streets of town like she'd done the night before. On her way home from the café that afternoon, she'd stopped at the Book Mart and the Red & White. No one had seen Clare since she and her mother had come back from Kelso on Sunday night. Wally told her he thought he saw her walking to school that morning, but wasn't sure. At the Red & White, Nell said it wasn't like Clare to have not picked up orders for George Sizemore and the others she helped by delivering their groceries and mail.

It wasn't as dark as the night before and the air was calm. The full moon was a week away, but there was enough light from a half-moon in the cloudless clear sky to see the dark outline of the mountains resting to the south like behemoths keeping watch on the silent town.

On Madrona Street, the Dolan house was once again dark. When Katherine knocked on the door there was silence within. She continued up Madrona, down the alley between Madrona and Linden, up Linden, and down the alley between Linden and Birch, until she'd covered the town, eight blocks east and west, eight blocks north and south. There was no sign of Clare and she muttered "darn you, come out, come out wherever you are," as she walked up Second Avenue toward home.

One block from Main Street, she was crossing Ash Street when she saw a brown conversion van driving slowly west on Main Street. She clenched her fists and wished the van would stop and turn towards her. *Come on,* she thought, *come this way so I can kick your butts.* She crossed Main and walked home down the alley. It was past midnight when she came in the back door where Winston was waiting on the kitchen table. "No luck tonight, old boy. No Clare anywhere," she said as she reached out to pet him and he jumped off the table. "OK, have it your way. I'm going to bed."

✧ ✧ ✧ ✧ ✧ ✧ ✧ ✧ ✧ ✧ ✧ ✧

The next afternoon Katherine fell on the sofa when she got home from work. She was exhausted after two nights of little sleep, wandering the streets, looking for Clare. She groaned when someone knocked at the front door a few minutes later. She opened the door to a courier in a dark blue uniform and a truck parked in the front with lettering on the side that read "Four Winds Bonded Couriers." She signed for a small carton festooned with *Fragile* stickers and a printed label with "J. Lindsay" typed above the return address of Pushkin, McDonald & Fishkin, Attorneys at Law.

She sat at the dining room table and carefully cut the packing tape with a pair of scissors while Winston sat on the table and watched. Inside was a gift wrapped box and a note card with a pen and ink drawing of a ferry on the front with a caption that read *MV San Mateo, The Last Steam Ferry on Puget Sound*. She opened the box before she read the note and gasped when she pulled out the porcelain brown-haired angel clock which had been wound and set to the correct time before it had been packed. She opened the note card and read:

> Dear Katherine:
> I saw this angel with brown hair in Silas Peavey's shop and all
> I could think of was you. I've tried to come up with something
> clever to write about you and time and eternity, but no luck. It's
> easier just to say I love you and miss you very much.
> Jack

Then the blubbering started and continued as she carried the clock into the living room and sat on the sofa holding it with both hands. She finally put it on the coffee table and stared at it, but the blubbering wouldn't stop. It went on until she heard Winston's loud meow reminding her that he hadn't been fed. She walked to the kitchen, opened a can of tuna fish and filled his bowl. When she sat back on the sofa and looked at the angel, she started crying again.

Finally she put the clock on the credenza next to the piano where she could see it and sat playing from the Johnny Mercer songbook until she realized it was nearly six o'clock and time for choir practice at Trinity. She gave Winston another can of tuna fish and hurried out the back door in to the dark alley. As she glanced down the alley toward the café, she saw the taillights of a van turn left from the alley onto Yarmouth Avenue towards the stoplight.

It was less than three weeks before Christmas and Brett Smallwood was working himself into a state of nervous anxiety, a state the veteran choir members had come to dread, fussing as he did over every bit of minutia associated with the Christmas pageant and the Christmas music concert. This year the choirmaster was determined to showcase the voice of the newest member of the choir at both the pageant and the concert.

But his enthusiasm was quelled before they got started when Katherine took him aside and told him she didn't want a featured role with the choir. She just wanted to be a regular member of the group. When Brett's face started to turn red and he sputtered that everyone in the choir was expected to rise to the occasion, Katherine said she was happy to do her part as a member of the choir, just not as a lead singer. Father Tom finally settled the matter after practice when he got the temperamental choirmaster to admit Katherine needed time to learn the finer points of being a choir member before she assumed a larger role with the group.

Katherine left the church and walked home at eight-thirty, an hour later than usual. On Second Avenue, she met Maude and Milos coming home with Rascal after their evening walk. Maude wanted to know what the courier from Seattle had delivered that afternoon and Katherine invited them over to see what Jack had sent. They took Rascal home and walked back to Katherine's.

Maude and Milos sat on the sofa as Katherine went to the kitchen to put on some coffee. But Maude said they couldn't stay.

"Just show us what you got," she ordered while Winston sat purring on Milos' lap.

Maude, who exuded the air of having seen and heard everything, gasped when Katherine handed her the Austrian angel clock. She carefully examined every inch of it and then handed it to Milos who did the same and placed it on the coffee table. Katherine handed Maude the note card. Maude read the note card several times and then handed it to Milos who read it and shook his head in unison with Maude.

"I told you. You've got to let him know how you feel," Maude ordered as she got up from the sofa. "That angel means business. It's hardly a trinket."

Will knocked on the front door an hour after Maude and Milos left. Katherine had just started getting to make another foray through the streets of town to look for Clare. Will stood on the steps and said, "I've found Clare."

They drove through town in Will's unmarked cruiser, north on Yarmouth Avenue to Walnut Street and east two blocks toward the library. Will stopped at Walnut Street and Ridge Avenue, a block from the library and turned off the headlights. He said Clare had gone into the library annex a little after nine o'clock with a sleeping bag and backpack.

"I don't want to scare her," Will said handing Katherine a small Maglite flashlight. "Go in and talk her out. She'll trust you."

"Then what?"

"I don't know. Can she stay with you until I figure something out."

"Of course," Katherine said and got out of the car.

The library was on southeast corner of Walnut Street and Mountain Avenue with the main entrance on Mountain. The annex was attached to the back of the building and extended past the width of the library, so the entrance looked onto to the street. Katherine walked a block down Walnut to Mountain and crossed to the library side of the street. There were two streetlights on either side of the buildings, one at the corner and one in the middle of the block. The incandescent bulbs cast a dim, eerie light that made the flashlight unnecessary.

Katherine went slowly up the walk to the annex entrance and up the rickety wooden steps to the door. She stopped for a moment and listened. Silence. She turned the doorknob and slowly pushed the door open to the large, cold room. Clare sat at the near end of a large conference table in the center of the room. A rolled up sleeping bag and a backpack were under the window behind her.

"Hello Katherine," Clare said, sitting at the table with her hands folded. "I saw you coming up the sidewalk. Am I going to get arrested for trespassing?"

Katherine walked in and sat down across the table from Clare who was bundled up in a heavy black wool pea coat and a black watch cap.

"I'll have to check with the authorities," Katherine with a wan smile. "No, of course you're not going to get arrested. I'm just glad you're safe."

"I saw you walking through town last night. It was late. Were you looking for me?"

"Yes Clare. I was looking for you. And I was looking for you the night before."

"I lied Katherine. I lied to you. I lied to everyone. I'm ashamed of myself," Clare said with a trembling voice. "Everything isn't ok, like I kept saying. My dad doesn't have a job. He's in jail. Curtis ran away. My mom drinks all the time. Guys from the tavern come home with her after work. That's why I stay here at night."

Katherine reached across the table to take Clare's hand, but she moved it away.

"I understand why you might be ashamed," Katherine said. "Of course you wanted everything to be ok. Who wouldn't?"

"I'll be fine, Katherine," Clare said. "I can take care of myself."

"Unfortunately taking care of yourself right now isn't an option. And if your mother isn't going to be there for you, someone else needs to be."

Clare raised her voice, "I know what you're doing. You and Chief McCann are going to shove me in a foster home with a bunch of other poor kids and tell me to shut up and be happy with a couple of sleazy foster parents who are just in it for the money. That's worse than jail. I'm running away."

Katherine sat silent. Clare sat silent. Their expressions were grim.

Katherine finally spoke. "Remember the first time you came to my house and we agreed to be friends? And remember last Saturday when I taught you the secret of Katherine Baker's pancakes. That's serious stuff. Would I let my best friend be sent to a foster home? Would I let a trusted member of the inner circle be mistreated? I take care my friends. The inner circle won't be trifled with."

Clare sat silent as Katherine continued. "I want you to stay with me for a couple of days. Chief McCann is going to talk to your mother. No. He's not going to arrest anyone. He's just going to tell her that you'll be staying at my house. No one's done anything wrong, but you need to be safe. You need to be with me and Winston for a couple days until we can figure this out."

Katherine stood and held out her hand to Clare who sat shaking her head and wiping tears from her cheeks. She didn't move. Katherine walked over and picked up the sleeping bag and backpack. She held out her hand again.

"Come on, let's go home."

Clare stood and took Katherine's hand. "Here, let me take the backpack," she said as they walked out the door and down the steps.

Will sat in his cruiser and watched the two walk hand in hand down Mountain Avenue toward Main Street. He waited until they were out of earshot and then drove over to the alley behind the Madison Café. He parked behind the restaurant in Larry's old spot and waited for them to pass, making sure they got home safely.

Clare talked all the way to Katherine's. She said Curtis had gone to California. She'd given him the $78 she'd saved from reading to Beata Holmgren and running errands for other people in town. He'd left Kelso for Los Angeles on a Greyhound bus. He'd promised to let her know as soon as he found a place to live. Maybe she'd go to Los Angles too because she was pretty sure she couldn't stay in Cedar Mills.

When they got home, Katherine chirped to Winston who was waiting on the kitchen table, "Look who's here you big old lug." Winston jumped off the table and walked over to Clare and looked up at her.

"You're all better now, Winston," Clare said reaching down to pet him, but he moved away before she could touch him.

They both laughed as Katherine led Clare into the spare bedroom. All the boxes of Luther Moody's trove of old music had been cleared out. The bed was freshly made with a new quilted flower print bedspread. and a pair of flannel pajamas were folded on top. A pair of fluffy slippers whose fronts were cat's heads sat on floor beside the bed. There were two piles of new clothes, jeans, shirts, and blouses, folded on the dresser at the foot of the bed.

Katherine said the clothes were Christmas presents for Clare but this was as good a time as any for her to have them. Clare put her sleeping bag in a corner and started unpacking her backpack. She told Katherine she'd packed clothes for school in the morning along with her toothbrush and some other things including her 1940s-vintage large black Big Ben alarm clock with chipped paint and a chrome alarm stem on the top.

Clare sat on the bed, wound the clock and set the alarm for six. "The hands are coated with phosphorus so they glow in the dark, sort of," Clare said. "The ticking puts me to sleep."

Before they went to bed, Katherine gave Clare an extra key to the back door and told her she'd be leaving for work at four-thirty but she'd be back home to see Clare before she went to school. When Clare said that really wouldn't be necessary, Katherine answered she knew it wasn't necessary but she wanted to see her off to school in the morning.

Katherine sat in the living room reading while Clare got ready for bed. She was tired of trying to understand Alan Lindsay's ecclesiastical reflections on faith and the Nicene Creed so she'd returned to Wally Berger's list of important American fiction from which she'd selected Theodore Dreiser's *Sister Carrie*. But she had trouble concentrating, half listening to Clare talking to Winston, who was sitting in the hallway watching her getting ready for bed, and thinking how she had to write Jack to let him know how she much she loved the porcelain angel clock and how much she loved him. A phone call wouldn't be enough.

A tear came to her eye when Clare walked out in her flannel pajamas and slippers and sat beside her on the sofa. Clare patted her on the leg and told her how thankful she was to have a friend like Katherine and how happy she was to be there. Katherine leaned over and gave her a hug. She told Clare she felt the same way, she was very happy Clare was safe with them. When Clare got up, said good night and walked into the bedroom, Winston was right behind her. Not long after, just before she went to bed, Katherine pushed open Clare's bedroom door enough to look in to see that she was already asleep and Winston was curled up on the bed at her feet.

A Little Girl in a New World

Will was at the café at six the next morning to find out how things had gone with Clare the night before. He told Katherine after he'd seen them home safely, he'd gone to the Scenic and told Sophie that Clare was too scared to stay at home and had been sleeping in the library annex. It was all news to Sophie whose theatrical expressions of shock were unconvincing. Will told her Clare was staying with Katherine for a couple nights and she'd acted relieved.

At seven o'clock, Katherine walked home to see Clare off to school. Clare was sitting at dining room table reading. Katherine asked if she'd fixed breakfast and Clare said no. She wasn't sure if it would be all right if she used stuff in the kitchen so she'd just had a couple of oatmeal snack bars.

Katherine held up a white paper bag from the café. "Of course it's all right to use the kitchen. But this morning I brought you this. It's a power breakfast sandwich."

"What's a power breakfast sandwich?" Clare asked.

"Just the right amount of egg, sausage, and cheese with a special sauce on a Bateman's Bread bulkie roll. It's one of my secret recipes to power you up in the morning," Katherine said.

"It sounds like you've got a lot of secret recipes," Clare said with a smile.

"Of course I do. There wouldn't be any need for the inner circle if I didn't," Katherine said as she brought Clare a glass of milk and a plate for the breakfast sandwich.

Clare ate the breakfast sandwich with gusto, making Katherine think she should have brought home two. She said, "I'm going to the Ravensdale Mall after work to buy some shoes for our new cook. Why don't you come with me. We'll stop for dinner somewhere on the way home."

Clare nodded in assent. Katherine showed her how the house key worked on both the lock and deadbolt. They parted in the alley and Clare said, "I'm all powered up and ready to go. I'm not used to having someone around to make sure I eat breakfast and see me off to school. Thanks for everything Katherine. See you this afternoon."

There was a steady stream of visitors coming through the kitchen to Katherine's office all day. Nils Holmgren said he was glad Clare was safe and handed Katherine an envelope. It was Clare's reading money for the past week plus another ten dollars. They'd moved Beata over to their house because she was having trouble eating and sleeping. They wouldn't need Clare to read for a while and he thought she could use the extra cash.

Norah Wineskin brought in a large coffee-table picture book about horses for Clare and said she was relieved that Clare was safe. Marty Birch came over from the Toggery with a blue denim cowgirl shirt with pointed pocket flaps and shiny pearl-colored buttons. He and Len thought Clare might like it. Carl Wilfong brought by a sketch pad and a set of charcoal pencils from the variety store because he knew Clare liked to draw. Nell called from the Red & White and asked Katherine to tell Clare they'd finally been able to get more of her favorite cereal, Frosted Oat Kibees, and that she'd put away a couple of boxes for her.

When they were closing, Joyce Woolley told Katherine and Sadie she'd never worked in a place where the kitchen was a public meeting place. Katherine laughed and Sadie told her that was just the way it was at the Madison Café, you wear Chuck Taylors and the kitchen is open to all.

Clare was already back from school when Katherine got home after stopping at the Red & White to pick up the Frosted Oat Kibees. Nell had told her in a authoritative voice that Clare didn't like Frosted Rice Kibees, or Frosted Corn Kibees, or Frosted Wheat Kibees. Just Frosted Oat Kibees.

She put two large shopping bags on the kitchen table and called to Clare. Katherine first handed her the envelope from Nils Holmgren. Then out came the book from Norah, the shirt from Marty and Len, the sketchpad and pencils from Carl Wilfong, and the Frosted Oat Kibees from Nell.

Clare stood silently shaking her head. Then she hugged Katherine hard, holding on like she wasn't going to let go. Katherine stroked Clare's hair and said, "I think a lot of people in town missed you," as they watched Winston jump on the table and carefully inspect everything, taking inventory with his nose.

❖ ❖ ❖ ❖ ❖ ❖ ❖ ❖ ❖ ❖ ❖ ❖

It was an hour's drive to the Ravensdale Mall in Kitsap County. Katherine and Clare drove most of the way in silence. Clare only murmured a soft "Okay," when Katherine told her about Will telling her mom where she was. When they got to Ravensdale, Clare took Katherine's hand as they walked slowly through the mall. She wanted to stop at every store and peer in the windows. She said she'd never been shopping like this before.

They finally got to McMurphy's Active Footwear where Katherine found some size eleven light blue Chuck Taylors for Joyce Woolley. Then she saw a display of cowboy boots in the children's section. Clare walked out of the shoe store wearing a pair of brown cowboy boots with gold and silver embossed stars on the uppers. For the first time in several days, she was smiling. When they passed the Sylvia Tormé Dress Shop for Girls and Young Ladies, Katherine stopped and motioned Clare over to the window.

"How many dresses do you have?" Katherine asked.

"I don't have any dresses. Just jeans and one pair of shiny black slacks my mom got at the thrift store," Clare said.

"Well what if you were ordered to an audience with the Grand Poobah of the Inner Circle? Big problem if you didn't have a dress to wear," Katherine said. "We're going to have to fix that."

"Who's the Grand Poobah of the Inner Circle?" Clare asked as they walked into the store.

"You'll be told when the time comes," Katherine answered. "Right now we need to be sure you're ready."

It was an hour before they finished deciding on two dresses and two skirts with matching blouses that Clare liked and that Katherine deemed appropriate for an audience with the Grand Poobah. They made one final stop at Molly's Shoes because Katherine told Clare that wearing anything but a nice pair of Mary Jane's in front of the Grand Poobah would be considered a serious violation of Inner Circle etiquette. They walked out to the car with one pair of black and one pair of brown shoes to go with Clare's new outfits.

"Now let's have dinner on the way home," Katherine said, feeling happier than she had since before Thanksgiving.

They stopped a few miles north of the mall at The Stuffed Onion Steakhouse which was another new experience for Clare. She told Katherine she'd never eaten in a restaurant that fancy. She intently studied the menu until Katherine asked if she had any questions. Clare had a lot of questions. What was an appetizer? What was the difference between a Delmonico steak, a sirloin steak, and a New York Strip steak? What did *au gratin* mean? What was a *vinaigrette?* What are *haricot verts?*

They went over the entire menu as Clare asked questions until, after the waiter had been to the table several times to ask if they were ready, they finally ordered. They had a crab and artichoke dip appetizer and then shared a medium-well Delmonico steak with two baked potatoes. For vegetables, which they shared, Clare ordered haricot vert with toasted almonds and Katherine had blackened kale with kelp butter and pine nuts.

Everything was new to Clare. She told Katherine that she felt like she'd been transported to another world in a space ship. When their entrees were served, Clare stared at the baked potato wrapped in aluminum foil. Finally Katherine told her it was the potato and showed her how to unwrap it. Clare ate with a serious, investigative air, hardly saying a word until they finished their dessert of brownie sundaes.

"I couldn't imagine anything like this, Katherine. I never thought I'd eat such good food with such strange names," Clare said as they climbed into the car. "Every time we do something together, it's the best time I've ever had."

"It makes me happy to see you smiling," Katherine answered.

Not long into their drive home through the dark December night on Route 104, a thin two-lane gray ribbon that sliced through the mountain forest of towering Douglas fir, Clare fell asleep. Occasionally, the headlights of a stray car coming in the opposite direction would break Katherine's train of thought as she tried to figure out how to talk seriously to Clare, how to give her advice without making her think she was being critical. She didn't want to scare her away. A few miles past the Hood Canal bridge, Katherine saw the sign for the turnoff to Gosport and thought of Jack for the first time that day. I *wish you here with me, Jack,* she thought. *You could help me figure out how to save this little girl.*

At home, after Clare's new clothes had been carefully inspected and hung on hangers in the bedroom closet and a cranky Winston was fed, Katherine announced that Clare should stay in the living room or her bedroom, while she made her special lime Jell-o salad to take to the farm in the morning.

"It's a very secret recipe," Katherine told her. "You're such a new member of the inner circle, I don't know if you're quite ready to learn how to make it. What do you think?"

Clare looked at her quizzically, trying to figure out if Katherine was serious. "Well, if I'm part of the inner circle now, I think I should learn everything there is to know. And it can't be that hard to make Jell-o and put shredded carrots and celery in it."

"You'd be surprised," Katherine said. "Come on then, if you think you're ready."

After the lime Jell-o was mixed and cooling, Katherine put Clare to work shredding the carrots and celery, explaining that the medium shredding side on the four-sided aluminum shredder was the only one to be used.

"Is this another one of those times when the second cook of the inner circle does most of the work?" Clare asked.

"It's the only way to learn," Katherine answered.

Once the shredding was finished, Clare opened the refrigerator and took out the square glass pan of still-liquid lime Jell-o and got ready to spread the carrots and celery around the pan.

"Oh my gosh, no," Katherine said. "You can't just dump the carrots and celery in the Jell-o now, they'll sink to the bottom. You have to wait for the critical moment, when the Jell-o is still a little gooey, to put in the vegetables so they'll float in the Jell-o and not sink."

"I didn't know it was this hard," Clare said.

"Nothing is simple in the world of the inner circle," Katherine intoned as Clare laughed. "Remember. You don't put in the carrots and celery until the critical moment."

Twenty minutes later, after Katherine had announced the arrival of the critical moment and Clare had added the carrots and celery to the Jell-o, Clare went to get ready for bed. Katherine sat at the piano softly playing a

Chopin nocturne. Over the music, she could hear Clare talking to Winston, who was at his post in the hallway watching. She came out of the bedroom in her pajamas and sat on the sofa. She was still wearing her new cowboy boots.

Katherine laughed and asked if she was going to wear the boots to bed. Clare said no, but she had to break them in. She held up the copy *Sister Carrie* and asked "What's this about?"

"I haven't read that much of it yet, but so far it's about a young woman named Carrie Meeber who leaves home and goes to the big city, Chicago, to find a job."

"That's what I might have to do," Clare said. "Leave here and find a job."

Coming from a little girl like Clare it sounded funny but it wasn't. Katherine sat down on the sofa. "You're eleven years old, Clare. Eleven year-olds don't go to the city and find jobs."

"Of course they do," Clare said. "Anyway, I'm twelve now."

Katherine asked when she'd had her birthday. Clare told her she turned twelve on November 20, the Monday before Thanksgiving, the day after her mom and dad had left with Uncle Tim.

"You mean they weren't here for your birthday?" Katherine asked.

"They just forgot," Clare said. "It's ok. Let's not talk about it."

They sat quietly staring at Winston who was sitting on the coffee table staring back. Katherine broke the silence, "I ran away once. When I was a kid. Older than you, but still a kid."

"How long were you gone," Clare asked.

"I never went back. I just kept running. For years," Katherine said, debating whether or not to continue. "We're friends right?'

Clare nodded and Katherine said, "Then I'll tell you everything. Things I've ever told anyone before."

Clare sat sideways on the sofa and leaned against the arm. She sat motionless as Katherine told her about Johnny Herrera and how she'd got pregnant at the chorus festival, how she'd fooled a high school teacher into thinking she loved him so he'd take her out of town on the night she graduated from high school. How he dumped her in Los Angeles and how she lived on the streets until the nuns took her in. How she gave the baby girl up for adoption as soon as it was born and how she lived for two years addicted to alcohol and drugs until she ended up in jail and learned how to be a cook. How she drifted around for ten years after that.

"I just kept running," she said. "Running from myself."

"Why'd you stop," Clare asked.

"I ended up working for a guy in Oregon who helped me see I wasn't a loser. He taught me about self-respect. And then I ended up back here. Maybe to meet you."

Clare moved next to Katherine and put her head on her shoulder. Katherine put an arm around Clare's shoulder. They sat that way until Clare fell asleep and Katherine carried her into bed, taking off her cowboy boots before she covered her up. She closed the bedroom door halfway and looked back in. Winston had jumped on the bed. He was curled up at Clare's feet.

The next morning when Katherine woke up, Clare was at the dining room talking to Winston who was sitting on the table watching her draw him with her new sketch pad and pencils. She was still in her pajamas and wearing her new cowboy boots.

Clare said. "I already had a bowl of Kibees but can we make pancakes before we go to the farm?"

"Of course, as soon as I take a shower," Katherine said as she wandered into the kitchen and found that Clare had already made a pot of coffee.

"Isn't that what second cooks are supposed to do? Get things going in the morning?" Clare asked.

"You learn fast," Katherine said with a laugh.

When she got out of the shower, Katherine heard Clare talking to Maude in the dining room. Still in her pajamas and cowboy boots, Clare was going back and forth from her bedroom, bringing out the clothes they'd bought at the mall to show Maude and Milos who were sitting at the dining room table. Then she showed them the book from Norah, the shirt from Marty and Len, and sketch pad and pencils from Carl.

"So many people in town care about you, Clare," Maude told her. "That reminds me. Milo, I forgot that book for Clare."

Milos went out the back door and by the time he'd returned with the book, Katherine was dressed and asking Maude if they wanted to stay for pancakes.

"Can't do it," Maude said. "We've already had breakfast and Milo's got to go home to meet the Beavers. They're going to clear some trees for him."

She handed Clare the book Milos had retrieved, "It's a box that looks like a book. Look inside."

The faux book was fashioned to look like an antique. The front and back boards were marbled and laminated. The front corners and the hubbed spine were leather. "A Book of Days" was embossed in gold at the top of the spine. Clare laid it on her lap and opened it. Inside was another book, a leather bound diary with a front strap that locked and embossed gold lettering on the front that read "Clare Dolan."

Whenever she thought back to the that Saturday not long before Christmas, Katherine remembered how Clare sat with her new diary, staring at it and quietly rubbing the embossed "Clare Dolan" on the front. Then she got up, walked over to Maude and hugged her around the neck. Maude unwrapped herself from Clare's embrace and told her to look in book box, to pull up the false bottom with the strap on the inside. In the bottom of the box was pen and pencil set, four five-dollar bills, and the key to the diary. When Clare unlocked the diary and opened it, she read aloud the inscription Maude had written on the inside end sheet:

For Clare Dolan, an exceptional girl. What you write here won't always be happy and won't always be sad, but let it always be from your heart. Your friend always, Maude Doud.

Katherine stood at the living room window watching the three of them walk across the street as Milos wheeled Maude home. At Maude's back door, Clare solemnly shook hands with Milos and tearfully thanked Maude with a hug.

❖ ❖ ❖ ❖ ❖ ❖ ❖ ❖ ❖ ❖ ❖

Katherine and Clare were just sitting down to their Saturday morning breakfast of pancakes when Will knocked on the back door and walked into the kitchen. Clare looked distressed. He said he'd smelled pancakes and bacon and thought he'd invite himself for breakfast. They set a place for him at the table and Katherine joked to Clare about another Saturday breakfast interrupted by visitors. Last week it was Randy Weaver and this week it was Will.

Clare kept looking across the table at Will as they ate and finally asked "Chief McCann" if something was wrong. Will smiled and said nothing was wrong, he'd just stopped by to see how things were going. Clare answered, "Things are going very well, Chief McCann. Thank you for asking," and continued watching him with suspicion.

Will said he had some news, however. He pulled out a copy of the Arts and Entertainment section of the *Seattle P-I* and read to Katherine and Clare:

Folklore Society Hits Pay Dirt Once Again

In what has become a much-anticipated holiday event for the anti-Nutcracker crowd in these parts, last night's tenth annual fundraising concert for the Northwest Folklore Society was a smash hit. It was a standing-room-only crowd at the UW's Meany Auditorium where this year's salute to world music was peppered with some old familiar faces and some fresh new surprises including one that left the audience hollering for more when the concert ended.

Most of the usual suspects were on the bill. Orville Wing and his twelve-string guitar put the audience in an upbeat mood with his soulful renditions of the old labor movement favorites, "Dump the Bosses Off Your Back," and "Going Down the Road Feeling Bad." Tacoma's own Sylvia Ratchford sang a haunting eighteenth century Finnish courtship ballad; the Mt. Si Consort, an ensemble of bladder pipes, sac buts, and crumhorns, brought their medieval instruments into the nineteenth century with a thoughtful medley of Stephen Foster songs, and the Grand Coulee Dulcimer Crackerjacks performed a clap-your-hands version of "When the Saints Go Marching In." One of the more singular performances came when Seth Shapiro, a welder from Lynden, played transposed Makah Indian whale hunting chants on his handmade flugelhorn which he'd made out of scrap aluminum from the old Roberts Brothers' mustard factory.

But once again this year, the Skagit River Ramblers, four
transplanted North Carolinians, came out of the mountains
near Burnt to bring the house down with their authentic
bluegrass music. And this year there was a double whammy
when they brought a special guest, Tennessee Jack Lindsay,
who by day masquerades as a maritime lawyer for a downtown
law firm. Forged in the Great Smoky Mountains, his haunting
voice and his virtuosic command of the bluegrass mandolin,
brought the audience to their feet as he led the Ramblers in
two gospel favorites, "Drifting Too Far From the Shore" and
"Hello Central, Give Me Heaven."

The crowd insisted on an encore and Tennessee Jack didn't
disappoint. In a poignant moment before he did the last song of
the night, he dedicated his performance to his Uncle Roy and
Aunt Hazel Willit, saying they'd taught him everything he knew
about music. Then he led the Ramblers in "The Darkest Hour
is Just Before Dawn" with a high lonesome voice of searing
emotion that was matched only by the crushingly plaintive
strains of his mandolin.

We can only say in closing that we need to hear more from
the Skagit River Ramblers and Tennessee Jack Lindsay. And
bring along Uncle Roy and Aunt Hazel if you can.

– Joel Zepp

Will handed the paper to Katherine. Her cheeks flushed as she read the review while Will and Clare cleared the table. Will washed the dishes and Clare dried. Winston sat on the kitchen table staring down a leftover piece of bacon on the counter. Clare made Will laugh when she told him she didn't know he could wash dishes. By the time they were finished, a bond was forming between them, prompted in part by Will's surprisingly avuncular manner.

Katherine had moved to the sofa in the living room. She was still reading the article about Jack while Clare showed Will her new clothes and the things people from town had given her. Will asked if she was going to learn how to ride a horse out at the farm now that she had some real cowboy boots. Clare told him she was thinking about it, but she had to get her nerve up before she talked to Hazel and Roy about riding lessons. He told her he'd been out to New Morning Farm a couple days ago to talk to Hazel and Roy.

Clare asked if they were in trouble. Will laughed and said no they weren't in any trouble.

As Will was leaving, Clare packed the lime Jell-o salad in its special insulated tote which Katherine said had been designed by a member of the inner circle just to carry the Jell-o salad. Clare nodded thoughtfully and carried it out to the car. They stood at Katherine's car saying goodbye to Will when Clare blurted out like she was confessing to a crime, that she was going to Kelso with her mother that night. They were going to visit her father at the jail on Sunday and stay overnight with her grandparents, Jesse and Roberta Dolan. Her mother told her they all had to go to court on Monday morning for a hearing, to show that her father had a real family behind him.

Will said he'd already heard about the upcoming bail hearing for her father. Clare said she *had* to go to Kelso with her mom. She had to help her family. They needed her more than ever now that Curtis was gone. Then she shook hands with Will and thanked him. "Everything will be fine," she'd said with a smile as they got into the car.

Katherine asked about her grandparents as they drove. Clare told her they were old, her grandfather was in a wheelchair, and they were a little cranky. But they were ok. All the way to the farm, she kept saying it would be fine; it was just for two nights. Katherine kept quiet until they parked at Hazel and Roy's. Then she put a hand on Clare's shoulder before they got out of the car and said, "You call me if you need anything when you're down there."

"It'll be ok," Clare said with a patronizing smile, and patted Katherine on the knee.

Katherine and Hazel sat in the farm office looking out the large rear window, watching Clare and Roy talking while they sat on the long bench next to the horse barn's front entrance. Clare had put the lime Jell-o salad in the refrigerator as soon as they got there and gone out to find Roy, telling Katherine and Hazel she thought she had her nerve up now and wanted to talk to him about learning how to ride.

Hazel said she had lots of news. First, the transfer of the land and horses had been formalized the day before. They'd met with Anne at Stamp & Grubb and signed the papers. They were now the owners of New Morning

Farm, less Anne's ten acres.

Afterward, Anne, who looked happier than Hazel could remember, left for Sea-Tac and a flight to Tampa where she was going to spend two weeks with her cousin Bonnie over the Christmas holiday. Then it was on to the Mediterranean for a month. She and a friend had rented a villa on Crete and after that, who knew? She'd said nothing about Jack.

They watched Donny lead a dark gray donkey with a limp in its right front leg out of the barn and over to the bench where Roy and Clare sat. Clare jumped off the bench and put her arms around the donkey's neck. Donny handed her a brush and showed her how to brush the donkey while Roy walked to the house.

He joined them in the office and told Katherine, he'd decided to bring Grajek's lame donkey out to the farm to treat her infected hoof. He said "Grajek keeps calling that animal a burro. A *burro* is a wild donkey. A donkey is domesticated. I told him that ten times but he won't listen. He's as stubborn as a mule."

Roy paused and looked at Hazel. "Did you tell her about Will McCann's visit?

Hazel shook her head. Roy said the constable had come out on Thursday out of the blue and asked if they'd consider being foster parents. It was like a bolt of lightning.

Will told them he wanted a good place for Clare to stay when the Dolan mess became a full-blown disaster, which was going to happen soon. He couldn't think of a better place than New Morning Farm. He explained they'd have to file an application for certification by the state and said he might be able to expedite the process. In the meantime they could be provisionally certified with an order by a circuit court judge. He said Maude had already phoned Judge Carl Haley in Port Smith and told him what had to be done. The judge said he'd arrange a visit to New Morning Farm by someone from the state department of human services on Monday. If the report was positive and after a favorable interview with Hazel and Roy in his chambers on Tuesday, he'd issue them a provisional certificate to be foster parents.

Hazel said she and Roy had been up most of the night on Thursday talking it over. First they decided no. They wouldn't know what to do with a little girl in the house no matter how much she needed a place to live. Then they decided yes. They'd give it a try, after all, they'd half-raised Jack. Then after the closing at Stamp & Grubb on Friday, they'd gone to Port Smith with Harry and with his help, filed an application to be foster parents.

Hazel said, "We decided to do it only if you'd be part of it. We'll need your help."

Katherine brushed away a tear and said, "Of course, I'll help."

Hazel and Roy knew a few things about Clare. They'd heard Katherine's stories about the Dolan kids running through town at night looking for food, how they'd stolen the two bottles of vodka from her tool shed, and how Clare had rescued Winston the cat after he'd been abandoned and injured. And Hazel had met Clare's mother Sophie, after which she'd told Katherine you've got to watch those Southern girls who pretend to self-deprecating shyness, they're just plain sneaky.

Katherine told them that Clare had been taking care of herself for at least two years, since her parents had joined the resident boozers at Lou's Scenic Tavern. She washed and ironed her own clothes, she never missed a day of school, she and her brother Curtis had to scrape to find food to eat, and she earned a little money by running errands for people in town. When Katherine told them about Sophie and Bud missing Clare's birthday and how she and Curtis spent Thanksgiving with frozen Turkey dinners on the holiday, both Hazel and Roy had tears in their eyes.

Katherine went on to tell them how every day after school, Clare went to the town library to do her homework. Some days afterward, she'd deliver groceries or pick up the mail at the post office for older folks who couldn't get out. She was loyal to her family who she refused to criticize. All she would say is she had to help her mom and dad because they were sick.

Katherine finished by telling them about last week, when Clare had gone to school during the day but had disappeared every night, afraid to stay at home because her mother was bringing men home from the tavern. She told them how she'd walked the streets looking for Clare, how Will had finally found where she was sleeping, and how Katherine had brought her home. She told them how the next day people dropped things off at the café for Clare: the book from Norah Wineskin, the pad and pencils from Carl, the shirt from Marty and Len, Nils Holmgren's extra "severance pay," and Maude's gift of the diary.

When she finished, Hazel was sitting with her head in her hands sobbing. Roy was standing behind her, rubbing her shoulders.

"I guess any of our doubts about taking her in don't mean a thing," Roy said. "Maybe we just ought to keep her here now. She'd be better off by a long shot."

Hazel and Katherine ignored his attempt at humor. Hazel raised her head and wiped her eyes, "For now, let's just go out and show her how to ride on a horse. With God's help, everything else will take care of itself."

❖ ❖ ❖ ❖ ❖ ❖ ❖ ❖ ❖ ❖ ❖ ❖

Clare had told Katherine more than once that every time they did something together, it was the best day of her life. But on that Saturday afternoon, after she'd finally taken Major's reins and slowly rode him around the field with Hazel riding next to her on Hannah, she wasn't the only one who thought it was one of the best days of their life. Afterwards, the others all said it was an unforgettable moment, watching Clare perched in the saddle, gravely holding the reins as Major steadily marched around the field. Afterwards, Clare had her first lesson in taking care of your horse after a ride under the tutelage of Roy and Donny.

When they were all back at the house, Clare asked Katherine for the copy of the review of the Folklore Society concert they'd brought and asked everyone to sit in the living room while she read.

"I'm going to skip all the first part," Clare announced with an endearing formality. "I'm just going to read the most important stuff." Then she read aloud:

*But once again this year, the Skagit River Ramblers, four
transplanted North Carolinians, came out of the mountains
near Burnt to bring the house down with their authentic
bluegrass music. And this year there was a double whammy
when they brought a special guest, Tennessee Jack Lindsay,
who by day masquerades as a maritime lawyer for a downtown
law firm. Forged in the Great Smoky Mountains, his haunting
voice and his virtuosic command of the bluegrass mandolin,
brought the audience to their feet as he led the Ramblers in
two gospel favorites, "Drifting Too Far From the Shore" and
"Hello Central, Give Me Heaven."*

*The crowd insisted on an encore and Tennessee Jack didn't
disappoint. In a poignant moment before he did the last song of
the night, he dedicated his performance to his Uncle Roy and
Aunt Hazel Willit, saying they'd taught him everything he knew
about music. Then he led the Ramblers in "The Darkest Hour
is Just Before Dawn" with a high lonesome voice of searing
emotion that was matched only by the crushingly plaintive
strains of his mandolin.*

*We can only say in closing that we need to hear more from
the Skagit River Ramblers and Tennessee Jack Lindsay. And
bring along Uncle Roy and Aunt Hazel if you can.*

Hazel exclaimed, "What on earth! Tennessee Jack Lindsay?"

Clare told them Will had brought the paper over that morning and read
the article to them over breakfast.

Roy just shook his head with a smile and Hazel said, "Tennessee Jack
Lindsay! I've got to tell May and Archie."

That night as they drove back to town, Katherine told Clare how much
she enjoyed watching people's first reaction to the lime Jell-o salad which
usually included wrinkling their nose and asking what it was. Then after
they'd eaten some, they always said how much they liked it. Clare said,
"Don't forget the mayonnaise, which is a garnish to make it look inviting,"
and they both laughed loudly like secret sisters do when they're members
of the inner circle.

It was almost nine o'clock when they turned onto Second Avenue and
stopped at Katherine's so Clare could get her sleeping bag and backpack
for the trip to Kelso. "You really miss your friend Jack, don't you?" Clare

said. "I was watching you when Hazel and Roy were singing "The Darkest Hour is Just Before Dawn" after dinner. You had tears in your eyes. Were you thinking of him?"

"Oh never mind," Katherine said with a smile, giving Clare a hug. "Wait till you're part of the inner, inner circle to talk about that stuff."

Sophie was pacing on the front porch when they stopped at Clare's house. She was bundled in a brown anorak spotted with grease stains and smoking a cigarette. A short man with straight blonde hair down to his ears and wearing jeans and a denim jacket, came out of the front door. He looked to be in his late twenties, at least ten years younger than Sophie. He smiled a leering grin at Katherine and she saw he was missing a front tooth, the right lateral incisor, which in the dim shadows of the bare front porch light made him look all the more sinister. He told Sophie with a laugh to call him again if she had any more plumbing problems. Then he turned to Katherine with a wink as he passed. He said he was Merle the Plumber and to give him a call at the Scenic if she needed any help with *her* plumbing.

Sophie flicked her cigarette into the front yard. She opened her arms to Clare and hugged her hard, saying how much her dad was going to love seeing her. Then she held out her hand to Katherine with a wan smile and thanked her for all she'd done for Clare. She thanked the dear Lord every day that Clare had a friend like Katherine. The family had been through a lot lately but things were going to get better. Curtis would be home in no time and Bud would be working soon.

Katherine felt like a criminal, leaving Clare on the front porch. But Clare was with her mother now. Her mother said things were going to get better. Her mother said they were going to have a good time in Kelso with Clare's grandparents. Her mother said they'd have a good visit with Bud on Sunday at the jail and Clare would have a day off from school on Monday. Things couldn't get much better.

That night, Katherine sat at the writing desk in the corner of the dining room and wrote Jack a note, telling him how much she loved the angel clock. On the front of the note card was a color photo of the Gosport waterfront that included the ferry dock and Harvey's Little Oyster. Before she'd started writing, she'd stared at the photo thinking back on that Saturday afternoon of their first date, and how she knew then that whatever happened, she was in love with him forever.

> *Dear Jack:*
> *I love the angel clock. I probably shouldn't be doing this*
> *because it's an antique, but I carry it with me everywhere. It's*
> *on my desk at work, it's on my nightstand when I'm in bed, and*
> *it sits on the sideboard next to the piano when I'm playing.*
> *But I haven't wound it since it stopped the day after it arrived*
> *because to me, time has stopped until I see you again. My life*
> *won't really resume until we're together. Please remember that*
> *"the narrow way leads home." I love you, Jack, always.*
> *Katherine*

Before she got into bed, she walked into the second bedroom and turned on the light. She looked in the closet at Clare's new clothes. She sat on the bed and watched Winston sleeping at the foot of Clare's bed. *I miss Clare too,* she thought as she turned out the light and went to bed. Before she fell asleep, she prayed for Clare to come home safe and sound.

Into the Good Night

Maude died in her sleep during the early morning hours of Sunday, December 10, two weeks before Christmas eve. The cause of death, according to the medical examiner, was a blood clot in her brain. She was found by her brother Lonnie at 9:30 that morning, when he and Elizabeth stopped to take her to church for the first time since she'd first been hospitalized with appendicitis in October.

Katherine was walking home from Trinity Episcopal after the service and had just turned onto Second Avenue when she looked across Main Street and saw the volunteer fire department's emergency vehicle parked at the side of Maude's house. Behind it were Lonnie and Elizabeth's Mercedes and Greeley's pickup. She started running, shouting "No, no" as she crossed Main Street, oblivious to oncoming traffic.

By the time she reached Maude's, Ray Kesecker and Chip Franklin had closed the rear doors of the emergency vehicle, climbed into the cab, and were slowly driving off. Katherine ran in the back door, through the kitchen and into the living room where Lonnie, Elizabeth, and Greeley sat in silence. The house felt different, it wasn't just quiet, it was empty. Its life spirit was gone.

"She died in her sleep sometime last night," Lonnie said.

After a few minutes of silence that seemed like an eternity, he said they'd better get to the hospital to the sign papers or whatever had to be done. Katherine asked if Milos knew and Lonnie shook his head no. Maude had sent Milos home on Saturday night and ordered him to take Rascal.

Katherine said she'd go tell Milos. Elizabeth took her arms and said, "Maude loved you like a daughter. She was so proud of you." Katherine put her head on Elizabeth's shoulder and broke into guttural sobs.

Lonnie said to tell Milos they'd get through this together, he was part of the family. "He's an emotional old cuss," Lonnie said with a sob as he got into the car.

Katherine drove up Cedar Street to Fourth Avenue and turned left, heading up the hill toward Milos' house. She saw a solitary figure in the distance, walking down the hill. She pulled over, got out of the car and started running toward him. Milos walked steadily towards her. He didn't stop when they met. His expression didn't change when he saw her tears. He said nothing as he took Katherine's hand. They walked past her car and on to Maude's.

Katherine stood in the kitchen while Milos paced through house with his hands behind his back, shaking his head and muttering in Yiddish. Finally he said, "She is gone, there's no reason for us to be here."

They walked together through town for a while in the cold, gray December morning until Katherine told him to come home with her. She expected him to decline with his characteristic brusqueness but he silently acquiesced with a nod. Katherine sat at the piano playing from *Chopin: Nocturnes, Polonaises, and Sonatas* while Milos sat on the sofa with his eyes closed and Winston on his lap.

Later, they drove out to Yarmouth and sat on the driftwood in front of the Blue Heron staring out across the windy Strait where a leviathan container ship with MAERSK on its side and containers piled five-high the length of its deck, was standing in toward Seattle. In spite of the wind, the low throb of its engine could be heard through the water. Milos absently asked, "What is in all those boxes, I wonder. Dreams for the multitude."

Later, when they drove to New Morning Farm and gave the news to Hazel and Roy, Milos and Roy walked out to the barn to see the donkey while Katherine and Hazel sat silently in the kitchen. Only twenty-four hours before, the house had been filled with the happiness Clare had brought to the farm.

In the late afternoon, Hazel fixed something to eat, but Katherine couldn't remember what. They sat at the dining room table eating in silence until Katherine told Milos that Clare had named the donkey Stormy the day before.

Milos said with a wan smile, "Stormy? Why?"

Katherine shrugged and said he'd have to ask Clare.

Later at his house, Katherine and Milos sat talking in the car, Milos pointed to the tree line of Douglas firs on the north side of his yard toward the water. He told her the Beavers were going to cut the trees out so he would have a full view of the Strait. After his first visit to New Morning Farm and his walk through the fields with the view of the water, he didn't want to live in a dark, enclosed milieu anymore. He wanted to see some of the world.

He told her that Maude knew her time was short. In early November, she'd started visiting Harry Stamp once a week, sometimes more. When he asked why, she'd told him to mind his own business. Milos laughed as he did a poor imitation of Maude gruffly ordering him to, "Mind your own beeswax, boyfriend." He said he'd wake up on the sofa in the middle of the night and see her in the bedroom, sitting at her desk writing. She spent hours at her desk writing. "She knew," he said as he got of the car and said goodnight.

Katherine watched as Milos walked slowly up the steps and opened the front door. Rascal ran through the open door barking and jumping up on his legs. Milos scooped up the little dog with one hand and nuzzled him as he closed the door. Two old men who would never see their girlfriend again.

Monday Morning Blues

Katherine got to work late on Monday morning. She might not have gotten out of bed at all if Winston hadn't insisted on it. At three forty-five, thirty minutes later than usual, Winston stationed himself inside the bedroom door and made a raspy meowing sound which finally woke her up. She got to the café an hour late and everyone was quietly working without the usual Monday morning chatter about the weekend.

The dining room was full not long after the café opened. Some of the regulars were forced to sit in the old booths in the front part of the café. A few were even sitting at the counter. Bobby and Muriel pulled a table out of the storeroom to add to The Table, which for the first time had an SRO section along the wall. Katherine spent the early morning working the dining room, helping Muriel and Bobby.

It was a circuitous sharing of collective grief that filled the café that morning. A stranger wouldn't have guessed the town had just lost one of its pillars. People didn't have to talk about Maude' passing. They were there just to be together.

A big snow was predicted for Christmas eve. The high school basketball team had beat Gosport for the eighth year in a row. The Japanese freighter, *Bashō Maru*, was in at Port Smith for a load of Lonnie and Walt's Genjisan lumber. Nils Holmgren had a new line of portable color televisions with remote control just in time for Christmas. Katherine heard only one offhand mention of Maude's passing when, at The Table, Marilyn Smallwood whispered she'd heard the funeral was going to be on Thursday.

By midmorning, when things quieted down, Katherine gave Joyce Woolley the pair of Chuck Taylors she'd bought at the Ravensdale Mall on Friday. Joyce sat in Katherine's office putting them on. She held the shoe box in her lap and said "I'll be honest. At first when I was in here last week, I didn't want the job. You seemed too young to be running a place like this. But then I could tell you've been around. You know the score."

Katherine looked embarrassed. "Thanks. That means a lot. I hope you'll stick around."

"I'll stay. At least until my new shoes wear out."

Katherine and Joyce started laughing which attracted Sadie, Bobby, and Muriel. Joyce was nonplussed when Bobby, who was a head shorter than her, marched over and gave her a hug, saying "Welcome to the team. Now it's just me and all these women."

Katherine ushered them out and closed the office door. She'd called Jack the night before to tell him about Maude but had to leave a message on his answering machine. Now she dialed his number at work and was told by Jack's secretary, A.L. Barney, that Mr. Lindsay was out of the office. Katherine told her to have Jack call her as soon he could. Maude Doud, a close family friend had passed away.

While she helped in the kitchen during the lunch rush, Katherine told Sadie that Hazel had called the night before with news about Larry. She'd just got off the phone with her sister. May had called from Bristol and said Larry had just left their place for North Carolina, for the Outer Banks.

He'd arrived unannounced and spent two nights. He was half lit when he got there and was that way when he left. On Saturday night, he and Archie had a few slugs of Archie's private stock of TVA moonshine and headed for the Four Aces where they'd ended up in a head standing contest with two outlaw bikers. May said she hadn't seen Archie act like that since his sister Addie married the chiropractor from Huntsville. They were glad to see Larry hit the road.

"Sweet mother Mary," Sadie said, "They say you've got to hit bottom before you can start back up. Sound like the bottom isn't even in sight."

Later in the afternoon when the phone rang in her office, Katherine took a deep breath and whispered, "Let it be Jack."

But it wasn't. A loud voice announced it was Hercules Pushkin. Jack's secretary had told him about Maude's passing. He'd already called Lonnie with his condolences and told him to have his son, what's his name, Smiley, Wally, or whatever, to get an obit over to the *Times* and the *P-I*. People had to know. King and Maude Doud were two of his oldest friends, went all the way back to the UW. He and King were fraternity brothers and rowed on the crew. He'd be over on Thursday for the funeral and would like to have a look at the crazy piano of hers while he was in town. Oh and by the way,

Jack Lindsay had left for Kodiak that morning to finish a deal on a crab boat. He'd be back in a few days.

After Pushkin hung up, she closed the café and walked up the alley toward home. The world had changed. She knew loneliness. She'd lived it for years on the road. But this was different. A desolation borne from an unrecoverable loss. She felt a chill when she opened the back gate and looked over at Maude's darkened house. There was no one there keeping an eye on things, keeping a watch over her, making sure all was well. There'd be no news updates on the phone, no pre-emptive visits with nosy questions, and no more of the love that was conveyed by all Maude did. A piece of the world and a piece of her heart were gone.

In the Aftermath of an Earthquake

That night, Katherine sat at the piano playing the andante from Mozart's Piano Concerto No. 23 over and over, remembering how playing it had brought tears to Maude's eyes on her first visit. It was the only time she'd seen Maude show a hint of tearful emotion.

The phone rang as she got up to get ready for bed. It was Will calling from the hospital in Port Smith. She could hear Clare shouting in the background. Will said to get there, pronto. Clare needed her. And he could use a little help too.

Later, Will told her the details of the accident that nearly killed Sophie and Clare when Sophie drunkenly sideswiped an oncoming car a few miles outside of town on their way home from Kelso. After visiting Bud in jail on Sunday afternoon and then spending the night at the Dolan house, things took a turn for the worse the next morning after Bud's appeal for bail had been denied.

They'd left the courtroom and gone back to the dingy Dolan house, a ramshackle Cape Cod with peeling blue paint which sat between two rows of barracks-like apartments next to the Burlington Northern railroad tracks that ran on a levee along the Cowlitz River. Bud's mother Roberta, who'd always whined that Bud had been a good boy until he'd come home from the Army with that white trash floozy from Missouri, ordered Sophie and Clare out of the house and tossed their things out in the packed-dirt front yard. She opened another can of beer on the front steps and told Sophie and Clare to never come back.

On the drive back to Cedar Mills, Sophie left Clare in the car in the parking lot of the Deep River Tavern in Chehalis while she spent a couple hours inside. Later, they stopped at a convenience store south of Shelton where Sophie bought a twelve-pack of sixteen-ounce cans of Olympia. It was five o'clock and just getting dark by the time they got to Port Contingency, twelve miles out of town. Sophie was driving with one eye closed and weaving back and forth across the center line. A terrorized Clare was stretched out in the back clutching the edge of the seat.

As she approached the Y where U.S. 101 merges with the road from Gosport and swings around the bottom of Contingency Bay, Sophie swerved toward an oncoming car, scraping its side before she turned the steering wheel hard to the left and slammed the passenger side of the car into a utility pole. Clare wouldn't have lived if she'd been in the front passenger seat.

Sophie staggered out of the car unscathed but Clare, though not unconscious, had been thrown around in the backseat enough to be dazed. She had some scrapes and cuts on her arms and legs, and a badly bruised left shoulder. By the time Will got there, State Patrolman P. T. Langley had Sophie in the back of his cruiser and was on his way to the Cedar County jail. Clare was lying on a stretcher being wheeled into the back of the volunteer fire department emergency vehicle by Ray Kesecker and Chip Franklin who were headed for the hospital in Port Smith.

Clare spent three hours under observation in the emergency room. Will sat beside the bed while Clare laid on her back, mutely staring at the ceiling. Finally, when it was determined it was unlikely she'd suffered a concussion and could be released, Will told her he'd take her to Katherine's.

Clare jumped out of bed and started putting on her clothes. She told Will he wasn't taking her anywhere. He wasn't going to trick her. He wasn't taking her away to some foster home. She could take care of herself. It went downhill from there until Will went out to call Katherine, while two nurses sat with Clare, trying to calm her.

Will was standing outside the emergency room entrance when Katherine got to the hospital. He led her into the Clare's room. She was sitting on the bed with a nurse on each side. She jumped off the bed and ran to Katherine, putting her arms around her and sobbing, "You did come. You did come."

Katherine put her chin on the top of Clare's head, stroked her hair, and said "Come on, let's go home." They walked out to the waiting room hand in hand. Will walked behind them, carrying Clare's backpack and sleeping bag. Katherine stopped at the door and turned to Clare. "Nothing's going to happen to you. You're coming home with me. Winston and I've missed you."

They drove the thirty minutes to Cedar Mills in silence while Will followed in his cruiser. Clare sat in the front seat with her hands folded, flinching when an oncoming car passed. It was after one o'clock by the time Clare climbed into bed after telling Katherine she wasn't hungry, she just wanted to get into her pajamas and go to sleep. She didn't even say hello to Winston.

When Katherine got into bed, Clare was standing in her bedroom doorway. "Can I sleep with you tonight?" she asked in a tearful whisper.

"Come on, get in here," Katherine said, patting the other side of the bed.

Clare climbed into bed with Katherine and lay on her side next to her. Katherine was on her back and put her arm around Clare, who rested her head on Katherine's shoulder, and they fell asleep. When he figured they were both safely asleep, Winston jumped onto the foot of the bed and curled up between the feet of the two sleeping sisters of the inner circle.

That was how Hazel found the three of them the next morning at eight o'clock after she'd let herself in the front door and started a pot of coffee. Katherine slipped out of bed and they sat in the kitchen drinking coffee. Hazel said Will had called the night before to tell them about the accident. Now Roy was at Kesecker's Handy Mart getting gas and then they were on the way to meet with Judge Haley to discuss becoming foster parents.

❖ ❖ ❖ ❖ ❖ ❖ ❖ ❖ ❖ ❖ ❖ ❖

Clare didn't get out of bed until noon and spent the day in her pajamas and cowboy boots. She sat for a while at the dining room table with her new sketch pad and pencils and then solemnly announced she was going to start writing the first entry in her new diary. Katherine sat in the living room reading *Sister Carrie* while Clare sat at the writing desk in the corner of the dining room alternately looking out the window and writing in the diary.

Hazel came by later and said she'd be back in the morning to stay with Clare while Katherine went to work. They talked softly in the living room while Clare worked in the other room. Judge Haley had been receptive to their request to be foster parents. He'd already heard about the accident and Sophie's arrest. He said he'd issue the provisional foster parent certificate that afternoon.

Clare finished writing, closed the diary, locked it, and took it into the bedroom. She came out and sat with them in the living room. She asked Hazel if Stormy was feeling better.

Hazel said Stormy's hoof was much better thanks to Roy's special ointment and Donny's help. She told them how the donkey had got into trouble the day before when she absconded with one of Roy's boots.

She said, "Stormy's started following Roy everywhere. Yesterday, when he came in for lunch, he left his boots on the back steps. Stormy snatched one of the boots and took off running for the horse barn with Roy chasing after her in his stocking feet. It was pretty funny."

Clare's sallow smile wasn't much, but it was encouraging.

"I'll be here tomorrow, we can go out to the farm and see Stormy if you want," Hazel said.

"I'll see," Clare said. "I don't much feel like doing anything right now."

The next morning before she left for work, Katherine told Hazel that Clare had gone back to bed after Hazel left the day before, and stayed there, alternately dozing and lying on her back staring at the ceiling. Finally Katherine had talked her out of bed for a dinner of grilled cheese sandwiches and tomato soup which she ate in silence and then went back to bed. By seven o'clock she was asleep with Winston curled up at her feet. She hadn't moved since.

Hazel sat knitting in the living room. Finally she heard Clare in the bathroom brushing her teeth and talking to Winston. Then she was in the living room doorway in her pajamas and cowboy boots. Hazel said good morning. Clare offered a soft "hello," and went into the kitchen. She poured a bowl of Frosted Oat Kibees and milk and carried it into the dining room where she sat quietly eating, pausing every now to look over at Hazel. When she finished, she cleared the table, washed the dishes, and disappeared into her bedroom. She brought out an armful of dirty clothes and carried them to the washer on the closed-in back porch.

Hazel got up and went out to the back porch. "Do you need help getting the washer started, " she asked.

"Actually, yes I do, if you wouldn't mind," Clare said. "I was going to ask but didn't want to interrupt you."

Back in the living room, Hazel asked Clare if she always washed her own clothes. She told Hazel she'd been doing it for two years. She'd decided it was part of the way to avoid getting caught by the child welfare people. Always wear clean clothes, never miss school, and get good grades. So she'd started washing and ironing hers and Curtis' clothes when she was ten, never missed a day of school, and always did her homework.

"That was very smart," Hazel said.

"Thank you," Clare said. "We had to do something. Our mom and dad were sick and couldn't take care of us. We were scared to death of getting sent to a foster home. Now I don't know what's going to happen."

Hazel put her hand on Clare's, "There's a lot of people who care about you. A whole town to be exact. We're all going to make sure you're ok."

"There's something personal I'd like to tell you if you don't mind. Something that I just wrote in my diary."

"It's ok. You don't have to tell me." Hazel said.

"I want to tell someone and I can't tell Katherine. I don't want her to be mad at me."

"I don't see that happening," Hazel said with a smile.

"All those times I kept saying everything was ok, that my dad had job and my mom was doing great, working at the tavern, and that Curtis was going to find a place to live in California and send for me, and our trip to Kelso would be fun and all of that. None of it was true. It was all lies."

Hazel motioned her over to sit on her lap. She gave Clare a hug and said, "It really doesn't matter. I think Katherine suspected you were having a tough time. The important thing is you're safe."

At noon, they walked down the alley to the café for lunch. Clare wore her new cowboy boots, a new pair of jeans and the western shirt from Len and Marty. Hazel took her hand as they walked and said she looked like a real cowgirl now. Clare gripped her hand tight and asked if they could go out to the farm after lunch.

Hazel and Clare walked in the front door of the café and sat at the middle booth. Anyone who noticed, which was just about everyone, said they'd never seen Katherine smile like she did when she saw Clare and Hazel. While the three of them sat eating the Wednesday special of chicken-fried steak with mashed potatoes and gravy, Clare told them she'd heard the nurses in the hospital talking about Mrs. Doud and she'd heard Katherine on the phone the night before talking about the funeral the next morning. She asked if she could go and Katherine said "Of course."

Nora Wineskin came in for her take-out lunch and gave Clare a hug. Carl Wilfong walked past on his way back to the variety store and with an overacted expression of surprise, exclaimed "oh my goodness, it's you, you're back!" Clare smiled and told him she'd already drawn three pictures of Katherine's cat Winston with the sketch pad and pencils.

Katherine took them into her office after lunch and closed the door. Katherine said to Clare, "You've probably already heard us talking and we want you to know what's going on. Hazel and Roy want you to come live with them at the farm. They want to be your foster parents."

Clare look at Hazel, "Do you really want to? Really?"

Hazel put an arm around her, "Roy and I can't wait to have you with us at the farm. We're all going to meet with Judge Carle Haley on Friday to sign the documents and then it'll be official."

Clare started sobbing. She hugged Katherine and then Hazel.

"I'm going to be at the farm all weekend, to help you get used to things." Katherine said.

"I'll try my best," Clare blubbered.

The Weather on Thursday: Lachrymose

Even at her own funeral, Maude was still running the show. Before she died, she'd written out the program in painstaking detail and given copies to Greeley and Father Tom, with orders it was to be followed without deviation. It wasn't easy, but they'd done their best to follow her wishes and put together a funeral service based on the *Book of Common Prayer's* "Burial of the Dead, Rite One," with a few modifications. As Maude had requested, Greeley persuaded Buck McCready to be part of the service. Father Tom had convinced Roy that his playing the mandolin prelude at the service was all but mandatory and Katherine reluctantly agreed to sing the two solos Maude had selected for her.

The café was closed for the day on Thursday. That morning, Katherine and Clare sat at the dining table after breakfast, trying to concentrate on a game of Scrabble while they waited for Hazel and Roy, but both were finding it difficult to keep their mind on the game.

Will had called earlier to tell Katherine that Sophie Dolan had jumped bail. She hadn't shown up for a plea hearing the morning before. She'd made bail with the help of her boyfriend Merle Snead, aka Merle the Plumber, on Wednesday. They'd gone straight to Sophie's house, threw two duffle bags in the back of Merle's pickup and left town, heading east on U.S. 101 just before noon.

Will had watched them leave but had waited until late afternoon to report it. He wanted to give them a good head start. The farther they got from Cedar County the better. Katherine told him that didn't sound much like a lawman. Will said it was pragmatism, pure and simple. Sophie Dolan was nothing but trouble and for now, Clare was better off with her mother out of the picture. He'd heard they were headed east of the mountains, for Chewelah, Merle's hometown, and then into Canada.

Then Will dropped the other shoe. He said the brown conversion van had been in town again. The fun bunch, as he called, Susan Owling, Mitchell Lodong, and Art Fletcher, had been back at the Duchess Tavern two nights in a row. They'd been thrown out the second night and Susan Owling had threatened to sue as she was hauled out to the van by Lodong and Fletcher.

"I get rid of one bunch of skunks and another bunch moves in. Just wanted you to know." Will said and hung up.

Katherine waited until Hazel and Roy arrived before she said anything to Clare about her mother. Then before she and Roy left for Trinity Episcopal to get ready for the service, Katherine gathered them around the dining room table and told them about Will's telephone call, that Clare's mother had left town the morning before and was now a fugitive from justice.

She took Clare's hand across the table. "It's better you should know now," she said with a tear in her eye. "No one knows where she is."

Clare looked around the table to Katherine, to Hazel, and then to Roy. "Now I'm really alone," she said quietly. "I'll have to face up to it. Thank you for being my friends."

Katherine and Roy got to the church as Greeley was carrying a box in from his pickup. He'd just came from Port Smith with the new batch of programs. They'd had to be reprinted overnight because the governor had announced the day before he'd be attending and asked to give the eulogy. And equally important, the musical director' name was printed as "Bert" instead of "Brett" Smallwood, a dangerous typo that could have triggered the choirmaster's immediate resignation.

After Katherine and Roy left, Hazel and Clare sat on the sofa talking. Clare brought out the thick red leather combination *Book of Common Prayer and Holy Bible* that Hazel had given Katherine at Thanksgiving. She said Katherine had shown her how the whole funeral service was spelled out in the prayer book, word for word. She'd been studying it so she could understand what was going on during the funeral.

"Katherine told me you'd made this book," she said.

Hazel said, "Well, sort of. My job was to take the printed pages and run a machine that stitched the pages together. I worked in the bindery part of a big book factory in Tennessee. I guess you might say I helped make it. I've got a whole bookcase full of books I put together. I'll show you when we get home."

She pulled a long, black barrette out of her bag and asked Clare to get her hair brush. Clare stood while Hazel brushed her hair and then fastened the barrette in the back. Then she went to the hall closet and brought out a black wool coat with leather trim.

"I bet you and Katherine forgot about a nice winter coat when you were shopping at the mall. But I didn't," Hazel said handing it to Clare.

Clare blushed and said "Thank you, Hazel. I'm not used getting all these new clothes." She slipped the coat on over her black skirt and black and white blouse. She walked into Katherine's bedroom and stared into full length mirror while Hazel stood in the doorway and watched.

"You're the prettiest twelve-year-old on the planet," Hazel said.

"Thank you, Hazel. My Mary Jane's are very nice, but don't you think my cowboy boots would look better?" She looked at Hazel with an impish grin and Hazel laughed.

"I really don't know that girl in the mirror," Clare said.

"Well maybe she'll get to know you," Hazel answered as she took Clare's hand and they started out the back door.

❖ ❖ ❖ ❖ ❖ ❖ ❖ ❖ ❖ ❖ ❖

The choir was assembled at the back of the church waiting for the processional when Hazel and Clare arrived. They were ushered to their pew by Marilyn Smallwood's daughter, Marsha, who was dressed in her Girl Scout uniform. Margie Parker and Roy were playing the prelude: "Do Not Hasten to Bid Me Adieu: Variations on 'The Red River Valley'" which Brett Smallwood had obediently arranged according to Maude's orders. Margie sat at the spinet piano they'd wheeled out from the choir room and Roy sat out of sight at the end of piano playing the mandolin. It was a simple, haunting rendition of the cowboy tune that Milos remembered from Treblinka.

Katherine, who was gathered with the rest of the choir at the front of the church, had hardly recognized Milos when he'd come in with Lonnie and Elizabeth. He wore a black overcoat and fedora which gave him a somber European air. Katherine caught his eye as he walked by, but he'd looked away, giving her no sign of recognition. They were seated in the right front pew and Katherine watched as Elizabeth put her hand on his shoulder before she and Lonnie went back out to the front of the church to wait for the governor.

At first, the small crowd outside the church didn't know Governor Del Welker had arrived when his car pulled up a few minutes before the service started. He got out of the front passenger side of the unmarked state patrol cruiser and leaned in to thank the driver as though he'd just a hitched a ride from Olympia. When the four state patrolmen, two on either side of the sidewalk, saluted, everyone realized that Del Welker had arrived, alone, without an entourage.

He shook hands as he came up the walk. He gave Lonnie a hug and Elizabeth a peck on the cheek, saying how sorry he was that Maude was gone. The three were led by Marsha Smallwood and the other usher, Greg Lundgren, who wore his Boy Scout uniform, to the front pew where they sat with Milos and waited for the service to begin.

Next on the program, after the prelude, was Buck McCready, who would say Kaddish "in tribute to Milos Grajek's devoted friendship for Maude and her dog Rascal." Milos thought to himself, *You still know how to embarrass me, even when you're gone, you old yenta.*

Buck walked heavily out to the lectern. His trademark jeans and cowboy boots had been replaced by a black serge suit and heavy black oxfords, his cowboy hat supplanted by a black yamaka. Buck was incensed when Greeley had called and asked him to be part of Maude's funeral. When Greeley cited the piece in the paper last year about him saying Kaddish at Sam Weinberg's funeral after his Sekiu neighbor had died in a boiler explosion at the Black Forest plywood mill in Sappho, Buck had said the Weinberg funeral was a one-time thing, he wasn't in the business anymore.

But Greeley was adamant. He reminded Buck that his research into Luther Moody's life had also unearthed facts about McCready. He knew young Myron Lantz had been a student of Cantor Moishe Hersman at the Temple Emanu-el on Mercer Island until he'd decided to go into show business as Ron Lantz, Impresario. Buck was flattered and caught off guard when Greeley brought up his mentor, who'd been known as the Jan Peerce of Puget Sound. Mention of the great Hersman was enough for Buck to give in and be a part of Maude's funeral service.

Now Buck's Hebrew filled the church and while everyone tried to follow along with the Hebrew and English versions printed on an insert page.
Milos closed his eyes and silently moved his lips in unison with Buck. The
prayer was burned into his soul. He'd heard it every day in the camps. When
Elizabeth glanced sideways and saw his lips moving, she took his hand and
held it until Buck had finished.

The processional cross was carried by Chip Franklin's son, Tommy,
who was followed by Father Tom ahead of the casket borne by six pallbear-
ers, arranged by height front to back. Mayor Phil Nunn and Ezra Franklin,
Chip's father, were in the lead. In the middle were the two Dalrymple brothers, Coy and Floyd, who had both been in love with Maude in high school.
Randy Weaver and Greeley were in the rear.

The choir followed the coffin and as Katherine passed the pew where
Clare sat between Hazel and Roy, she gave Clare a little wave, but Clare
didn't see her. She was concentrating on following along in the prayer book
and glancing at the program to see what was next while trying to rest the
hymnal on one knee. She whispered to Hazel that she didn't realize it was
going to be so much work.

At Maude's request, the full communion service, which would have had
everyone kneeling at the altar rail to receive the bread and wine, had been
eliminated. She'd written that non-church members shouldn't be made to be
uncomfortable or feel left out during the proceedings and more importantly,
she didn't want the ceremony to drag on *ad infinitum*. But at the risk of in-
curring Maude's wrath from above, Father Tom changed the service slightly
by eliminating his homily, replacing it with the governor's eulogy.

After the opening prayers and the first lesson, Katherine sang the first
hymn, "In The Garden," a cappella and alone, as Maude had ordered.
Hazel took Clare's right hand and Roy took her left. They sat together, three
as one, as the echoes of Katherine's voice, which some later claimed was
divinely inspired, rang in their hearts.

❖ ❖ ❖ ❖ ❖ ❖ ❖ ❖ ❖ ❖ ❖

There were three speakers that morning. The first was Winifred Smith, the town librarian who smiled at Clare when she saw her in the audience. Winifred told of Maude's anonymous support of the library after King had died. How she'd established a fund for purchasing new books for the library in his honor to make sure at least two copies of every book on the *New York Times* bestseller list were purchased. She'd made it clear that although the fund was in King's honor and funded by her, it was to be listed in the library's annual report as "from an anonymous donor."

Marty Birch started his tribute by describing Maude as a generous and caring person until Friday night, when it was time for duplicate bridge. There was a ripple of laughter when he described her as a hungry shark on those nights at the bridge table and with a smile toward Greeley, said it was especially difficult for her partners if they couldn't keep up with her competitive intensity.

He ended by telling the story of how Maude had started what she called one of her slush funds, this one to buy clothes for children whose family was struggling financially. Swearing Marty and Len to secrecy, she made a monthly contribution so the two owners of the Toggery could buy the clothes. The three of them selected the recipients each month. She eventually enlisted business owners on Main Street to donate to the clothing fund and asked them to keep its existence secret because she didn't want the needy families to be embarrassed by taking charity.

When Marty was finished, Governor Del Welker rose and walked to the lectern. Speaking without notes, Welker began his eulogy by saying as far as he knew, Maude rarely left Cedar Mills after King died. A few people in the audience started to shift restlessly and sigh when he continued by saying her life reminded him of a long-forgotten anecdote about Henry David Thoreau and Ralph Waldo Emerson. When Emerson advised Thoreau that he should get out of Concord and travel more because it would give him a better perspective on the world, Thoreau had cryptically said, "I have traveled a great deal in Concord, Ralph."

The governor said like Thoreau, Maude had traveled a great deal in Cedar Mills. She stayed at home but her influence was felt far beyond the Peninsula. There was a ripple of laughter when he said Maude probably had the largest phone bill in the state and any politician who understood the art of survival always took a phone call from Maude Doud or suffered the consequences. Many people made the mistake of thinking she lived in the shadow of her husband. But, the governor said to a wave of approving laughter, if the truth were known, it was the other way around. King may have been taller, but Maude's shadow was longer.

She'd served on the Cedar Mills school board for years and been elected to the town council twice. She had been president of the Western Washington Girl Scout Council, had been a member of the Swedish Hospital board, and president of the local Soroptomist Club. After King's passing, she'd taken his seat on the Bank of Cedar County board of directors to name a few of her public achievements.

But, the governor said, much of her most important work was done behind the scenes, and reflected her most endearing quality, the desire to remain anonymous whenever she helped someone, something she'd done countless times over the years. He told the story of how not long after he'd been sworn in as governor, Maude had called about a problem she wanted him to "look into," as she'd put it.

The owner of a restaurant in town was embroiled in a legal action with the state. The highway department had ordered the Chicken in a Basket be closed because it had been built too close to U.S. 101. It all had to do with the prescribed setback from the road and an error in the original survey done over fifty years before. When the governor had his staff look into it, they discovered that more than two miles of highway had been surveyed incorrectly. It wasn't just Jerry Zampini's lot that was incorrectly platted, it was several dozen lots on the east edge of town that could be considered in violation of the law.

When the governor ordered the highway department to issue a variance until the problem could be settled without any loss to the property owners, Welker told Maude he'd make sure Jerry Zampini know she had helped save his business. But she'd told him to leave her out of it, he could take the credit.

Del Welker finished his eulogy with the words of Dylan Thomas, "Do not go gently into that good night," saying that although Maude has gone into that good night, the rest of us would not go gently from here without her. That her passing diminished us all.

The governor took his seat and Katherine stepped out of the choir box and walked to the center of the nave. The service ended with her solo of "Ave Maria" and then the blessing by Father Tom, who afterward said Maude would have been pleased that the ceremony had only lasted an hour, the amount of time she'd prescribed.

✧ ✧ ✧ ✧ ✧ ✧ ✧ ✧ ✧ ✧ ✧ ✧

Hazel, Roy, and Clare stood in front of the church watching the casket being loaded into the McDougal Funeral Home's hearse while they waited for Katherine. Will brought Governor Welker over to meet them, saying as soon as the mayor was ready, they were going to give the governor a walking tour of Main Street on their way to the Odd Fellows Hall for a community party that Maude had dictated was to take place immediately after the funeral service. The whole town had been invited.

Will first introduced Clare, who, rather than shaking the governor's outstretched hand, put her hand on top of his and made a small curtsy, saying it was honor to meet him. She turned to Hazel and Roy and said, "Governor, I'd like to present Mrs. Hazel Willit and her husband Mr. Roy Willit." As the governor shook hands with Hazel and Roy, Clare said, "Hazel and Roy are going to be my new foster parents."

Governor Welker said he hoped she was going to make them proud. He went on to say he'd already heard about Hazel and Roy, explaining that his daughter was a producer at KUOW, the Public Broadcasting television station in Seattle, and had coordinated the taping of the Northwest Folklore Society's concert the Friday before. She'd given him a copy of the tape because he was a bluegrass gospel fan, telling him he had to see The Skagit River Ramblers and Tennessee Jack Lindsay. He told them the concert was going to be broadcast on Christmas Eve.

Hazel's and Roy's faces both turned red. Hazel said she didn't know when and how Jack had come to be called "Tennessee Jack" but the governor was welcome at New Morning Farm anytime. She and Roy would be sure he got to hear some of his favorite gospel songs played live.

Katherine came out of the church just as the governor started off on his walking tour. Clare took her hand and said she was glad Katherine had taught her what to do if she was ever introduced to the grand poobah of the inner circle because she'd just met the governor who must be right up there with a grand poobah. They all laughed and headed off down Fourth Avenue for Katherine's house in the bright December sun.

Just before they turned the corner at Main Street, Katherine looked up Fourth Avenue and saw in the distance a solitary figure dressed in black marching up Pleasant Valley Hill. She suppressed the impulse to take off after him. Milos wouldn't want company now and he certainly wouldn't want condolences. Hazel saw him too and told Roy, "We'll go up and take him out to the farm. He needs to be with someone."

Hubba Hubba Ding Ding

Clare changed her clothes at Katherine's and then left for the farm with Hazel and Roy, who'd steadfastly refused to go with Katherine to the celebration at the Odd Fellows Hall. They said they could meet Jack's boss Hercules Pushkin some other time. Right now they wanted to give Clare a tour of the house and her new bedroom.

Katherine hung up her coat in the foyer of the Odd Fellows Hall and walked into the ballroom where Lonnie, Elizabeth and Greeley were standing at the entryway greeting people. Lonnie was talking with a white-haired man in a suit that said "city" all over it. She knew it was Hercules Pushkin when she saw a flash of red suspenders under the suit coat.

Suddenly Elizabeth had an arm around her and was saying she looked stunning in her black dress especially with the black cardigan sweater, gold chain necklace and matching bracelet.

"That's just because you've never seen me dressed like this before, " Katherine said, a little perturbed. "In fact, I can't remember when I've ever been dressed like this."

"Well you look exquisite sweetheart. And if you don't believe me, look around, I think you've caught everyone's attention, especially that one," Elizabeth said, nodding in the direction of Randy Weaver who was gawking at them from across the room. "I think the doctor might want to make another house call."

Katherine forced a smile and watched Elizabeth walk over and point her out to Hercules Pushkin, which added to her growing ill humor.

Then Sadie snuck up behind her. She put her hands on Katherine's shoulders and whispered, "Hubba hubba, ding ding, baby you've got everything."

"Watch your language!" Katherine said with a reproachful tone. "I didn't think I'd see you here."

"I'm just repeating what Sam Crouch said when you walked in," Sadie said.

"Sam Crouch is ninety years old and can hardly see," Katherine retorted.

"Every male in the room stared with their mouths open when you walked in, sweetie," Sadie chuckled. "You've given a whole new meaning to the basic black dress."

Sadie said she hadn't planned to come but when the piano had been delivered that morning, she wanted to come and thank Katherine. A delivery truck from Sherman Clay had pulled up at ten in the morning with a new upright piano. She'd had to have the two delivery guys help her move furniture to make room for it. She asked them to find out who'd bought it and one of the men called the store in Seattle. He was told it was gift, that's all they'd tell him.

"You said you were going to look for a piano. I thought you meant a used one," Sadie said. "Danny's going to be beside himself when he sees it. But I've got to help you pay for it."

Katherine told her she hadn't bought the piano. "If I had, I'd make sure you knew it was from me," she said with a laugh. "Now I can start Danny on his piano lessons."

"That's all Danny talks about. Piano lessons," Sadie said. "He kept telling his mom you were going to give him lessons when I took the boys down to Gig Harbor last weekend."

"We'll start first thing in January. How's Vicki doing?

"Horrible. That's another story. But that reminds me, Tommy Lowry's back in town. Just wanted to warn you. He'll be back hanging around the café trying to mooch off Greeley."

"He's going to be disappointed now that the place is under new management. No free breakfast. Times have changed."

By the time Sadie left and Lonnie brought Hercules Pushkin over to introduce him, Katherine was visibly irritated. She regretted coming, sorry she'd become a spectacle.

A smiling Hercules Pushkin held out his hand said, "What the deuce! It's an honor to finally meet you, Katherine Baker. Not only is your voice that of an angel, you're looks are that of a goddess. No wonder Jack Lindsay's been acting lovesick since Thanksgiving."

Katherine frowned and shook his hand as Del Welker joined them. "Well, hello Mr. Mayor. I haven't seen or heard from you in…I can't remember."

Pushkin said, "That's because I don't want anything."

Welker laughed as he said, "You're the only one in the state who doesn't want something." Then he turned to Katherine and held out his hand. "Del Welker, Ms. Baker. You're as beautiful as your voice is pure. What a pleasure it was to hear you sing this morning."

Katherine nodded as she shook the governor's hand. She tried to smile but couldn't.

"How'd you get mixed up with Herk anyway? We all call him The Mayor in honor of the primary election fight where he came in third in a field of three. King Doud said Hercules redefined the term 'a distant third.' "

Pushkin shook his head with a smile, "You just lucky I didn't jump into the governor's race," and Welker laughed.

Katherine told the governor, her friend Jack Lindsay, was a lawyer in Mr. Pushkin's law firm.

The governor said he knew who Tennessee Jack Lindsay was and he'd just met his Aunt Hazel and Uncle Roy. "I hope you get to see that concert when it's on television. He wowed everybody." he said before he left. "And by the way, think about singing at my inauguration in January. I'll have someone get in touch."

The governor was gone and Katherine started for the door. She'd had enough. Hercules Pushkin started after her, asking about the piano.

She turned and said, "The piano's not part of a carnival side show and neither am I." She took her coat and walked out onto Main Street toward home.

✧ ✧ ✧ ✧ ✧ ✧ ✧ ✧ ✧ ✧ ✧ ✧

Katherine was still in a funk when she drove out to the farm later in the afternoon. She wanted Jack there with her. She wanted to tell him how going to Maude's wake had been a disaster. But all she knew was he was somewhere in Alaska. Then there was the message Harry Stamp's secretary had left on her answering machine saying that the executor of Maude's estate requested her presence at the reading of the will tomorrow afternoon. Lonnie was the executor. Why hadn't he said something to her at the Odd Fellows Hall instead of having Harry's office call her with the formality of a government official?

The farmhouse was empty when she walked into the kitchen. She called out a loud hello as she carried in the food for dinner only to be greeted by silence. She'd brought chicken and biscuits from Jerry Zampini's, something Clare had asked for when she found out Katherine was bringing take out, and a tossed salad she'd made at home under Winston's supervision. She unpacked the "Towering Tub" of chicken and placed the pieces on a cookie sheet, covered it with foil and put it in the oven on warm.

She called out another hello and there was still only silence. After covering the biscuits and putting them on top of the stove, and putting the salad in the refrigerator, she walked through the empty living room and then upstairs to peek at Clare's new room. While Hazel and Roy were at the funeral, Donny, Danny and two high school friends had replaced the old furniture with a matching bed, chest of drawers, and vanity that were more suitable for a twelve year-old girl. The writing desk at the picture window with a view of the mountains and the two bookcases had been left intact.

Katherine went back downstairs and into the farm office. Out the back window she saw Donny, Hazel, and Clare putting up wire mesh fencing on the side of the horse barn. Clare was wearing her cowboy boots, jeans, and a new denim jacket. She and Hazel were holding up temporary metal fence posts while Donny pounded them into the ground with a sledgehammer. Stormy the donkey, now sporting a red bandana around her neck, was standing nearby watching.

Katherine sat and watched as they finished up with a what looked to be a large pen, something she was pretty sure Stormy was not going to like. Clare acted like she been doing farm work all her life. When Donny took the tools to the barn and Hazel walked with Clare toward the house with her arm on Clare's shoulder with Stormy keeping up the rear, Katherine started to cry.

In the kitchen, Hazel told Katherine the new fencing was a goat pen. When they'd gone up to get Milos to come home with them after they'd left Katherine's, they'd found him out petting his goats while Rascal chased the chickens around the yard. He'd told them the goats, Shlomo and Malachi, were lonely without the burro. It didn't take long before Roy had agreed to take the goats out to the farm for a while. They'd come home and Roy had taken a trailer back to Grajek's to get the goats while Donny, Hazel, and Clare put up a temporary goat pen. Donny promised he'd have a permanent pen in place in a few days.

Clare took Katherine's hand and asked Hazel if she could show Katherine her room.

"Of course," Hazel said. "But don't you want to take off your jacket now."

"No thank you Hazel, not just yet. Look at my new jeans jacket with silver snaps, Katherine. Just the thing to go with my cowboy boots. Hazel and Roy gave it to me," Clare said as she led Katherine through the living room and up the stairs to her new room. They walked around the room inspecting each piece of furniture. At the vanity, Clare confessed she didn't know what to do with it.

"Here, I'll show you," Katherine said and walked over to the vanity. She sat down in front of the large oval mirror, took a hair brush and started brushing her hair as she stared into the mirror and spoke with a pretend British accent, "Oh, I wonder how dear Katherine and Winston are. I must call them soon."

Clare had burst out in a great loud laugh and hugged Katherine around the neck. "Come on, I've got a surprise for you. She led Katherine back downstairs and into the kitchen and ordered her to cover her eyes. Hazel proudly watched as Clare opened the refrigerator, took out a square glass pan covered with foil, and put it on the counter.

"Ok, you can look now," Clare said. "Guess what this is?"

Katherine looked surprised and said, "No, it can't be."

But it was. Clare proudly took the foil off and held up the pan of lime Jell-o salad which she bragged, she'd made all by herself. Katherine pretended to give it a thorough inspection and said it looked like Clare had waited for the critical moment to add the shredded carrots and celery so they wouldn't sink to the bottom. "If you keep this up, you're going to make first cook in no time," she said giving Clare a hug.

There were six of them at the dinner table that night, Hazel, Roy, Clare, Katherine, Donny and Milos. When he'd gone back to get the goats, Roy had told Milos he wasn't taking Shlomo and Malachi to the farm unless Milos came along for dinner. Milos had reluctantly agreed saying Roy would have to haul three old goats out to the farm instead of two. But there was little talk except for Hazel and Roy both saying they were surprised, the chicken and biscuits were better than they imagined.

It had been a long day for everyone and Katherine was ready to head home shortly after dinner. She said she'd take one of old goats back to town with her and everyone laughed. It was the first time Milos had shown any emotion all day. Clare insisted she and Katherine go for a walk before she left. They walked up to the horse barn and stood watching Shlomo and Malachi at the far end of the new pen staring across the fence at Stormy.

"My first night at the farm," Clare said. "I hope I'll be ok."

"If you ask me, I think you're going to be just fine. I'll be back tomorrow night and spend the weekend. And I want to hear all about your meeting with Judge Haley."

"Thank you for helping me, Katherine. You're my best friend."

Katherine held Clare tight and whispered, "I'm proud to know you Clare. You've given me more than you can imagine."

Hazel, Roy and Clare walked Katherine and Milos to the car. Clare stood between Hazel and Roy and waved as they watched Katherine drive off in the early December night. The twelve year-old girl and her new foster parents.

Great Expectations

Just as Hazel and Roy had been surprised the week before when they'd met Judge Carl Haley, Clare was caught off guard when she met the judge in his chambers on Friday morning because he didn't look like she'd imagined. He wasn't a white-haired grandfatherly type with a stern visage and he wasn't wearing his robes.

Carl Haley was at his desk in a brown business suit when Hazel, Roy, and Clare were escorted into his office by his administrative assistant Mike Finch. He got up with a smile and shook hands with them. He introduced his clerk, Abigail Baumgartner and Clare's caseworker from child protective services, Carol Gray. They sat on the side of the room next to Will McCann who stood and nodded hello. Judge Haley ushered Hazel, Roy, and Clare to three chairs in front of his desk and asked Abigail for Clare's file.

The judge opened the folder, looked up at Clare and smiled. As he skimmed the documents, a thick straight shock of brown hair kept inching its way down the left side of his forehead, until with a practiced swipe, he pushed it back before it touched his glasses. He was a large man in his forties with the athletic looks of someone who spent a good deal of time outdoors. But it was his brown eyes that caught people's attention. Nothing escaped their purview even when it seemed he was in deep concentration.

Clare tried not to fidget as she anxiously watched the judge read. But as she sat between Hazel and Roy with her feet off the floor, she couldn't help swinging her cowboy boots back and forth as she waited for Judge Haley to break his silence.

There had been some discussion about the boots when Clare came down stairs that morning. She and Hazel had been in her bedroom for nearly two hours trying to decide what she should wear. They finally settled on a long light brown prairie skirt and flower print blouse, an outfit Clare said would be perfect with her cowboy boots. Hazel couldn't say no. But she asked Roy what he thought about the boots, saying she didn't think it was appropriate to wear them to a meeting with the judge. But Roy disagreed. He said she should wear them if she wanted. They couldn't manage every little detail of her life.

Judge Haley told them it was unusual for him to meet with children going into foster care. But he'd heard a great deal about Clare Dolan and wanted to meet her. He told her she'd done nothing wrong. On the contrary, from what he understood, she was something of a local hero in Cedar Mills, admired by many people for her bravery and resourcefulness, not to mention her generosity.

He went to say that everyone present needed to know where things stood with Clare's parents and why it was necessary for her to live in a foster home. Her father, Arthur "Bud" Dolan was still in the Cowlitz County jail. If he accepted the plea agreement he'd been offered, he was facing eight years in prison without parole. If he went to trial and was convicted, he'd be in prison longer.

Clare took Hazel and Roy's hands and stared at the judge as he spoke. She'd spent months defensively telling herself and others that things were fine or if they weren't, they were going to get better. Now to hear a recitation of the stark reality of it all was crushing. Hazel reached over and patted her hand and whispered, "You're with us now. Everything's going to be fine."

"As for your mother, Clare" the judge said, taking off his glasses. "Your mother is missing. She posted bail on Tuesday and hasn't been seen since. There are unconfirmed reports she's left the county. She didn't appear at a plea hearing on Wednesday which makes her a fugitive from justice. I debated whether or not to tell you this, but it's best you know the facts."

Clare looked at Hazel and then looked at Roy. When she turned to look at the judge, she started to sob. "It's mostly my fault. I should have done better. They needed help and I let them down." Roy put his arm around her and handed her a handkerchief while she continued to cry with her head bowed.

Judge Haley waited until Clare's sobbing subsided. When she finally dried her eyes and looked up at him, he beckoned her to the side of his desk, "Please come over here and stand next to me for a minute, we need to have a heart-to-heart talk."

Clare got up and walked to the end of his desk with her head down. "I'm sorry your honor, it won't happen again."

The judge took her hand and said with a smile, "The first thing I'd like you to remember is, as I said before, none of this is your fault. You didn't let anyone down. Quite the opposite. Your parents have let you down. Now let's change the subject and talk about you. You'll be surprised what I know about you. It also may come as a surprise that I first heard about you well before this current situation."

He explained that Beata Holmgren was his godmother. She and her late husband Augie had been close friends of his parents. He and Nils Holmgren had grown up together, they were like brothers. The judge had visited Beata a few months ago and all she could talk about was the little girl, Clare Dolan, who had started coming three nights a week to read to her. Later when he'd seen Nils at the Sons of Norway, Nils had told him the most important thing in Beata's life was the reading hour with Clare.

Clare blushed and said, "I loved reading to Beata. She was very kind to me."

"I also know that you delivered groceries to older people who found it difficult to get to the store and that you also picked up their mail for them. You also helped Winifred Smith at the library shelve books and ran errands for folks on Main Street. I know that the week before the car accident, you were too frightened to spend the night at home and had to roam about town with your sleeping bag looking for a place to sleep."

Clare looked down and said sheepishly, "I'm sorry you honor, I don't mean to be disagreeable but I knew where to sleep. I really didn't roam around *looking* for a place to go to bed."

The judge smiled, "Well be that as it may, there was plenty of roaming around at night because you didn't have a decent place to live with food on the table."

Clare nodded and the judge continued, "Which brings us to the reason we're all here. As of today, you are the foster child of Hazel and Roy Willit. Now what do you call them, how do you address them?"

"They've asked me to call them Hazel and Roy," Clare said.

"Then with their permission, I'll also call them Hazel and Roy," the judge said nodding to the new foster parents. "Let's start at the beginning and make sure we understand just what 'foster parents' are supposed to do. The word 'foster' comes from the Old English word 'fostrian,' which means 'to nourish or nurture, to bring up, to cultivate and cherish.' So foster parents, in this case Hazel and Roy, are charged with nurturing you, with bringing you up. As their foster child, you are the one who is going to be nurtured, the one who is going to be cared for.

"Now by the way Clare, by 'Old English,' I mean the English that was spoken over a thousand years ago, which was considerably different than the Modern English we speak today. I don't want you to be confused."

Clare managed a smile and said, "Yes, your honor."

"Well , if you have any questions, don't hold back, feel free to ask," the judge said. "I've given this situation a lot of thought. In my opinion, the promise of your new life with two loving people like Hazel and Roy at New Morning Farm couldn't be better. And by the way, I like your cowboy boots. It looks like you've already started to adjust to being around horses."

"Yes, your honor, I had my first riding lesson last week," Clare said.

"My only concern is this, a lot has happened in the last few weeks. You've been through more trauma than anyone deserves. You've been living a life that can only be called Dickensian in nature. Because of parental neglect, you've been free to do as you pleased most of the time. You've had to make your own decisions and you've done so with an immense amount of perseverance and a rare measure of perspicacity. But now you're going to have another kind of freedom. With Hazel and Roy's guidance, you're going to have the freedom to be a young girl, to do things a young girl should be free to do. But in exchange, you're giving up that life of living on your own, making your own decisions, deciding to do whatever you need or want to do. Do you understand? Your life is going to be very different."

Clare said, "I think I understand, your honor. I know I'll have to do what Hazel and Roy want me to do. I'll try to be a help to them."

The judge nodded with a smile and said, "I'm glad to hear that. You have a wonderful future ahead of you. Everyone in this room is quite pleased about it. Now, does anyone else have anything to add."

Clare looked around the room and waited until she was sure no one else was going to speak, "You honor, I have one question, please. What did you mean when you said that my life was Dick. . .Dicken. . ."

"Dickensian in nature," Judge Haley said. "Perhaps you've heard of Charles Dickens, the English writer. You probably know about *Oliver Twist* or *A Christmas Carol*. 'Dickensian' means like something out of one of his novels. He wrote about street life in London and he wrote a lot about children growing up in bad circumstances who had to fend for themselves. In the way I used it, I meant your life was very much like the life of a child in a Dickens novel."

"What book by Charles Dickens do you think I should read to learn more about a life that is Dickensian in nature?" Clare asked.

The judge's laugh was loud enough to be called a guffaw, "Well, given that you're the one that's asking, I'd want to say *Bleak House,* because you remind me of the main character, Esther Summerson. But the book might be too long for your first encounter with Charles Dickens, so put *Bleak House* second on your list. I'd recommend *Great Expectations.*"

"Thank you, your honor. I'll ask Winifred if it's at the library."

Judge Haley beckoned Abigail over to his desk and handed her Clare's file. He asked her to have Michael Finch step in for a moment. When his administrative assistant came in through the rear door of his chambers, the judge whispered to him and Finch disappeared. He came back a few minutes later with an old leather bound book and held it up for the judge to see.

"No not that one," the judge said. "The new one, the Oxford Illustrated edition."

Michael Finch returned with the book the judge had requested and put it on the desk in front of him. The judge held it up for Clare to see and said, "I'll save you a trip to the library, here's a copy of *Great Expectations*. Let me sign it for you and you can be on your way."

When Judge Haley got up and handed Clare the book, she laid it on the end of his desk and said, "I guess I'm not supposed to, but. . ." and she gave him a hug, her head coming halfway between his belt and his chest. "Thank you. I don't know what to say, Judge Haley. Thank you."

"We're all looking forward to hearing how you're doing out at the farm," the judge said walking Clare back to Hazel and Roy. It was now official and after a round of handshakes, hugs, and congratulations, the new family was on their way home.

You've Got to Walk It By Yourself

Katherine went to work early on Friday morning. She'd hardly slept the night before, lying in bed thinking about Maude's funeral and the reading of Maude's will that afternoon. But her thoughts kept returning to Jack. She wanted him beside her. So much had happened since he'd been gone. She was sorry she'd walked out on Hercules Pushkin at the wake, he could've told her more about Jack.

She left the house at four a.m. and started down the alley to the café. She stopped and looked warily behind her. Last night, when she got home from the farm, a brown conversion van was idling in the alley behind her house. She'd turned on the back porch light and the van had slipped slowly down the alley. She knew who it was.

Now in the early morning, there was another rogue vehicle in the alley, a pickup parked in Larry's old spot behind the café. It was Tommy Lowry. He was passed out in the cab. An empty bottle of vodka rolled out when Katherine opened the driver's side door. Tommy's head was resting on the steering wheel. She shook him and his head flopped back against the seat.

He muttered, "That you Greeley?"

"No it's not Greeley, meathead. There's no free breakfast anymore. Now get out of here."

Tommy didn't move. He slurred, "Bitch."

"Ok, my friend, we'll do it the hard way," Katherine growled.

She started pulling Tommy out of the truck when Joyce Woolley drove down the alley. Katherine left Tommy hanging half outside the truck and walked over to Joyce's car. "Leave your car there for a minute and help me move some trash."

They got Tommy out of the truck and into the back where they propped him up against the cab, his head just below a bumper sticker on the rear window that read, *Don't like my driving? Call 1-800-Eat-Shit.* Katherine got in and started the engine. She backed the truck out and drove the half-block down to Yarmouth Avenue, turned right and parked it just around the corner, a block from the stoplight on Main Street.

The café was packed that morning. Everyone was talking about the funeral and the wake until Will and Charlie arrived for breakfast an hour later than usual. They were peppered with questions about Tommy Lowry, how he'd ended up passed out in the back of his pickup on Yarmouth Street. All Will said was at least the truck's battery had been disconnected so he couldn't drive it if he'd come to. Ray Kesecker said it was strange because earlier he'd seen the truck parked behind the café with Tommy passed out in the cab.

Katherine, who was in the front helping Bobby try to decide where the newly arrived Bateman's Bread plastic pastry case should be placed, smiled at Joyce, who just shrugged when Sadie asked her with a wink if she knew anything about what happened to Tommy Lowry.

Greeley came down from his office, looking more pale and tired than he had yesterday. He and Katherine sat in her office. He said he had to cancel the café staff Christmas party at his house that weekend. He wasn't up to it. Katherine said she'd figure something out. Then he handed her Hercules Pushkin's business card, saying Pushkin had asked him to give it to her, he needed to tell her something.

"I don't know why the devil he can't remember my name," Greeley said. "He kept calling me Smiley and then Willy. Lonnie thought it was hilarious."

Katherine laughed. "Did he say it was about Jack?"

"He said nothing about nothing. Just that he wanted to talk to you," Greeley said as he got up to leave. "Listen, why don't we walk together to Harry Stamp's this afternoon for the reading of the will. Give us a little time to talk."

"Ok by me. Guess this must be the other shoe that's ready to drop."

"Something like that," Greeley said, trying to smile.

She called Hercules Pushkin as soon as Greeley closed her office door. She was surprised when his secretary said "Of course" when she was told who was calling, "Mr. Pushkin said to put you right through."

Katherine apologized for walking out on him the day before but Pushkin just laughed. "It isn't the first time a beautiful woman's walked out on me."

"Greeley said you had something to tell me. Is it about Jack?"

Pushkin laughed again. "No, it isn't about Jack. But since you asked, he was supposed to be back here today, but the weather's a mess up at Kodiak. Plane couldn't get out. Says maybe he'll get to Anchorage tomorrow. No, I wanted to talk to you about the piano."

Katherine bristled. "I told you yesterday…"

"I know what you told me and I don't really give a hoot about seeing your piano. But you need to know about this Canadian kook who thinks it's his. We can't tell if he's serious or seriously off his rocker, or both, or what he's capable of. Anyway, name's Paul Merrick. Dark-skinned Indian-Englishman-Canadian. Sharp dresser. Jack can tell you more. Just beware. I said something to your sheriff, Will what's his name, yesterday."

"Just what I need, another crackpot who's fixated on my piano."

"I'm going to ignore the crackpot part. Anyway, I've got to go. I'm sure Jack will call as soon as gets back."

The morning brightened when she came out of her office and saw Clare, Hazel, and Roy sitting in the middle booth with menus in hand. Katherine slid in next to Hazel waiting for a full report about their meeting with Judge Haley.

Roy looked at Clare with a smile, "Well, you go first."

There was a description of Judge Haley, a recounting of the new words she'd learned like *perspicacity*, and how Old English was spoken over a thousand years before. When Clare got to the part when the judge had said her life had been Dickensian in nature, she asked if she could go out to the car and get her new book.

She came back in and proudly handed it to Katherine. "I'm going to take it back out to the car before we eat because I don't want to spill stuff on it," she said. "But read what Judge Haley wrote."

Katherine took the Oxford Illustrated edition of *Great Expectations* and opened the front cover to the judge's inscription on the inside endpaper. *For Clare Dolan, with my respect and admiration for a remarkable girl with great expectations. I wish you the very best as you embark on your new life. Judge Carl Haley, Port Smith, Washington.*

"So you're going to start reading Charles Dickens," Katherine said approvingly. "I think you'll like this."

"He said the second book on my list should be *Bleak House* because I remind him of Esther somebody, I don't remember," Clare said excitedly.

"Esther Summerson," Katherine laughed. "It sounds like you got an education this morning."

"I've got an awful lot to write about in my diary," Clare said.

They didn't stay long. They were going to Katherine's to pack Clare's things and get her moved to the farm. Katherine joked they should probably take Winston too and said she'd be out later, after the reading of Maude's will. It was the first time she'd said anything about being asked to the reading. She hadn't wanted anyone to know.

But it was old news to everyone else in town and later, after lunch, Will poked his head in the office door and whispered, "We're all waiting to hear what happens at the reading this afternoon."

Greeley was waiting for her when Katherine got back from the bank just before three. He said it was a little early to be heading for Harry Stamp's, but he wanted to take a detour and walk over to Madrona Street to take a look at the Dolan house and have a talk on the way.

"I've got to do something with that house now that Sophie and Bud have decamped," he said. "Maybe I can start getting some money out of it. They hadn't paid rent for months and I've been paying the utilities so the kids had a place to live. I don't think those two drunks even noticed."

They stood in on the sidewalk in front of the house while Greeley debated whether or not to go in. But he decided against it, saying he'd better talk to Will about the legality of removing anything yet. Across the street was Luther Moody's empty house, which like the Dolan's was another bungalow-style two-story home with a wide front porch. Greeley said he wanted to buy it from Rex, Luther's brother who was still in San Francisco, but he didn't want to sell. He wouldn't say why.

They started walking again and Greeley said, "Before we get to Harry's, I want to tell you something about Maude. How she felt about you, all the way back to high school and that... you know...that kerfuffle."

Katherine said, "Kerfuffle...kerfuffle? By 'that kerfuffle' you mean when I left town with a high school teacher on graduation night and how he dumped me on the streets of L.A. when he found out I was pregnant? That kerfuffle?"

"Well, yes, that's the one," Greeley said. "I wasn't here then. Janis and I were in Wenatchee. But I heard all about it."

Maude was president of the school board then and she took the whole thing personally. She'd told the other board members that someone should have seen warning signs that something was wrong with Katy Owling. She proposed a program to help troubled students. But Ezra Franklin, another member of the board, said the school district wasn't a welfare agency, some kids screwed up and others didn't. Katy Owling had screwed up. End of story. Everyone else agreed.

But Maude never forgot Katy Owling and ten years later, she was stunned when she came back to town as Katherine Baker. Greeley described with relish how in spite of her new look and her new name, Maude immediately knew who she was, regardless of what game she was playing with her identity.

"Do you remember when you pulled into town in that old Toyota square back with everything you owned stuffed inside. Wearing your uniform, Frye boots, jeans, and lumberjack shirts," Greeley chuckled.

Katherine huffed, "So what's your point? That I was some kind of freak?"

"Hey, lighten up. I'm trying to say something good here," Greeley said, putting a hand on her shoulder.

"Well get to the point and leave Katy Owling out of it."

"Well my point is, you were the first person that ever confounded Maude. She didn't know what to do when you came back. It took her a long time to approach you. And when she finally did, you weren't at all what she expected."

Greeley told her Maude came to understand why he'd hired her at the Madison Café when she saw how Katherine had saved the place from his blundering attempts to start a restaurant. Then Maude was confounded again, only this time with remorse, after the meltdown.

"She blamed herself and was sure you'd leave town again"

"Meltdown...meltdown?" Katherine asked. "By 'meltdown,' do you mean when she showed me the old newspaper clippings about high school and I couldn't handle it. I didn't want her or anyone else to know I was that little twerp Katy Owling. So I got mad, stormed out of her house, missed work, packed up my car, all ready to leave but the car wouldn't start? Is that the 'meltdown' you're talking about."

"That's the one," Greeley answered.

"Well we worked it out. Or more to the point, I got over it,." Katherine said. "I finally understood she wasn't being mean. I came to love her like a grandmother."

"The feeling was mutual. She loved you dearly."

They stopped on the steps of Harry Stamp's office. Katherine asked, "So we've discussed the kerfuffle and the meltdown. Is there more?"

"Nope. That's it. Let's go find out's what going on," Greeley said a laugh.

The offices of Stamp & Grubb occupied a small one-story white stucco building on Yarmouth Avenue next to the Town Pharmacy which fronted on Main Street at the stoplight. There were two doors, one on each side of the recessed entry. On the left was the door to Harry Stamp's office. On the right was the door to the office of Milton Grubb, Harry's father-in-law who was in his eighties and rarely came to work. In the rear, a large conference room spanned the width of the building.

It was exactly three-thirty when Katherine and Greeley walked into the conference room. They sat opposite Elizabeth and Lonnie while Harry Stamp sat at the end of the table listening to Lonnie describe how Milos had adamantly refused to attend in spite of their insistence that Maude had wanted him there. Roberta Peebles, came with the accordion folder labeled *The Estate of Maude Doud*. Harry opened the accordion folder and pulled out a file folder labeled *Will of Maude Doud* and Lonnie stopped gabbing.

People in Cedar Mills knew the Douds had plenty of money and that it had come from King Doud's shrewd dealings in timber leases and real estate. Combined with years of careful investing in the stock market and their unpretentious lifestyle, everyone in town figured Maude was worth a substantial amount of money. But no one, except the Martins, knew how extensive it really was.

So Lonnie, Elizabeth, and Greeley who had gone over the will with Maude many times, were not surprised when Harry Stamp began to read the list of Maude's bequests. Katherine was stunned, however, when Harry came to Paragraph Twelve which began, "To Katherine Baker is bequeathed the following." The first sub-paragraph gave her a cash gift of $50,000. The last three sub-paragraphs outlined the terms of a $250,000 bequest with the following stipulations. The first $150,000 was to be used to purchase the Madison Café from the current owner. The remaining $100,000 would be placed in a cafe reserve fund to be used for future expansion, remodeling, and new equipment.

Katherine would have thirty days to decide whether or not to accept the bequest. If she decided not to purchase the restaurant, the $250,000 would be added to the $750,000 endowment for Swedish Hospital.

There were fifty-four bequests in Maude's will, including new office equipment for the city offices at the town hall and a new kitchen at the Odd Fellows Hall. There was money for expansion of the town library; the school district received funds to purchase three new buses; the fire department would have a badly needed new alarm and communications system; there was money for the town to purchase two new police cruisers; the American Legion's parking lot would be paved, and the list went on.

Finally, two new high school scholarship funds were established; one provided four years of college to a promising music student, preferably for but not limited to, a student of the piano. Another scholarship gave the same to an outstanding student who planned to attend a school of veterinary medicine.

The Martin family, Lonnie, Elizabeth, and Greeley, had insisted none of Maude's estate be directed to them, but nonetheless, she did remember Greeley tangentially with a bequest of $50,000 to the Cedar County Historical Society.

Everyone was staring at Katherine when Harry finished. Then Lonnie said they were going to vamoose so Harry and Greeley could have the floor. Before they left, he and Elizabeth came around the conference table and patted Katherine on the back.

"We're going to get you into the Rotary Club yet," Lonnie said with a grin.

Katherine smiled wanly when Elizabeth said, "It's a lot to absorb. But we'll all be here to help you."

Harry said, with her indulgence, he and Greeley would like a few minutes to talk about purchasing the Madison Café. Out of the accordion folder, he pulled three copies of what he called a draft sales contract. He handed her one, saying that they were certainly not trying to rush things along, but that the current owner was hoping, after careful consideration, she'd accept his offer.

"I can see you're not trying to rush things," Katherine said. "You two are moving very slowly, about the speed of a steamroller."

They both laughed as Katherine stared at the contract. Greeley said she probably wanted to talk to Harry alone, and got up to leave.

"I know it's overwhelming," he said. "We can talk about it as much as you need to. I know you'll make a good decision."

When they were alone, Harry said she should have another lawyer go over the contract. She could see how incestuous the legal work was for a lawyer like him in a small town. He knew what he'd advise, but they'd all feel better if she got another legal opinion. Katherine asked out of curiosity what he'd recommend and Harry said he'd take the deal in a heartbeat.

Harry told her it would help with her taxes if she took care of the paperwork for $50,000 gift as soon as possible, before the end of the year. He knew it was on short notice but he'd made an appointment for her with a trust officer at Elliott Bay Bank & Trust in Seattle on Monday morning, and he encouraged her to make the trip. She could also discuss the disposition of the money for the purchase of the café with the people in Seattle.

Katherine got up to leave and told Harry she'd go to Seattle on Monday morning.

He said, "Let me give you a little advice. You need to have money in a local bank but keep most of it out of the county. You don't want everyone to know your business."

Katherine laughed, "I understand completely, believe me, I do."

❖ ❖ ❖ ❖ ❖ ❖ ❖ ❖ ❖ ❖ ❖ ❖

A different Katherine Baker walked out of the offices of Stamp & Grubb. She wasn't the same. The town wasn't the same. What had Thoreau written at the end of *Walden*, "Things do not change, we change." *Well he was wrong*, she thought, *everything's changed, me and everything else*.

It was winter twilight now as she crossed Yarmouth Avenue and started up Main Street toward home. She felt completely alone, like she used to feel on the road as a gypsy cook in the San Joaquin Valley. The decisions she would make now would be hers alone, just like it was whenever she'd decided to quit a job and move on.

She was shaken out of her reverie when she passed Fitzpatrick's Furniture and Appliances. It was almost Christmas. The stores were open late tonight. She stopped and stared vacantly at Fitzpatrick's display window. A recliner surrounded by flashing colored lights was displayed on the left with a sign resting in the chair that read "For Him." On the right side of the display was a montage of things "For Her," which included a table-top mixer, two styles of vacuum cleaners, and an ironing board adorned with a shiny chrome iron.

She walked up the block to the Madison Cafe, past Lou's Scenic Tavern, Betty's Maternity Shop, the Christian Science Reading Room, and the Star Theater, which Greeley claimed he was going to renovate. She cupped her hands on the café's plate glass window and peered into the now dark space, just able to make out the row of booths on the right side and the end of the counter near the front door where she'd handed Jack his breakfast before he left for Seattle.

She walked across the street, stood in front of Wilfong's Variety and stared back at the café. It wasn't much to look at from the front. She liked it that way. She liked how people walked in for the first time thinking the three old wooden booths and a few stools at the counter was all there was to the place and then were surprised to find the brightly lit dining room in the back with the skylights and glass wall looking out to the stone garden.

But hers? The Madison Café? She turned down Second Avenue and walked past Maude's empty house. She'd never get used to Maude being gone. She walked down the alley to her back gate and stopped. Was there a rustling sound in the tool shed? She took a few steps up the walk to her back door when someone came from behind and grabbed her arms with a brute force that sent a searing pain through her shoulders.

It was Mitchell Lodong. He yelled to the tool shed, "I got her." The shed door swung open and Susan Owling sauntered out. She stood in front of Katherine, spewing a acrid cloud of boozy breath that made Katherine gag. Looking like a two-hundred pound sideshow attraction in her curly black wig, white fake fur coat, jeans and high heels, she waved a forefinger at Katherine and growled, "Where's my granddaughter? What've you done with her. I want her, you little tramp."

Katherine stomped on Lodong's left foot and he loosened his grip on her arms. She shook free, turned and kneed him in the groin. He doubled over and she grabbed him by the back of the neck and pushed him face first to the ground. Then she turned and shoved Susan Owling back into the tool shed, slammed the door shut, grabbed a dead branch and pushed it through the latch to lock the door.

Mitchell Lodong started to get up. She shoved him back to the ground and put her foot on his neck so his head was face down in the dirt.

"Listen carefully, Ding Dong or Long Dong, or whoever you are. I'm going to let you up and you're going to go find that toad who drives the van. You two are going to drive to the state store. You know the way. Wait for me in the parking lot. If that fat sow in the tool shed is sober enough so I can talk sense to her, we're going drive down and meet you. Now I'm going to let you up."

Mitchell Lodong staggered up and dusted himself off. "I'm Bishop Mitchell Lodong and you know it. Furthermore. . ."

Katherine stepped back and gave him a karate kick in the chest, knocking him over on his back. She put a foot on his cheek and pushed his face sideways into dirt. "Listen blockhead, we'll keep this up until you decide to do what I tell you. Now get up and go get Fletcher. I'll meet you at the state store."

Lodong struggled up and walked out the back gate. In the alley he turned left and walked across Second Avenue into the darkness behind Maude's house. Katherine left a sobbing Susan Owling locked in the tool shed and went into the house. She paced through the house for a few minutes and went back outside. She stood at the door of the tool shed trying to talk calmly.

"Listen to me, Susan. There's no granddaughter here. You may have seen a little girl with me but she's a foster child of some friends. My baby was given up for adoption when she was born in Los Angeles. I never saw her. You've got to go away and leave me alone. Do you understand?"

Loud sobbing came from the tool shed.

"I'm going to let you out now. We'll go meet your pals. I'll help you get out of town. It's either that or jail."

Katherine unlatched the tool shed door, ready to throw Susan Owling into a headlock if she tried to bolt. But she didn't. Her sobbing subsided and she took Katherine's outstretched hand. They walked around the house to the front where Katherine's car was parked. They drove slowly down Cedar Avenue, crossed Yarmouth, turned left on Mountain View and drove over to Main Street where Mountain View bordered on the state store parking lot. The brown conversion van was parked in the shadows at the back of the lot.

Katherine led Susan to the van, opened the rear side door and Lodong pulled her in. Art Fletcher was at the wheel looking terrified, his porcine features more pronounced in the dim light. He rolled down the window. Katherine told him to wait while she went into state store.

She came back with a cart filled with shopping bags. She told Fletcher to get out and help her load them onto the floor of the front passenger side. When they finished, Katherine told him, "You've got six gallons of vodka and two gallons of red wine. That should hold you for a while."

"I stopped drinking," Fletcher said. "And I'm going to dump these two anyway. I'm sick of them."

"Well get them out of here or you're all going to jail," Katherine said, pulling a roll of bills out of her purse. "Here's twelve hundred bucks. It's all the money I've got. Get them into California before you do your dumping.

Maybe Lodong will get rid of her."

Fletcher shook his head, "No chance of that. As long as she's got her ATM card and a monthly deposit, he sticks to her like flypaper."

"Just get them out of here."

Katherine watched the van ease out of the parking lot and disappear down Highway 101 going east. If Fletcher kept his word, they'd be heading south toward California in a half hour. *Happy holidays,* Katherine thought as she walked back to her car and drove home.

Jesus Christ Made Seattle Under Protest

Katherine was on the road for Seattle on Monday morning just after six o'clock. She planned to park the car at the Bainbridge Island ferry parking lot and walk on the 7:45 boat. Will had offered that advice before she'd left, saying it was a good way to avoid the hassle of parking in the city. He'd also said his sources had told him she'd gotten rid of that pack of skunks in the conversion van on Friday night.

"Only following your lead when it comes to eradicating skunks," Katherine had joked as they'd walked out to her car together.

As she drove out of town, east on U.S. 101, she thought of Jack heading for the city on those Monday mornings after he'd stopped at the café to pick up his breakfast. It seemed like a lifetime since she'd seen him. He hadn't met Clare. He hadn't met Winston. He didn't know about Maude. She hoped by now he was back from Alaska. She'd surprise him after her meeting with Hercules Pushkin. She smiled as she thought how she'd walk into Jack's office unannounced. He'd push his office door closed and sweep her into his arms. They'd fall together on the office carpet and make mad passionate love.

She'd left the café without much fanfare. Sadie had teased that on Thursday afternoon she'd been the vamp in a black dress and now she was the CEO in her Harris Tweed jacket and black wool pencil skirt. Everyone else kept quiet. By now, the whole town knew that Maude had left money for her to buy the café and that Greeley was eager to sell. Sadie, Joyce, Muriel, and Bobby were nervously subdued because of it. They knew change would come no matter what she decided to do.

Now on the road in the early morning light of December, with the classical music of KING-FM in the background, Katherine kept coming back to the question of Maude's generosity, because in no way did she deserve it, regardless of what Greeley said. How was she supposed to be the person Maude expected her to be? She'd have to shed the convenient, self-deprecating image she'd always relied on, that of the tramp short-order cook who had a drinking problem, only a step away from another bout with the booze.

She and Clare had talked about their new lives and trying to accept it all on Friday night at the farm. They'd sat on Clare's new bed in their pajamas and talked late into the night. Clare started blubbering when she told Katherine how scared she felt when she, Hazel and Roy, had loaded her things into the car for the move to the farm.

"It made me sad when I should have been happy," she said. "But I just felt like a piece baggage being shipped around from one place to another because I messed up."

For once Katherine sounded scolding, "You know better than that, Clare Dolan. Life in the inner circle can be tough, but sisters never feel sorry for themselves. They pick themselves up and take care of things."

She'd said she could see it was time for Clare to become an official sister of the inner circle and hopped off the bed, heading for her bedroom next door. She brought back three bibles from one of the bookcases that held the books Hazel had bound at the Kingsport Press. Back on the bed, Katherine and Clare sat cross-legged facing each other with the bibles between them.

"Ok, all new sisters have to swear on a stack of bibles that they'll always be true to the inner circle and true to each other. One hand on the bibles and one hand in the air."

Clare had smiled and put a hand on the bibles, "I never know if you're serious or not, Katherine."

"I couldn't be more serious. Now repeat after me: *Sisters never waver. Sisters never doubt. Sisters work together. Sisters never pout. We all pull together, that's what we're about!*"

With her right hand raised and her left hand on the bibles, Clare repeated the oath haltingly with Katherine's help. Then they did a double high five and double pinkies three times.

"Now you're officially a member of the inner circle. The grand poobah will be contacting you at the appropriate time."

By then, Clare was laughing. "Oh Katherine. I've never known anyone like you."

Clare had finally fallen asleep on Katherine's shoulder trying to listen as Katherine started telling her about acceptance, which in retrospect had sounded painfully pontifical, thanks to her generous borrowing from Alan Lindsay's books and Father Tom's sermons. Accepting ourselves, accepting the love of others, and accepting the love of God were the greatest challenges of all, she'd told Clare. Or was she talking to herself? Katherine's blather was too much for a twelve year-old girl and Clare had dozed off before she'd finished.

The next morning when they'd gone into town to meet Will at the Dolan house to see if there was anything Clare wanted to have before the house was emptied, Katherine and Clare both fought back tears. Katherine had waited in the car while Clare and Will went in. All Clare had brought back was a large brown manila envelope which contained two photographs. One was a black and white photo in a cheap gold frame of Bud and Sophie, Bud in his Army dress greens with his arm around Sophie who was wearing a sun dress and stood with her head cocked toward Bud and her free arm akimbo. The label on the back read, "Wedding day, Fort Leonard Wood, August 17, 1972." The other picture was an unframed school photo of Curtis, taken the year before, when he was thirteen.

It was getting light now as Katherine drove down the hill to the floating bridge at Hood Canal and when the car clattered over a metal grate and onto the bridge, she was jolted out of her ruminations about Clare's move to the farm. The glassy smoothness of the water on the right side of the bridge, the south side, was in stark contrast to the choppy waves on the north side which were fed by the wind off the Sound and bounced against the span. She thought that Greeley the English teacher could have used the scene to construct a clever metaphor for her state of mind.

The sun was just coming over the Cascade Mountains east of Seattle as Katherine drove down the hill through the little village of Winslow and into the ferry terminal parking lot. Foot passengers boarded the ferry down a covered walkway to the passenger deck of the boat. Katherine joined the crowd of commuters marching down the ramp to the ferry and was passed by most of them as they jockeyed for position en route to their special spot on the boat.

When she finally got a cup of coffee and found a place to sit in one of the long rows of chairs in the front of the boat, she thought of *Sister Carrie* and Carrie Meeber, the country girl taking the train to a new life in Chicago. But she wasn't a naïf from the sticks and unlike Carrie's experience on the train when she was waylaid by a roué traveling salesman, the only man Katherine wanted to see was Jack Lindsay. Today at least, she'd get to see where he worked.

On a whim, she'd called Hercules Pushkin's office on Saturday afternoon after she'd read Harry and Greeley's sales contract countless times. Surprised that he answered on a Saturday, she apologized again for walking out on him at Maude's wake and asked if she could meet with him on Monday.

"Is this legal or personal," he'd asked with a laugh. "I can't help you out with young Mr. Lindsay."

"I need a legal opinion. About a sales contract," she'd said. "It's a little complicated."

"About you buying the café? Lonnie told me a little about it last week. Sure I'll take a look at it but only if I get to take you to lunch afterward," Pushkin had said. "And who knows, maybe we'll get Jack to come along if he ever gets back here."

It was a beautiful, brisk winter morning when the *MV Colville* slid into the Colman Ferry Dock slip at Pier 52 on time at 8:15. Katherine had plenty of time before her nine o'clock meeting at the bank and as the cab growled up the steep incline of Columbia Street to Fourth Avenue, she remembered Will's recommendation: "Get to where you're going ahead of time and then find a place to have a cup of coffee and relax before your appointment so you're calm and collected for the meeting." She paid the cabbie and walked across Fourth Avenue to a coffee shop where she sat in a window booth staring across the street at the narrow five-story Romanesque Revival building that housed Elliott Bay Bank & Trust.

Just before nine, she crossed the street and stood at the bank entrance, staring vacantly at the bronze plaque beside the gold framed revolving door which described it as "one of the few buildings west of the Mississippi River designed by Henry Hobson Richardson." In spite of her anxiety, Katherine felt a flood of relief when she was finally inside the bank's hushed interior and was pleasantly surprised when the receptionist, who sat behind a large walnut desk just inside the entrance, immediately ushered her into the trust officer, John Melville's office at the opposite end of the lobby.

It was then, when she shook hands with John Melville and sat at the conference table in his office, opposite the angular banker with prematurely gray hair and a notable aquiline nose, that she had the fleeting thought she really was a Carrie Meeber, an artless bumpkin from the boondocks. But Melville, with a courtly civility thought to have disappeared a generation before, quickly assuaged her uneasiness and after a few polite questions about her trip over from the Peninsula that morning, got right to business.

Thirty minutes later they were finished. Katherine left the bank with an array of documents which barely fit into her scuffed zippered portfolio, an accessory she was certain Melville gazed at with a polite expression of noblesse oblige.

"Jesus Christ Made Seattle Under Protest," Katherine said softly as she walked out onto Fourth Avenue and went north toward Marion Street trying to calculate how many blocks it was to Pine Street. Years ago in high school, someone had said that was how you remembered the names of Seattle's downtown streets that ran up the hill from the waterfront. Jefferson and James; Cherry and Columbia; Marion and Madison; Spring and Seneca; University and Union; Pike and Pine. Six blocks to Pine Street and one block over to Third Avenue. Seven blocks to the offices of Pushkin, McDonald & Fishkin at Third and Pine.

She stopped at a luggage store a few doors down from the bank and bought a soft brown leather briefcase which she exchanged for the scuffed leather portfolio. The store clerk hesitated when Katherine had asked for a pair of scissors to cut off the price tag on the briefcase. He watched with a frown when she emptied her portfolio onto the top of one of the glass display cases and then carefully rearranged all the documents before packing them in the new briefcase. She left the store carrying the new briefcase and her old portfolio, which was deposited in the first trashcan she passed, something she did with a flourish.

She made one more stop at McGinty's Books at Third and Pike, a block from her destination. After a half hour of browsing, she bought two books for Clare, the Oxford Illustrated edition of *Bleak House* and Cooper Power-Lesley's *A Dickens Lexicon: Words and Phrases From the Novels of Charles Dickens.*

Pushkin's office was on the top floor of a compact, twelve-story office building on the southwest corner of Third and Pine, diagonally across the street from the Bon Marché department store. The security guard in the lobby phoned upstairs to confirm her appointment, walked her to an open elevator, and pushed the twelfth floor button. He was an avuncular elderly fellow, dressed in a gray business suit, who introduced himself as Tom Hansen. He told her with a flourish and a twinkle in his eye that he didn't do this for everyone, but she must be important if she was going to see the boss and he'd better mind his p's and q's.

Hercules Pushkin was waiting for her at the elevator. He escorted her down the hall and introduced his secretary, Alice Ridley, a large, middle-aged woman with short white hair who smiled as she gave Katherine a thorough inspection.

Hercules led her into his corner office which looked out over Elliott Bay to the west and Queen Anne Hill to the north. They stood at the window while Pushkin pointed out the neighborhood on the west side of Queen Anne Hill where he and Silas Peavey had grown up. Katherine looked across Belltown toward the Space Needle and saw Jack's apartment building at Second and Lenora where he'd fixed dinner at his condo for her and Elizabeth when Maude was in Swedish Hospital. *Jack, Jack, where are you now,* she thought.

While Pushkin read the contract, Katherine stood at the window staring out over Elliott Bay as two tugs nudged a loaded container ship toward Harbor Island. Pushkin motioned her to sit down. He had two issues with the contract. The first was straightforward. There was no precise description of what was being sold. The description of "The Madison Café building that occupies two lots on the north side of West Main Street," was hardly enough. Harry Stamp needed to insert the appropriate legal description of the property.

"An oversight probably caused by their rush to get something in front of you," he said. "Lonnie told me Smiley was hoping to close the deal before the first of the year."

Katherine laughed. "Not Smiley. Greeley."

The second issue was more complicated because of how it might affect her relationship with Greeley. He said Greeley shouldn't have open-ended usage of the office on the second floor "until such time as it was convenient for him to move." He needed to sign a ninety-day lease which could be renewed for period of thirty days. And the apartment, Larry's old apartment, should be vacated within thirty days after the sale. Pushkin said it was a way for her to declare some autonomy from Greeley's largesse.

Katherine shook her head no. She said it would derail their relationship not to mention the sale. But Pushkin disagreed. Lonnie had said Greeley wanted to be free of the place so he could devote more time to the historical society and to renovating the theater next door. Like everything else he'd done, he was bored and wanted to move on to something new. Yes, he might have his feelings hurt by the stipulation but he'd get over it.

Pushkin said, "If he doesn't and wants to walk away from the sale, then you're better off anyway. But I think he'll have a new respect for you. This is business not a marriage. You need to let him know you're going to chart your own course."

Pushkin said Alice would have someone downstairs rewrite the clause to spell out the terms for Greeley's use of the office and vacating the apartment. She'd have it ready for them after lunch.

"Now let's get out of here," Hercules said. "I've got a couple of guys I want you to meet at lunch. But first, I'll give you a tour of Jack's office. And by the way, there's good news and bad news. The bad news is Jack's not here. The good news is he's scheduled to land at SeaTac just before midnight."

They went down to the ninth floor to meet Jack's secretary, A. L. Barney, who was sitting at her desk outside Jack's office talking with Leah

Balfour. As they approached, she heard Jack's name and something about pissing contests, and then muted laughter. Hercules told them to behave themselves and introduced Katherine.

A. L. Barney, or Arlie as Pushkin called her, was a tall, thin woman in her mid-forties with strawberry blonde hair, blue eyes, and a winning smile. She was immediately likable, so much so that Katherine worried that she and Jack might have more than a working relationship. After the introductions, Katherine started to feel a little resentment about how Arlie and Leah Balfour talked about Jack with an air of possessiveness.

Leah told her with a proprietary pride how Jack had confounded all the folks at the Burnt Fire Hall when her Uncle George Neeley and Cousin Tut Burwell had forced him onto the stage without warning, thinking he'd make a fool of himself, but instead he'd brought the audience to their feet with his mandolin playing and singing. Then when Arlie said they were all very proud of "our Jack," Katherine was outright jealous and her face flushed with emotion.

"And this is where our wandering boy toils," Pushkin said, leading Katherine over to Jack's open office.

She looked at the carpet. It was a rough looking brown Berber, hardly suitable for rolling on the floor. She'd have to bring some padding. Unlike Pushkin's office on the top floor with its palatial view, Jack's window looked out across Pine Street to a parking garage. Who knew, maybe he'd start moving up a floor or two now that he was "their Jack." Their Jack indeed, she huffed to herself.

Hercules invited Leah Balfour to lunch, saying they were meeting her brother Eddie at the Duwamish Club. Leah declined. She shook hands with Katherine and told her how lucky she was. She patronizingly patted Katherine on the shoulder and joked that in spite of her efforts, Jack had made it clear there was only one woman in his life, Katherine Baker from Cedar Mills. Everyone laughed, even Katherine, who managed an unconvincing chuckle and tight smile.

The Duwamish Club was on top of the Carlyle Hotel at the corner of Stewart Street and Fifth Avenue, and as they walked, Hercules told Katherine he knew he'd sent Jack into the breach when he dispatched him to

Kodiak to babysit Bart Ladderback's purchase of a crab boat.

"But it was time to throw the kid into a shark-infested pool to see if he could swim," he said with a laugh. "Not only could he swim but he fought off the sharks. I'm glad Maude told me about this sharp young maritime lawyer from Chicago who wanted to move to the Northwest."

"So Maude engineered Jack's move to Seattle," Katherine said. "Why am I not surprised."

"Just more of her 'beneficent skullduggery.' She was always up to something." Pushkin said as they walked into the hotel and took the elevator to the Duwamish Club.

Eddie Balfour was already at their table and Katherine found him to be a charming antidote to his sister's brash assertiveness. When Hercules introduced him as Professor Edward Balfour of the University of Washington where he was an Associate Professor of Maritime History and a maritime consultant to Pushkin, McDonald & Fishkin, Eddie smiled and softly recited Will and Joey's refrain of "Eddie it was, Eddie it is, and Eddie it always shall be" as he held out his hand to Katherine.

They all ordered the special of the day, black cod ravioli with seaweed salsa verde and arugula with papaya pesto. Then Eddie elaborated on his sister's story about Jack's visit to the Burnt Fire Hall for Uncle George Neeley's birthday party, confessing he was the one who talked Jack into going even though he knew the North Carolinians would like nothing more than to give the unsuspecting boy from Tennessee a bad time. Katherine said she'd seen the review of the Folklore Society concert in the paper and how she, Hazel and Roy had all laughed about his new sobriquet of Tennessee Jack.

Then Hercules got serious, saying he wanted to warn her about this brown-skinned Englishman, Paul Merrick.

"He's convinced your piano is filled with a trove of his grandparents' jewels," Pushkin said. "He talks like a complete screwball and he could be dangerous."

He went on to tell Katherine the whole story, how Merrick had first contacted Eddie, ostensibly searching for the remnants of the *Arctic Maid* and how Eddie had told the Englishman about Silas Peavey's knowledge of early Puget Sound maritime history and then, after they'd found the location of the hulk with the help of his mentor, Jim Underwood, Eddie had taken Paul Merrick to Lake Union, thinking the piano might still be on the ship.

Eddie said it all sounded preposterous anyway, a piano with hollow legs. But Katherine said it was true, the front legs of the piano had indeed been hollowed out but were empty by the time the piano got to her house. Then there was Randy Weaver's conclusion that East Indian satinwood was used to construct the mechanism's extra legs that allowed the originals to swing free.

"It doesn't take Philip Marlowe to figure out that something from the South Asian subcontinent had been stashed in those piano legs at one time," Hercules added. "The problem is the nut log Merrick thinks Katherine has the goods."

"Speaking of Philip Marlowe. . ." Eddie said, waving at well-dressed man in the dining room's doorway. "Nick's here."

Nick Geyser came over and sat down as they were finishing lunch. Hercules introduced him to Katherine, telling her Nick and his partner Homer Tan were partners in Geyser & Tan Research Associates, "a bunch of gumshoes who do work for us. I asked Nick to stop by to give us an update on Merrick's whereabouts after he stormed out of my office last week."

Nick got right to the point. Paul Merrick had spent the past week on a sales trip through the state, first east to Spokane, then south to Portland, peddling his line of yoga gear, Ghandiwear. He'd been tailed out of Portland by Homer Tan's cousin Virgil who'd lost him somewhere around Olympia.

"That was three days ago," Nick said. "Right now we don't know where he is."

Pushkin was still fuming by the time they were all out on Fifth Avenue after lunch, "Well, Nick, what the deuce, you've got to find this Merrick before he gets to Katherine."

"We'll do our best," Nick said, shaking hands with Katherine and turning up Stewart Street.

When they said goodbye to Eddie Balfour at the parking garage across Pine Street from Pushkin, McDonald, & Fishkin, Katherine felt like she'd known the young professor for a long time. When she told him that her last stop that afternoon was Silas Peavey's clock shop, Eddie told her how

Peavey had taken Jack in like one his own.

"Silas will be beside himself when he finally meets you," Eddie said, taking her hand. "I wish I could be there to see it."

Back at the office, Alice Ridley had copies of the revised contract ready for Katherine. Hercules sat at his desk and reviewed the document while Katherine stood at the window watching the Bremerton ferry emerge from Rich Passage on the south side of Bainbridge Island and lumber across the Sound toward Colman Dock. She remembered Jack's postcard when he'd taken that boat on a trip to nowhere, and now she wanted him somewhere. *Get back here, now!* she thought as Hercules got up and handed her the papers, saying everything looked in order.

They stood at the window while Pushkin pointed down Pine Street to the north end of the Pike Place Market and explained how to find Silas Peavey on the second lower level. He walked her out to the elevator and when he held out his hand, Katherine put down her briefcase and shopping bag and embraced the startled lawyer with a bear hug. It was Pushkin's turn to blush and when Katherine looked back as the elevator door was closing she saw his face was as red as his suspenders.

In the lobby, Tom Hansen was talking to a tall Chinese man in a black trench coat. It was Horace Tan, Homer's younger brother, who was an associate at Geyser and Tan. Katherine was told by Hansen that he'd been assigned to escort her to the market at Mr. Pushkin's request. When Katherine protested, saying she could walk the three blocks to the market and find the clock shop on her own, Horace smiled and held the door for her. Tom Hansen bid her farewell with a smile saying, "The boss man's orders."

Katherine and her escort started down Pine Street toward the market. When they crossed the alley a few doorways down from the office building, Horace Tan said he knew Pushkin was watching from his office window, making sure all was well.

"If Uncle Herk saw you walking alone, I'd probably lose my job," he said.

Katherine smiled and said, "Well I wouldn't want you out on the streets jobless just before Christmas."

Hercules Pushkin was indeed watching from his office window, glad to see his orders had been followed. He'd been tempted to call Silas Peavey and tell him Jack's girl was on her way but decided against it. *She's a singular woman,* he thought as he watched the pair disappear into the market, *Jack had better get the lead out when he gets back and make sure she doesn't get away.*

Horace Tan walked Katherine through the upper market level, with its seafood stalls, fruit and vegetable stands, through the hollering and the strange smells, the jostling and offers of a bargain everywhere. The corridor to the lower level shops was dank and dim and wound down through the bowels of the market forever. Katherine was finally glad to have Horace Tan's company. They parted in front of Silas Peavey's shop with a warm handshake and "happy holidays." Katherine stood hesitantly at the front window peering into the interior and finally walked in.

Silas Peavey, who ignored the jangling bell when Katherine opened the shop door, was behind the display counters, sitting at a large table in front of the plate glass window that looked out over Elliott Bay. He finally glanced up into round rearview mirror to get a look at the intruder and muttered, "I'll be with you in a minute." A large, blonde-haired man sitting next to Peavey, turned his head and nodded with a smile before turning back to a notebook on the table.

Peavey was looking through a large telescope mounted on a tripod. He said "*Hanseatic Meteor,* standing out at one fifty-seven p.m. on December 18, Bob. It's that old tramp that brought in coffee beans from Matarani. The *Shipping News* says she bound for Osaka with a cargo of hops. Two Mars Brothers tugs, the *Ellen B.* and *Marcy Jo*. Pilot registry says Dewey Santini is taking her out to Port Smith. You got that Bob?"

Peavey turned his swivel chair toward the front of the shop and gazed at Katherine. He got up and walked toward her with a twinkle in his eye, looking every bit the jovial Santa. A broad smile spread through the whiskers.

"Paint me blue, and call me Lester. It's you, isn't it? You're Katherine Baker."

Katherine reached across the display case and offered her hand to Peavey. In a chivalric gesture, he took her hand and bowed. "Every time I say I've seen everything, I'm always wrong. Please, come around back here and sit down for a minute. Tell us why you've graced our humble shop with a visit."

Katherine walked around the display cases to the back of the shop already feeling at home by the warm welcome. Peavey escorted her to a chair in front of the window and yelled to Bob, who had already disappeared into the other room, "Bob, you rounder, please bring us some tea, and don't dally you blackguard. We haven't been so honored since Princess Sonja was here from Norway."

They sat at the window and talked as Bob brought out a pot of tea and a basket of warm scones. Peavey wanted to know why she'd come to the city and his genuine interest and warm countenance encouraged her to tell him in detail about her trip to the city and lunch with Hercules Pushkin and Eddie Balfour. He smiled and nodded as she ended her monologue, telling him Jack had been in Alaska for an eternity.

"Oh, he'll be back soon," Peavey said consolingly. "We're all pretty proud of our friend Jack."

Bob piped in, "He's from Tennessee, you know."

Katherine laughed out loud and said, "Oh yes, I know. Believe me, I know."

Peavey walked her around the shop showing her some of his favorite time pieces and she picked out three Christmas gifts. There was a mantel-size nineteenth-century English elm grandfather clock from London for Hazel and Roy. The pendulum was a gold violin behind which was painted a music score. Clare was going to get a small round gold clock nestled in the middle of a sleeping gray and white Porcelain cat. Jack's gift, if she ever saw him again, was a brass ship's chronometer in a mahogany case which Peavey said came from the Pacific Coast lumber schooner *Penelope Montgomery,* which had sailed between Puget Sound and San Francisco in the 1870s.

Katherine got ready to leave, saying she wanted to catch the three-fifteen ferry. Peavey said he'd have the gifts delivered on Wednesday. As they started toward the door, the shop door burst open and Will and Joey ran in, both carrying back packs.

"You hooligans, what are you doing here?" Peavey shouted as they ran past him and into the back room. "You're supposed to be home with Beatrice, you scurrilous dodgers."

They came back and told him Gran Beatrice went Christmas shopping. She'd dropped them off after school. Peavey introduced them to Katherine, saying she was Jack's friend, Katherine Baker, the one he'd bought the angel clock for. They both giggled and shook Katherine's hand. Then Peavey ordered them into the back room to do their homework and they disappeared again. Katherine blushed when she heard them chanting, "Jack bought an acre for Katherine Baker. Katherine Baker, his wife he's going to make her and never, no never, ever forsake her."

"Pipe down you rambunctious ragamuffins or it'll be bilge water and hard tack for dinner," Peavey yelled. "Bob, Bob, you copperhead, where the devil are you?

Bob came around the corner and Peavey told him to call Mort Laxalt. "Tell him to have a car upstairs in ten minutes. Bob, you ride with her to Pier 52 and make sure she gets on that ferry or you'll walk the plank at sundown."

Katherine had protested once that afternoon about having an escort but she didn't do it again. Peavey offered her his hand before she started for the door but she put down her things and gave him a hug. She turned around before she walked out the door and waved to Peavey who was blushing the color of a Santa Claus suit.

At Colman Dock, Bob hopped out of the front seat of the car, opened the back door for Katherine and took her things, telling the driver not to wait, he'd walk back to the market. He escorted her up the stairs to the passenger terminal walkway. At the top, he stopped and asked her to turn around and look up the hill toward the market.

"I know you don't know what window it is, but Silas is up there at his telescope keeping watch," Bob told her. "Give him a big wave so he knows all is well."

Katherine waved toward the market. Then she gave Bob a hug, walked through the terminal and onto the boat just as the ship's deep horn bellowed its impending departure. As the *MV Enumclaw* slowly left the slip, Katherine walked out onto the observation deck in the rear and waved again, this time to Hercules Pushkin, Eddie Balfour, Silas Peavey, Bob, Will and Joey, and even to A. L. Barney and Leah Balfour.

Homecomings

Katherine wanted to be back in Cedar Mills before five o'clock so she could leave the revised sales contract with Harry Stamp before he went home. But it was almost five-thirty and getting dark by the time she got to town. She'd had to drag across Bainbridge Island and through Poulsbo, part of an endless line of cars from the ferry. Then there was a delay at the Hood Canal Bridge, which was just closing after the interminable process of opening to allow another submarine from Bangor, the mysterious naval base down the Canal, to escape out to the Strait and the Pacific Ocean beyond.

She'd sat at the bridge thinking of her trip to the Ravensdale Mall with Clare a few weeks before and their stop for dinner at the Stuffed Onion Steakhouse. An eternity had passed since then. After that, at Contingency Bay, she saw the "Yield" sign was still bent and Sophie Dolan's skid marks were still visible at the Y where U.S. 101 meets the road from Gosport. Katherine shuddered when she thought of what might have happened to Clare that night.

She was surprised to see Harry Stamp's lights still on when she drove up Main Street. She turned onto Yarmouth and parked in front of the Stamp & Grubb office. Harry was sitting at the reception desk talking on the phone when Katherine walked in.

"She just walked through the door," he said and hung up.

Katherine pulled the revised contract out of her briefcase and handed it to Harry. "I've decided to buy the café if the current owner will accept two changes to the contract. I'd like to get it all done before the end of the week. Who was on the phone?"

"Good, good. I'll let the current owner know right away. I'm sure we can get this thing done before Friday," Harry said. "He's as eager as you are to make the deal."

"Who were you talking to?"

"Oh, on the phone?" Harry said sheepishly. "Will asked if you'd shown up yet?"

"So Will's tracking me? What going on?" Katherine laughed.

"Well, he'd called earlier to tell me about the bridge delay. Said you'd probably be a little later getting back to town, so I decided to hang around awhile. See if you'd show up."

"How does Will know where I've been?"

"Will says there's an issue at your house. Needs you there right away. The current owner called before Will. He called it an imbroglio in the tool shed."

Katherine shook her head. "An issue. An imbroglio in the tool shed. I can't wait. Give me the short version."

Harry said it had all started that morning after Katherine had left for the city. There'd been a heated discussion at the Table about why Katherine went to Seattle. Everyone knew part of the reason concerned the money in Maude's bequest. Lonnie said he was sure she was also going to take Greeley's contract offer to Hercules Pushkin for his opinion and to prove it, he'd called Pushkin to find out. Not only did the lawyer confirm his meeting with Katherine but called Lonnie later to let him know that, according to his operatives, she'd caught the three-fifteen boat for Bainbridge Island and hoped to drop off the contract at Harry Stamp's when she got back to town. Lonnie immediately relayed the news to Greeley.

"So the current owner called me late in the afternoon to say you'd probably show up before I closed." Harry explained. "If you did, he was hoping to stop by the house this evening to take a quick look at your changes to the contract. Then Will called to say he'd heard the bridge was backed up. Then the current owner called again with the news about the tool shed. Then Will called back to say he needed you at the house right away."

"You've had a busy afternoon, Harry," Katherine said before she headed for the door. "See you later."

" I'll let you know what the current owner has to say. Give you a call in the morning."

Katherine drove up Yarmouth, turned on Cedar Street, and drove the two blocks home. It was dark now. She parked in front, behind Will's cruiser. The house was dark, but between the houses, she could see through to the alley and the blue flashing lights of Charlie Sizemore's patrol car.

She took her things in the front door, switched on some lights, picked up the mail from the living room floor and tossed it on the dining room table as she went to the back door. She turned on the back porch light, took a deep breath, and slowly opened the door. Will was standing in front of the tool shed with his arms crossed. A padlock secured the latch on the shed door. Inside Katherine could hear someone mumbling.

Charlie Sizemore had just closed his patrol car door and was walking toward Will with a shotgun in the "present arms" position.

"For Pete's sake Charlie, put that thing back in the car," Will ordered. "Find me a Philips head screwdriver. This guy isn't going anywhere until we pull him out of there."

Will ushered Katherine back into the house. They stood in the kitchen and Will told her that Paul Merrick was in the tool shed.

"The crazy Canadian who's after my piano," Katherine said. "I'm afraid to ask how he got locked in the tool shed."

"Tommy Lowry locked him in late this afternoon. He'd brought Merrick up here to dig up the floor of the tool shed looking for the lost jewels from the piano legs. The guy started acting squirrely so Tommy put the padlock on the door and called us. Now Tommy's half in the bag at the Duchess and can't find the key."

"Of course, it all makes sense now," Katherine said. "Tommy Lowry and this Merrick character digging up the tool shed. I should have known it might happen."

Will explained that Merrick had come to town that morning, stopped at the Handy Mart for gas and struck up a conversation with Tommy who was filling his truck at the next pump. Merrick wanted to approach Katherine's house incognito so he'd persuaded Tommy, with the help of fifty dollars, to take him there later that afternoon. Then when Merrick showed up at the Madison Café on a scouting mission, he'd overheard Lonnie joking at The

Table about Katherine not needing any money, she had all those jewels from the piano buried in the tool shed. So late in the afternoon, Tommy drove Paul Merrick down the alley to Katherine's. Armed with a spade and a grub hoe, they started digging up the dirt floor of the tool shed.

Will told her: "I'm going to put Merrick in the holding cell here in town. In the morning I'll take him to Port Smith and put him on the first boat to Victoria. Let the Canadians deal with him. Charlie's going down to the Duchess and haul Tommy in. He'll be in the hoosegow for a while."

"What do you want me to do?" Katherine asked.

"Nothing. Just stay out of the way. I wanted you here as a witness so you could swear this nut log had broken into the tool shed."

Thirty minutes later, Katherine was finally alone after watching Will unscrew the latch to the tool shed and pull out a bedraggled Paul Merrick, who looked half-crazed with his dirt-streaked face and disheveled three-piece suit. He stumbled out of the shed ahead of Will with his hands cuffed behind his back. Will poked him in the back with a night stick as they made their way to the front of the house where Will pushed him into the back of his cruiser. Katherine stood on the front porch wanting to shout something but couldn't think of anything to say.

Back inside the house suddenly felt empty. Winston was gone. The day before, on Sunday afternoon, she and Clare and taken the cat to the farm with the caveat he could come back to town if he didn't like it. Katherine chided herself for feeling abandoned. He was just a cat and he belonged at the farm with Clare.

Hazel had stopped by when she'd come to town that morning and left a note on the dining room table. Katherine read it out loud:

> *Dear Katherine,*
> *Thought you might like to have something for dinner if you*
> *got home late, so dropped off some tamale pie. Clare had her*
> *riding lesson early this morning before breakfast. Then she and*
> *Roy went into town to the Feed and Seed for goat feed even*
> *though we all know Shlomo and Malachi will eat anything.*
> *Winston seems to have taken to the farm already. I'm in town to*

see Mrs. McDermott and get Clare's school assignments. Hope
your trip to the city was ok. Looking forward to having you with
us at Christmas.
Love, Hazel.

She thumbed through the stack of junk mail on the table and trembled when she found two postcards from Jack. Both were postmarked from Anchorage. One was a color photo of the Anchorage International Airport terminal with "Air Crossroads of the World" printed across the bottom and read *Hello Dear Katherine: This has been my home the past 24 hours waiting for the fog to lift. I love you.* Jack. The second card was reproduction of an old color postcard with a cowboy riding a giant King salmon which was arching out of the water. The caption read, "Roundup time at Bristol Bay, Alaska." Jack's note read, *Still Anchorage. Still socked in but supposed to be out of here soon. Sat awake all night thinking of you. I love you always. Jack.*

Katherine spent the rest of the evening at the piano where she'd propped the two postcards on the music rack and kept reading them as she absent mindedly played everything she knew by heart, the Mozart concertos, the Chopin nocturnes, Schubert and Schumann, Haydn and Handel, Beethoven, Grieg, and Dvorak. When she finally went to bed, she lay awake thinking about Christmas at the farm with Clare, Hazel, and Roy, and how much she wanted Jack to be there. She thought back to the solitary Christmastimes on the road when she felt she deserved nothing more than being alone in a cheap room in some ragged town fighting the urge to get drunk.

She fell into a half-asleep state and Katy Owling's Christmastime returned. It was December in Cedar Rapids, her mother's favorite time of year. First came the Advent Calendar and arguments with her sister Karen to see who got to pull open the next flap. Then came the boxes of Christmas paraphernalia. Wax snowmen and Santas, ceramic painted angels and reindeer, not to mention hard-carved wooden cast members from the Nutcracker, all of which were spread around the house and crowned by the heirloom nativity set that had belonged to Grandmother Owling. It was triumphantly displayed on a special raised mahogany table in the living room.

They always had a Christmas tree with lights but no outdoor lights. Pastor Ron was on the governing board of the local Keep Christ in Christmas

Committee. He wanted no outward suggestion that the Owlings worshipped the crass commercialism of Xmas. As an antidote to his wife's obsession with what he called the cheap trappings of Christmas which he sanctimoniously insisted was nothing more than idolatry, Pastor Ron placed a miniature wooden billboard in the front yard with a border of white lights that highlighted a simple message for the holiday. It quickly became a model for the anti-Xmas faction in Cedar Rapids. The first year's message was the ubiquitous "Keep Christ in Christmas," followed the next year with "There is no 'X' in Christmas." And then "He's the Reason for the Season" followed their last year in Cedar Rapids with "We're Spending Our Christmas With a Carpenter From Galilee."

Katherine woke up in a sweat at three o'clock. She got out of bed and walked through the house, lit the oil stove in the dining room, started coffee in the kitchen, and sat at the kitchen table shivering. *Be gone Katy Owling, be gone. You're not welcome here,* she thought as poured a cup of coffee and got ready for work.

It was four o'clock when she walked out the back door. It was dark but she could still see inside the open tool shed. The door wouldn't close now because mounds of dirt blocked the entry. There was a hole in the middle of the dirt floor. She mumbled something about screwballs and their obsession with her piano. *This better be the end of it,* she thought as she turned down the dark alley.

She got to the café an hour before the others and sat in her office with the only light from the banker's lamp on her desk. It was a relief to be there in the quiet, alone, back from the city after what seemed a week rather than a day. She smiled as she read the notes scribbled on a yellow legal pad which has been carefully positioned at the edge of the desk in front of her chair, under the lamp, just to make sure she saw it first thing.

> *Bobby and Bert have news about pastry. Bobby*
> *Low inventory: flour, yeast, baking powder. Bobby*
> *Norah wants to talk to you. Muriel*
> *Are we going to get more coffee cups? Bobby*
> *A dark Canadian came in for breakfast. Sadie*

Someone broke a pot pie dish! Bobby
Nils called. Joyce
Took care of bank deposit. Hope all "went well" in the city.
Want to hear all about it. G.

She'd come to love these people and this place. Her people. Her place. She was jolted out of the reverie by the phone ringing. It was a quarter to five in the morning. It was Jack.

"I called your house, but got the answering machine," he said softly. "Thought I'd try work."

"Oh Jack," she whispered.

"Just got home a few hours ago. I've missed you. I've been such a fool. I got your card. I love you."

"Oh Jack," she whispered again.

"I'll be over as soon as I can. Hercules owes me some time off after this."

"Oh Jack, " she whispered. "I'll be here. I love you."

"I called the office before I left Anchorage yesterday. Arlie told me you'd just left after a meeting and lunch with Hercules. Couldn't believe it."

There was too much to tell him on the phone. "I was there. Got to see your office too. Met A.L. and Leah Balfour. Then Hercules took me to lunch at the Duwamish Club with Eddie Balfour."

Jack laughed. "He's never taken me to lunch at the Duwamish Club."

"So much has happened Jack. I'll tell you all about it when you get here. Clare Dolan's living with Hazel and Roy now, there's Maude's death and funeral, Winston the cat, this goofy Merrick digging up my tool shed. I can't tell you much now. The gang's rolling in to work. Just get over here. I love you."

"I love you too. I'll be over soon," Jack said.

"I'll be here," Katherine whispered as the lights in the kitchen and dining room came on, announcing the arrival of Sadie, Bobby, Joyce, and Muriel.

✧ ✧ ✧ ✧ ✧ ✧ ✧ ✧ ✧ ✧ ✧ ✧

Jack's return to the offices of Pushkin, McDonald, & Fishkin later that morning had the trappings of the return of a hero. After he'd sifted through his voice mails and poured over A. L. Barney's notes, Pushkin called him up to his office. He told Jack he'd represented Bart Ladderback in the way Pushkin, McDonald, and Fishkin always took care of their clients. Straining for a tone of modesty, Jack said the preliminary tally of his billing hours was sizable.

Hercules laughed and said, "In light of what you did for Bart, he'll gladly pay double whatever we bill. Now, have you talked to Katherine yet? Did she tell you about our lunch yesterday?"

"She told me you'd taken her to lunch at the Duwamish Club."

"What the deuce, man!" Hercules bellowed. "She such a fine person. I'd hate to see you let her get away. She's one in a million."

"That's why I was hoping you'd let me leave a little early for Christmas and get over to Cedar Mills, maybe tomorrow. Compensatory time off?"

Hercules guffawed. "What the deuce! Of course not. You've got to stay in town until Ladderback gets back from up north on Thursday. He wants to celebrate getting his hands on the *Bering Dawn* thanks to his new favorite lawyer. Going to throw some catered affair here in the lunch room for us all. You've got to be here."

Then he told Jack about meeting Katherine at Maude's funeral and what he knew about Maude's gift to Katherine so she could buy the Madison Café.

Pushkin said, "I took her down to see your office and introduced her to Arlie and Leah Balfour happened to be here. Katherine marched into your office and gave it a thorough inspection. She kept looking at the carpet for some reason."

That night after work, Jack sifted through the mail he piled on his desk and ignored when he'd got home late the night before. Most of it was junk. But there was a card from Katherine, postmarked the day he'd left for the north. There was a letter from the law offices of Stamp & Grubb in Cedar Mills and there was a hand-addressed envelope with no return address on the front. He turned it over and read the embossed blue lettering in the middle of the flap, "Office of the Governor. Olympia, Washington."

He read Katherine's card first.

> *Dear Jack:*
> *I love the angel clock. I probably shouldn't be doing this*
> *because it's a priceless antique, but I carry it with me*
> *everywhere. It's on my desk at work, it's on my nightstand when*
> *I'm in bed, and it sits on the sideboard next to the piano when*
> *I'm playing. But I haven't wound it since it stopped the day*
> *after it arrived because to me, time has stopped until I see you*
> *again. My life won't really resume until we're together. Please*
> *remember that "the narrow way leads home," to me. I love*
> *you, Jack, always.*
> *Katherine*

He read the note several times and then went to the living room window overlooking Elliott Bay. It was dark, but he could see a faint black outline of the mountains looming over the twinkling lights of Bainbridge Island. *I love you, Katherine,* he thought. *I'll be home soon.*

He held the envelope from the governor's office and stared at the back flap. Del Welker had made a cottage industry out of writing personal notes to his constituents since he'd been a county commissioner in Kitsap County. As he neared the end of his first term as governor, one wag at the *Seattle Times* claimed that over fifty percent of the households in Washington state had a personal note from Welker. To Jack he wrote about seeing the video tape of the Folklore Society concert and how much he enjoyed Jack and the Skagit River Ramblers. He continued:

> *I've been a lover of bluegrass gospel music for years, since I*
> *saw Bill Monroe and the Blue Grass Boys in Pensacola when I*
> *was in the Navy. Nobody played mandolin like him, put you're*
> *getting there. By the way, I had the honor to meet your aunt*
> *and uncle, Hazel and Roy Willit, when I was in Cedar Mills for*
> *Maude Doud's funeral. Also had the pleasure of meeting their*
> *new foster daughter, Clare Dolan and a special friend of yours,*

*Katherine Baker. The Willits promised me some live gospel
music when I visit and maybe we can talk you into being there
too. All the best for the holidays,
Del Welker*

The enevelope from Stamp & Grubb contained a short letter from Harry Stamp "In Regard To The Estate of Maude Doud." Harry wrote that Mrs. Doud had included a bequest for Jack in her will. He asked Jack to make an appointment to discuss the matter at his earliest convenience.

❖ ❖ ❖ ❖ ❖ ❖ ❖ ❖ ❖ ❖ ❖ ❖

Katherine's cheeks were flushed and she felt flustered after talking to Jack on the phone, the first time she'd heard his voice since Thanksgiving. She opened her office door and stood in the kitchen entry watching everyone quietly working with an exaggerated concentration not unlike they'd done the morning before when she'd left for Seattle. Sadie and Joyce were at the grills getting them ready for breakfast. Muriel was loading the coffee urns. Bobby was in the dining room wiping down tables he'd probably already cleaned before closing the day before. Their hellos were friendly but stilted. No one asked how her day in the city had gone.

By the time Katherine herded everyone into her office and closed the door, the anticipatory silence was heavy in the air. They were all nervous.

"You may or may not have heard about my chance to buy the café from Greeley, thanks to help from Maude Doud," she said.

"We've heard a few rumblings about it," Sadie said, giving the others a wink.

Katherine got right to the point. She explained the terms of Maude's bequest, making sure they understood she hadn't been given the money outright. If she didn't use it to buy the café, the money would go to Swedish Hospital.

"I don't get to keep the money and walk away from the restaurant," she said. "Besides, I want to be the new owner and if Greeley and I can agree on a couple things, it should happen soon, maybe by the end of the week."

There was a minute of silence and then Bobby shouted, "Hooray for

Katherine Baker." They encircled her in a scrum, all talking at once and patting her on the back. Then Katherine told them there was more.

First, like last year, the café would be closed the week between Christmas and New Year's. They'd close on the coming Friday and would reopen on Tuesday, January 2. But this year they'd be paid for the time off. That was Katherine's Christmas present to the staff. Secondly, the Christmas party would be at her house on Friday after work instead of at Greeley's. He wasn't up to it after Maude's death.

Bert Peck was at the front door with his morning delivery when the meeting broke up. She listened to Bert and Bobby's upbeat report that the first offering of pastries, six butter horns, six maple bars, and six bear claws had sold out in an hour the morning before. She patted them both on the back before Bobby disappeared to fill the pastry case. Bert stood in the office door and whispered, "Anything else going on?"

Katherine told him there was nothing new.

"I hope you don't think I'm being too nosey, but I hope the deal goes through," he whispered with a conspiratorial air.

Katherine thanked him as she edged past, into the kitchen. She snuck up behind Sadie who was standing at the service window and gave her a light slap on the rear. Sadie jumped and said, "You're asking for it, Suzy Q! The last hombre that did that is still on life support. You learn that stuff in the big city?"

Katherine laughed. "That and a lot more."

"So why was Jack calling so early in the morning?"

Katherine laughed again. "Why do you think it was Jack? Maybe I was making an appointment to have my teeth cleaned."

"Very funny. The way you looked, there was only one appointment you were thinking about. What'd he say?"

"Nothing. None of your business."

Sadie laughed and looked at Joyce. "I know what he said. He said he loved you like crazy and he was going to get you where you belonged, between the sheets for a day or two."

Joyce was standing at the grill down the line chuckling as Katherine blushed and walked out to the front counter. She watched Muriel open the dining room door to Ray Kesecker, Marilyn Smallwood, and Lonnie, who took their turns at the coffee urn and sat down at The Table.

"Good to see you made it back in one piece." Lonnie said. "It can be rough in the big city."

As more of the regulars drifted in, everyone studiously avoided asking her about Seattle, feigning a disinterest in where she'd been. Yesterday, the café had been filled with talk of her trip to the city and the sale of the café. Today, with Katherine there, everyone avoided the subject as though she'd not gone anywhere.

Later, when Lonnie was up for his second cup of coffee, he came through the kitchen and stood in her office door. "Everything copasetic in Seattle?"

"All is well," Katherine said noncommittally. "I saw everyone I needed to see."

"I heard through the grapevine you met with Pushkin. Let me know if you need anything."

Katherine got up from her desk and put a hand on Lonnie's shoulder, "Thanks for everything you've done, you and Elizabeth."

"Mox nix," Lonnie said. "That's what we're here for. Gotta skedaddle. Don't do anything I wouldn't do."

❖ ❖ ❖ ❖ ❖ ❖ ❖ ❖ ❖ ❖ ❖ ❖

Katherine still hadn't seen Greeley by lunch time. He hadn't had coffee with Will and Charlie at breakfast and he wasn't in his office. She'd been listening for him on the stairs or shuffling around upstairs. When she left for the bank just before two o'clock, he still hadn't come in and she started to get nervous. Was he mad about her revisions to the contract and ready to withdraw his offer to sell the café? She started to regret taking Hercules Pushkin's advice.

After she left the bank she detoured down Main Street to see Nils Holmgren. Cedar Country Appliances was awash in Christmas decorations and the two large display windows were filled with gift suggestions, a matching washer and dryer filled most of one window. A large sign rested against them on the floor that read, "Hers and Hers." Radios and portable televisions flanked the appliances. The other window was crowded with three large console televisions arranged in a staggered column and adorned across the top by a brightly painted sign that read "Get him what he wants! Get him what he needs!"

Nils had a large gift wrapped carton on the counter. He said it was for Clare from all the Holmgrens, especially Beata. They all wanted her to have something special in her new home. He said, "It's state of the art. A portable stereo CD player and radio. The latest in entertainment on the go. Andy calls it a high-tech puppy."

Katherine said she'd come back after work and pick it up. Nils looked around the store and whispered, "I saw Greeley over at Harry Stamp's office this morning. How are things going?"

Katherine whispered, "No big news."

When Katherine walked home up the alley after work, Greeley and Harley Beaver had just pulled a small cement mixer out of the back yard and were hitching it to Harley's pickup.

Katherine shook her head and asked, "What now?"

Greeley laughed, "Well as your landlord, I thought I'd better take care of that mess in the tool shed. Harley and I just finished putting in a new floor. You'll need a jackhammer to get through that baby."

"Darn. I guess I won't be burying any more treasure in there," Katherine said. She stood in the shed door admiring the wet, glistening cement.

Greeley followed her into the house after Harley left. He sat at the kitchen table while Katherine started a pot of coffee. "This Canadian kook really ran off the rails yesterday. The whole town was stirred up by the time Will and Charlie showed up here and nabbed him," he said.

They sat in the kitchen with their coffee while Greeley told her how when Paul Merrick pulled into the Handy Mart for gas, Scooter Markham's wife, Tonya, who ran the register, had called Ray in the middle of his breakfast at the café. Tonya told Ray in a panic that a black man was pumping gas and asked what she should do, she'd never seen anyone that color before.

Ray testily told her to take his money and hung up.

Then Paul Merrick showed up at the café. He ate breakfast at one of the booths in the front where he'd heard Lonnie joking how Katherine didn't need any money, she had all that loot buried in the tool shed. He'd left after breakfast, tracked down Tommy Lowry at the Duchess, and armed with a grub hoe and spade from Tommy's truck, they'd proceeded to the tool shed.

Greeley continued, "Evidently, in the middle of the digging, this Merrick character just lost it, according to Tommy. Started swinging the shovel at him, swearing that he'd been duped, and then got down on his knees and started praying. Tommy ran out to his truck, found a padlock and locked the buzzard in the shed," Greeley said with amusement. "I guess you know the rest."

Katherine said, "I know the rest," as Greeley got up to leave.

"Thanks for the coffee. And by the way, the changes to the contract are fine. I told Harry we should get this done by the end of the week."

Katherine walked Greeley out to the back gate. They both looked up the alley, across Second Avenue to Maude's dark house. Greeley shook his head in silence and Katherine put a hand on his shoulder. She started to say something but didn't. He started off down the alley toward the café with his head down. Before she went into the house, she opened the tool shed door and stared at the still-wet concrete. A few minutes later she had a small stick. She knelt down at the shed door and reached around as far as she could, almost to the front left corner of the shed. The cement was starting to set up but it was still workable. She drew a large heart in the cement and then "KB + JL" inside it. It made her laugh.

That Lonesome Valley

An hour after she'd said good-bye to Greeley in the alley and embellished the tool shed's new cement floor, Katherine was walking down Second Avenue and across Main Street on her way to choir practice at Trinity Episcopal. She was halfway there before she realized it was only Tuesday and not Wednesday when the choir's final rehearsal for the Christmas Eve service was scheduled. She walked to the church anyway.

It was dark and cool inside. The only light came from a small spotlight in the ceiling above the altar which gave the gold altar cross a muted glow. She sat along the aisle in a pew a few rows from the back. She stared at the cross and let the overwhelming quiet flow through her body, creating a softening peacefulness she had never known. For the first time she understood how the church was a sanctuary, a safe shelter, a refuge.

After she fled the town and her family, she'd never considered going into a church again. But now, back in Cedar Mills, in Trinity Episcopal alone on this night, after the events of the past week, the church gave her peace. There'd been Maude's funeral, Clare's adoption, the possibility of owning the Madison Café, her trip to Seattle, Paul Merrick's raid, and Jack's telephone call that morning which had made her want him more.

She stared through the darkness at the altar. Her lips began to move as she softly recited the Nicene Creed, "I believe in one God, the Father Almighty, Maker of heaven and earth, And of all things visible and invisible..." She didn't know if she believed any of it but she loved the rhythm of the words. "...And I believe in one Catholic and Apostolic Church: I acknowledge one Baptism for the remission of sins: I look for the Resurrection of the dead: And the Life of the world to come. Amen." She sighed when she finished and thought of Alan Lindsay's *The Platonic Ideal of Faith: There Isn't One*, which had been called a "recondite dissection" of the prayer. It hadn't helped her understand it and it didn't matter. It was the rythm of the words she found enchanting.

She was startled by a gust of wind rattling the front door of the church. She suddenly felt scared and alone. Clare was safe now with Hazel and Roy at the farm. Jack was home from Alaska but not with her. Winston had moved to the farm. And Maude was gone. No, she *couldn't* be gone, but she was. And Milos was brooding up in his aerie on the hill, stubbornly refusing to acknowledge that his heart was broken once again, this time by his girl-friend's passing. And where was Larry when she needed him the most? Another gust of wind rattled the door. She stood in the church aisle and stared at the cross. "Thank you, God," she whispered before turning for the door.

The wind was blowing hard now as she walked up Fourth Avenue toward Main Street. Someone at the café had said at lunch that gale warnings were going up out on the Strait. It was a classic winter Pacific sou-wester, one of the giant storms that pummeled the Northwest this time of year. Rain was slanting into her face when she turned onto Cedar Street and walked up her front steps.

Inside the house, she didn't turn on any lights but went straight to the bedroom and put on a pair of flannel pajamas. After her nightly routine in the bathroom, she knelt at the side of the bed and prayed for the first time in years, "Dear God, thank you for this day. Please help me be a better person. Please bless all those around me, especially Jack, Clare, Hazel and Roy, and everyone at the café. I thank you God. Amen."

She climbed into bed and that's where Hazel found her the next morning a little after eight o'clock. Katherine was curled up in a fetal position with her eyes half-closed. She opened them when Hazel walked into the bedroom.

"I'm glad to see you're getting some good use out of that Tennessee quilt. You need it on a morning like this," Hazel said neutrally.

Katherine, lying motionless, closed her eyes again and said nothing.

"We missed you for dinner yesterday and nobody answered when I called last night, so I went to the café this morning to say hi before I went to see Clare's teacher for her school assignments." Hazel said. "You weren't there so I thought I'd get snoopy and see what's up. Coffee's made and the oil stove's going."

Hazel went out to the living room and sat at the piano. Katherine lay in bed listening as Hazel softly played "When You Walk Through a Storm," a song her grandmother Owling always said was her favorite, even over Red Foley's version of "That Lonesome Valley."

❖ ❖ ❖ ❖ ❖ ❖ ❖ ❖ ❖ ❖ ❖

It was ten o'clock by the time Katherine got to the café. She and Hazel had sat on the sofa drinking coffee for an hour after she'd forced herself out of bed and got ready for work. As they talked, Katherine kept waiting for an admonishment or at least a hint from Hazel that she'd let everyone down by not coming to the farm for dinner the night before or shown up for work that morning. And when Katherine said with an approval-seeking tone that she hadn't been drinking, Hazel brushed it off with "I'm glad to hear it."

Hazel did most of the talking. She retold the story of the Dunn sisters' escape from Clinch Mountain on the coal train to begin a new life in the big city of Kingsport and how scared she was. Then she told Katherine about the dark days after she and Roy had left Tennessee for the Pacific Northwest.

She said, "About a month after we got here and started to get settled a little, I just shut down for the first time in my life. Could barely fix Roy his meals. Could hardly get out of bed in the morning. I took long naps or just sat on the front porch staring out across the valley at those mountains. Boy did I hate those mountains."

She told Katherine "those mountains" looked nothing like her Smoky Mountains, all rounded and smooth, enchanting and inviting. No, these mountains here were sharp and hostile. Ugly to her. Threatening and intimidating.

"But that was just the beginning. I hated everything here," Hazel said with a laugh that made Katherine smile. "For one thing, everyone talks so fast up here. I swear I couldn't understand half what they were saying. People probably thought I was a half-wit. I'd stare at them and say 'what'd you say?' I hated going to town, afraid I'd have to talk to someone."

Katherine laughed. "Do I talk too fast?"

"All you Yankees do. I'm pretty much used to it now. At Thanksgiving, May told me I was starting to sound a little like one of you. Anyway, Roy got real worried and called May. Asked her to come out from Bristol. But May said no. Told Roy to let me be. Said I was a Dunn sister. I'd come out of it."

"It doesn't sound like you," Katherine said. "It doesn't sound like you at all."

"It was just too much all at once." Hazel said. "I just conked out for a while. Overload. I worked it out with Roy's and the Lord's help. It's all behind us now. And as for you, you'll figure it out. You're going to be fine."

"I don't know. I'm scared all of a sudden. Maybe I won't be able to handle all this," Katherine said.

"Get out of here! You can handle anything. Come on, I'll drive you down to work."

They sat in the car on Main Street in front of the café for a few minutes before Katherine went in. They both laughed as they watched Sadie, Bobby, Joyce, and Muriel alternately come to the café window and offhandedly glance out the window. Hazel had Katherine laughing as she described how that morning, when she'd walked into the dining room through the alley door, something she'd never done before, Lonnie had escorted her over to The Table and insisted she join them. They all wanted to know how Clare was doing.

"I told them she and Roy were supposed to be coming in for lunch today so they could see for themselves. By the way, that's supposed to be surprise so don't say I told you."

"My, my," Katherine laughed. "You've been inducted into the grand realm of The Table society. Nothing to be taken lightly. We're going to turn you into a Yankee yet."

They hugged before Katherine got out of the car.

❖ ❖ ❖ ❖ ❖ ❖ ❖ ❖ ❖ ❖ ❖

The morning rush was over when Katherine walked into the café. She stood at the front window waving to Hazel as she drove off, just as Greeley and Norah Wineskin were coming down the stairs from his office. Their chatter stopped when they saw her turn and look at them with a smile. Before Norah went out the front door, Greeley patted her on the shoulder said he'd see her that afternoon.

He told Katherine, "We've been working on the preliminary plans for my new digs in the old theater office next door. Norah was a feng shui consultant back in Brooklyn."

Katherine laughed. "Does she know anything about dim sun?"

"Very funny. Let's go to your office. I've got news."

Sadie and Joyce were in the kitchen at their stations, cleaning up after breakfast and getting ready for lunch. When Katherine walked past, Sadie said to Joyce in a stage whisper, "Banker's hours now I guess." And they both laughed.

"Everyone's a comedian," Katherine muttered and poked Sadie in the back.

In the office, Greeley told her he'd already opened up the door in the hall upstairs across from his office that led into the theater office. "I've got Lonnie and the Beavers lined up for the week after Christmas. And with Norah's help, I'll be moved by January first."

"Norah's help? That's a new twist," Katherine said, trying not to sound sarcastic.

Greeley ignored her mocking tone. "Now, the big news. The closing's slated for ten o'clock on Friday morning at Stamp & Grubb."

Katherine took a deep breath. "That's the day after tomorrow."

"Harry says it's all routine. We'll be out of there in less than an hour. Then Lonnie will be waiting to sign you up for the Rotary Club."

Katherine smiled. "Let's do it. I can't wait."

After Greeley left, Katherine sat with her back to the desk, staring absently at the wall. *Let's do it. I can't wait. Let's do it. I can't wait.* She kept repeating it to herself until Sadie startled her when she walked in and sat in the chair at the end of the desk, staring at the floor. Katherine thought, *Oh no. The other shoe's about to drop.*

The door was closed and the office was quiet until Sadie said, "I've got something to tell you and I'm not sure how to say it. I just want to thank you for giving me a chance to better myself a little. I know it's no big deal, being a short-order cook in a joint like this. But it is to me."

Katherine was surprised and confused. Sadie continued, "I've been slinging hash for over twenty years. I'm so far over the hill, it's all flat behind me. But you gave me a chance to change that a little. Thank you."

Katherine started to say, "Sadie, I really didn't…"

"Shush," Sadie said. "Let me finish. You've done so much for all of us. Look at Bobby, what you've done for him. And both Muriel and Joyce say they love it here. We all do and it's mostly because of you. That's it. I've got to get out there."

They both stood. Katherine reached to give Sadie a hug, but she stepped away. "No, no. I've got to get back to work." Before she opened the door, she turned back to Katherine and said, "Just remember what you mean to us. Don't be afraid of what's to come. We're here for you." Then she was back in the kitchen, chattering with Joyce.

The Eagle Has Landed

Just before eight o'clock on Friday morning, Katherine put on her coat and slipped out the kitchen service door. "I've got to get something from home," she whispered to Joyce who nodded before the second cook yelled, "Order up."

Two days before, on Wednesday afternoon, the presents she'd bought at Time Pieces on Monday had been delivered as Silas Peavey promised. Along with the delivery was a large box addressed to "Katherine Baker and The Madison Café." She had waited to open it, wanting to have it at the café after the closing at Stamp & Grubb when they'd all open it together.

Katherine started up the alley toward home in the bright sunshine. The storm that had lashed them for two days had ended the night before. There was new snow on the mountains and the air was freshly brisk. She had the heebie jeebies and was relieved to be out of the café where everyone, including her, was surreptitiously counting the minutes until ten o'clock when she was supposed to sign the documents making her the new owner of the Madison Café.

But she kept walking, past her back gate, up to Fourth Avenue where she turned left and headed south toward Pleasant Valley Road. It felt good to be moving. She'd get the box on her way back. Now she wanted to see Milos and the changes to his property. Roy and Clare had told her how all the trees were now down in front of his house so he had a panoramic view of the Strait, thanks to the Beavers.

Roy and Clare had come in for lunch on Wednesday afternoon after running errands that morning, first to Port Smith to pick up a part for one of the tractors and then back to town to East End Feed and Seed for a couple of bags of chicken feed which they'd taken up to Milos at Lonnie's request. While they were there, Milos had told them he needed to find a home for the chickens. They were lonely now that Stormy and the goats were at the farm.

Everyone at the café said Clare's transformation was astonishing. Her blue jeans were tucked into her cowboy boots. She wore a denim jacket over a red denim shirt. Her hair was in a pony tail which was tucked through the back of a green John Deere baseball cap. She was a real farm girl.

It was Clare's talking about the chickens and her description of all the trees down at Milos' place that had inspired Katherine to pay him a visit. Milos opened the front door before Katherine started up the front steps. She was pleased to see him smiling. But Rascal, usually animated and incessantly barking when visitors came, silently stood in the doorway and stared at her.

"No car. You're walking now," he said, with a twinkle in his eye. "I saw you huffing up the hill."

Katherine laughed, "I wasn't huffing. I can't stay. I just wanted to see your new view. It's impressive," Katherine said, standing behind the large drawing table which sat in front of the picture window looking out over the town and the Strait five miles beyond.

"It is all new to me. A view of the world now, instead living in the shadows."

Milos proudly pointed to the telescope mounted on a tripod on the drawing table. It had been delivered the day of Maude's funeral. He didn't know who'd sent it. Walt Beaver had told him about the Strait Gawkers, an informal group of strait watchers who kept logs of the marine traffic moving in and out of the waterway that connected Puget Sound and the Pacific Ocean. He'd shown Katherine with an uncharacteristic note of pride, how he'd started his own log, recording details of each ship he'd spotted.

Rascal's basket was on the floor next to the drawing table where he slept most of the day while Milos monitored the Strait. Katherine thumbed through the log as he talked. There was an entry for the *Hanseatic Meteor,* standing out on Monday. She told Milos she'd seen the ship leaving Elliott Bay on Monday afternoon when she was in Seattle.

"She's loaded with hops for Osaka," Katherine said authoritatively.

Milos stared at her, trying to decide whether or not she was serious. "Hops, you say," he exclaimed. "Where does this information come from?"

She liked shocking him for once with something he didn't know. She told him about her trip to Seattle and how Silas Peavey told her about the weekly *Puget Sound Shipping News*. Milos said he'd talk to Wally about getting him a subscription.

Katherine declined his offer of tea and Christmas cookies, saying she had to get going.

"From Clare," he said, holding up a plate of cookies. "She brought me cookies the other day when she and Roy brought the chicken feed. What a dear girl and how she's changed so suddenly."

Katherine told him about the meeting that morning with Greeley to close the sale of the café and how afterward, after the café closed, there was a small celebration at her house. "Hazel, Roy, and Clare insisted on catering. You'd better be there or I'll huff back up the hill to get you."

Milos laughed and said he might come. At the door, he said, "Tell me this. What is a McDonald's farm? Roy said they didn't have a McDonald's farm when Clare asked him about taking the chickens."

Katherine's laughter echoed down the hill. "I'll explain it this afternoon. Or better yet, ask Roy when you see him. I'm going to be late."

❖ ❖ ❖ ❖ ❖ ❖ ❖ ❖ ❖ ❖ ❖ ❖

Fifteen minutes before ten o'clock, Greeley came down the stairs from his office looking for Katherine. She wasn't in her office or anywhere else in the café. No one had seen her for a while. Joyce said she'd gone home to get something around eight o'clock but hadn't returned. Greeley called her house and was surprised when Hazel answered. She told him she, Roy and Clare were there getting ready for the Christmas party that afternoon. They hadn't seen Katherine. He called Harry Stamp's office and Roberta Peebles said, no, Katherine hadn't arrived yet but Harry was already in the conference room waiting for them.

"For Pete's sake," Greeley muttered as he walked out on Main Street, heading for Stamp & Grubb. "Is the other shoe about to drop?" Greeley walked into the law offices saying to Harry, "Houston, we have a problem. Our prospective buyer may have disappeared." Then they sat silently in the conference room listening to the great oak wall clock tick its way to three minutes past ten.

Harry was getting ready to deliver his stock philosophical observations about real estate closings, how anything can happen until the last document is signed, when they heard the front door open. It was Katherine. Roberta was on the phone. She put her hand over the mouthpiece and pointed to the conference room and whispered with a smile, "They're waiting for you."

Just before Katherine closed the conference room door she thought she heard Roberta say in a low voice, "All clear Mr. Martin. The eagle has landed. One more left. Lindsay at one o'clock."

When Katherine sat across from Greeley at the conference room table, he nodded to Harry and they said in unison, "The eagle has landed." Roberta came in with her notary public stamp and thirty minutes later, they were all shaking hands, congratulating Katherine and wishing her well.

Afterward, Greeley and Katherine walked up Main Street as far as the bank and paused at the entrance where he complimented her on adding the clause about vacating his office, calling it a nice piece of work. He told her Larry's things were already out of the apartment and she could decide whether or not to keep the furniture. Lonnie and the Beavers would move it out if she didn't want it. He said again he'd be out by New Year's.

She knew that everyone with a window on Main Street was watching when they stood on the sidewalk in a long embrace and then witnessed him giving her a peck on the cheek. Then she stepped away and shook his hand before he went into the bank. She didn't want anyone to get the wrong idea.

Instead of walking up Main Street to the café, Katherine turned left on Yarmouth Avenue and walked over to Cedar Street, heading for home and thinking about Jack. She and Jack had talked every day since he'd been back from Alaska on Monday night, sometimes twice, and yesterday, he'd told her he'd be over on Friday as soon as he could, but he hadn't said anything about a meeting at Stamp & Grubb. Her heart beat fast as she thought of them being together soon.

Hazel and Clare were busy in the kitchen when she walked in the front door. They were chattering away while they worked and didn't hear her come in. She stood in the kitchen doorway watching until Clare turned and saw her.

"Oh my. You're here!" Clare shouted and ran over for a hug. "Hazel just said she didn't know if we could get all this done in time."

"Well, unfortunately, as grateful as I am for you all doing this, I can't stay to help," Katherine said. "But I'll be back as soon after three as I can. It's supposed to start at four."

"We're not telling you what we're fixing, are we Hazel," Clare said. "It's all going to be a surprise. And Roy's gone to Port Smith for the smoked salmon. Whoops. At least some of it's a surprise."

Hazel and Katherine exchanged smiles as Katherine kissed Clare on the cheek before she started out the back door with the box from Seattle. "Did Jack say anything about a meeting with Harry Stamp when you talked to him?" she asked Hazel.

Hazel shook her head. "No, he just said he'd be here sometime today. Didn't know when. Why? You getting anxious?"

Hazel laughed and Clare laughed. Katherine's face turned red as she walked out the back door.

Unwrapping

Bobby opened the box from Seattle with Katherine's help after the café closed and the cleaning was complete. Everyone stood around a table in the dining room waiting for Katherine to bring the box out of the storeroom. She'd spent the day in the dining room, helping Muriel and Bobby, and shaking hands with all the well-wishers who congratulated her on being the new owner of the Madison Café. She'd started every time she heard the front door open, each time thinking it might be Jack. But it wasn't.

Norah Wineskin told her how she'd been helping Greeley upstairs with his new office and said "We're so happy for you," which caused Katherine to raise an eyebrow. But she kept her mouth shut.

There were plenty of people who told her how great Clare seemed when she'd been there on Wednesday. Everyone said how thankful they were that Katherine had done so much for her.

Lonnie was effusive with his good wishes. He said he'd been on the phone with Roberta when she'd walked in. "Music to my ears when Roberta announced the eagle had landed. Boy, you had Greeley sweatin' bullets there for a little while."

Katherine laughed. "Good for him. Did I hear something about Lindsay at one o'clock? What's that all about."

"My lips are sealed. As executor of Maude's estate, I gotta keep my trap shut. Maybe you'll find out and maybe you won't," he said impishly.

Now finally it was almost three o'clock when Katherine handed Bobby a pair to scissors to cut the tape on the carton from Seattle. "Katherine Baker and The Madison Café. Does that mean all of us?" Bobby asked.

"It means all of us, especially you," Katherine said. "Now let's see what it is."

The package inside was gift wrapped with paper covered with images of clocks. On the gift tag was printed "Another unique gift from Time Pieces, Pike Place Market, Seattle, Wash." On it was written, "Best wishes to Katherine and the café staff. Silas Peavey and Hercules Pushkin."

Katherine, Sadie, Muriel, and Joyce all patiently watched as Bobby carefully pulled the tape from the wrapping, piece by piece. Then Katherine helped him open the box and lift out a large round wooden clock, two feet in diameter that looked like it might have once been a frosted doughnut. The red lettering on the top of the doughnut read, "Madison Beanery." On the bottom was, "Seattle 1905."

"It's beautiful!" Katherine exclaimed.

Bobby shook his head. "I don't get it."

Joyce stepped over and picked it up. "It's an antique, Bobby. There's nothing to get. Now see the two chains hanging down. Pull the short one down to get it running. When the longer one becomes the shorter one, you pull that one."

Bobby shook his head while the other four debated where to hang it.

Finally Katherine said they'd decide when the café reopened and took the clock into her office.

"Let's get out of here," she said. "I'll see you at my house in an hour."

❖ ❖ ❖ ❖ ❖ ❖ ❖ ❖ ❖ ❖ ❖ ❖

Katherine walked up the alley alone in the winter afternoon sun. The world had changed again. She was now the owner of a restaurant. She'd almost told Nolan Beane about it when he'd called from Roseburg the morning before to announce more visitors from Cedar Mills had stopped at the Log Cabin Restaurant a couple days ago. But when she realized he was describing her mother as a drunken sow accompanied by an equally drunk preacher who he'd thrown out of his place with the help of their driver, a fat little man who at least was sober, she'd abruptly ended the conversation. Now she shuddered as she opened her back gate and thought of the ruckus in the tool shed with her mother and Mitchell Lodong the week before. Another thing to tell Jack when she saw him.

Katherine quietly came in through the back porch door and walked to the open kitchen door. Clare and Jack were standing at the stove with their backs to her. They hadn't heard her come in. They both had aprons on. Clare was telling Jack that as second cook, he'd have to wrap the wieners in the puff pastry and bake them for five minutes. When they cooled a little, he could slice them into bite-size pieces.

"That's how Katherine told us to make pigs in blankets," Clare said authoritatively. "While a batch is baking, you can roll some more wieners to get them ready."

When Jack said it sounded like the second cook did most of the work, Clare told him that's just what she'd told Katherine and Katherine had said the first cook's job was to accept the responsibility for making sure everything was done correctly. She'd called it a key ancillary duty.

"Sounds like some pretty big words to me," Jack said rolling a sheet of puff pastry around a wiener.

"Well, if you want to make it into the inner circle, you have to do what you're told. But I shouldn't be talking about the inner circle right now. I don't really know you."

Clare told him there were two kinds of wieners, regular and turkey. Hazel gave strict orders that Roy only got the turkey wieners but you had to watch him because he loved to sneak the real ones, what he called the "good stuff."

Jack laughed. "Poor Roy. No good stuff."

Clare turned and saw Katherine in the doorway with a forefinger to her lips. Clare smiled and told Jack she had to ask Hazel something and left for the dining room. Katherine crept across the kitchen and locked Jack in a bear hug from behind. He turned to Katherine and they kissed, really kissed for the first time. It was a kiss that spanned a thousand years, a kiss that had traveled a million miles and by the time it ended, Hazel, Roy, and Clare were standing in the doorway. Clare had turned away in embarrassment and Hazel whispered to Roy, "It's about time."

The café Christmas party started out as a quiet affair. Bobby and his grandparents were the first to arrive punctually at four o'clock just as Jack, with Katherine's help, finished baking the last batch of pigs in a blanket. Sadie and Danny arrived a few minutes later. Sadie said Donny had told her he'd come if he could, but there was still a lot to be done at the farm. Joyce and Muriel came together, both noticeably uncomfortable being at Katherine's for the first time. Roy was at the piano playing Christmas songs and Hazel was everywhere, making sure people had a plate of food while Clare carried platters from the kitchen into the dining room.

Just before people arrived, Clare had taken Jack out to the tool shed so he could help her carry in the two large dishes of lime Jell-o salad which Hazel had put outside in the shed to chill in the winter cold. Clare had acted theatrically secretive in front of Katherine when she took Jack's hand and led him out the back door. "I've got something else to show you too, besides the you-know-what," she'd stage whispered so Katherine could hear.

Katherine stood in the back porch door watching as Clare opened the shed door and turned on the light. She pulled Jack in and pointed to the left front corner of the new cement floor. "Look what I found," she said, pointing to the heart and initials in the concrete. She looked back at Katherine and giggled.

Jack said, "This looks new. What's it say: 'KB + JL?' Who did that?"

Clare laughed out loud, "Oh, I think we know."

Within an hour, the quiet café Christmas party had turned into an impromptu open house attended by what seemed like most people in town. Folks came in a steady stream to wish Katherine well as the new owner of the café. Milos came with Lonnie and Elizabeth. Greeley and Norah Wineskin stopped by for a few minutes. All the Main Street regulars came and went until well after six o'clock.

One of the highlights of the afternoon was when Hazel and Roy finally succumbed to the demands of Bobby and many others for some real country music, starting with "The Wasbash Cannonball." After a few more songs, Joyce shyly asked Hazel if they knew "The Orange Blossom Special." Of course they knew it. Pulling a harmonica out of her purse, Joyce said it was one of her favorites and launched into the opening huffing of the engine as it rolled down that Seaboard Line, while everyone clapped and whistled.

By seven o'clock, everyone was gone. Katherine and Jack were finally alone. They stood in the living room with their arms around each other. It was an awkward moment until Katherine said she'd make some coffee and Jack sat at the piano. She came back from the kitchen while he was playing "I'll Be Home for Christmas" in a soft lounge piano style. She smiled and said she had an early Christmas present for him and headed for the bedroom.

A few minutes later, she stood in the dining room doorway dressed in a sheer nightie with string straps and flared at the bottom at mid-thigh. A black bra and bikini panties were visible underneath. She stood for a minute leaning against the doorway with a hand on her cocked hip and said, "Don't you want to unwrap your present?" Then she turned and walked into the bedroom. She didn't have to wait. Jack was right behind her.

Katherine whispered "Merry Christmas," as they fell together on the bed.

How Deep Is The Ocean

Hazel was surprised the next morning when she called Katherine at ten o'clock and got the answering machine. "Aren't those two up yet," she muttered to herself and hung up without leaving a message. But Katherine and Jack had been up for hours and were long gone, seventy miles west, at the ocean.

It was Jack's idea. After being entwined naked in bed talking most of the night and after two reprises of their first union, he'd coaxed Katherine out of bed at six, telling her they had a trip to make. They were returning to Third Beach. And she didn't resist. She was with Jack now and they'd go anywhere together.

It was a dull gray morning, overcast with marine stratus clouds hanging over the Peninsula like a wet blanket. The mountains hadn't been seen for two days. They stopped for breakfast to go at Port Smith, breakfast sandwiches from the Old Port Diner that both agreed were hardly comparable to the Madison Café's power breakfast sandwiches.

Jack kept bringing the conversation back to Clare as they drove. "She's devoted to you, you know," Jack said. "All afternoon yesterday it was, 'Katherine said this, Katherine told me that, Katherine knows how to do this, Katherine can do that.'"

Katherine blushed. "I think it's more the other way around. Clare has changed us all." She told Jack about the nights Clare had gone missing and how she and Will had found her in the library annex. She'd been so determined to take care of herself. "We were a step away from losing her then," Katherine sighed. "Another night and she might have left town on her own. It's scary to think about."

Jack reached over and took Katherine's hand, "I'll never let anything like that happen to our kids. I promise."

Surprised, Katherine hesitated and then said, "What if we say *we'll* never let anything like that happen to our kids," she whispered and squeezed his hand.

Jack laughed. "Agreed. And talking about having an effect on people, you cut a wide swath on your trip to Seattle. When people weren't asking me about the Ladderback deal, they were telling me about your visit. Hercules is president of your fan club."

"Get out of here," Katherine said. "I was just someone new who broke the monotony."

Katherine was proud of her self-discipline. She hadn't said a word about Jack's meeting with Harry Stamp as they lay in bed the night before, exchanging stories about their time apart. But now, as they cleared the west end of Lake Crescent, she finally had to know.

"How was your meeting with Harry Stamp yesterday?" she asked, trying to sound casual. "Were you interviewing for a job?"

Jack laughed. "No. Something far more important," he said cryptically.

"Are you going to share?"

"In due time. It's tangentially related to our trip this morning. Sort of."

It was Katherine's turn to laugh. *"Tangentially* related. Pretty big word, counselor."

"Well, your honor, I only use big words when the situation warrants it," Jack said with a smile as they drove into the empty parking lot at the trailhead to Third Beach.

A gauzy mist hung over the trees as they started the mile and a half trek through the thick forest to the beach. They could hear the roar of the waves just before they stepped out of the woods and when they did, they immediately wrestled with the ocean wind. The weather wasn't as wild as it had been on their first visit, but it was tumultuous compared to where'd come from. They made their way down the beach the way they'd gone before, holding on to each other, as low scudding clouds swirled around them.

Jack was a seasoned hand at helping build a makeshift shelter from driftwood this time and in a few minutes they were sitting close together in the sand inside their transitory haven with Jack's arm tightly around Katherine. How long were they there? They might have said an eternity, watching the waves roll onto the beach, spotting the bald eagle out on the point to their right, feeling the salt mist on their faces, bonded together as one.

The spell was broken when Jack finally stood and paced back and forth in front of the shelter, alternately looking at a mystified Katherine and out to the roaring waves. He finally returned and knelt on one leg in front of her holding a ring box which he opened. It was a diamond ring; a brilliant, two-carat oval, in an antique white gold setting. Katherine gasped.

Jack took her left hand and held it gently. "Dear Katherine. My dear Katherine. Will you marry me?"

Katherine gasped again. "Oh Jack. Oh no. I mean, oh yes. Of course. Of course I'll marry you."

He slipped the ring on her finger and they fell together in the sand, holding each other tightly as Katherine sobbed "I love you," and Jack whispered, "I love you forever."

The car was quiet when they started toward home and it stayed that way until just before Sappho, when Katherine suggested they stop for lunch at Jake's Forest Diner. "Then let's cut over to Sekiu and see if Buck Mc-Cready's around."

They walked hand in hand into the diner, bumping each other's shoulders as they walked. The only sign of Christmas inside was a small plastic Christmas tree at the far end of the long Formica counter, its tiny white lights flickering bravely in the low light. They sat at the same table near the front window. Katherine ordered a Rueben sandwich and Jack ordered a BLT, both of which Katherine said were benchmarks of authenticity for a greasy spoon.

Jack laughed out loud when Katherine whispered, "The Rueben better be plenty greasy and the BLT better have crisp bacon and be loaded with mayonnaise."

The hot, black coffee tasted good after their morning at the beach and they sipped it silently, staring at each other, their eyes gleaming with love. Katherine held up her left hand and gazed at the ring.

"So counselor. How did you know my ring size? Or was it just plain luck?"

"Well, if I may approach the bench for a sidebar, I'll share a few details of this case with your honor."

Katherine laughed and said, "Approach at will, counselor."

Jack told her that he'd bought an engagement ring as soon as he'd returned from Alaska. "I had no idea what your ring size was. I was getting ready to call Hazel and see if she could find out, but then thought better of it," he said. He'd bought the ring anyway, hoping it would fit. "But that's not the ring," he said pointing to Katherine's hand. "This is where my meeting with Harry Stamp comes into play."

Katherine looked amused. "Does this have anything to do with Maude?"

"It has everything to do with Maude Doud, your honor." Jack answered. He explained that Maude had named him in her will, leaving him the ring, a family heirloom. "To do with as I see fit," Jack laughed. "I'll show you the letter she wrote to me. It's out in the car in my briefcase."

Katherine graded their lunch as they walked to the car. "A B-minus for the Reuben. Thousand island dressing instead of Russian. Provolone instead of Swiss cheese. Greasiness just adequate. A B-plus for the BLT. Bacon freshly fried. Lettuce fresh but tomato near gone. Barely enough mayonnaise."

Jack laughed. "You're going to teach me all kinds of things, your honor."

"You better believe it, counselor," Katherine said as they climbed into the car.

Just past Sappho, Jack turned off U.S. 101 onto State Route 113 which would take them north toward the Strait and Route 112, the road to Sekiu. The ten-mile trip on the unpaved road through the dense growth of Douglas fir was longer than normal because of the low clouds and pockets of fog. Katherine read Maude's letter out loud as the car crawled through the wilderness.

Dear Jack:
This ring was my grandmother, Martha Boyle Martin's
engagement ring given to her by my grandfather Darius Martin
when she was eighteen. Darius was master of the coastwise
lumber schooner Matilda Fitzwater *which was owned by*
the Pope & Talbot Lumber Company at Port Gamble. When
he married Martha Boyle, the daughter of a San Francisco
customs broker, in 1879, he left the sea and they built a grand
house along the Strait at Old Yarmouth, not far from Bert
Peck's place. A few years later, Darius started Martin Lumber,
one of the first business operations in the Cedar Valley and
they moved to just outside what is now Cedar Mills. Lonnie
and Elizabeth live in the house Darius and Martha built there
in 1883. My grandmother Martha gave me this ring after King
and I were married, saying she hoped that it would eventually
be worn by my daughter or daughter-in-law. As you know, King
and I had neither. And now it comes to you. Don't ask why.
Some questions don't have answers. I had the ring cleaned
and refitted and sized for Katherine Baker's ring finger. Blood
doesn't always define family relationships and Katherine is
as much a granddaughter to me as anyone could be. I'm not
telling you what to do with this ring. I just want you to have it
as something to remember me by. I'm so happy I told Hercules
Pushkin about a young lawyer in Chicago who wanted to move
to Seattle and might be a good addition to his firm. With love
and admiration,
Maude Doud

Katherine read the letter again, this time more slowly because of the tears
in her eyes. Then they both looked at each other and laughed out loud when
Katherine said, "Who's running this show anyway?"

Now, just two days before Christmas, Sekiu was deserted. There were only
a few fishing boats in the marina and fewer cars scattered around the clus-
ter of houses that comprised the village. Buck McCready and Roger Farnsworth weren't home. They were down the hill at Dick and Carma Lee

Watson's for an afternoon of canasta and Dick's celebrated vodka nog. Later they planned to adjourn to Buck and Roger's for dinner, where in the oven, Roger had a venison standing rib roast glazed with key lime and salmon berry chutney.

Buck was just telling Dick and Carma Lee how things were looking up in the new year with two weekend Sasquatch expeditions already booked for late January, when they heard the "doorbell" gong at Buck's ring out over the little settlement. Someone was up the hill whacking the weathered copper cylinder that hung on the front porch.

Roger jumped up first and ran to the Watson's back porch with a pair of binoculars. By the time Buck joined him, Roger was muttering, "It's them again. That couple from Cedar Mills."

Buck took the binoculars and gasped in panic as he saw Katherine and Jack on the front porch examining the metal tube. Katherine was standing on a chair, tipping the top of the cylinder down, trying to look at the top. Jack was measuring its length with a tape measure. "Holy moly, Roger," Buck whispered. "We've been had."

By then Katherine had climbed down from the chair and was looking out over the marina toward the Watson's back porch. Buck and Roger ducked down and crawled back into the house, afraid they'd been seen.

Katherine took Jack's hand and looked back at the copper cylinder before they started down the stairs toward the car. "I was right. That's the missing inner leg. Buck and Luther Moody knew about the piano legs and never told anyone. They probably got the treasure."

"Does it really matter," Jack asked. "What shall we do, call the cops? Get Will out here to arrest him?"

Katherine laughed. "You're right. Arrest him for what? Let him have his secret and whatever was hidden in the legs. Or maybe they were empty when Luther and Buck found them. I don't care. Just leave my piano alone."

They talked about the piano legs on the drive back, wondering what Luther Moody had done with his share of the boodle from India if it existed. Katherine, who kept shifting her left hand around for different perspectives on her new ring, said she'd always thought there was something strange about the way Buck McCready had behaved when Greeley had complained to him about the Canadian cousins poking around, looking for the piano.

Katherine said, "I thought it was odd when Buck stopped at the café on his way back from Seattle, claiming he just wanted to meet me. Now I think he was on a fishing expedition, and not for salmon. He wanted to find out if we knew anything about the piano's secret compartments."

Jack laughed. "The plot thickens. Maybe there's hidden loot in Luther Moody's house. There might be a treasure map," he teased.

It was Katherine's turn to laugh. "Very funny counselor. But keep this in mind. According to Greeley, Luther's brother Rex refuses to sell his brother's house. Maybe he knows something."

It was mid-afternoon, just after three-o'clock, when they got home. Katherine shook her head when she saw on the caller-ID that Hazel had called three times and not left any messages.

"Something's up," she said. "I told her we'd be there sometime today and stay for dinner. It's not like her to keep calling like this."

But Jack was back outside at the car and didn't hear her. She watched as he opened the trunk and pulled out two suitcases and a clothes bag and she went out to help carry them in.

"Hercules told me to get lost for a week, until after the new year," Jack said. "Do you think I can stay here?"

Katherine grabbed a suitcase and said, "Only a week? I thought it was going to be forever."

"The forever part comes a little later," Jack said.

When they got his things in the house and unpacked, Jack sat on the sofa and Katherine stretched out with her head on his lap.

"Your love makes me want to be better, Jack Lindsay, and I love you for it. I love you madly," Katherine whispered, looking into his eyes.

He stroked her forehead and said, "Better? How can you improve on perfect. You've given me so much. I was just another lonely guy until we met."

Katherine gave him a soft punch on the chest and laughed, "I knew it. I knew you were a lonely guy when I saw your apartment. That's when I decided to take you under my wing."

Jack guffawed as Katherine jumped up. "Let's get going. Let's see what's going on at the farm.

❖ ❖ ❖ ❖ ❖ ❖ ❖ ❖ ❖ ❖ ❖ ❖

There was a shiny, new Buick sedan parked at Hazel and Roy's between Hazel's Ford Ranger and Roy's pickup. Katherine spotted Clare up at the barn, standing in front of a new chicken wire fence.

"I'm going to go see Clare," Katherine said. "You go in and find out what's happening."

They kissed long and hard before Jack turned for the house. He stopped and pointed to the Buick, "That's got rental car written all over it. I know who's here."

But Katherine was halfway to the barn and hadn't heard. Winter twilight was just starting to fall as the late afternoon sun started to slip behind the mountains. Clare was standing with her right arm around Stormy's neck, saying something to the donkey, who quietly nuzzled her. Winston sat on the ground between the two staring through the fence.

"This is all new," Katherine said as she approached.

Clare turned and shouted. "You're finally here! We've been waiting all day! I've got so much to tell you, Katherine. Aunt May and Uncle Archie are here. They came last night. All the way from Tennessee. Uncle Archie taught me how to stand on my head. Aunt May said they came just to meet me. I don't believe it. We're getting the chickens from Mr. Grajek tomorrow. We just finished the pen."

As they walked toward the house each with an arm around the other, Clare told Katherine she and Donny had spent the morning lining the inside of one of the horse trailers with chicken wire so they could transport the chickens in the morning. Lonnie and Greeley were going to bring the chicken house on one of the flatbed trucks from the lumber yard.

"It's a wonderful Christmas present. Fourteen chickens!" Clare said, hugging Katherine. "But Roy said that was it. He was putting his foot down. No more animals, even though Donny wants to get cows."

Hazel and May stood at the picture window in the farm office at the back of the house, watching Clare and Katherine walk slowly toward the house with Stormy and Winston following. Clare was excitedly waving the arm that wasn't around Katherine as she talked non-stop.

The two Dunn sisters stood at the window holding hands.

"Who would have thought we'd travel this far when we hopped on that coal train up on the mountain, heading for Kingsport." May said. "Two little hillbilly girls, alone in the world."

"And who would of thought we'd be this blessed," Hazel said. "Those two girls are miracles for Roy and me."

❖ ❖ ❖ ❖ ❖ ❖ ❖ ❖ ❖ ❖ ❖ ❖

Hazel saw Katherine's ring first and gasped. "Oh my land! Is it true? This is a Christmas miracle," she said talking Katherine's left and hand and holding it up for the others to see as they all gathered in the kitchen, circling Katherine and Jack, hugging them both. Both Hazel and May had tears in their eyes while Clare clung to Katherine, smiling proudly.

"I knew something was up when I saw those initials on the tool shed floor," Clare said, and everyone laughed.

Then Roy announced that they were going to watch a video tape from the governor before dinner and they all adjourned to the living room. Governor Welker had sent them a copy of the video tape of the Folklore Society concert where, a few weeks before, the Skagit River Ramblers and Tennessee Jack Lindsay had brought the house down. The governor's accompanying note read:

Dear Hazel and Roy:
I wanted you to have a copy of this so you could watch your
nephew Tennessee Jack perform that beautiful rendition of
"The Darkest Hour is Just Before Dawn," he dedicated to you.
I hope I'll have the honor of hearing you all do it live sometime.
All the best."
Del

The room was silent as the Ramblers and Jack did "Drifting Too Far From the Shore," and "Hello Central, Give Me Heaven." Then there was Jack dedicating the next song to his Aunt Hazel and Uncle Roy, who by now both had tears in their eyes. The room was silent for a moment afterwards and then everyone started clapping and slapping Jack on the back.

Archie said, "Son, I didn't know Yankees could play like that."

"They're from North Carolina, Uncle Archie. Moved here years ago," Jack said.

Archie laughed. "Like I said, I knew Yankees couldn't play like that."

Roy said grace when he got everyone quieted down at the dinner table, thanking God for bringing Clare and Katherine into their lives, for bringing Jack home and the blessing of his and Katherine's upcoming marriage, and for May and Archie coming all the way from Bristol. He prayed for those who weren't with them. Annie, who was somewhere in Europe. And his guardian angel, Larry Bradford, who he hoped would find his way back here. "Please let him know that guardian angels don't have to be perfect." Roy said in ending.

When the food was being passed around the table, Clare suddenly jumped up and ran into the kitchen. "I forgot something. Something for Uncle Archie," she said, returning with a glass serving dish. "It's the you-know-what," she said looking at Katherine. "Uncle Archie asked me to make it last night."

Archie laughed out loud. "Well, it was your big sister over there who got me hooked on this wonderful stuff," he said, pointing to Katherine.

Katherine smiled and told Clare, "You've mastered the lime Jell-o salad and it's time you're promoted to first cook of the inner circle."

Everyone laughed as Clare stood and bowed.

Jack said, "Now don't forget about the Four Aces, Uncle Archie. Clare hasn't heard that story."

Clare looked around the table and said, "This is the best Christmas ever, and it isn't even Christmas."

About The Type

The text type is set in Times New Roman which was designed in 1931 when *The Times* of London commissioned the Monotype Corporation's Stanley Morison to design a new typeface to replace its Times Old Roman. Drawn by Victor Lardent of *The Times'* advertising department under Morison's supervision, Times New Roman debuted in the newspaper in 1932. In 1992, when Microsoft released Version 3.1 of the Windows operating system, Times New Roman was used as the default font, making it the most widely used typeface in the United States.